A Stormy Peace

David McDine

First published in 2019 by Endeavour Media Ltd.

Table of Contents

1

A Quiet Night at the Mermaid

Flickering candles stuck in wax-encrusted bottles gave off just enough light for Joe Maggs, landlord of the Mermaid Inn, to survey his little empire and keep an eye on tonight's few customers.

It was a large but cosy bar-room, with rickety chairs, upturned barrels as tables, and a few fly-blown pictures on the once white-washed walls, long stained brown by tobacco smoke.

Like many a publican in the Channel ports, Maggs had once earned his living afloat. His left forearm bore a fading blue-inked tattoo featuring a ship of the line and his right — appropriately — a mermaid, also outlined in blue, with only her lips and nipples picked out in red, matching the crudely painted sign that swung outside.

Which came first was known only to him, but while the one on the sign remained slim and seductive as the day she was painted, the tattooed version had grown fatter and more wrinkly over the years as the landlord himself increased in girth.

He had the broken nose common to seaport landlords, acquired keeping order among over-indulging customers when they were in funds. He drank himself, though never to excess, preferring to squirrel his money away against the day when he would sell up.

Maggs had been at the Mermaid for longer than any of his customers and his mind was beginning to turn to retirement, perhaps to the row of seaside cottages overlooking the harbour.

Giving up the drudgery of running the pub was growing ever more appealing. It was a life many of his regulars imagined as a kind of paradise, with free drink on tap, a steady income and the pleasure of not having to roll off home to a scolding wife or mother at closing time. But the reality was quite different.

The early shine had long since worn off. The daily routine involved cleaning and cellar work before the first thirsty customer crossed the threshold. And the rest of the day was spent serving a string of regulars, each of whom only stopped off for a wet or two to be replaced by a steady stream of others while the landlord himself remained 'watch on, stop on', as they called it in the navy.

Then, into the evening, the pub was either dead — in which case he still had to hang about waiting for drinkers who might or might not appear — or he would be rushed off his feet with a rowdy room-full.

All to be repeated the day after and the day after that, it seemed, ad infinitum.

How sweet the prospect of giving it all up and spending his days idly fishing off the beach seemed, coupled with the pleasure of dropping into his old pub whenever he chose for a glass or two with his old cronies whenever it suited him.

He had resigned himself to a quiet night tonight, but then two naval officers and a couple of fishermen had drifted in, followed by a stranger who had the rolling gait and whiff of the sea about him.

So, Maggs reckoned, although there were only a few customers his takings would still make it worthwhile staying open.

The two officers who had taken root at the table near the door ordered some of his best French wine, acquired free of charge from smugglers in payment for some favours he had been able to do for them.

Lieutenant Anson, of the local Sea Fencibles, whom he liked, and the new divisional captain who also seemed to be a decent type, were clearly in celebratory mood and would no doubt order a second bottle: pure profit.

The two fishermen, elbows on the bar counter and pewter tankards in their fists, were knocking back the ale and the stranger who had entered just after the officers was nursing a double rum served to him by Kitty, the young skivvy who did the washing up and cleaning.

There was something vaguely familiar about the newcomer, but by the candlelight Maggs was unable to place him and turned his attention back to the fishermen's talk of the day's catch.

*

Over in the nearby Sea Fencible detachment building, Sam Fagg, lately foretop-man in one of His Majesty's men-of-war and now game-legged boatswain of a bunch of — in his words — 'ragged-arsed 'arbour rats', was in contemplative mood.

He leaned back in his chair, stuck his well-worn sea boots on the table, puffed at his evilly smoking clay pipe and gave the unit's master at arms the benefit of his wisdom.

'Y'know, Tom,' he observed, 'if this 'ere peace what they keep goin' on abaht breaks aht, I fink I might give up the sea. Swallow the anchor, like.'

Not one to jump to instant conclusions, his companion Tom Hoover fingered his ear and weighed the bosun's comment carefully.

There were indeed rumours of talks between the British and the French to end the war that had been raging across Europe and the world's oceans for the past decade, but nothing firm.

Having given the matter of peace some thought, Hoover, a smart marine sergeant who would never dream of putting his highly polished boots on any table, was sceptical of his mate's stated intention to swallow the anchor. 'Thought the sea'd already given you up, Sam, on account of that peg leg of yours.'

'It ain't a peg leg. A peg leg's when they cuts it orf if it won't work proper and starts goin' sceptical. Then the pusser issues yer wiv a wooden one. *That's* a peg leg.'

Hoover raised his eyebrows. Although born in America, he hailed from a New England loyalist family and spoke the King's English properly, albeit with what was usually mistaken for an East Anglian drawl. His correct use of the language came thanks to the custom at his childhood school for pupils to read words aloud together as one class — and to fix the meanings in their minds.

Fagg, however, had learned his fractured version of the language as an urchin on the mean streets of the naval dockyard town of Chatham, where aitches were few and far between and if you weren't sure of the correct word you came up with something that sounded like it — sceptical being a case in point.

Noticing the marine's wry grin, he protested. 'Nah, yer know full well I still got both me legs, 'though I 'ave to hadmit the duff one ain't no good fer friggin' abaht in the riggin' no more. Mind you,' he touched his nose conspiratorially with his index finger, 'I can still get it over, like, if ye get me drift.'

Hoover, bought up as a good Baptist, got his drift sure enough, but chose to ignore the crude innuendo.

'So, if you give up the sea or it gives you up, what d'you plan to do?'

'Well, there's runnin' a pub. Always fancied that, I 'ave. I'd get free drink, see, an' all the tarts would be round like flies on a cowpat.'

'It wouldn't be free — the drink, I mean. And before you start knocking it back, you'll have to buy a pub in the first place, so how're you going to do that?'

The bosun considered. 'Yeah, well, I see what yer mean, but the drink'd be only what I pay the brewers and as fer buying a pub, well, we got prize money coming our way, ain't we, from that there privateer?'

'Mebbe, but I'll believe it when I see it. Right now, it's pie in the sky.'

'But if we do get it, quite a lot of money like, what'll yer do with yours?'

Hoover smiled. 'Well, if there really is going to be peace between us and the French and the marines don't want me anymore, why, I reckon I'll find myself a wife and a place in the country, like a smallholding, and settle down to a nice peaceful life.'

It was Fagg's turn to grin knowingly. 'And you got a gal in mind, ain't yer?'

It was no secret that Hoover fancied Sarah, daughter of Phineas Shrubb, the Baptist preacher, apothecary, and sometime surgeon's mate in the navy who now looked after the Seagate detachment's sick and hurt.

The marine smiled but held his tongue. Sam Fagg and the rest of them would find out soon enough, subject to three ifs: if peace was declared and the service decided it no longer required his services; if the prize money for the detachment's capture of the Normandy privateer materialised — and if the girl in question said 'yes'. But these were big ifs.

*

Over in the Mermaid, Oliver Anson clinked glasses with his particular friend and now his divisional captain — Amos Armstrong — and they drank a quiet toast to the many brave men lost during the Boulogne fiasco.

Ever since the raid, while convalescing, Anson had suffered a black depression, absorbed in his own gloomy thoughts and unable to talk about the operation to anyone — other than Armstrong — who had not been there and shared the experience with him.

This even included his dear friend Josiah Parkin and niece Cassandra, who had cared for him and helped him pull through.

The raid failed because Nelson hadn't known that the crescent of ships defending Boulogne had been chained together and could not be cut out.

And Anson, who had discovered this vital intelligence while on a secret mission in the Pas de Calais just before the attack, blamed himself for not ensuring that it got to the admiral.

True, he had reported it to the chain of command — in his case the then divisional captain, the pompous, pumped-up Captain Arthur Veryan St Cleer Hoare. But only when it was too late did Anson discover that his report had got no further.

Hoare had chosen not to inform Admiral Nelson because he did not want to appear lily-livered, an accusation he had instead levelled at his own 'underling' — Anson.

But things had changed. Hoare's fatal failing had evidently been uncovered, along with his pretence to have played a major part in the earlier capture of the privateer.

Captain Hoare was now kicking his heels as resident naval officer in the Isles of Scilly, the furthest west the Admiralty could send him.

And Armstrong had at last been released from his lonely signal station eyrie atop the Sussex Downs to replace the disgraced Hoare in command of all Sea Fencible detachments along the coast from the North Foreland to Beachy Head — including Anson's Seagate unit.

Now, in his cheerful company, Anson permitted himself to relax fully for the first time since Boulogne.

He raised his glass again, this time to wish his friend joy of his promotion. True, it was not a sea command, but they would both be in the front line if the French invaded.

However, that seemed an unlikely prospect at present and the only cloud on their joint horizon was all the talk of pending peace.

Although a common toast among officers in the navy was to 'a bloody war or a sickly season', so that they could climb the promotion ladder in dead men's shoes, it was invariably proposed tongue in cheek.

No-one in their right mind could really wish for conflict or disease, but without them advancement in the navy was snail-like and no war at all meant laying up ships and casting sea officers up on the beach.

Asked what he would do if peace did break out, Armstrong pondered. 'There's a role for me of course, managing the family estate.'

His family, descended from the border reivers, the robber barons who in earlier centuries held sway over the country between England and Scotland, had an extensive estate in Northumberland.

And his father, he had told Anson, was reduced to 'being pushed around in a Bath chair by a sturdy maid', so he would no doubt inherit in due course, and most likely sooner than later.

Armstrong sighed at the thought of taking on the responsibility, when he would far sooner stay in the service. 'Yes, I suppose it will come to that, but first I should like to travel to places we've been denied access to during this war.'

'Like Paris? You were there before The Terror, I recall.'

'Yes, my wise old father sent me there to learn the language — and certain other skills, of a romantic nature.'

'And you'd like to return?'

'Of course, mon vieux!' He had addressed particular friends that way ever since his Paris days. 'I'd love to find out what's happened to the crowd I ran around with, mostly aristos of a sort. I fear many will have lost their heads to the guillotine, but you never know. And then there's the girls... they may still be around.'

He savoured the thought, but then remembered he had declared an interest in Anson's sister Elizabeth, so quickly changed the subject, asking, apparently innocently: 'But what about you, mon vieux? Will you enter the church like your father and brother?'

Anson spluttered. 'The only way I'll enter the church is in a coffin. Religion's one thing, but I can't abide church politics. It sickens me, as does the tithe system where poor men are taxed so that the likes of my father and brother live lives of ease off the fat of the land and the sweat of other men's brows.'

Armstrong was startled by his friend's vehemence. 'I was only joking, mon vieux!'

Anson shook his head and confided: 'My father gave me an allowance when I joined the navy, y'know.'

'Many an officer gets some sort of allowance from their family. I do myself, and some consider it essential to supplement our miniscule pay.'

'But I took my father's money without realising it came from the iniquitous tax forced on poor farmers and smallholders by the church. I know now — and I've stopped taking it.'

'Is that part of the reason for breaking with your family?'

'In part, yes, although the main reason was them trying to force me to marry Charlotte Brax.'

'Of course,' Armstrong nodded. He knew Anson had been cornered by the oafish local squire's spoilt daughter, desperate for a suitable husband before, as her own father had put it, 'she ran to fat like her mother'.

'Anyway, we won't go there. The fact is that since all that I've vowed to pay it back, every penny, and when I do, I intend to shame my father into using it for the poor of his parish.'

Armstrong refilled their glasses. 'Steady on, mon vieux. Precisely how do you intend to pay it back — certainly not out of your naval pay?'

'Chance would be a fine thing. That barely covers my living expenses. I even tried to sell my horse but thought better of it. No, don't forget the detachment is expecting prize money. If that comes through, I'll certainly be able to pay back at least some of the allowance.'

Armstrong spread his hands in mock surrender. He well knew that when Anson had made his mind up about something he could not be shifted. It was a stubborn streak that occasionally defied logic.

'Well, I know it's the weevil nearest your biscuit right now, but let's forget all that for a while and enjoy this very fine wine, no doubt courtesy of some of those free traders you have recruited into your detachment!'

Anson grinned. He could name every one of his men who smuggled as a side-line, but there was no way he would ever finger any of them, telling himself, probably correctly, that the economy of half the county would collapse without their efforts.

And anyway, whoever had heard of Kentish wine? Maybe in the distant future someone would start producing some that was drinkable, but for now — war or no war — France was the only ready source of it, and of the brandy English gentlemen consumed in such quantities after enormous dinners.

As they chatted away amicably, sipping some of the wine in question, neither took notice of the short, thick-set man, with tattooed neck and a nose that had clearly been broken several times, who had come in after them and was now sitting in the corner nursing a double tot of rum.

The landlord, who knew most of those who frequented the Mermaid, had not recognised this old salt with his coat collar turned up and floppy hat pulled down low obscuring his battered features. Indeed, from his rig he could be taken for just another piece of sea-faring human flotsam that inhabited the Channel ports.

2

Revenge

As he bent over his rum, the stranger stole a glance at the two officers chatting and sipping their wine. He didn't know the captain, but the young lieutenant's face, although considerably more scarred than when he last saw him, was imprinted on his memory.

Nor would he ever forget his name: Anson, the officer he blamed for his downfall.

Sipping his drink to avoid the possibility of being recognised by the landlord if he called for another, the stranger waited until at last the fishermen at the bar downed the dregs of their drinks and went off noisily to get their supper.

Heart thumping, he now had only to wait a few more minutes to make sure they were well clear of the pub, and then he would make as if to leave himself, cudgelling the sandy-haired captain as he passed and stabbing Anson through the heart.

Then, one by one, he would deal with the rest of his betrayers and revenge would be all the sweeter for the length of time he had brooded on it while at sea.

Job done, he would melt away once more — and his future plans did *not* include a return to naval slavery.

*

Over in the Sea Fencible building, Tom Hoover had managed to divert the conversation from his marriage prospects to the arrival of the new divisional captain.

'Yeah, that Captain Armstrong's a real gent,' Fagg commented. 'Thank Gawd they got rid of that bastard Hoare. The Silly Islands is about the right place for 'im — about as far away as ye can get.'

Hoover shook his head. 'It's the Isles of Scilly, Sam — not the Silly Islands.'

'Daft name t'call 'em whichever way you says it, but them islands sounds ideal for the likes of 'im.'

'Anyway, it's good to see Lieutenant Anson back.'

'Got to agree wiv yer there, Tom. But 'e ain't properly fit yet, is 'e? Phin Shrubb'd take one look at 'im and order 'im back to bed, officer or no orficer. Anyways, let's get over to the Mermaid. It ain't every day the likes of us gets to 'obnob with orficers.'

Hoover may have had an American loyalist upbringing, but he subscribed to the new order created by the Declaration of Independence that 'all men are equal' and snorted. 'You Brits do too much forelock-touching for my liking and neither of our officers worry themselves about that kind of thing. They're not jumped up like that idiot Hoare.'

'Orlright, lobster, ye've made yer point. Let's get on over to the pub and if we're all equal like what you say then we'll let 'em buy us a drink!'

*

Satisfied that the fishermen were by now well clear of the pub, the stranger downed the remains of his rum and rose slowly to his feet and made his way slowly towards the door.

The two officers were so wrapped up in conversation that they paid him no attention. But their convivial chatter froze as Armstrong was whacked across the back of the head an crashed to the floor.

The landlord had his back turned to the bar, handing empty tankards to young Kitty in the back room, but the noise of the officer's wineglass smashing on the flagstones made him spin round shouting: 'What the hell!'

Anson, equally shocked, started to his feet, but the snarling attacker had already pulled a knife from his belt and slashed at him, forcing him back.

It was then that the penny dropped.

'Good grief, MacIntyre!'

The man grinned evilly, as if pleased that he'd been recognised, and hissed viciously: 'That's right, ye fuckin' southern worm. Thought ye'd seen the last o' me, didn't ye? But Billy MacIntyre's come back to haunt yous!'

It had been two years since Anson had caught the former boatswain of Seagate Sea Fencibles fiddling the detachment's books and blackmailing men by threatening betrayal to the press gangs and condemning them to naval servitude unless they paid for the protection.

But some of his victims had entrapped him and dumped him miles away in Rye where, following a tip-off, the local press gang had found him, still confused from the blow he had taken, and carted him off to a receiving ship.

He had been unable to protest because doing so could have marked him as a deserter. And the navy's punishment for anyone caught after 'running' was having their back flayed with a cat-o'-nine-tails.

No, he had sense enough to bite the bullet, give a false name — William Black —to the impress men, allow himself to be sent off to serve in a ship of the line and hope to escape the navy's embrace when the chance arose, as it just had when they put in at Chatham.

Now there were scores to settle. And Anson, the officer who rumbled his lucrative scams, was first on the list.

Anson realised his only chance was to keep his assailant talking to win time for Armstrong to recover his wits or the landlord to come to the rescue with his smuggler's bat — the long-handled club he was known to keep behind the bar to deal with troublesome drunks.

'What d'you want, MacIntyre? Money?'

The Scotsman grinned evilly. 'Ye'll need yer money for your funeral, ye bastard!'

'So what do you want?'

'I wanna see the colour of yer blood and yer innards spewing out on the deck for what yous did t'me.'

Still playing for time, Anson protested as calmly as he could. 'I merely got rid of you because of the scams you were running. I could've had you court martialled and flogged for striking an officer — me! I'm not responsible for what happened to you after that.'

MacIntyre snarled. 'Mebbe not, but it started with yous — and ye fixed with yer arse-lickers to get rid o' me.'

The bar was frozen like a tableau. Anson dared not lose eye contact with his attacker; Armstrong was still on the floor, dazed and winded, and the publican was rooted behind the bar, trying to reach for his bat without attracting attention.

No-one noticed that young Kitty had slipped out of the back door, bumped into Fagg and Hoover as they made their way to the pub and breathlessly warned them what was happening.

The Scotsman, grinning in anticipation of a kill, growled. 'Anyways, that's enough of the talkin'. I wanted yous t'know it wus Billy MacIntyre who did for ye. Best say yer prayers!'

Club in his left hand and knife in his right he took a step forward and Anson seized the moment to lunge at him.

Taken off balance, MacIntyre managed to strike him a glancing blow to the side of his head with the club and slash at his neck with the knife.

As he fell, Anson raised his right arm to protect himself and cried out as the cold steel penetrated his jacket and seared his forearm.

Half stunned, he looked up to see his assailant standing over him, triumphant, but the door was flung open and Hoover burst in, closely followed by the limping Fagg.

Enraged, MacIntyre reckoned he could finish the officer off before tackling the newcomers and pinned Anson to the floor with his booted foot to prevent his victim squirming away.

Knife pointing down in his fist, he raised it to deliver the fatal blow. But he had miscalculated. Instantly taking the situation in, Hoover grabbed the bat from the landlord, flung it at the attacker's head and charged after it.

The club struck MacIntyre's shoulder, a hard-enough blow to make him drop his knife and stagger back, freeing Anson to roll away.

Hoover rushed forward, but MacIntyre had the presence of mind to push a chair in his path, partially tripping him, and made for the door. He still had his cudgel and although Fagg tried to bar his way he was brushed aside by the burly Scotsman who fled out into the night.

The marine extricated himself from the broken chair and overturned barrel table, but by the time he reached the door MacIntyre had disappeared and there was precious little chance of finding him in the dark in the maze of Seagate's back alleys.

3

'Needlework'

'Sam! Mister Anson's wounded and so's the captain. You'd best go find Phineas. He'll still be at Ned Clay's place, seeing to his leg.'

The bosun, who had been caught totally by surprise during the mayhem, was anxious to make up for lost time.

'Right y'are, Tom!' He set off for the local blacksmith's house where the apothecary had gone to check on Clay and others wounded on the Boulogne raid.

Hoover and the landlord helped Captain Armstrong to his feet and sat him in a chair where he sat gingerly feeling the egg-sized lump on his forehead.

'Good job you've got a tough skull, sir,' the publican offered. 'A blow like that could have put many a man out cold.'

Armstrong grinned ruefully. 'Thank you for the compliment, if that's what it was. Many a senior officer has told me I'm thick in the head. But leave me and see to Mister Anson.'

The landlord produced a towel and Hoover knelt, pulled back the injured man's sleeve, and bound the cloth round it to stem the flow of blood.

'How bad is it?' Armstrong asked.

'He's got a deep six-inch cut to his arm and he's bleeding a bit from the side of his head where that ruffian coshed him, but he'll live. Landlord, can you fetch some water?'

Armstrong added: 'And a glass of spirits?'

At a nod from the publican the serving girl poured a large tot and returned with a bowl of water.

To her surprise, it was the captain who grabbed the glass and emptied it with one gulp, muttering, 'I needed that!'

Hoover dipped the bloodied towel in the bowl and washed the worst of the blood from Anson's hair.

Still feeling the lump on his own head, Armstrong asked: 'Who was that fellow? Clearly not some casual robber.'

Hoover shook his head. 'No, sir, it was MacIntyre. Black Mac they call him.'

'Ah, yes. He was the Seagate detachment's bosun, was he not?'

'That's right, but when Mister Anson took over, he got rid of him for blackmailing the boys. But he got his comeuppance when some of them clobbered him, took him down to Rye and shopped him to the press gang.'

'Poetic justice, eh?'

Hoover looked up from tending Anson's wound. 'Yeah, last we heard he was in a man-of-war. Reckon he must have deserted and come back here to get revenge.'

Shrubb came hurrying in with his daughter and Fagg, taking a quick look at the lump on Armstrong's head, announced that he would live and turned his attention to Anson, who had been helped to a chair.

Blood had soaked the makeshift bandage, and the apothecary told him: 'I want you to raise your arm to shoulder level, to stop the blood running out of you.'

He turned to his daughter. 'Sarah, Mister Anson has been badly cut by a blade. Look, a classic defence wound. Once again, he's in dire need of your needlework skills, but I'll need to put a tourniquet higher up his arm before you can get to work.'

She nodded. It had not been long since she had stitched the accidentally self-inflicted sword cut to his cheek, acquired when Anson leapt aboard a French vessel during the Boulogne raid. That neat piece of 'needlework' as her father called it, had been carried out on the shingle beach at Deal. At least this time they were under cover.

From his bag, Shrubb took a leather strap and tightened it round Anson's upper arm. He loosened the blood-soaked towel carefully to confirm that the tourniquet was doing its work and cleaned the wound.

The landlord, still shaken by the attack, watched the proceedings, muttering, 'Bloody cheek of the man, attacking me customers in me own pub! And the bastard didn't pay for his drink neither! Typical bleedin' Scotchman!'

Shrubb raised a hand. 'Pass me the bottle of shepherd's purse from my bag, Sarah.'

She handed it to him and the apothecary explained to his patient, 'This is a tea made from a plant. We use it to clean wounds and stop bleeding. Poultices of common plantain or silverweed would do just as well, but neither is to hand.'

Dabbing the wound with his concoction, Shrubb announced, 'It's clean. Now Sarah, if you'd kindly get to work.'

Hoover supported Anson's arm to keep it steady while Sarah worked her needle and she blushed when she looked up for a second to see the marine's eyes focused on her rather than the officer's wound.

While his daughter plied her needle, Shrubb took the opportunity to lecture his patient, a privilege that in the service was strictly reserved for an officer's seniors — and men of medicine.

'What are we to do with you, Mister Anson? Always into scrapes and getting your skin punctured!' He clucked: 'And now this, on top of your Boulogne wounds from which I respectfully suggest you have not fully recovered.'

Wincing from the stitching, Anson protested weakly. 'Hardly my fault this time, Phineas—'

'And now, despite Sergeant Hoover's quick work in stemming the blood, you have again lost a good deal of it.'

'An armful at least,' Fagg offered, unhelpfully.

Armstrong had recovered sufficiently himself to get Kitty to fetch a bottle and held a glass out to Anson. 'Here, mon vieux. Take a drop more wine. It'll take your mind off the stitching, eh?'

As a Baptist preacher, Shrubb foreswore alcohol except for the small beer that, being boiled, killed off most of the miniscule creatures that swam in the drinking water, and was therefore not only permissible but highly recommended if you wanted to avoid myriad diseases.

He observed: 'I fear that wine, however red, will not replace the blood your friend has lost, Captain Armstrong. Allow me to advise you that in the first place, Mister Anson has returned to duty far sooner than he should have after his Boulogne wounds, and now that he has been injured again and lost so much blood, he should be sent off immediately to recuperate.'

Sarah had finished her work and together she and her father bandaged Anson's arm, both ignoring his insistence that he was still fit for duty.

Armstrong cut his protests short. 'Just listen for once, mon vieux. I am your divisional captain and, having taken expert medical advice—'

'Thank you,' Shrubb interjected.

'Having taken expert medical advice, I rule that you are not physically fit for duty and will therefore be sent on leave for—'

The apothecary offered: 'One month might do it, although ideally he should have six weeks and he needs plenty of rest and good food.'

'Very well, six weeks.'

Anson protested. 'But what about MacIntyre? He must be found and dealt with before he attacks other members of the detachment. He's mad enough to try, despite failing this time. Do we know who's most vulnerable?'

The bosun touched his nose. 'Me an' 'oover know, but best you don't know, sirs.'

There was no way he was going to going to name those who had a hand in MacIntyre's removal from Seagate. And he added, enigmatically, 'Them as don't know can't tell, not that you'd tell even if ye did know, which ye don't and won't.'

Armstrong, clearly becoming slightly exasperated, held up his hands to silence Fagg and told Anson: 'Leave this MacIntyre fellow to us. I'll call on Lieutenant Coney of the impress service first thing in the morning and tell him to make a thorough search of Seagate, Hythe and Folkestone. The wretched deserter will no doubt be holed up somewhere local.'

'But what about warning the others?'

'Sergeant Hoover will do that, will you not?'

'I'll go around and warn those I reckon most at risk right now, sir.'

'Good man! Now, mon vieux, we must look to where you can go to convalesce. We'll get you back to your room at the Rose tonight and I'll stay there myself to make sure that maniac doesn't make another attempt. In the morning we'll send you off somewhere safer. You'd be well looked after at home, I'm sure, but I suppose...?'

'You suppose right. There's no way I would go there after the break with my family. No, if I must go anywhere, I'll go to Ludden. I know Josiah Parkin would be pleased to take me in again.'

'And his delightful niece?'

Anson chose not to respond, but admitted to himself that that the prospect of seeing Cassandra again so soon almost made the night's drama worthwhile.

*

Billy MacIntyre stayed hidden behind a pile of nets in an open-fronted fisherman's hut down by the harbour, in case the fracas in the pub sparked an immediate hue and cry.

He squatted, still clutching his cudgel, hunched against the back wall of the shed where he would be able to deal with anyone who came searching.

Mulling over his failure to kill Anson, he consoled himself that there would be other opportunities to finish the job — and punish the others who had brought about his downfall.

For now, his biggest regret was that he had lost his knife in the struggle.

After an hour or so he had heard no sound of a pursuit or search of the hotchpotch of fisherman's shacks and turned his mind to what to do next.

'Best make yerself scarce, Billy boy,' he muttered to himself, 'else when it gets light the fishermen'll come after their gear.'

He pushed himself to his feet, cudgel in hand, and crept to the front of the hut. Still no sign of anyone searching, so he slipped away, crunching along the pebbled beach heading towards Dungeness and the wild expanse of low-lying sheep pastures and dykes of Romney Marsh.

4

Sick Leave

Next morning, young Tom Marsh turned up at the Rose with his pony and trap and Armstrong helped Anson, his arm heavily bandaged, aboard.

Seeing him off, Armstrong warned amiably: 'If I see you again before six weeks are out, I shall have you court-martialled, mon vieux, friend or no friend!'

Anson tried to touch his hat in ironic salute but winced with the pain and instead mouthed, a mite sarcastically, 'Aye, aye, sir.'

'Fear not,' Armstrong assured him, 'if that MacIntyre creature is still hanging around we will catch him. Coney and his men are already on the case. But until he is caught kindly avoid strange men with Scottish accents and stay out of public houses!'

Anson managed a chuckle and turned to Tom Marsh, who flicked his whip and ordered his pony: 'Walk on.'

It was mid-afternoon by the time the pony and trap turned into the familiar gates of Ludden Hall.

Negotiating the long, curving driveway they passed the small willow-fringed lake where he had left the French royalist — Gérard Hurel — in hiding after his fake funeral on Dead Man's Island, only for the wretched man to reveal himself to a passing gamekeeper by wishing him 'Bonjour.'

Anson smiled at the recollection. The garrulous Hurel had been a pain to keep under wraps, but on their joint reconnaissance of Boulogne in preparation for Nelson's raid he had proved heroic, invaluable — and an amusing, if sometimes infuriating companion.

Josiah Parkin, retired banker, avid antiquarian and naturalist, was in the rose terrace beside the house, magnifying glass in hand, attempting, so far unsuccessfully, to identify a curious hovering wasp-like insect, when he heard the crunch of iron-shod wheels on gravel.

Recognising Tom Marsh's pony and trap, he hurried to the broad paved steps, fronting the iron-studded oak doors framed by imposing Doric columns, ready to meet his visitor.

'Anson, my dear fellow! How very good to see you, although I must confess I had not expected you back quite so soon, knowing that you were anxious to get back to your Sea Fencible command after so long away. Do tell me all is well?'

Anson disembarked from the cart gingerly, favouring his injured right arm. He had chosen not to wear a sling but now wished he had.

Although he felt weak and depressed, Anson put on a brave face. 'Indeed, sir. I had fully intended to remain there making sure training is going apace — and that the families of those lost and the wounded from the Boulogne raid are being looked after properly.'

'And are they?'

'Yes, thanks to my bosun, master at arms and Phineas Shrubb, the apothecary, who's done wonders patching up the wounded. And they have the full support of my particular friend, Commander, now Captain, Amos

Armstrong, who I'm delighted to say is my new divisional captain.'

'Replacing that charlatan, Hoare?'

'Yes, the not-so-gallant Captain Arthur Veryan St Cleer Hoare has evidently been unmasked, but is no doubt by now regaling the entire population of the Isles of Scilly with tales of his imaginary heroism.'

'Scilly?'

'Yes, it appears he could not be trusted with a sea-going command and evidently St Mary's was the furthermost point their lordships at the Admiralty could think of to banish him to as resident naval officer.'

'Hmm, the Scillies, a habitat favoured by the Dartford warbler, *Sylvia undata*, one of our rarest breeding birds, among a number of other species of interest. And your friend has replaced Hoare on the Kent coast?'

'Indeed, and on promotion, I am pleased to say. But I am afraid Armstrong is the cause of my returning here so soon. There was a brush with a disgruntled former bosun: no more than a scuffle really, and I took a cut to my arm.'

'Wounded again! After the injuries you suffered at Boulogne, Doctor Hawkins was adamant that you should take things easy for a good while.'

Anson smiled ruefully. 'Armstrong is of the same mind and has banished me from my command for six weeks. Ridiculous, of course, but I had no option other than to obey. So here I am.'

'Capital, capital! But I'm afraid you have missed Cassandra. Once you had returned to Seagate, she decided to go off to stay with her cousins. She will be sorry to have missed you, but will be back in a few weeks, so we may well have her company for the last part of your leave.'

Trying to hide his disappointment that he would not see her immediately, Anson merely nodded. Parkin's butler-cum-coachman, Dodman, appeared and touched his forehead in salute to the visitor. 'Good day to you, sir. Shall I take your bag?'

'Yes, Dodman, kindly carry Lieutenant Anson's dunnage up to his room. I'm afraid he is incapacitated once again.'

'Blessed Frogs agin, was it, sir?'

'No, actually this time it was one of ours who winged me — well, that is, a Scotsman.'

'I'm not surprised, sir, they're a heathen lot! I mind the time I met a Scotchman in —'

Parkin cut him short. 'Thank you, Dodman. You can save that tale for some other time. Kindly take charge of Lieutenant Anson's bag.'

Anson's host appeared to notice for the first time how pale and tired his visitor looked. 'Forgive me, dear boy. You look exhausted. Why don't you refresh yourself and take a rest before we meet for dinner and catch up on each other's news? I have a particularly fine natterjack toad to show you. Newly stuffed, of course.'

Tongue in cheek, Anson murmured, 'A rare treat, indeed.'

But his host failed to notice the gentle sarcasm and called after his manservant: 'Dodman! Inform cook that we will be two for dinner.'

5

The Looker's Hut

Waking with a start, Billy MacIntyre wondered for a moment where the hell he was.

Then he heard sheep bleating outside and remembered. After the unsuccessful attempt to kill Anson, he had fled along the beach towards Dungeness.

He knew he needed to get as far away from Seagate as possible before the inevitable hue and cry got under way, and he had forced himself along until his legs ached from the effort of near wading along the loose shingle.

Realising that he could not keep up such a pace any longer, he had eventually cut inland and — despite the thin moonlight — come perilously close to falling into several of the dykes that criss-crossed the Marsh before he had come across a small brick-built, tile-roofed 10-foot square hut and took shelter there.

Inside, in the dark, he had tripped over what proved to be a low truckle bed and lay down on it, panting and near exhaustion from the efforts of the past few hours.

Gradually his breathing had become more even and sleep soon overcame him.

Daylight was now seeping in through cracks in the hut's old wooden door and the shutters of what appeared to be a glass-less window. There was a small open fire grate under a brick chimney breast, a pile of kindling and log-wood, tinder box, a tin mug and plate, and an old iron cooking pot. Leaning against one corner was a shepherd's crook, and there was a pair of dagging shears hanging from a nail.

This must be what he knew the Marsh-men called a looker's hut, one of the hundreds dotting the Marsh, and used by shepherds — known locally as lookers — tending to the flocks at lambing and shearing time and in bad weather.

Slowly he eased himself up off the bed and, still stiff from last night's exertions, staggered to the door. Cudgel in his left hand, he worked the latch, opened the top of the stable-style door a few inches and peered out: nothing but grass, sheep and dykes.

The bleating that had woken him was coming from a lamb trapped in a nearby thorn bush. There was no sign of its mother.

Billy MacIntyre was suddenly conscious of how hungry he was. He had last eaten before going to the Mermaid — and that must be well over 12 hours ago.

He approached the bush cautiously, anxious not to startle the lamb into breaking free, and mouthing soothingly: 'There, there, wee lamb. Come to Billy and ye'll be just fine.'

At the last moment he flung himself on it and dragged the terrified creature from the bush. It struggled frantically, but there was no way its captor was going to let go of this meal ticket.

Looking around, all MacIntyre could see was the almost featureless land, devoid of trees and hedges and intersected with water-filled dykes. It was if he was the last man on earth. The only living creatures apart from himself and the doomed lamb were two herons standing sentinel along the dyke banks, a few seagulls passing overhead, and sheep — hundreds, maybe thousands, of sheep.

'Och, well,' he told himself, 'this wee lassie will na be missed,' — and he carried the wriggling, bleating lamb inside.

Half an hour later, the messily-butchered carcass was simmering away in the pot perched on bricks in the fireplace. Having killed it with a blow from his cudgel, he would dearly have loved to be able to skin and dismember it with his knife. But that had been lost in the fracas at the Mermaid, so he had to do his clumsy butchery with the shears.

His chief fear now was that some-one would notice the smoke from his fire rising from the chimney, but with a westerly breeze scattering it he reckoned there was little chance of that.

Anyone who did spot it might well assume that the local looker was staying there, and if the man himself turned up and protested, well, MacIntyre had the wherewithal to silence him and dispose of the body in a dyke.

His hands covered in blood and grease from preparing the lamb for the pot, he looked the part of a crazed would-be murderer now, right enough, and would have scared the living daylights out of any unsuspecting caller who came across his temporary residence.

Jabbing the meat impatiently with the shears from time to time, he finally reckoned it was cooked enough to eat and set about it ravenously, drinking some of the boiled fatty water when it cooled.

For a man who had so recently escaped from the navy, found his way to Seagate, been in a desperate fight, spent half the night wading through shingle and negotiating the dykes in semi-darkness, it was a rare feast.

Satisfied at last, he made himself as comfortable as possible on the truckle bed and fell once more into a long, deep sleep.

6

Some Welcome Intelligence

Over morning coffee in the summerhouse, Anson and his host perused the newspapers brought by the carrier from Faversham.

Anson chose *The Times*, while Parkin leafed through the county newspaper, the *Kentish Gazette*, clucking occasionally at items of news.

One article in *The Times* jumped out at Anson. 'Good grief! So the rumours are true. There's a piece here about talks in London between Lord Hawkesbury and some Frenchman called Otto.

'Hawkesbury, the secretary of state for foreign affairs?'

'One and the same. And this Citizen Louis-Guillaume Otto is apparently the commissary for the exchange of prisoners.'

'So their talks are about prisoner exchanges?'

'No, according to this report they've been discussing preliminary articles between us and the French!'

'Articles?'

'Articles of peace.'

'Great heavens! So, the war could soon be over?'

'If we are to believe that, we'll believe anything. But then there's no doubt the war has reached stalemate. Both us and the French are pretty well exhausted and need to recuperate.'

'Especially the French?'

'Well, it certainly suits them to take a breather in the war at sea where we're a constant thorn in their side, blockading their ports, taking their overseas possessions and whatnot.'

'As a former banker I can tell you that our national debt has soared above £500 million, which is unprecedented — unimaginable a decade ago. Food prices have almost doubled and the newspapers are reporting riots in pretty well every major city, including London. No doubt it's much the same in France, so it's understandable that both sides want peace.'

Anson was sceptical. 'Quite so, but I reckon any peace is likely to be of short duration. If it does happen, I doubt it will last. Bonaparte would merely use it to draw breath.'

'Really?'

'I believe so. Lifting our blockade would give the French the chance to get their ships to sea, move troops, import vital war materials that they lack and so forth.'

'Until they're ready to start it all up again?'

'Precisely. I just hope that if these so-called articles of peace are signed, we don't give away too much and do the normal thing that our politicians do the minute the guns fall silent...'

'Run down the army and navy?'

'Yes, 'twas ever thus. Some call it the peace dividend. I call it wanton folly.'

'However, they're calling these merely preliminary talks, are they not? In which case, knowing how slowly these things proceed, even a temporary peace could be a good way off.'

Tutting, Parkin returned to his perusal of the *Kentish Gazette*. 'Here's a thing. Your former ship, HMS *Phryne*, is reported to be in Chatham Dockyard completing some repairs and taking on stores before returning to duty in the Channel.'

Anson's first thought was the naivety of the Admiralty in allowing such items to be published. Even in the frontline county of Kent the local newspapers were full of similar items about ship and troop movements. And it was a well-known fact that smugglers regularly took English newspapers across to France where no doubt much military and naval intelligence was extracted from them.

If he had had his way he would have dearly loved to return to *Phryne* after his escape from France following the St Valery raid, but his boots had been filled by someone else and he had been posted to command the Seagate Sea Fencibles instead.

He admitted: 'I miss my old shipmates, but I suppose life doesn't stand still and we have to play the cards we are dealt. At least being banished ashore has enabled me to see more of you, and...'

'Cassandra?'

'You have smoked me out, sir. Yes, and I plead guilty to feeling disappointed that she is away.'

'I can assure you that she wouldn't have given a thought to visiting her disagreeable cousins if she'd known you would be back here so soon. You care for her a lot, don't you?'

'I do, but I am also aware that it's important to bide my time. I fear I have a pretty poor record as far as my brushes with the fair sex are concerned.'

Parkin smiled sympathetically.

'Yes, we sailors come ashore and generally behave like idiots where women are concerned. It's the lack of women at sea I suppose — apart from the odd gunner's wife, who is usually built like a gorilla and certainly as hairy. And so, when Jack goes ashore he falls for the first female he sees, squanders his money and is left older, impecunious, but no wiser, ready to repeat the whole sorry process when next allowed ashore.'

'But you surely don't equate yourself with Jolly Jack Tar in that sense?'

Anson sighed. 'I'm afraid my own few liaisons have been no more successful. You are aware of the Charlotte Brax affair. She was actively hunting for a husband and I foolishly allowed myself to take on the role of fox pursued by her, her ghastly father and my own parents and brother in full cry.'

'Your reluctance to marry such a female out of lust and for money is very understandable, commendable even, but it's a pity that it has led to a breach between you and your family.'

'So be it. As you are also very well aware, I do have feelings for your niece, strong feelings, but as I said, after what happened regarding the Brax affair I am anxious not to rush my fences.'

Knowing that his young friend was no better at horsemanship than he was at handling husband-hunting females, Parkin smiled. 'There's little danger of that. You must know that she is extremely fond of you. We both are.'

'Yes, fondness is all well and good in friendships and in both your cases it is most certainly reciprocated. The question I ask is at what point does that fondness become love? Between man and woman, I mean.'

'Ah, that is a matter of complete mystery to an aged bachelor such as myself. What *is* love? A mixture of attraction, passion and friendship, or something more?'

'I'm afraid I'm not qualified to answer that, sir. The first two were certainly present in my brief relationship with, well, you know who I mean... although on my side it was mostly the lust we foolish sailors so easily seem to succumb to when we step ashore. But there was never any friendship.'

'And your feelings for my niece?'

'Quite different. Attraction and friendship of course, but I already feel there is something more, something purer than my previous encounters with the fair sex. It would be good to spend more time with her — with you both, but...'

An idea was forming in his head. 'You tell me that my old ship is in Chatham and I would dearly love to see my former shipmates and trade stories with them. A lot of water has passed under our bridges since I left them in somewhat of a hurry on the Normandy raid.'

'And you would like to visit the ship while she's at Chatham?'

Anson agreed: 'I believe visiting them and perhaps staying on board for day or two while they are alongside would do me the world of good.'

Parkin nodded. 'Why not, indeed! Dodson could take you in the carriage and I'll give him the wherewithal to put up at a coaching inn so that you can spend a day or two with your friends. Who knows, by the time you return Cassandra might be here. There's a limit to the amount of time she can put up with her cousins!'

And so it was decided. It took no time at all to put on his uniform and re-pack, and within the hour Dodman had brought the carriage round to the front steps ready for the off.

Parkin was clearly reluctant to see him leave again so soon, but wished him joy of re-visiting his old shipmates.

As he climbed aboard, he turned to shake Parkin's hand but thought better of it when the stitches reminded him of his wound. Instead, he raised his hat with his left hand the old gentleman did the same.

And as Dodman flicked the horses into action Parkin cautioned: 'Take care not to lose any more blood, my boy!'

Peering back out of the window, Anson smiled and nodded as the coach crunched down the driveway.

7

The Crooked Billet

Many hours after his lamb feast, Billy MacIntyre awoke with an urgent need to relieve himself.

He opened the shutters a few inches and peered out of the window. Over in the west the sun was setting but otherwise he could see nothing but grass, dykes — and sheep.

Outside, he answered the call of nature and contemplated his next move.

There was enough of the boiled meat left for a meal or two and there was no shortage of water on the Marsh, so he could hole up for a couple of days in the looker's hut — as long as the shepherd didn't make an appearance.

He had already made up his mind that taking revenge on those who had fingered him would have to be put on hold for a while. Stabbing a sea officer would not be taken lightly and what's more, he had been recognised. No doubt the whole of Seagate would be on the alert searching for him, so it would be foolhardy to reappear there for a while.

There was no point in hanging about the looker's hut either. It would likely be only a matter of time before his presence was noticed, and he knew that if the navy got its claws back in him, he risked extreme punishment — especially as the officer he'd attacked knew exactly who he was and that he had been marked as 'run' twice now.

No, he couldn't face that. Instead, an idea occurred to him. Since he was now well outside the law there was only one way he could think of that would enable him to stay free and at the same time make money to keep body and soul together.

But first he must find the kind of men who could help him — smugglers.

*

It was early evening when he came upon the pub with a creaking sign announcing it as the Crooked Billet, opposite the old churchyard in a small Marsh village.

He waited outside beside the churchyard wall for a while and then plucked up courage to go into the pub, hat down over his brow and cudgel under his jacket.

A noisy group of men playing cards occupied a large round table in the corner, but otherwise the bar was empty except for the landlord behind the counter pouring drinks for them and a farmer who had dropped in for a wet on his way home after checking on his flock.

It was one of the scruffiest and most disreputable pubs he'd come across since his Glasgow youth — the kind of establishment, he supposed, where you could walk out leaving a dead dog on the bar and no-one would notice.

Sidling up to the bar, he pointed to a rum bottle, but the gnarled old publican looked to the occupied table.

The men's leader, a tough-looking ginger-haired man with a scarred cheek, full beard and door handle ears, gave the newcomer the once-over and nodded.

Given the go-ahead, the inn-keeper pushed a heavy glass across the bar and half-filled it. MacIntyre signed for him to top it up and the publican obliged.

To avoid suspicion that he might try to leave without paying, MacIntyre slapped a handful of coins — all he owned in the world right now — on the bar and the landlord took what was owed and left the rest.

The other men drinking at the corner table glanced at the newcomer from time to time. Clearly, he was a sea-farer of some kind, but then so were most of those hereabouts who weren't shepherds. Some were both smugglers and shepherds — the bat-men who provided protection for smuggling runs and the pack-men who were called upon to take the contraband inland.

This was owlers' territory, where men had been evading the revenue for countless generations. The free trading had once been in the very wool produced here on the Marsh and those who smuggled it to France where it was worth far more were known by their signal — the hoot of an owl.

Wool had been Britain's most important and profitable export and the loss to the revenue through smuggling was so serious that those caught running it faced the death penalty. But that had only bred more desperate and harder generations of free traders, ready and willing to deal ruthlessly with anyone who might inform on them.

With the full cooperation of the sheep farmers who themselves benefited from the illicit trade, the owlers had long fostered an atmosphere of fear among the scattered Marsh communities. Those who cooperated and played an active part, however small, were rewarded — but anyone suspected of disloyalty would disappear.

Now it was luxuries: brandy, wine, tobacco, tea and lace that were the main contraband, but those involved in the trade were just as ruthless as their forebears.

It was only natural that a stranger appearing in one of the Marsh pubs would be scrutinised. And the Crooked Billet was well known as a haunt for smugglers, like the group sitting around the corner table haunting it right now.

Their leader finished a hand of cards and looked the interloper over more closely. Those with him fell silent, too. The farmer at the bar sized up the situation, quickly finished his ale and left hurriedly. The less you knew about what went on hereabouts the healthier life was.

MacIntyre took a slurp of his rum, well aware that he was being closely observed.

After a while the smuggler's leader shrugged and sipped his own drink, satisfied that at any rate the newcomer did not have the look of a revenue man. He was more of a bruiser — a thick-set man, with the look of an old salt, short but with muscular shoulders, shaven head, tattooed neck and nose that had clearly been broken perhaps more than once and had set slightly askew.

After a long pause the ginger-haired man called out: 'So who might you be, stranger?'

MacIntyre bit back the sharp retort he would have liked to make. There were half a dozen of them, all apparently armed and on their home turf, so he answered, civilly enough. 'Just a poor seaman, down on his luck.'

'Irish?'

'Scottish.'

'Navy man, is it?'

'Was.'

'So, a deserter, then?'

'Just takin' a wee bit o' leave.'

His inquisitor laughed, the rest joined in and MacIntyre forced a grin. The ice was broken.

'So, what's your name, mister wee-bit-o'-leave man?'

His real name might be known out this way from his Seagate days, so he chose to give them the one he'd been using since he was pressed. 'Billy Black.'

'Now tell us what you're doing sniffing around these parts, Billy Black. How do we know you're not spying on the likes of us so you can 'peach us to the revenue men?'

MacIntyre knew they had reached a critical point. If these men believed he was some kind of informer he had no doubt they would have no hesitation in disposing of him, so he chose to level with them.

'Look, boys, I'm no on leave. I've run.'

There was a murmur of surprise from the gang. They'd suspected as much, but had not expected him to admit it.

He added earnestly: 'So y'can see, there's no way I want t'mix wi' the revenue or anyone official like.'

'You're a long way from Scotland, Billy Black. So how come you've washed up on our patch?'

'I'm here because I want t'get into the smuggling game.'

This provoked a bigger laugh, and the leader countered: 'You've got some cheek, I'll say that for you, coming here offering to join like you was 'listing for the army! How d'you know we ain't off-duty revenue men, or a navy press gang?'

His men laughed heartily at that.

MacIntyre grinned too. 'Well, I know full well what a press gang looks like and ye don't act like revenue men. Ye're all armed, ye're in a Romney Marsh pub and ye've been talking 'bout yer next run, so I reckon ye must be smugglers. Gie me a chance an' ye'll no regret it.'

Amused, the leader asked the others: 'What d'you say, boys?'

The smugglers, entertained by the repartee, wasted no time in agreeing to give the new recruit a trial run. It was obvious that a hard-looking nut like him could be useful as a bat-man protecting the landing beaches and keeping the inland villages on their smuggling route toeing the line.

So, in short order MacIntyre was downing more smuggled spirits, contemplating a comfortable bed at the inn and looking forward to starting his new career on the next run.

Revenge on his Seagate enemies could wait, for a while at least.

8

HMS *Phryne*

Wedged in a corner of the carriage with his feet braced against the rear-facing seats to steady him as they jolted over potholes, Anson gazed at the familiar Kent countryside.

In just over an hour they had passed Sittingbourne and reached the village of Gillingham. Ahead he could see the Medway — the river that by tradition separated the Kentish Men from the Men of Kent. Having been born south of the river, he counted himself among the latter.

They descended the long hill into Chatham, where Dodson urged the horses along, occasionally shouting 'Make way there!' to encourage idlers out of their path.

Soon they were in Chatham High Street, familiar to Anson with its chandleries, pubs, tailors, tobacconists, tattooists and others who fed off the navy, including the inevitable ever-present cruising whores.

He was eagerly anticipating seeing his old shipmates again — or at least those not dead, time-expired or posted in the meantime — and was especially looking forward to renewing his acquaintance with his particular friends, the first lieutenant, John Howard, and Ned McKenzie of the marines.

Enquiries of the gate-keepers, whose role appeared to be more to do with preventing dockyard mateys making off with official stores than keeping people out, sent him to the gun wharf where the frigate was loading shot.

He remembered with a wry grin the stunt he had pulled a couple of years earlier in jumping the queue to obtain guns for the Seagate battery. His role in helping to end the mutiny at the Nore had stood him in good stead then — plus a sweetener or two for the hammock-counters, of course.

Phryne's lines were unmistakeable. She had the look of a French frigate, which she had indeed been until her capture and recommissioning for service in the Royal Navy some years before. She was older and carried less armament than the now standard French frigate but nevertheless she was sleek, beautiful and a good sea-keeper. The French naval architects knew their business.

It was the first time Anson had clapped eyes on *Phryne* since the boats drew away from her off the chalk cliffs of Normandy on their way to attack St Valery-en-Caux.

Before that, he had enjoyed a memorable prize-taking Mediterranean foray in her and he much regretted that he had not been allowed to return as second lieutenant and ended up commanding Sea Fencibles instead.

The arrival of Parkin's carriage alongside stirred the officer of the watch into action. A carriage hinted at a visitor of some importance and the lieutenant sent a midshipman scurrying off to find the captain.

'Kindly wait here, Dodman, and I'll let you know how things stand once I've reported on board.'

Parkin's coachman tapped his hat with his whip. 'I will, sir. It'll give me the chance to give these here horses their nosebags and a drink.'

By the time Anson emerged from the carriage and made his way up the gangway and on board to the squeal of a bosun's call, the captain had been sent for and a small reception party had been hurriedly assembled.

Captain George Phillips, telescope under his arm and hastily-donned hat at a precarious angle, peered in disbelief at the newcomer. 'Great heavens! Is it you Anson?'

Anson raised his hat with his left hand. 'It is indeed, sir. My apologies for my long absence and may I say what a great pleasure it is to be back on board *Phryne* at last!'

He held out his left hand. Slightly puzzled, Phillips nevertheless shook it vigorously and called to the first lieutenant who was busily engaged with some dockyard men: 'Howard! Look who it is, young Anson back from the dead, albeit with a rearranged face!'

The first lieutenant shrugged the dockyard men aside and joined his captain. 'Oliver Anson, how very good to see you! We had heard that you had survived France and taken charge of some Sea Fencibles, but we're dying to hear all about—'

But Phillips interrupted. 'We'll save all that for later. For now, we must press on to get everything loaded and shipshape ready to sail on the ebb tide in the morning. You'll stay on board tonight, Anson?'

Disappointed to hear that the frigate would be sailing so soon, Anson thought that at least one night would be better than nothing and responded, 'I'd very much like that, sir.'

'Splendid. Meanwhile Midshipman Foxe here appears to be desperate to renew your acquaintance and he can make himself useful by showing you round the old tub. You'll find little has changed since you left us so hurriedly. There are quite a few new faces, but still a good many you'll recognise.'

'Thank you, sir. I do indeed remember Mister Foxe very well indeed, although I had expected to see him at least an admiral by now!'

Foxe grinned with delight. 'Not quite yet, sir. I sit my lieutenant's exam when we get to Portsmouth.'

They set off on a tour of the upper deck and Foxe observed, 'You appear to have been in the wars, sir.'

'I acquired these scars at St Valery and Boulogne.' He patted his arm. 'But I'm afraid *this* wasn't caused by enemy action. Some discontented former member of my Sea Fencible detachment disliked me enough to make his mark on my arm with an extremely sharp knife. However, they tell me I'll live.'

'Now, sir, if you'll step this way we'll see if you recognise some of the old hands.'

One such was the armourer's mate Abel Grist, taking advantage of the afternoon sun by squatting on deck cleaning a rack of muskets.

'Good day to you, Grist. The last time I saw you was the night before the St Valery raid, sharpening bayonets, cutlasses, half pikes and boarding axes.'

Grist knuckled his forehead. 'That's right, sir, and we wus right sorry to hear you'd been killed.'

'That report was a little premature, I fear.'

'Never mind, sir, 'tis good to see you back from the dead!'

They moved on and came upon the master with the bosun inspecting the rigging. 'You'll remember Mister Tutt.'

'I do indeed. He knows the Channel and its tides, currents and other foibles better than any man alive. A pleasure to see you again, Mister Tutt. You were spot on with your deductions about the currents off St Valery but at the time I didn't foresee that I'd not be returning to the ship.'

'But you're back now, sir, and we're right glad to see you. Will you be staying with *Phryne*?'

'I'm afraid not. Their lordships decided otherwise and I'm trapped in a shore appointment. Nevertheless, it's a great pleasure to be back on board, even if only for a brief visit.'

Wherever Anson went, above and below deck, he was greeted warmly by the old hands — especially those who had taken part in the abortive boat action in Normandy.

Among a group mending sails, another familiar face greeted him, instantly recognisable as one of the St Valery veterans.

'Welcome back, sir. Good to see you didn't snuff it on the mole, like we thought.'

'Coppins, isn't it? Very good to see you, too. The last glimpse I had of you was when you were helping the first lieutenant after he injured his leg jumping ashore.'

'That's right, sir.'

'But do I detect that you've been promoted?'

Coppins grinned. 'That I have, from sail-maker's mate to being the main man himself!'

'Excellent! Your warrant is thoroughly deserved I'm sure, and I wish you joy of it.'

He was chatting to another group of boat raid survivors when a midshipman who looked all of twelve years of age, came panting up, touched his hat and squeaked: 'Captain's compliments, sir, and he requests the pleasure of your company in the great cabin.'

*

Captain Phillips was at his desk, pouring himself a large glass of brandy, when Anson knocked and entered.

'Forgive me, Anson, but I've been so damned busy trying to get all the ducks in a row ready for sailing tomorrow that I haven't had a moment to devote to you. However, Howard and the bosun have everything well in hand, so here I am. Will you take a wet with me?'

'Thank you, sir, I will if I may.'

Phillips poured him a brandy and ushered him to a seat. Anson asked: 'I take it you've been refitting, sir?

'No, not a proper refit. Merely getting the dockyard people to put right some of the wear and tear we've suffered remaining so long on blockade duty.'

The captain sipped his brandy and Anson nodded sympathetically.

'You'll recall what a hammering our ships endure in the Channel and the Bay of Biscay, eh? So we needed to come in to replace broken and warped timbers, stop up leaks with oakum and pitch — that sort of thing. We've got new sails to replace torn and rotten ones, new ropes and so on. Plus, we've been taking on stores of course.'

There was a knock and the purser, new to Anson, appeared, seeking the captain's signature.

Signing the paper without reading it, Phillips turned to his visitor again. 'So, we're delighted to see you again, Anson, but forgive me for asking: is there some particular reason for your visit other than merely to see the good ship *Phryne* and renew old friendships?'

Anson took a gulp before answering with a splutter as the spirit burned its way down. 'To be honest with you, sir, I am not sailing under full canvas at present. I was wounded during the Boulogne affair and then attacked by a disgruntled former bosun of my Sea Fencible detachment.'

'In the wars again, eh? And winged by one of your own?'

'Indeed, sir. At any rate, against my will I've been ordered to take six weeks off and I'm staying with a friend of mine down near Faversham to convalesce. It was he who spotted an item in the newspaper about *Phryne* refitting at Chatham and suggested a visit might do me good.'

Phillips snorted: 'Damned news-sheets — always giving away information about our deployments to make things easy for the enemy! And what's worse, it's pretty well the only kind of thing the confounded scribblers get right!'

'Couldn't agree more, sir, but on this occasion it was the paper that sparked the idea of visiting *Phryne*.'

'Of course.' The captain nodded understandingly. 'So a chance to visit us and get some sea air to clear out your lungs and lift your spirits as well, eh?

'Just so.'

'Well, I'm afraid you'll breathe precious little clean sea air here at Chatham. All you'll get here is the malodorous stink of river mud mixed with sewage!'

There was no arguing with that. The receding tide was already uncovering the filth-strewn mud-banks allowing the familiar nauseous stench to drift ashore. It took Anson's mind back to Dead Man's Island and the mock funeral he had been called to witness before his Boulogne adventures. The smell had impregnated his clothing for days.

The captain eyed him sympathetically. 'Look Anson, we're going to be flat out until we sail and I fear we won't be able to entertain you properly. If, as you say, you've been ordered to take time off, why not come with us to Portsmouth?'

The idea had already been in Anson's mind but he had not wanted to suggest it himself in case it was not welcome. But now...

'Well, sir, I have been recommended to get plenty of fresh air and I suppose there's no better way than taking passage round the coast.'

'Just so. You'll be supernumerary, of course. No work to do and as much rest as you need. But there'd be plenty of fresh air — and fresh food, thanks to this visit to Chatham and pigs and sheep we'll be embarking in the Downs.'

'And I could coach it back from Portsmouth?'

'Precisely. Not least it would be good for us all to have someone on board who can entertain us with tales of something other than our own boring ship's routine, the weather, what we'll do if peace comes, how many rats the midshipmen have caught so far this week, and so forth. Why don't you give it some thought?'

It did not take Anson long to mull the offer over. He could send the old gentleman a note explaining what was afoot and Cassandra was not going to be at Ludden for a while anyway.

'Most kind of you, sir. No need to think it over. I accept with gratitude. I will need to write to Mister Parkin, my host at Ludden, explaining what I'm up to and why, and send it via his coachman who's waiting to find out if I'm staying on board tonight or not. I took the seamanlike precaution of bringing my dunnage with me, so I have everything I need.'

'Very wise of you. I always say a good sailor is never parted from his kit — except when joining a cutting out expedition off the Normandy coast, eh Anson?'

'Good point, sir, although at the time ending up wounded and a prisoner of the French was furthermost from my mind!'

'Nevertheless, you made it home.'

'Yes, largely because I had taken the precaution of sewing coins in the lining of my second-best coat. They opened a good many doors.'

'If you wish to write to your host best do it here in my cabin, away from all this hustle and bustle. I need to be on deck, anyway.'

There was indeed a good deal of noisy activity going on as the ship's stores were replenished and dockyard men helped the carpenter and his mates complete last-minute repairs.

Seated at the captain's desk in the great cabin, Anson allowed himself to savour the thought that one day he might be there by right — or maybe captain of a ship of the line, or even flying his flag as an admiral, the nation's destiny in his hands.

But he shook off the presumptuous thought, reached for a pen, dipped it in the inkwell and wrote:

From HMS Phryne *at Chatham*

My very dear sir,

I hope you will not think it ungrateful of me, but much as I was enjoying your kind hospitality, I have been invited to embark in my old ship HMS Phryne *when she sails from Chatham tomorrow to remain with her as far as Portsmouth, and I have accepted.*

Sea air is said to be wonderfully restorative and being back on board among my old shipmates has already lifted my spirits.

With fair winds we will reach Portsmouth within the week and while there I will take the opportunity to call upon my agent before returning to Ludden via the mail coaches. By that time I very much hope that your niece will be back from visiting her cousins and the three of us will be able to spend an agreeable time together before my sick leave is up and I return to duty.

Yours affectionately

Oliver Anson

He addressed his missive to Josiah Parkin Esquire, Ludden Hall, folded it, melted a blob of wax and stamped it with the ship's seal.

9

Back to Sea

Settled into one of the miniscule cabins alongside the gunroom, Anson rested for a while before the evening meal which was to be a Spartan affair, he was told, owing to the need to catch up on everything before sailing.

Being a mere frigate, *Phryne* did not run to a wardroom as in ships of the line, and the gunroom housed all the officers excepting the captain.

At dinner the first lieutenant told him, 'Our mutual friend Ned McKenzie has gone off to the marine barracks to select some replacements. He's gone himself to ensure they don't try to fob us off with anyone with two left feet, or whatever.'

'Very wise. My bosun will never live down recruiting a man who hid his wooden leg under a pub table!'

Howard laughed. 'You'll see McKenzie later and of course you've already met your replacement, Lieutenant Allfree, and young Foxe, but otherwise the gunroom inhabitants are mostly new faces. Tempus fugit, you see.'

With last-minute work continuing and stores still being loaded until late there was little chance of a convivial evening and, tired from his travels and still weak from the loss of blood, Anson turned in early.

But he was up and about early to watch the boats being lowered to pull *Phryne* out into Upnor Reach, to take advantage of the ebbing tide and begin her slow progress down the Medway.

Rounding St Mary's Island, Anson looked ahead, paying particular attention to the prison hulks moored along the river below the village of Gillingham in line of sight of one another and rising only a few feet above the glutinous mud even at high tide. He knew them as overcrowded hell-holes in which French prisoners and their allies were confined.

They included famous old British warships, among them *Bristol*, *Hero*, *Eagle* and *Camperdown*, and captured ships including the *Vryheid,* Admiral Jan de Winter's flagship at the Battle of Camperdown, where Admiral Duncan defeated the Dutch so decisively just after the Nore mutiny.

All masts, rigging and sails had been removed from the hulks and haphazard superstructures, erected to house prison staff and stores, cluttered the top decks.

They were bedecked overall but with washing, rather than flags, hanging from lines slung all over the deck. He had once visited one of the hulks, overcrowded floating hell-holes that he believed shamed the nation with inhumane treatment of prisoners-of-war.

But he dismissed the thought to concentrate on the frigate's passage down river.

This was a nervous time for the sailing master, Josiah Tutt, the senior warrant officer on board responsible for setting courses, monitoring the ship's position and pilotage. He and his fellows throughout the service were the Admiralty's main source of hydrographic information and were charged with noting and reporting any new shoals or underwater rocks they discovered.

He and the captain shared a natural horror of running aground and were constantly checking and rechecking the chart and Tutt's pilot's notes, carefully recorded over many a year.

Their attention was on one of the old hands who stood in the main chains, heaving the seven-pound lead forward. The line, knotted at one fathom intervals, was vertical when it bottomed, giving him the depth of water which he reported in sing-song fashion.

A diminutive midshipman, clearly fresh out of school, stood beside Mister Tutt, noting the depths — barely three fathoms to begin with, but gradually increasing to the relief of Captain Phillips. Getting stuck on a mud-bank and having to be pulled off almost within musket shot of the dockyard would hardly enhance his reputation.

Unflappable, Tutt was comparing the depths with his chart. It was a help in determining their position but not totally reliable in a tidal river known for its shifting mud-flats.

Running seawards with the tide, they carried minimum canvas — merely enough to give them steerage.

Anson knew this stretch of the Medway well, having been rowed down it to join HMS *Euphemus* during the Nore affair and helping the loyal hands on board to make a dash for freedom. It had been a nail-biting exploit, but they had come through it successfully — and thereby helped bring about the collapse of the mutiny.

Channel markers placed by Trinity House, which was responsible for the provision and maintenance of navigational aids including the Nore buoy and lightship, were of great help to river traffic. But Anson wondered if they took full account of the additional hazard: the presence of wrecks, some perhaps deadly hangovers from the navy's shameful defeat when the Dutch raided the Medway more than a century before.

He had grounded on a mud-bank not far from here himself when taking *Euphemus* into Sheerness and there had been hell to pay kedging the ship off under fire from some of the mutinous ships. It was not an experience he ever wished to repeat.

But now, despite all the hazards, all went well for *Phryne* and before long they had left Hoo Island behind them to larboard as they entered Pinup Reach, with more than three fathoms under them.

Anson remained on deck taking a keen interest in their progress, although feeling a little frustrated at not having any proper work to do.

Down the Long Reach and Kethole Reach, with Burntwick Island to starboard, he could see ahead to the sinisterly-named Dead Man's Island, little more than a tidal mudflat, where he had attended the fake funeral of Lieutenant Gérard Hurel, a French royalist officer from the prison hulks.

The charade had been engineered to make Hurel's fellow prisoners believe he was dead, leaving him free to accompany Anson on a spying mission to Boulogne in the run-up to Nelson's raid. It had been a clever plan, well executed, but, Anson mused, such a tragedy that although he and Hurel had brought back vital intelligence it was not acted upon and the raid had turned into a disaster.

Seated on a grating with nothing but the view and observing the careful working of the ship down the middle of Saltpan Reach to occupy him, Anson extended his telescope, one of Messrs P and J Dolland's six guinea superior three-foot achromatic models paid for out of his own pocket, and surveyed the Isle of Grain to the north.

Herons and egrets stood sentinel on the banks and wildfowl of various types abounded. How Josiah Parkin would enjoy such a view.

Ahead now lay the dockyard town of Sheerness — unkindly known as 'Sheer Nasty' by some in the service — on the Isle of Sheppey, with Garrison Point marking their entry into the Thames estuary.

Beyond lay the Great Nore Anchorage and the North Sea, a welcome sight for all on board and a massive relief for the captain and master who could now congratulate themselves on having avoided the ignominy of running on to any of the many mud-banks.

Picking up a light westerly off the land, *Phryne*, now under full sail, made good progress along the north Kent coast. They passed Faversham, a few miles from Parkin's home at Ludden, and then the small fishing port of Whitstable, the twin towers on the site of the Roman fort at Reculver, and the town of Margate, where Drake had returned from pursuing the Spanish Armada up the North Sea two centuries before to report victory.

The breeze favoured them until they rounded the North Foreland, where it backed with what Tutt called 'a bit of south in it' and there was nothing to be done now other than claw their way upwind past Ramsgate and Sandwich into the Downs anchorage.

It was here that not long since Nelson's squadron had sailed for the doomed Boulogne attack and limped back, frustrated, many of the ships' boats full of casualties — Anson among them.

Now, he leaned on the ship's rail, looking shoreward, remembering that dreadful time as if it were yesterday. Even without a glass he could clearly see the exact spot where his Seagate gunboats had been run up on the shingle. It was there that Parkin and Cassandra had found him badly wounded and taken him to a house they had hired in the small fishing port of Deal close by.

Other wounded officers had been similarly accommodated, including Nelson's favourite, young Edward Parker, who had commanded the division that included the Seagate boats.

The young hero, only 23, sword drawn at the head of his men, had been struck down by a blast of grapeshot and musketry.

Anson had recovered sufficiently to be taken back to Ludden Hall to convalesce, but Parker had not been so fortunate — and some weeks later Nelson had followed his coffin to Deal Church, weeping unashamedly.

10

A Fancy Dinner

A presence at his elbow startled Anson out of his reverie. It was Captain Phillips.

'You may well gaze impotently at Deal, Anson. It's a sight that's going to become all too familiar by all accounts.'

'Really, sir?'

Phillips nodded. 'The first lieutenant just spoke to one of the fishing boats and the mackerel-hookers kindly informed him that this pestilential south-westerly will likely trap us here for several days at least, along with all the rest.'

He indicated the forest of bare masts of the warships, merchantmen and coasters sheltering in the wide anchorage framed to seaward by the Goodwin Sands.

'At least the Deal boatmen will be smiling, sir. I've spent some time here recently, both ashore and afloat, and I reckon the locals must pray to the god of prevailing winds to keep them fully occupied rowing around the anchorage running errands, bringing stores, passengers and whatnot.'

Sighing, Phillips acknowledged this. 'Frustrating for us, but not an ill wind for them then.' He shrugged. 'No matter, seeing as we're trapped here and you have returned to us from beyond the grave, as it were, albeit for a few days, we must use the opportunity to celebrate.'

The first lieutenant joined them, smiling. 'Did I hear the magic word, celebrate? A fancy dinner, eh?'

'We may as well, since we're going nowhere for a while and we're not likely to be attacked or collide with anything swinging round a buoy here. It's one of those rare occasions in the service when we don't have to keep our wits about us and can afford to down a few wets.' He smiled at the thought.

Howard beamed. 'Capital! Do I take it that you are formally inviting the officers to dinner in your cabin, sir?'

Phillips, far from being the richest officer in the service — or on board his own ship, come to that, screwed his features into a rictus grin. Hoist with his own petard.

The thought of a table's-worth of hungry and thirsty officers and gannet-like midshipmen devouring his precious private stores was alarming.

But he was not born yesterday.

Hesitating for a moment, he announced: 'Yes, we'll dine in the great cabin, but best send the pusser ashore to procure the necessary articles — fresh meat and suchlike — and no doubt the Deal smugglers can supply him with some decent French wine, for a price!'

Howard raised an eyebrow. So the captain was providing the venue but not the victuals, which would be paid for from other purses, including his own. But no matter, as the scion of a rich and aristocratic family he could well afford it.

*

And so the scene was set for a merry evening. The officers exercised their razors and dug out their best figs, midshipmen were instructed to wash behind their ears, a task deemed unnecessary by some as they were generally reckoned to be wet behind them anyway.

After downing an agreeable sherry they repaired to the table, resplendent in their immaculate undress uniforms and took their places as directed by the first lieutenant.

Cruikshank, the captain's steward, ushered Anson to the seat on the left of Phillips and the only other guest, Captain Mordecai Merton, a rotund merchant navy skipper, was seated on the right.

After grace, shrilly squeaked by the youngest midshipman, Phillips engaged Merton in polite conversation for a while before turning to his former second lieutenant.

'So, Anson, here you are — yet we've laid you to rest at a memorial service. Why, I unveiled the memorial plaque to you myself!'

Howard and McKenzie exchanged grins at the memory of the ensign enveloping their captain when he performed the unveiling ceremony.

Anson smiled. 'Kind of you, sir. I would have enjoyed being there myself, but I was detained in France at the time, of course.'

'Tell me, was the memorial taken down when you showed up very much alive?'

'No, sir. Apparently, in the interests of economy, my clergyman brother decided it should merely be covered up until such time as I do shuffle off this mortal coil and the date and place of death can be amended.'

The copious refills of wine were beginning to take effect and Anson's remark provoked some jocularity among the diners.

Phillips observed: 'Hmm, yes, I do recall that your brother — Augustine, isn't it? — was quick to present your brother officers with the bill for that damned memorial, so I suppose we have a vested interest in what happens to it!'

Howard held up his hand. 'Might I suggest, Anson, that you arrange to be killed somewhere with a very short name? It would save on the stonemason's bill!'

Amid further hilarity, Anson smiled wryly. 'Thank you, gentlemen. Your kind consideration for my well-being is much appreciated. However, I aim to outlive you all, so the memorial plaque will remain covered long after the rest of you have left the planet!'

As the laughter subsided the captain tapped his glass and Anson was invited to take wine with him.

Their glasses were quickly refilled by the hovering Cruikshank, who himself appeared to have been imbibing, and they raised them in salute and drank.

This being the first formal dinner on board for some while, the cooks had excelled themselves, wisely opting for a Kentish theme to take advantage of the ingredients that were readily available locally.

Whitstable oysters, obtained from one of the many fishing boats keeping company with *Phyrne* in the Downs anchorage, had set the meal off on a high note.

Next came an excellent rich, eagerly-slurped fish soup, also courtesy of the Deal fishermen's overnight catch in return for some plugs of tobacco.

Dover sole followed, fried in butter and perked up with juice from lemons brought on board by Captain Merton.

Next came freshly-slaughtered beef and fresh vegetables — a rare treat for men accustomed to lengthy periods at sea, far from cabbage, sprout or carrot.

Undoubtedly smuggled wine, readily available in a fishing/smuggling town like Deal, flowed freely throughout the meal and conversation grew louder and less and less inhibited as consumption mounted.

Having downed a splendid suet and fig pudding known in the service as figgy duff — but to most as 'drowned babies' because of their puffy, glistening new-born appearance — the diners downed the dregs of their wine and ship's decanters of port and Madeira began their larboard voyages.

Both fortified wines that were now fortifying the company came, again, from their guest, Captain Mordecai Merton, whose Indiaman had recently touched at Funchal and Porto on her way home from the Far East.

The final flourish from the cooks came in the form of bowls of freshly-picked cherries purchased from a bumboat, carried in with some style and set between the diners.

Howard tapped his glass. 'Gentlemen, the King!'

All responded: 'The King.'

The loyal toast duly drunk, seated as was the custom in the service owing to the very real danger of crashing already fuddled heads on low bulkheads, the decanters continued to circle the table and the captain tapped his glass again.

'A further toast, gentlemen. It is my pleasure to welcome on board our current next-door neighbour Captain Merton of the good ship *Delivery* — a fine representative, if I may say so, of our nation's mercantile fleets, and we thank him for the excellent port and Madeira that is even now warming the cockles of our hearts.'

'Hear, hear!'

'Kindly raise your glasses.'

Merton beamed, rose unsteadily to his feet, and nodded to the captain and each of his fellow diners in turn. 'Think nothing of it, dear sir, gentlemen. You have done me great honour by inviting me. We merchant fellows are mere tradesmen, pedlars of the seven seas, and we bow, as ever, to the nation's real heroes — of the Royal Navy!'

The ship lurched at anchor and he staggered but managed to keep his feet by grabbing the table, provoking mirth by admitting that 'Robust beverages, port and Madeira, gentlemen, are as you can see, extremely quick-acting on middle-aged fellows like me!'

Captain Phillips, his cheeks shining from the effects of the food and wine, caught Anson's eye and clicked his fingers. 'Damn me, I clean forgot! It being a Sunday, I'd meant to propose a toast to absent friends and those at sea, but I'm reminded that one of our friends is no longer absent! So we'll couple it with our former shipmate Oliver Anson, returned from the dead!'

All eyes turned to Anson and glasses were emptied in salute to him.

Phillips put down his glass, wiped his hand across his mouth and announced: 'Now, gentlemen, I call upon our former shipmate to explain in detail why it has taken him so long to return on board after his run ashore at St-Valery-en-Caux.'

Anson sighed and spread his hands. 'Must I, sir?'

'Certainly! The last I saw of you, my boy, was when you climbed into one of the boats off the Normandy coast, although of course Howard and McKenzie reported back what had happened on the mole.'

Nodding, Anson recalled the high hopes they had of cutting out a troublesome privateer — hopes that were dashed when they found the French had been alerted.

He offered: 'The raid could well have succeeded, sir, but as I subsequently learned ashore, quite by chance a

71

battalion of French infantry had arrived in the area and bivouacked nearby. We weren't to know that and without them the mole would likely have been at best lightly defended and penetrating the inner harbour and cutting out the privateer would have been relatively straightforward.'

Relieved, Phillips ventured: 'So it's your opinion that Admiral Leng's plan was realistic?' In posing the question the captain, whether by accident or design, was making sure his officers understood that no blame for the failure of the raid could be attributed to him personally.

It was the admiral commanding the blockade who had ordered *Phryne* to undertake the mission after receiving intelligence from a French royalist sympathiser that the privateer pestering merchantmen off England's south coast was lurking at St Valery.

'Absolutely, sir. I have no doubt that we would have succeeded with minimum casualties. As it was—'

Howard interrupted: 'We lost five men killed, several wounded in the boats, and you and two others wounded on the mole and captured.'

'That's about the size of it. Our lads did all they could, but the odds were overwhelming.'

'But fortunately you were able to escape.'

'Once we had recovered somewhat from our wounds. It was relatively easy to get away before we arrived at a prison camp, but I doubt I'd have managed to get to the coast and make it back across the Cannel without the support of Hoover and Fagg.'

McKenzie asked: 'My Corporal Hoover, the American?'

'One and the same, although he's a sergeant now — master at arms of my Sea Fencible detachment. As reliable and resourceful fellow as you'll ever find.'

The Scot nodded enthusiastically. 'That's good to hear. We train 'em well in the marines, you know!'

'Hoover is an exceptional man. But for the fact that his father was killed fighting the rebels in America, he could well have had an easier start in life and become an officer. Still could and should in my opinion.'

McKenzie looked doubtful. It was not just the fact that Hoover was an American by birth. Commissions from the ranks were rare, even in the marines, and almost unheard of in the army where the system was bedevilled by the purchase system. It was well known that anyone short of a congenital idiot could buy his way in and up the rank ladder.

Phillips enquired: 'The other man, Fagg, wasn't it? I remember him as an excellent foretop-man, albeit a mite too cheeky for his own good, but then he was from Chatham.'

'Indeed, sir,' Howard observed. 'He was one of those artful devils you suspected of all sorts of mischief but were never actually able to catch at anything,'

Anson grinned his now lop-sided grin. 'Quite so, but he also proved to be just the sort of man to have with me when attempting to escape from France — annoyingly cheerful, quick-witted, and able to scrounge from the French without having a word of the language, well, no words they would have understood! He's now my detachment bosun.'

Phillips laughed. 'So you've got 'em both promoted! Well, a spot of nepotism never did the navy any harm!'

Anson raised his hands in mock surrender. 'Guilty as charged, sir. But when taking command of a bunch of Sea Fencibles who'd been badly led, I was advised to have about me one or two men I could trust — and Hoover and

Fagg had proved to me beyond doubt during our escape from France that they were such men.'

'Now tell us about this stone frigate of yours and these strange Sea Fencible creatures you command.'

'Well, basically they're a bunch of harbour rats, mainly men who earn their living by the sea and rather than serving afloat they volunteer for the fencibles. No doubt the main attraction is that they are given a protection against being pressed, so there's no shortage of recruits.'

'Presumably they're paid, too?'

'Yes, a shilling a day for training with the great guns — we have our own shore battery, y'know — and with musket, half pike and cutlass. And we have two newish gunboats armed with carronades.'

'And the role is mainly to prevent French landings?'

'It is. If the French were to evade our ships and invade, our role is to frustrate any attempts to land — and of course to protect the coast from enemy privateers. Some call the fencibles man-of-war dodgers, but without them the Normandy privateer would not have been taken. What's more, every man jack of my detachment volunteered for the Boulogne raid — and paid in blood when it all went wrong.'

*

The decanters continued to circle and Anson was persuaded to recount the circumstances of the capture of the privateer, which he did with some reluctance, playing down the heroics.

Nevertheless, Howard and McKenzie, who had both been in the thick of the unsuccessful and costly St Valery raid, were not to be fooled.

The marine declared: 'Damned brave, boarding and taking a well-armed and well-manned brig like that!'

Howard concurred: 'And with a bunch of harbour rats!'

'Yes,' the captain agreed, 'but *British* harbour rats!'

More drink flowed and Anson escaped further swinging of the lamp about his exploits since leaving the frigate by recounting the story of the stuffed birds he had sent his particular friend, the naturalist and antiquarian Josiah Parkin, from Gibraltar.

To the huge amusement of all, he explained that all that could be found of the stuffed hoopoe, blue-cheeked bee-eater and greater short-toed lark when Parkin opened the box back in England were a few feathers, bones and glass eyes — the work of *Rattus rattus*, alias the black or ship rat.

The by now well-oiled diners subsided into helpless mirth, and first Allfree, then others, followed up with tall stories of exploding rats that had been at a ship's powder store, midshipmen's ratting expeditions — and moved on to tales of weevils and other creatures that inhabited their nautical world.

Captain Merton was prevailed upon to recall exotic dishes served up by his cooks and his mention of Clive of India reputedly calling the pungent lizardfish 'Bombay duck' sparked the first lieutenant to counter with 'Spithead pheasants':

'The navy's nickname for kippers,' he explained to the puzzled merchant captain. 'We made good use of 'em when I was a middie in the old *Unforgiveable*. The first lieutenant was a real tartar, hated by the gunroom. He'd masthead or cane us for the slightest thing. But we got our own back.'

'How did you do that?'

'One of the other mids overheard the captain agreeing that the swine could go ashore to meet some lady friend when we reached Devonport. So a few days before he went, we purloined his best coat, unpicked the lining, put half a kipper in each of his coat tails and sewed them up again.'

'Good grief!' Anson exclaimed. 'Didn't he notice?'

'Not 'til the kipper started rotting, but by then he was ashore no doubt being followed about by an extremely nasty smell emanating from his nether regions. I imagine it had an adverse effect on his love life. Coitus interruptus, you might say.'

Anson winced. The last time he had heard *that* expression, it had been blurted out by the dreaded Charlotte when they were caught by surprise dallying on the terrace during the Brax Hall ball. It was *not* something of which he wished to be reminded.

He swept the image from his mind. 'Surely your first lieutenant must have found out what was causing the evil smell, put two and two together and taken his revenge?'

'That's the strange part. We're sure he did eventually track the smell down and got rid of the kipper, because when he came back on board his jacket had clearly been freshly laundered and he reeked of eau de Cologne.'

'But didn't he punish those responsible?'

'He must have had his suspicions, of course, but he never did discover who'd done it and if he'd punished the entire gunroom the captain would have wanted to know the reason why. The whole story would have come out and made him a laughing stock. In any event, we reckoned he'd learned his lesson and realised that if he cracked down on us youngsters too hard, we had ways of getting back at him.'

Captain Merton chuckled. 'I have to say, gentlemen, that discipline in the merchant service is an altogether different animal, but then we rarely have to lock horns with an enemy. We carry sufficient by way of guns to deter would-be plunderers, but fortunately we have the legs on most men-of-war and privateers and at the first sight of a strange sail we cut and run.'

Phillips offered: 'With a valuable cargo to protect, that's the sensible thing to do.'

'Thank you, sir, kind of you to say so. Some might accuse us of being lily-livered, but the owners require us to forego heroics and bring their ships home intact.'

Mordecai Merton took another swig of his drink and enquired: 'Having heard of Mister Howard's kipper exploits as a midshipman and observed the relaxed atmosphere on board *Phryne*, I take it this is a happy ship by comparison?'

Phillips waved his hand dismissively. 'Not for me to say, sir, but we are fully manned and many of the ship's company have been with me for a good while. I venture to suggest that the same would not be true in an *un*happy ship.'

'Very true, captain — and I am much relieved to hear that you are not in want of hands.'

'Relieved?'

'Indeed. I have a confession to make. As soon as we hove to in the Downs, I sent my best hands ashore in a Deal bumboat to avoid the press. It's well known that short-handed warships using this anchorage send boats to filch men from merchantmen sheltering here.'

Knowing looks were exchanged by his hosts, most of whom had been involved in doing just that at some time or another when short-handed.

'Yes, gentlemen,' Merton continued, 'the shipping companies have had it decreed that the navy must not press masters, mates, boatswains and carpenters of vessels of fifty tons or more, but even they can be taken if they set foot ashore unless on company business. Hence sending 'em off with packages addressed to the company.'

'Wise of you, sir, very wise. If I didn't have a full complement, I wouldn't be averse to winkling a few out myself.'

'It's an occupational hazard for us merchant types, especially when returning from a deep-sea voyage. I've known merchant ships with specially constructed hiding places where hands can lurk if navy boats come near.'

'But you prefer to send 'em ashore?'

'I do, giving them the wherewithal to enjoy a spot of leave while my purser holds on to most of the pay they're due to make sure they return once we're safely alongside in the London docks.'

Howard asked: 'Have you had any scares yourself?'

'Last voyage we were scarcely into the chops of the Channel when a British man-of-war ordered me to "Heave-to in the King's name" and sent a lieutenant and a tough-looking boat's crew to board me looking for men to press.'

'And you lost some men?'

'Only a few bad hats: drunken, truculent fellows who'd given me nothing but trouble from the moment we sailed. I entertained the lieutenant liberally in my cabin and told my first mate to make sure all the boat party had a few wets. They left as happy as sand-boys carrying with them the men I would cheerfully have thrown overboard myself if such things were permitted!'

'Good for you, sir. I've no doubt both sides came out of it well. You got rid of your trouble-makers and the navy got some hard bargains who could no doubt be licked into shape and prove to be useful in a scrap!'

Midshipman Foxe produced his fiddle and the company continued well into the night with songs of the sea and recitations by several of the officers.

The decanters continued their voyages round the table, and it was not until the early hours that Captain Phillips dozed off in his chair, sliding slowly down until he was in imminent danger of slipping below the table.

The merchant skipper had already left saying he needed to relieve himself and instead wisely crept away to his waiting boat to return to his ship. He was due to sail for London in the morning, the south westerly being in his favour.

The first lieutenant signed to the rest that it was time to depart and led them unsteadily out of the great cabin, shushing any who made a noise — not that anything could be heard above their leader's loud snores.

11

The Morning After

Next morning the officers of His Majesty's frigate *Phryne* were not so merry.

The captain himself, when he eventually appeared on deck, confided in his first lieutenant. 'I must admit I don't feel too clever this morning, Howard.'

Tongue in cheek, Howard observed: 'The wine went down well enough, so it must have been something you ate, sir, the oysters perhaps?'

Phillips growled. 'The truth is, I'm getting a bit past staying up all hours knocking it back with you youngsters. You'll find the time comes when it begins to catch up on you.'

The first lieutenant smiled wanly. He was but a few years younger than his captain and didn't feel too clever himself after the night's carousing.

'The pusser has procured some excellent coffee from one of the merchantmen. May I suggest you repair to your cabin and instruct your steward to make you a strong brew of it? I'd not refuse a mug of it myself. There's precious little for any of us to do until this wretched wind changes direction.'

'You're right, as ever, my dear boy. I'll heed your advice, but pray do not hesitate to call me on deck should anything untoward occur.'

'Untoward? Here at anchor, sir?'

'Yes indeed. A plague of locusts, the sudden appearance of the four horsemen of the apocalypse, some stray admiral poking his nose into our affairs, a favourable breeze — that sort of thing.'

Howard smiled affectionately. He and his captain had covered many a league together and each understood the other as well as, if not better, than a married couple. And unlike most of those joined in holy matrimony, they seldom became irritated with one another.

'Rest assured, sir. I have the weight.'

*

With no duties to perform and nothing much else to do, Anson spent a good deal of time at Josiah Tutt's side, quizzing him about his vast knowledge of the Channel and its foibles. Truth be told, the vagaries of wind and tide, indeed the whole business of navigation had never been Anson's strongest subject and he used the opportunity to educate himself a little better, courtesy of the master.

Tutt was one of a special breed. They were charged not only with navigation but all the complexities of stowage, rigging and trim — and were expected to provide their own navigational charts, books and instruments, including a sextant, dividers and parallel rules.

In absorbing Tutt's vast knowledge, Anson paid particular attention to the currents to be encountered entering ports both sides of the Channel. During this lull, the kindly pilot patiently answered his many questions and permitted him to copy navigational notes from his personal sailing bible, the product of many years roaming these waters.

Anson copied selectively, recording the information in his pocket-sized leather-bound journal, concentrating on the French ports around the Pas de Calais and the Normandy coast.

Most valuable, he reckoned, were the detailed sketches Tutt had made of the approaches to each of them, from Calais round to the Normandy seaports as far as Cherbourg, giving not only the geographical features, but also the currents, depths and so on. These excellent representations he copied to the best of his ability, making a fair job of it thanks to the basic sketching training he had been given as a midshipman.

It was time, he thought, well spent. If not of immediate use, such information would most surely be of value at some time in the future.

Meanwhile, *Phryne* and the many other vessels stuck in the Downs continued to swing at anchor awaiting a change of wind to allow them to continue their westward journeys.

*

A day after Anson's note was received at Ludden Hall, another letter arrived for Josiah Parkin.

He took it to his study, called for cook to bring his morning coffee, settled into his favourite armchair and broke the seal. Somewhat surprised to see that it was from Oliver's father, the Reverend Thomas Anson, rector of Hardres-with-Farthingham, he read:

My dear sir

I write craving your indulgence as a fellow-antiquarian and friend of my son Oliver, to ascertain his whereabouts and well-being following Admiral Nelson's attack on Boulogne in which I understand he took part and was wounded.

It grieves me to explain that just before the above action an unfortunate rift occurred between Oliver and our family over a private matter which, in the interests of all parties involved, it would not be proper for me to disclose in detail.

I had hoped that by now there would have been some contact, but Oliver has not responded to my letters.

May I therefore request your assistance by telling him that the question of a proposed marriage to a certain lady of his acquaintance no longer applies as she has since married another. The matter is therefore closed and I hope we can now forgive and forget.

I seek your goodwill in persuading him to meet me at any time and place to suit him so that we can set about healing this breach. Please assure him that it is not my intention to include his mother or brother Augustine in any such meeting.

I have a further, I hope not impertinent, favour to ask of you. Conscious of the friendship between you, your niece and my son, and the fact that he has always been close to his own sister Elizabeth, I wonder of you would consider inviting her to stay at Ludden Hall? You will fathom, as Oliver might say, that I believe if the two were together for a while well away from the rectory the seeds of reconciliation might be sowed. I hasten to add that Elizabeth had nothing whatsoever to do with the dispute and is devastated that he is apparently now lost to her, as, I might add, am I.

I pray that you will kindly forgive this appeal and act upon it out of the affection I know we share in equal measure for Oliver.

I will await you response in hope.

Your obedient servant

Thomas Anson DD

*

Strolling in the gardens, Parkin pondered long and hard how to respond. He knew that Oliver's breach with his family had been serious, perhaps terminal, and there was an opportunity here to play peace-maker. But would his young friend thank him for it?

The breach, he understood, was brought about by Oliver's mother and priggish, self-seeking older brother Gussie attempting to push him into marriage with the scary Charlotte Brax, and the rector had no doubt been coerced into going along with them.

But that was all water under the bridge now. The Brax girl had married someone else and Oliver was off the hook.

So might a reconciliation now be possible? With his father, perhaps, but Parkin doubted that Oliver would ever feel able to bury the hatchet with his mother and brother — nor vice versa. However, he felt he could happily agree to the request for Elizabeth to spend some time at Ludden Hall.

It was a matter he would dearly have loved to discuss with Cassandra, but with her not expected back for some time it was down to him.

What would Oliver have wanted him to do?

He made his way to the arbour beside his small lake and sat alone, thinking it through as he watched dragonflies darting about and damsel flies mating over the water lilies.

When the time came to stroll back to the house for lunch, he had made up his mind. He would not agree to act as an intermediary, but would offer to tell Oliver on his return that his father wished to see him. Other than that he would stick to facts and avoid comment, and as he walked, he composed a response in his head.

*

After a couple of days the south-westerly slackened to be replaced by a light northerly breeze, a welcome occurrence that set the hotchpotch collection of vessels in the Downs all of a flutter.

But with the northerly came fog, prompting Captain Phillips to summon the master. 'What d'you make of it, Mister Tutt?'

Tutt touched his hat. 'I've seen this many a time before, sir. This is what you get when warm moist air coming up the Channel meets a cold nor'-easterly.'

'And condensation equals fog, eh?'

'Just so, sir. And, sir...'

'And what?'

'Well, what with the fog and all and being in the midst of all these merchantmen with so many wanting to get under way after wasting a lot of time stuck here in the Downs, there's likely to be a lot of what you might call, well, confusion—'

'And every chance of colliding with one or more of 'em and red faces all round, eh?'

Tutt nodded. The possibility of colliding with one of the undermanned merchantmen was a very real danger. 'That's about the size of it, sir. I recall that back in '82 Nelson himself was here in the Downs preparing to sail in the old *Albemarle* with a convoy. A sudden violent squall blew in from the north and drove an East India store-ship into her, carrying away her bowsprit, foremast head and much of her sails and rigging.'

'Hmmm...' Phillips stroked his chin and announced: 'So it would be a good seamanlike precaution to make a quick getaway.'

'Indeed it would, sir.'

'Very well Mister Tutt, let's get under way quickly and cleanly.'

He beckoned the first lieutenant and Anson over. 'We're going to sail immediately, gentlemen — before all these clod-hopping merchant wallahs clutter up the Channel.'

Howard was of like mind. 'Very wise, sir.' And he called to the bosun, hovering nearby. 'Look lively, Mister Taylor, and let's have all hands on deck to up-anchor and make sail. Let's show the traders how the proper navy does things!'

The bosun grinned. He and his mates were charged with seeing '…that the men go quickly on deck when called, and that, when there, they perform their duty with alacrity and without noise or confusion.' And he was highly skilled at doing just that, he and his hard-nut mates encouraging the men with calls, cries — and rattan cane or rope's end when necessary, although in *Phryne* both the captain and first lieutenant viewed 'starting' as a last resort.

Taylor put his bosun's call to his lips and blew *call all hands*, backing it up by hollering: 'Do you hear there? All hands! Lively now!'

A stampede followed throughout the ship as his mates echoed the call and men raced to their stations, glad that the boredom of swinging at anchor was over.

Tutt raised his hand to get the captain's attention. 'You'll want to cruise off and on down to Portsmouth, sir? Should be plain sailing except for this blasted fog.'

Off and on meant keeping close to shore and sailing off and on it, and it made sense to Phillips. Sighting landmarks from time to time would at least confirm where they were.

He wrinkled his eyes and peered seawards. 'Quite, so be sure to have plenty of look-outs posted. Men with sharp eyesight and not afraid to sing out if they so much as glimpse another vessel or we run too close to shore. I don't want to end my career being court-martialled for bumping into a Newcastle collier or running aground!'

Tutt chuckled. 'Never fear, sir. If anything comes anywhere near us, you'll be the first to know.'

*

Anson went on deck to see *Phryne* weigh anchor but suddenly felt giddy and, head down, clutched a rail for support. He had clearly still not fully recovered from his wounds.

'Are you alright, sir?'

He looked up to see a marine eyeing him anxiously.

'Thankee, yes, 'twas just a dizzy turn.'

'Can I help you below, sir?'

He nodded and the marine took his arm, causing him to wince. 'Best take my left arm.'

Below, he collapsed on his cot and quickly drifted off into a deep sleep.

*

Phillips paced the quarterdeck until he was confident that the hurly-burly of the anchorage was well behind them and they had given the treacherous Goodwin Sands a wide enough berth.

Much as he would have preferred to remain on deck, the captain had long recognised that it was important to show trust in his subordinates. Left to their duties they would make the decisions, right or wrong, without deferring to him at every twist and turn.

And so he left the quarterdeck to the first lieutenant, officer of the watch and the sailing master. Like Howard, Tutt not only had a wealth of experience but was renowned for fine judgment. And Allfree, who had the watch, was a sensible fellow. The ship could hardly be in better hands.

Nevertheless, as he sat at his writing desk composing a letter to his wife back home in Pembrokeshire, he kept an ear out for any shout from above that would warn of another vessel looming up out of the thickening fog.

12

Josiah Parkin's Response

As was his custom, it being a Wednesday, the Reverend Thomas Anson, rector of Hardres-with-Farthingham and distant kinsman many times removed of the late, great, circumnavigator and reformer of the navy, Admiral Lord Anson, walked down his shingled driveway to await the arrival of the local carter.

Hezekiah Champion could be relied upon to come by with the mail, newspapers and sundry items ordered from the Canterbury shops around 11 o'clock on Mondays, Wednesdays and Fridays, rain or shine.

Today, being a trifle early, the rector settled himself on the wooden bench seat beside the iron gates and while waiting turned the matter of his estranged son over in his mind.

The falling out had been most unfortunate. It was not of the rector's doing and he had come to realise that he had been foolish to allow himself to be brow-beaten into taking sides with his wife and elder son Gussie against his favourite. However, he had now taken the first step towards healing the breach and was anxiously awaiting a response from his fellow-antiquarian Josiah Parkin.

At last Hezekiah's cart rounded the bend and, seeing the rector sitting beside the gate, the carter called out. 'Letter for you today as well as the papers, your reverence.'

Restraining his impatience to send the garrulous old man on his way, the rector listened for a few minutes to the inevitable local gossip the carter had picked up along the way before excusing himself.

Back in the rectory he told his butler-cum-steward George Beer that he did not wish to be disturbed and shut himself in his study on the pretext of writing his weekly sermon.

Nervously he broke the seal on the packet the carter had delivered, smoothed it out and read:

Dear Sir

I respond to your enquiry regarding the whereabouts and wellbeing of your son Oliver.

I am pleased to say that although he has not yet fully recovered from wounds sustained during Admiral Nelson's late attack on Boulogne, he is on the mend. He has been ordered by his superiors to convalesce for a further six weeks, but, as you might expect, he has interpreted that instruction in his own way.

Currently he is a guest on board his former ship, HMS Phryne, in a supernumerary capacity, enjoying some sea air en route to Portsmouth. His intention, I believe, is to disembark there and return to stay with my niece Cassandra and I at Ludden Hall.

Regarding your request that I act as an intermediary and attempt to mend the unfortunate rift that has occurred between you, I am very much afraid that I must decline as I believe he will see any such intervention by me as unwelcome interference in his personal affairs. However, I will certainly mention to him on his return that you have written seeking reconciliation with him. Whether or not he chooses to respond is of course entirely a matter for him.

As to your request that your daughter Elizabeth be invited to stay with my niece at Ludden for a while, Cassandra is away visiting her cousins at present but I am sure she will be delighted to acquiesce. She has heard a great deal about Elizabeth from Oliver, who is clearly particularly fond of the elder of his two sisters, and will be thrilled to make her acquaintance. Not least, I am sure she will brighten up the dull lives we country mice lead when your son is away. As soon as Cassandra returns, we will write again to make the necessary travel arrangements and suggest Elizabeth plans to stay for at least a month so that she is sure to be here when Oliver returns.

I look forward to renewing my valued acquaintance with you at the next meeting of the county antiquarian society.

Meanwhile I thought you might be interested to see the enclosed sketch I have made of some old stone foundations our gardener has uncovered in the grounds of Ludden Hall. From the odd coin and broken pot discovered over the years I had long suspected that there might be some Roman connection but further excavations will be necessary and now that peace is rumoured I very much hope that Oliver will be interested enough to assist me.

I am, sir, your obedient servant
Josiah Parkin

13

The Captain's Visit

A welcome visitor down at Seagate was the jovial Captain Amos Armstrong, permanently cheerful now that he had been promoted and escaped the confines of the Sussex signal station he had endured for so long.

As the new divisional captain overseeing all Kent Sea Fencible units from the North Foreland to Dungeness, he was making it his business to pay particular attention to the Seagate detachment in the absence on sick leave of his friend Lieutenant Anson.

Sam Fagg, trying to make sense of columns of figures recording how many king's shillings had been dished out to the Seagate fencibles for each day's training they had put in over the past month, jumped to his feet and knuckled his forehead in salute as the captain entered.

'Ah, Bosun Fagg! Caught in the act of massaging the figures, eh?'

From Armstrong's detested predecessor, the haughty, egotistical, social-climbing Captain Hoare, this would have raised hackles. But the new captain was known to be a proper officer with a sense of humour and an easy manner with his underlings.

Unfazed, Fagg grinned. 'Perish the thort, sir. I take as good care of these 'ere shillens like as if they wus me own children what I ain't got, well, so fer as I know that is, on account of their muvvers not informin' me, if you follow my drift.'

Armstrong chuckled. 'I'm not sure I do follow your drift, bosun, but I think I have fathomed your sentiments. Anyhow, I'm not here to check up on your book-keeping. Prefer to leave that to the sea-grocers and hammock-counters. No, in the absence of Lieutenant Anson I am here merely to cast a friendly eye over his domain and make sure morale is high, the boats haven't sunk, boots fit and that sort of thing.'

'Very well, sir. Well, our morals is up to scratch 'cept fer the odd bit of drunkenness, womanising and so-forth like what you'd expect, normal like. The boats is still afloat and boots is not on issue, so you could say that the ones what we ain't got don't fit on account of our not 'avin' any, well, not pusser's boots anyway.'

Armstrong, struggling slightly with the twisted logic, held up a hand. 'That's all to the good, bosun — all to the good. Therefore all I need do is get you to take me through the nominal roll, updating me on recruiting, the progress or otherwise of the men wounded during the Boulogne raid, what's being done for the widows of those killed, etcetera, etcetera.'

'Well, sir, recruitin' is pretty good on account of the prize money what we're expectin' from capturin' that there privateer and men wantin' to join after the Boulogny business.'

'The lure of prize money I can understand. It drives a good many in the service, especially admirals who get a large chunk of it even when they're usually far away from the shot and blood. But what makes men clamour to join to fill the boots of those killed or maimed in action eludes me.'

'Like I said, sir, the pusser don't issue no boots.'

'It was a figure of speech, bosun, merely a figure of speech. And you have expressed a double negative, by the by. If the purser doesn't issue *no* boots, that means he must issue you with *some* boots.'

Fagg shook his head. 'Oh no, sir, beggin' yer pardin. Like I said, he don't issue no boots.'

Armstrong sighed. 'Never mind the boots. Kindly take me through the nominal roll.'

They settled down to study the ledger recording the fencibles' names, ages, addresses, marital status, number of children — where applicable — and civilian occupations and date of joining.

First, Armstrong queried the fate of those whose names had been scored through and annotated: DD, naval shorthand for discharged dead.

In each case Fagg explained simply: 'Boulogny, sir.'

Nelson's disastrous Boulogne raid had indeed been a bloody affair. Altogether some 200 had been killed or wounded, including three local Sea Fencibles among the dead and half a dozen severely wounded, along with Anson himself.

'These three men killed. Were they married?'

'Brooke and 'ogben were, but Longstaff's wife left 'im years ago on account of 'is drinkin'. Liked a drink, did Longstaff, well lots o' drink, but whatever anyone says abaht 'im, 'e was as brave as anyfink at Boulogny.'

'And the widows?'

Fagg hesitated. 'Not supposed to tell, sir, on account of the gent involved wishing to remain a-nonymouse, like what I try t'be on board ship, but seein' as it's you... well, truth be told Lieutenant Anson's friend Mister Parkin 'as sorted out some sort of pensions for 'em. Don't know the

ins and outs, but word is they'll not want for nuffink —
nor will their kids.'

Armstrong nodded knowingly. From what he knew of
Anson's other particular friend, the wealthy former banker,
this was a typically generous gesture, looking after the
families of men he could not have known. It was clearly
enough for him to know that they were Anson's men and
they had died heroically for king and country.

'By the by, sir. One of our blokes, Billy Rogers, was wiv
us at Boulogny, and went wiv the boardin' party, but no-
one ain't seen sight nor sound of 'im since.'

'So, either killed or maybe wounded and captured?'

Fagg shrugged, unable to throw further light on the
matter.

'Was he married?'

'No sir, nor did 'e 'ave no father nor mother what
anyone knows abaht.'

'Miraculous!'

They moved on to the wounded and Fagg went through
the list.

'And are they, too, being looked after?'

'Agin, sir, Mister Parkin 'as seen 'em orlright. And I'm
given 'em a king's shillen whenever we 'as a trainin' day,
on account of they would he 'ere if they could but they
can't, what wiv missing bits, like.'

'Very good. I'm sure His Majesty wouldn't object to
that. Now, with rumours of peace in the offing I hope
we're not taking on any of these would-be recruits you
were on about.'

Fagg frowned at the prospect of an end to hostilities that
might put them all on the beach. 'Don't know nuffink
about all that politickin', sir. The Frogs 'as always been

our enemy and sure as eggs is eggs they ain't goin' to chuck it in now, are they?'

'The powers that be reckon that they might be willing to, as you say, chuck it in, if for no other reason to give themselves a breather and time to regroup. I doubt that any peace will last, but while it does the Sea Fencibles, volunteers and all will probably be stood down. His Majesty's government doesn't like to spend money feeding idle mouths. Hence, it would not be wise to fill our ranks with new recruits amid all the uncertainty.'

Fagg spread his hands in a gesture of helplessness. 'Too late, sir. We've just taken on a few and right good men they are, too.'

'How unfortunate, but then you were not to know. Who are these men?'

The bosun explained: 'This 'ere's the list. The ones we've took are good keen blokes.'

Armstrong scanned the list. 'What was wrong with these men listed as rejects?'

Fagg explained: 'This one, Wright, was, well, different...'

'What's different about him?'

'That is what's different, see, sir. Wright ain't a 'e, 'e's a she...'

'Good Lord!'

'It's like this, sir. Our surgeon bloke—'

'Phineas Shrubb?'

'One and the same. Well, 'e came along to vet this lot, see, and told us abaht Gladwish thinkin' 'e was King George, Pearse 'avin' a wooden leg, and Wright lookin' like a man wiv a beard and all, but 'e's got tits too — and other bits and pieces what shows 'e's a she!'

Armstrong scratched his head in bewilderment. 'I'm beginning to wish I hadn't asked. Look, I can understand why you wouldn't take a man who thinks he's the king — and some...', he groped for the word, '...person, with female attributes—'

'And a beard, sir.'

'Harrumph. Yes, thank you for reminding me about the beard. You rejected the man with a wooden leg, too, I trust?'

'No, sir, we took 'im on account of 'e can still get about well enough on 'is peg leg, and 'e's a right good seaman.'

Armstrong could not immediately think of a reply to that and while he was still deliberating, they were interrupted by the clatter of hooves on the cobbles outside.

Sergeant Hoover, just back from visiting the wounded men, went out to greet a blue-jacketed dragoon mounted on a sturdy grey. He returned with the messenger who saluted and reported: 'From Hythe signal station, sir. Lieutenant Dixon couldn't be sure a signal would have reached you with this fog about, so here it is, verbal like.'

'Jolly good. Verbalise away, Dragoon...?'

'Lewis, sir.'

'Thankee Lewis. So what's afoot?'

'Seems some fishermen have reported spotting a French warship off the coast, sir, most likely out of one of the Channel ports — Calais or Boulogne.'

'Headed?'

'Appears the fishermen couldn't be sure, sir, what with all this fog about.'

Armstrong reached for his telescope.

Fagg, who had poked his nose out of the door, offered: 'Don't fink you'll see a lot through that there glass, sir. I can't even see the effing Mermaid from 'ere.'

'Hmm, it's come to a pretty pass if you can't even see the nearest pub, bosun. Nevertheless, I'll give it a try.'

Outside, Armstrong swept the sea with his glass for signs of a sail, but after a moment or two accepted defeat and snapped the telescope shut.

'Where are you due next, Lewis?'

'Dungeness, sir. One of their dragoons'll have to take the message on from there.'

Armstrong nodded. As the former and most unwilling incumbent of the Fairlight signal station further down the coast he knew the routine only too well. When visual signals could not be seen the dragoons attached to each station would carry messages like this to the next signalling post and Sea Fencible detachments en route. One of the Dungeness dragoons would take it to his old station at Fairlight, and so on.

'Very well, you'd best get under way then.' He pondered a moment. 'But add to the message that the Seagate gunboats are launching as a precautionary measure.'

The dragoon remounted and touched his helmet in salute. 'Precautionary measure? Understood, sir, I'll be sure to add that.'

As the messenger rode off to the west, Armstrong turned to Fagg and Hoover. 'In this fog there's a simple choice. Either do nothing or get the boats out there.'

'So shall us get some of the men and launch, sir?'

'Quick as you can, bosun. And as soon as we have enough oarsmen, I'll take the first boat out with Sergeant Hoover here. You're handy with the carronade, sergeant?'

'Handy enough, sir, although I prefer my musket.'

'Take that too. If nothing else we can use it as a warning in the fog. And bosun...'

'Sir?'

'Follow us out in the second boat as soon as you have enough men.'

The bosun had already busied himself loading one of the battery's 18-pounders with wad only, clapped his hands to his ears and fired it. The gun lurched back and Fagg chuckled. 'Heh, Heh, that'll wake the town up and bring the boys a-runnin' dahn 'ere!'

*

No sooner had the gunboats pushed off than they lost sight of the shore — and each other.

Hoover, in *Striker*, cupped his hands and called: 'Ahoy *Stinger*! Row to the sound of my voice. We'd best be roped together for safety.'

Fagg's voice would be heard 'Aye-ayeing', oars splashed and *Stinger* appeared out of the fog.

A rope was thrown across and, now linked up, the two boats were rowed out to sea in silence, all ears alert for the sound of the mystery ship.

They had ceased rowing and been drifting for an hour or more, with carronades loaded, when Joe Bishop at the prow of *Stinger* called softly that he thought he'd caught a glimpse of a ship within musket shot.

Armstrong heard and called to Fagg. 'You're nearest. Did you see it, bosun?'

'No, sir, but Bishop don't make stuff up. Shall we fire the carronade?'

'No, no. It could be one of ours, or a merchantman. We'll have to take a risk and alert them.'

Fagg seized the initiative. 'Right ye are then, let's fire a bleedin' musket and see what 'appens.' He picked up the weapon he had brought along for signalling purposes — primed, but not loaded with ball.

Pointing it skywards he cocked it and pulled the trigger. But the damp had got to the charge and nothing happened.

''Effin' 'ell!' he swore. 'Ye know all further 'ope's lost when an angel pisses on the flintlock of yer musket!'

The boat's crew tittered at the timeless joke but some were clearly relieved that they hadn't drawn attention to themselves. What if the ship Bishop had spotted was the Frenchman they'd been warned about? One ball could sink them — or they could easily be taken and end up in a French prison dining on snails and frogs' legs for the foreseeable future.

After an hour or more drifting fruitlessly around in circles sighting nothing, Armstrong ordered both boats back to Seagate, to the relief of all concerned.

14

The Fog of Peace

Anson, awake early thanks to the noise of men holystoning the deck, was somewhat revived after a good night's rest.

He breakfasted and was on the quarterdeck chatting to the officer of the watch when one of the foretop-men sent aloft to keep watch in the fog shouted down: 'Deck there! Think I saw a ship ahead, but can't see anything now in the fog.'

Allfree shouted back: 'Warship or merchantman?'

'Couldn't say for sure, sir. Warship, I think.'

Allfree turned to Anson. 'This is one of those confounded dilemmas, ain't it? If I beat to quarters and rouse the captain it'll turn out to be a figment of the imagination and I'll be the butt of all the gunroom jokes.'

Anson smiled. 'But if you do nothing it could be a Frenchman about to give us a broadside? I know what I'd do.'

'Exactly! Bosun, beat to quarters!'

As if keeping step with the tattoo beat of the marine drummer, Captain Phillips came bounding hatless up onto the quarterdeck, telescope under his arm and attempting to button his coat one-handed.

'What's afoot, Mister Allfree? Kindly report.'

'Can't be sure, sir, but one of the look-outs reported a ship in the offing. He reckons he caught a glimpse of it but then it disappeared in the fog.'

Phillips harrumphed. 'Man-of-war or merchantman? Ours or theirs?'

'Don't know, sir.'

'Then call the man down and let's hear exactly what he thinks he saw.'

Bosun Taylor had anticipated the order and the lookout was already scrambling down the rigging.

He landed awkwardly, twisting his knee, and hobbled across to the captain who was sweeping the fog with his telescope.

'Well, Gubbins? What d'you think you saw?'

'A ship, sir, to larboard, close, mebbe pistol shot distance.'

'Merchantman or man-of-war?'

'Dunno, sir, but didn't look like a merchantman.'

'So a man-of-war. But French, or one of ours?'

'Sorry, sir. I just had what you calls a glimpse, like. Then it was gorn, like a ghost ship.'

Phillips raised his eyebrows. Sailors were notoriously superstitious and the last thing he wanted was for his men to be spooked by a phantom disappearing vessel, which the more imaginative among them would no doubt soon man with a skeletal crew with the devil in command.

'Nonsense Gubbins! There's no such thing and don't you start spreading daft tales like that.'

'Yes, sir. I mean no, sir.'

Allfree seized the opportunity to impress his captain. 'Was there anything at all that you noticed about her, Gubbins? Three masts, or two?'

'Three, sir, I'm pretty sure of that. And there was one other thing.'

'What?'

'I thought I saw some kind of white flag flying from her mainmast.'

*

Alone with the servants and his collection of stuffed creatures, Josiah Parkin missed the companionship of his niece and was pleasantly surprised when she arrived back earlier than expected, explaining that she had quickly tired of her cousins' endless chatter about fashions and possible suitors.

Privately, Parkin suspected that the real reason for her early return was to be at Ludden for whenever Anson returned.

Cassandra was clearly disappointed to hear that he was currently at sea, but as predicted, was delighted at the prospect of a visit from Elizabeth Anson. Oliver had often spoken of her as his favourite sister and she longed to become her friend.

Not least, Elizabeth would be the perfect chaperone when Oliver returned.

Cassandra helped her uncle compose a further note to the Reverend Anson making the necessary arrangements and before he sealed it, she added to the packet a note of her own:

My dear Elizabeth

I have heard so much about you from your brother Oliver and am thrilled beyond measure that you are coming to stay with us at Ludden Hall. My uncle and I so look forward to welcoming you and sharing time with you, and your brother of course. I am quite certain that we are destined to become the firmest of friends!

I attach a list with suggestions as to dresses etcetera that you may wish to bring...

*

With her guns manned and run out, boys hastening up from the magazine with cartridges and slow matches at the ready, *Phryne* sailed on in eerie silence broken only by the flapping of sails and slapping of waves.

On the quarterdeck Phillips went into a huddle with the first lieutenant, the master and Anson, who was embarrassed to be a mere passenger and anxious to take on whatever role he might be able to fill.

'We have a dilemma, gentlemen, and I don't like dilemmas. Gubbins is not the kind of hand who imagines he's seen something when he hasn't.'

'No, sir,' Howard agreed. 'He's a sensible man, not given to seeing things.'

'So we must assume he did indeed see a ship, a man-of-war.'

'And they must surely have heard us beating to quarters—'

'Yet they have not responded in kind or fired a signal gun, as one of ours would surely have done.'

Howard spread his hands. 'Quite right, sir. So, a Frenchman then? But the white flag Gubbins believes he saw. What can that mean? Surely they're not trying to surrender?'

Captain Phillips was something of a glass half full man and rejected the idea out of hand. 'Chance would be a fine thing, unless they're crippled in some way in which case surely they'd try to remain hidden in the fog.'

Anson raised his hand. 'As we know, sir, there was talk of peace before we sailed, so a white flag could mean that they want to parley.'

'You mean peace may have broken out and they know, but we don't?'

'Yes, sir, but it's merely a guess.'

'But a reasonable assumption nevertheless.' The captain frowned and fingered his chin, a habit of his when pondering a problem, Anson had noticed.

'Hmm, if this does mean peace it's more than I dare to break it or endanger it. If I do, I'll be running a Pembroke chicken farm quicker than you can say Jack Robinson. But if it is peace, I suppose I'll be doing that pretty soon anyway.'

Howard offered a new perspective. 'There's one other possibility. The French royal standard was a plain white ensign before the revolution — and that's what they fought under in the American War.'

'So?'

'So this ship, whatever she is, could have gone over to the royalists.'

Phillips was dubious. 'What do you think Anson? You've hobnobbed with the Frogs more than any of us one way or another.'

'That's true, sir. If you count being captured by them at St Valery and getting a bloody nose from them at Boulogne as hobnobbing, then I suppose I have. But no, I don't buy the royalist idea. Anyway, gentlemen, for whatever reason the white flag appears to indicate that they want to parley and, with respect, I suggest there's only one way to find out why.'

Howard spread his hands in a gesture of acceptance. 'Permission to launch the jollyboat, sir, and I'll go and investigate.'

'Is your French up to it?'

The first lieutenant hesitated. His French was known to be of little more than 'la plume de ma tante' standard. So Anson offered to accompany him. 'I have some of the lingo, sir, and I'd be happy to go with Howard.'

'Very well, so be it.'

The bosun, who had been awaiting a decision, hurried away to supervise the lowering of the jollyboat. Anson advised: 'Best carry a white flag too, sir, to show them we're unarmed and wish to negotiate.'

Howard shouted after the bosun: 'The men are to carry no weapons, Mister Taylor, and get the pusser to find something we can use as a white flag!'

While the boat was being lowered the drifting fog revealed the lookout's 'ghost ship' for a moment, hove to within pistol shot. But the brief glimpse was enough to confirm that she was indeed a French frigate with a dirty white flag flapping limply from her mainmast. Men could be seen in the rigging and on deck, but, importantly, her gun-ports were firmly closed.

Howard and Anson climbed down into the boat and Midshipman Finlay, at the tiller, ordered the coxswain to shove off.

The first lieutenant shushed the low chatter from some of the oarsmen. 'Keep the noise down lads and row smartly. The Frogs will be watching us closely. We think they want to parley so that's what we'll do, but you mustn't give them any lip while Mister Anson and I are aboard. Is that clear?'

There were muttered 'Aye ayes.'

'Mister Finlay. Take the name of any man who so much as sticks his tongue out at a Frog!'

The men chuckled and the grinning midshipman spoke up: 'Aye aye, sir.'

Howard and Anson exchanged a glance. Both were wondering: could this be some ruse or could they really trust the French?

Halfway across to where the outline of the enemy frigate could now clearly be seen, a thought struck Anson. He caught Howard's eye. 'I sincerely hope the French don't keep careful records of their escaped prisoners!'

Howard grinned. 'I doubt it, but if this white flag business is a trick, we'll no doubt both end up as guests of the French in Verdun or Biche.'

Anson smiled wanly. Both French prisons where captured naval officers were held had already achieved notoriety and were reckoned to be virtually escape-proof.

The frigate now loomed large out of the fog and the white flag could be seen. *Phryne's* lookout who thought he'd glimpsed it had indeed got good eyesight.

Howard muttered to Anson: 'That's no proper flag. See how scruffy and stained it is.'

Anson shrugged. 'A makeshift one, then. I don't suppose even the French go around with pristine white flags, waiting for a chance to surrender.'

Frenchmen could now be discerned peering down at them from the deck. Some had climbed the rigging to get a better view, but none appeared to be armed. Nevertheless, it was an uncomfortable feeling for those in the boat and every man jack — including Howard and Anson — could not fail to be anything other than apprehensive.

As one, the rowers had eased off without needing to be told as they closed on the enemy ship. And now, at a nod from Howard, the coxswain ordered: 'Cease rowing and hold station.'

With the oars in the water holding the boat in position it rocked gently in the swell.

Above them an officer leaned over the side and shouted through a speaking trumpet, 'Quel bateau?'

Howard looked enquiringly at Anson.

'Best tell them the name of the ship.'

Nodding, Howard cupped his hands and shouted: 'His Majesty's Ship *Phryne*. Je suis...' he hesitated and Anson prompted him. 'Lieutenant de vaisseau.'

Howard repeated: 'Je suis lieutenant de vaisseau.'

The French officer called down: 'Bien, approche, si'l vous plait.'

The coxswain ordered 'Pull alongside and ship oars', and as the jollyboat bumped against the frigate's side ropes were thrown down and secured. A rope ladder followed and the French officer called down, in heavily-accented English: 'Officer to come on board, if you please.'

Howard looked to Anson, who answered the unspoken question: 'You might need my French, such as it is. I'll come too.'

Clearly relieved, Howard muttered to Midshipman Finlay, 'Hopefully it won't come to this, but give us a while and if we don't reappear head back to *Phryne* and tell the captain we've been tricked.'

The midshipman nodded, but Anson raised a rueful eyebrow. How long was 'a while', and did Howard really believe the jollyboat would be allowed to escape if this was some kind of trick?

Howard grabbed the swinging rope ladder and started to climb. Anson waited until he had negotiated half a dozen rungs and then followed suit.

Immediately in pain from the stitches in his right arm he pulled himself up awkwardly taking most of the strain on his left and wincing from the effort.

A shrill bosun's call greeted Howard as he swung himself on the deck and he came to attention and raised his hat to the officer in charge of the side party.

Following on behind, puffing and blowing from the effort of the climb in his weakened condition, Anson followed suit and removed his hat, noting that the French officer was showing equal respect.

'Welcome on board, messieurs, and please to follow me to the captain's cabin.'

He led the way and as they crossed the deck Anson was surprised to see that there were no signs of hostility from anyone they passed. On the contrary, they were greeted everywhere with smiles.

He whispered to Howard, 'This must surely mean peace.'

Nodding, the first lieutenant replied, 'Nevertheless it's weird to be treated as a welcome visitor by the Frogs!'

It was indeed the oddest feeling and Daniel entering the lion's den sprang to Anson's mind, although today there was no sense of threat.

Reaching the captain's cabin, their escort waved the marine sentry aside and rapped at the door which was immediately opened by a steward.

A voice beyond hailed them. 'Do come in gentlemen, and when we've introduced ourselves, I hope you will join me in a toast to peace!'

The French captain rose from behind his desk and came to greet his visitors. Shaking hands with both warmly, he repeated: 'Welcome, gentlemen, welcome!' In near perfect English he explained: 'I surmised you might not have heard that our nations are now at peace. That is why I ordered a white flag to be flown.'

Howard looked smug. 'One of our look-outs spotted it, monsieur.'

But it crossed Anson's mind that the French must have smoked their proximity well before *Phryne's* look-out had glimpsed his 'ghost ship'.

The Frenchman smiled. 'I fear we had no proper white flag in our locker, so we had to improvise. What your man saw is merely a tablecloth stained with what I believe to be several spillages of wine and soup. In my experience, what with the motion of the ship and the absence of ladies, sea officers are not the daintiest eaters, n'est-ce pas?'

Smiling, Howard and Anson nodded in unison. Anybody who had witnessed midshipmen in particular wolfing down their food after a day of being run ragged by their seniors in the fresh sea air could but agree.

'When you were heard beating to quarters it confirmed to me that you must not know that the peace had been signed and we are no longer at war. No doubt you sailed before the news came through?'

'That's correct, sir.'

'From Chatham, I believe. Your English newspapers are so informative and usually accurate where naval matters are concerned.'

Howard and Anson shared a knowing glance. Their concerns about the 'inky-fingered' profession's carelessness with operational security were confirmed.

'Ça ne fait rien. At least you now know we are at peace. Please seat yourselves and permit me to show you the confirmation I have received from Paris.' He picked up a document from his desk. 'Would you like me to translate, or do you have any French?'

Howard indicated Anson. 'My, er, fellow officer here has some French, which is why he has come along.'

The French captain looked closely at Anson, ashen-faced and holding his injured arm across his chest.

'Are you unwell, monsieur?'

Howard answered for him. 'He was recently, er, wounded.'

'I am sorry to hear that, monsieur, and apologise on behalf of my countrymen.'

'No need. The wound was administered by one of our own.'

The captain gave a Gallic shrug. 'You English! Such a warlike race, so when you are not fighting us you fight among yourselves, n'est-ce pas? An affair of honour, perhaps?' And without waiting for an answer he handed the document to Anson who said, 'I think I may have enough French to make out the gist of it, monsieur.'

'Excellent. It is rare indeed to encounter an Englishman willing to try speaking our language. I have a copy for you to take away. However, I can tell you the main points are that all hostilities between us have ceased, Britain is to give up territories recently annexed including Malta and Egypt — and various others taken from Holland and Spain.'

Howard asked: 'And in return?'

Another Gallic shrug. 'We have agreed to recognise the neutrality of Holland, Switzerland and so on...'

Anson looked up from the document. 'I see that we are also giving up our base at the Cape of Good Hope — and most of our possessions in the Caribbean.'

'Bien sûr, and the lifting of your blockades means that our trade can get back to normal. But while you are studying the details allow me to offer you some good French wine to celebrate. No doubt you have not been able to enjoy any for some years.'

'Au contraire, monsieur, thanks to your turning a blind eye to the smugglers we have been well supplied throughout.'

'Eh bien, there has been some sense prevailing despite the nonsense of war.'

Having scanned the document, Anson told Howard, 'What the captain has told us is evidently perfectly true. Peace has broken out and we will need to re-draw our maps to take account of the changes to overseas possessions.'

Howard nodded and raised his glass to the Frenchman. 'Peace is good news of course, although a sad blow to all our hopes of further promotion. For many on our side of the Channel at least it will mean being on the beach on half pay with zero chance of further employment, promotion or prize money.'

The captain laughed. 'But I doubt it will be the same for us. I suspect this is merely a temporary peace which suits our political masters, eh? And while it exists our ships will be able to leave their harbours unmolested and there will be much sailing for our navy in order to assume control of our overseas possessions once more. Our First Consul has great ambitions, and there is much unfinished business.'

'You are most frank, sir,' Howard commented. 'So a respite only?'

'That is my opinion. But nevertheless a welcome pause during which we can put aside blood-letting.'

Anson had kept a low profile, leaving the conversation to Howard and the French captain, but now he caught their attention.

'Gentlemen, we may no longer be at war, but our people are not yet aware of that. To avoid the possibility of someone in *Phryne* accidentally starting it up again I believe we should return immediately and tell our captain the news.'

The Frenchman reacted with a resigned Gallic shrug. 'Very well, but I am desolé that you cannot stay longer to enjoy our hospitality — as sailor to sailor, not opponents.'

Howard tossed back the remains of his wine. 'Amen to that, but duty calls!'

'Ah, duty, the curse of we officers, is it not? But please, take back a barrel of brandy for your captain with my compliments — and as we sail away, we can then drink a toast to peace and the brotherhood of the sea.'

'You are too kind. Allow us to send back a barrel or two of Kentish ale in return.'

The Frenchman wrinkled his nose. 'I am very much afraid that my men do not have a very high opinion of your beer, monsieur. We had occasion to take some barrels of it from a prize, but I am desolated to say the men told me they found it quite disgusting, so we fed it to the fishes.'

Howard protested weakly. 'Perhaps it was past its drink-by date. I assure you that normally our beer and ale — from Kent at least — is of the finest and a new supply was delivered to us just before we sailed from Chatham. We have wonderful hop gardens, you see.'

'Nevertheless...'

'However, perhaps you would prefer a couple of fat Romney Marsh sheep, also brought on board only a few days ago. Your men will be able to enjoy some fine chops and mutton steaks, washed down with wine rather than our disgusting beer! I will send a boat back with the sheep the minute we arrive on board our ship.'

'That would be most kind, monsieur.' The French captain rose and Howard and Anson followed suit.

Showing them out, their host shook hands with both, telling them, 'Next time we meet, gentlemen, I very much hope it is while strolling about the streets of Paris or London with attractive ladies on our arms, rather than through a telescope in opposing ships with our guns run out.'

Howard smilingly agreed and Anson added: 'D'accord!'

The officer of the watch was waiting outside the captain's cabin and led them back on deck.

They raised their hats in salute and as they climbed back down to the jollyboat, in Anson's case very gingerly, a brandy barrel was rolled out and lowered after them. The Frenchman had not forgotten his gift.

Seated in the thwarts beside Anson, Howard nodded to Midshipman Finlay who ordered: 'Shove off and row smartly lads, the Frogs are watching!' and they headed back to *Phryne*.

As they pulled away Anson whispered to the first lieutenant: 'The boys'll be wondering what's afoot.'

But on occasion Howard was a stickler for protocol and this was one such occasion. 'I'm sure they're all agog, but this item of news is for the captain's ears first and I don't want him to be the last to hear after every other man jack on board.'

*

Back on board *Phryne*, they reported to the captain, showed him the document and Anson took him through it.

Phillips was clearly underwhelmed. 'So it's true then? My God, I can't believe how much our idiot politicians have given away. And now there'll be all manner of problems with the men. They'll be the very devil to keep in line once they hear it's all over — or think it is.'

'I'll take extra precautions with the rum, sir.'

'Quite right, Mister Howard. We all know what lengths Jolly Jack Tar will go to when he comes across an opportunity to celebrate. With luck we'll get to Portsmouth in one piece but once there I fear half the men will disappear.'

'Talking of the demon drink, sir, the French captain has sent you a barrel of brandy.'

'Thoughtful of him.' Phillips turned to his steward: 'Cruikshank, tap it and decant enough for dinner with all the officers in my cabin tonight.'

'Aye aye, sir.'

'But make sure the barrel isn't left where one of your shipmates can tap the other end of it.'

As an afterthought, he asked: 'Should we not return the compliment to the French?'

Howard nodded: 'I've sent the boat back with two of the live sheep we brought on board at Deal. The French wisely declined my offer of English beer.'

*

Word of the peace went round the ship quicker than a rat up a mooring rope and the mood on board vacillated from relief now that the prospect of death or losing one or more body parts to enemy action had evaporated, to be replaced by unease at the likely interruption — and perhaps end — of their careers afloat. The latter was a prospect that cheered some and depressed others.

There were mixed feelings, too, as the officers and warrant officers gathered for dinner in the captain's cabin that evening. Sampling the brandy after the dessert course and the loyal toast, Captain Phillips pushed back his chair and addressed his guests: 'Gentlemen. I thank you all for what you have done for king and country and for me in particular aboard *Phryne* these past few years. I doubt you

115

will receive more thanks from a grateful nation. However, I wish you all joy of the peace and may it bring you all you deserve.'

Glasses were raised and Howard added: 'Amen to that!'

15

Portsmouth

Steering for the point between the belfry of Gosport Chapel and the south-most sentry box under the ramparts of Blockhouse battery, *Phryne* ran serenely past the marker buoys and entered Portsmouth Harbour.

Anson was sad to be leaving his old ship. The passage from Chatham had reminded him how much he missed being at sea rather than making occasional forays on it from his shore-based command. It had been a particular pleasure to mix once more with his brother officers on and off watch, especially off. The camaraderie born of shared experiences, both dramatic and mundane, was difficult if not impossible to recreate ashore, where men went off to their homes or billets when off duty. Afloat, the ship was home and shipmates were family.

But now, peace having broken out, the chance of further sea service was remote. It seemed likely to Anson that the navy and army would suffer the usual cuts imposed by short-sighted politicians at such times.

The volunteer movement including the Sea Fencibles would no doubt be the first to go, followed by the laying up of ships and the disbandment of army units.

So, instead of an active role, he faced remaining one of the many naval officers already ship-less, cast up on the beach on half pay — half life.

It was a far from attractive prospect. Ashore, without a role, he feared he would be lost.

After having his stitches removed courtesy of *Phryne's* loblolly boy and making his farewells, Anson was rowed ashore in the jollyboat to the Spur Redoubt where the Channel fleet ships' boats came and went.

He felt at home here in 'Pompey', as the world's biggest and most famous naval base was affectionately known to sailors everywhere. The familiar forest of masts and the hustle and bustle of the place, with bumboats and myriad other craft fussing around the anchored warships like ducklings around their mothers, were meat and drink to a sea officer like him.

Still not fully recovered from his wounds, he employed a couple of urchins to carry his dunnage and made his way through the dockyard heading for the George, the coaching inn just outside the gates where he had stayed for a few days during the mutiny several years before.

Then, there had been a threatening atmosphere as groups of mutinous seamen gathered awaiting the outcome of demands made by the delegates chosen to represent them. Their grievances about low and irregular pay, poor provisions, inadequate treatment of the sick and wounded, and the lack of shore leave to visit their families, were reckoned by most to be reasonable, and their bellyaching had changed to euphoria at the news that the Admiralty had granted pretty well everything they had asked for.

The mood today was muted. Peace was welcome but, in a town where so many relied on the navy and the dockyard, any scaling down of the fleet would certainly result in tightened belts. Naval personnel, dockyard mateys, publicans, chandlers, tobacconists, tailors, barbers, tattooists, even the inevitable cruising whores — all would feel the pinch.

At the George, Anson gave the urchins-cum-porters sixpence each — to their astonishment and delight — and sought out the landlord who greeted him warmly. 'Mister Anson, isn't it? Never forget a name like yours — you being kin to the great circumnavigator, eh?'

Anson did indeed share his surname with Admiral Lord Anson, who had won undying fame for braving horrendous hardships to circle the globe, capture a Spanish treasure galleon — and rise to become the reformer of the navy. But the kinship was distant, and the latter-day Anson was tired of explaining it. So he chose not to challenge mine host. At least the imagined close relationship with such a national hero would ensure him a good room.

Later, sitting in the bar sipping a tankard of ale, he listened in to the cheerful conversation around him. The peace was on everyone's lips and despite the likely effect of it on people's pockets there was an air of celebration. In the main these were people who had every right to be bucked by the news, Anson reflected. Invasion fears had vanished at a stroke and there was every chance that the hated new-fangled tax on private income introduced to finance the war would be scrapped.

One chubby man of business sitting nearby was even proposing a toast to the fact that he and his cronies need no longer fear being forced to learn French and dine on frogs and snails.

Anson sat alone, moodily contemplating his future, but his melancholy thoughts were interrupted by the porky businessman. 'You, sir! Navy man, ain't you?'

Anson inwardly groaned. He was not in the mood for banter with self-important civilians with whom he had nothing in common.

'Most observant of you, sir. I imagine the uniform gave you a clue.'

The chubster chuckled. 'It did, sir, and I was speculating with my friends here that the likes of you navy men will be cock-a-hoop now that peace has broken out with the French?'

'Not exactly, sir. For one thing, I expect the politicos will now seize the chance to mothball our ships, and secondly, I have little faith in the peace lasting. The result will be that when war breaks out again, we will be unprepared.'

'Now those are gloomy thoughts! Surely even the French want peace as much as we do?'

'The people perhaps, but not Bonaparte. He needed a breather to get his colonies back and gird the nation up for the next campaign. If you want my opinion, I say it's merely a truce, giving them a chance to rearm and prepare while we disarm.'

'Tut tut! Come join us, sir, and we'll banish those dark thoughts with a glass or three!'

Anson shook his head. 'Kind of you gentlemen, but I was not long since wounded and must away to my bed. But I wish you well and that the peace delivers what you wish for and not what I fear.'

16

A Smuggling Run

Billy MacIntyre hefted the large club one-handed and tested it by smacking it down hard on his left palm. Calloused and desensitized as his paws were after years of holy-stoning decks and hauling on ropes, it still hurt like hell. Nevertheless, he grinned: pity the poor revenue man who got a clout round the head with a bat like that.

The weapon indicated MacIntyre's new status in life — a bat-man for a gang of Romney Marsh smugglers. His role was to protect those bringing the contraband ashore and accompany the pack animals as they took the goods to distant hiding places to await distribution to eager customers far and wide.

In his belt was a loaded pistol and he had acquired a new knife to replace the one lost when he attacked Lieutenant Anson in the Mermaid at Seagate.

It was the first time the smugglers had used him on a run and he relished the thought of being involved and reaping the rewards.

He stationed himself near the new lighthouse whose beam served not only as a navigational aid but, tonight, as a beacon to guide the smuggling vessels to the rendezvous with the team ashore. And it was a large team. Dotted around the wide shingle beach were maybe a score of other bat-men and as many more were waiting by the boats drawn up on the shingle. Close by were a dozen pack horses and their handlers. It would be a brave or foolhardy revenue man who would dare interfere with tonight's business — unless mob-handed or backed up by a troop of dragoons.

Preventative men were known to be overworked, outnumbered by the smuggling fraternity, poorly paid and therefore open to bribery. And there was no way they dare challenge the large gang of free traders carrying out tonight's run, anyway.

A two-masted vessel appeared in the bay and three boats were rowed out to meet it. They went alongside and MacIntyre could see casks being lowered into them.

With nothing to do except hang around watching for trouble, he looked up at the lighthouse, impressed by its powerful construction. One of the local men had told him that this was not the first, a tower with an open coal fire at the top having been erected near the shoreline almost two centuries earlier. However, the sea had receded so it had to be demolished and another built to replace it. But that too was eventually left too far from the water's edge and only a few years since — in 1792 — the present efficient lighthouse was erected.

It was built by Samuel Wyatt on a design similar to the Eddystone lighthouse. Its light was powered by oil and it was reckoned it could be seen from Cap Gris Nez in the Pas de Calais on a clear night. There was a cluster of single-storey buildings attached to its buttressed base, but there was no sign of the lighthouse keepers. No doubt they would be rewarded, either with spirits or coin, for looking the other way during the run.

MacIntyre's musing was interrupted by a passing pack-man, evidently on his way to the animals waiting for the boats to come ashore.

'Alright, mate?' the man asked.

'Aye, I dinna think we'll be needing our bats t'night, pal.'

The man paused. 'Scotch is it? Didn't know we had any of you lot down on the Marsh.'

He came nearer and peered closely at MacIntyre by the thin moonlight and the glare from the lighthouse that threw long shadows from anyone standing under it.

'Hang on a minute. I know you, don't I? You were the sod who gave my cousin Jacob Shallow a bad time afore they kicked you out of the fencibles and you went to the press gang! What the hell are you doing here? With the revenue now, are you, spying on us?'

MacIntyre cursed inwardly. Just when everything was going his way this moron had to turn up and recognise him, but he tried to remain cool. He countered the accusation. 'Don't be daft. Do I look like a revenue man? I'm on the run from the fuckin' navy meself!'

'So who are you?'

'I'm Billy Black and like I said, I'm on the run so I've joined yous lot.'

His inquisitor stared at him. 'Black? You're black right enough — Black Mac, they called you. I don't know what you're up to, but we don't like impress men down here on the Marsh as you'll find out when I tell the other boys who you really are...'

MacIntyre took a furtive look around. There was no-one close and the rest of the gang's attention was on the unloading of contraband.

He could not let this idiot shop him, and in an instant, he knew what he had to do and did it. He swung the bat and clouted the pack-man round the head with all the strength he could muster.

There was a crunch of bone and the man fell, pole-axed: dead.

Breathing hard, MacIntyre stooped, pulled the body into the shadow of buildings at the foot of the lighthouse and moved quickly away.

He stooped again to clean the blood from his bat with a handful of wet shingle and walked down to the water's edge where all eyes were on the incoming boats.

Putting the bat aside, he helped unload a barrel and roll it up the shingle towards the pack animals but the gang-master spotted him and shouted: 'Hey, you, Billy boy! You're supposed to be a bat-man, not friggin' about unloading barrels. The tub-men can do that. You couldn't wait to get at the brandy, eh?'

'You're right there, boss! Sorry, I'll get back to guarding.'

The tub-men were each slinging two tubs of spirits or wine from rope harnesses and carrying them up the shingle to where the pack-men were waiting with the horses, most borrowed from sympathetic farmers for a cut-back.

MacIntyre retrieved his bat and walked over to the pack animals, quietly delighted that he had been noticed well away from the murder scene. And when the body was discovered, as it surely soon would be, there was nothing whatever to connect him with it.

On the contrary, he had shown himself willing to get stuck into the smuggling game and the one man who could have queered his pitch was spread-eagled on the shingle, skull crushed by un unknown hand and very definitely dead.

17

Messrs Adkins, Woolsack and Adkins

A hearty supper and a good night's sleep at the George put Anson in a better mood and after a late breakfast he quizzed the landlord about the availability of mail and stage coach seats to London.

Learning that there were none to be had until next day, he set off for a stroll around the town before calling upon the prize agent.

He found the offices of Messrs Adkins, Woolsack and Adkins close by the dockyard and entered hoping against hope for positive news about the sale of the Normandy privateer.

An elderly clerk, bent over a large leather-bound ledger totting up figures, looked up and, recognising Anson's naval rank, ordered the office boy to show him straight into the adjacent lair of the three partners where the younger Mister Adkins was working alone.

Anson was greeted warmly by the junior partner and to his astonishment received confirmation that the sale of *Égalité* had indeed gone ahead.

'My father is dealing with it personally, sir. He and Mister Woolsack are presently visiting a potential client and then taking an early lunch, but if you are able to wait, I'm sure he will be able to quote figures and give you an idea of when the money will be distributed.'

Anson was delighted. It would mean that he could send his share to his father to repay at least some of the allowance he had received until their estrangement. And it would be good news for his fencibles. If they were indeed to be disbanded now that peace had broken out then at least they would have something in their pockets.

The young Mister Adkins summoned the office boy to bring coffee and found Anson a seat at one side of the large paper-strewn desk he assumed was shared by the two senior partners.

'Now, sir, while we are waiting, I should be obliged if you would recount the story of the capture of your privateer. Our work here is very dull, you know. We seldom hear of the daring deeds performed in capturing prizes. Our lives are inhabited merely by the legal niceties and figures, endless figures.'

And so, although he played down his own part in it, Anson allowed himself to be persuaded to recount the story of how his Sea Fencible detachment, with help from men from the impress service, had trapped and taken the troublesome Normandy privateer.

Already it seemed part of the distant past, the Boulogne affair being uppermost in his mind, and the sanitised outline he gave bore little comparison to the blood and guts of the operation.

Nevertheless, the young Mister Adkins was clearly enthralled. 'My, my! What lives you naval fellows lead...' He sighed and frowned: 'Yet how dull am I, trapped here with my ledgers, these plain figures hiding such tales of derring-do.'

Seeking to lift the junior partner's spirits, Anson assured him, 'Nevertheless, sir, think how helpless your naval clients such as I would be without you representing us, jousting with the prize courts, monitoring the sale of captured vessels and marshalling the resulting pounds, shillings and pence on our behalf!'

Young Adkins was touched. 'Kind of you, sir. Most kind. But we do well enough from our percentage without having to spill any blood.'

Anson, now in good spirits at the thought of the coming prize money, faltered slightly. He had heard of agents' and other costs involved in such cases swallowing up most of the returns from the sale of captured vessels.

But then, he consoled himself, the disposal of *Égalité* had been relatively straightforward and Messrs Adkins, Woolsack and Adkins had always been fair as far as his affairs were concerned. Being based in Portsmouth within pistol shot of the dockyard they would not have lasted long in the business if they acquired a reputation for being anything other than totally straight with their naval clients.

His thoughts were interrupted by the return of Messrs Adkins senior and Woolsack from what had clearly been a good lunch.

'Ah, Lieutenant Anson is it not, kin to the great circumnavigator?' asked the older Adkins, red-nosed presumably from the wine he had consumed and rather plumper than his client remembered him.

'Only very distant, I fear sir...'

'Nonsense my dear fellow. However distant, a relationship to be proud of and one that will stand you in good stead in the service. Why, I fully expect you to be made post at any moment!'

'Hardly, Mister Adkins. Their lordships are not exactly falling over themselves to promote mere Sea Fencible detachment commanders.'

'Ah yes, I deduce that a fencible command is a bit of a step backwards on the promotion ladder. But nonetheless, it gave you the opportunity to take that Normandy privateer, did it not?'

He rubbed his hands together in a gesture Anson had noted before as common among men who dealt with money.

'Anyway, it's good news, Mister Anson, good news indeed! As my son will no doubt have told you, the sale of *Égalité* went off successfully.' He consulted his ledger. 'Hmm, very successfully, I should say. In capturing her I see you took great care not to do much more than superficial damage and that has translated into a good sale price.'

Only superficial damage? Anson had a mental picture of the carronade shot from his gunboat smashing a hole in the privateer's side, sending a cloud of dagger-like splinters on their deadly path and felling a good many of the crew.

But he chose to play along. 'Yes, I suppose that once the odd hole had been patched up, the blood washed away and the garlic fumes had dispersed we did leave her in reasonable condition. The French had been kind enough to refit her not long since, you see, so she was in pretty good shape.'

'Capital, capital!' Mister Adkins senior wrung his hands again. 'Now, let's cut to the chase, eh? Now, as I am sure you are aware, to be eligible for prize money various conditions must be met.'

'Indeed. You no doubt recall that I gained some experience in the Mediterranean and so, once the dead and wounded had been removed, I ordered the hatches to be nailed down to prevent theft. My Sea Fencibles are not rich men and the temptation to rummage below deck would have been irresistible.'

'Wise of you, sir, very wise. So you met that condition — and of course there was no doubt whatsoever that she was an enemy vessel.'

'None whatsoever.'

'Now, as again I know you will be aware, the prize money is distributed according to a fixed scale. Normally three eighths of the sale price goes to the captain...'

Anson grimaced. The thought of the majority share going to the preening nincompoop of his then divisional captain — the odious Captain Hoare — filled him with disgust.

The agent raised a hand to catch Anson's attention. 'As I say, normally the captain gets the lion's share, but extraordinarily in this case Captain ...?'

He hesitated, scanning through the relevant document for the name.

'Hoare. Captain Arthur Veryan St Cleer Hoare.'

'Ah yes, rather pompous name, don't you think? Well, your Captain Hoare seems to have incurred their lordships' displeasure.'

Anson pretended ignorance. 'Really, Mister Adkins, in what way?'

'Who knows? In fact I see that they chose not to attempt to interfere with the machinations of the prize court but instructed the captain to renounce any claim on account of some irregularity.'

Anson smiled at the euphemism. 'The fact that he was not present until all was done and dusted?'

'At any rate, it's sufficient to say that the court has seen fit to decree that his not inconsiderable share—'

'Three eighths.'

'Precisely. That his three eighths should go to the officer in charge of the operation. In short, you.'

'Good grief! Me, sir? I was under the impression that I would get no more than one eighth — and would have been content with that.'

'Whatever, with Captain Hoare ruled out, it was adjudged that not only were you in locum parentis, as it were, but you were not acting under direct orders from a flag officer, who would have been able to claim one of your eighths. So, the lion's share falls to you.'

Anson was almost more gratified that Hoare's deception in claiming credit for the capture of the privateer had clearly been rumbled than he was to hear of his own good fortune, welcome though that would be.

He made a mental note to try to find out who had shopped Hoare to the Admiralty. But that was for later. Right now, he wanted to know how his men would fare in the prize money share-out.

Adkins consulted his papers. 'An eighth goes to the other officer involved. Bunny, or some such name?'

'Coney, the impress officer,' Anson corrected him.'

'Ah yes, knew it was something to do with rabbits. A further eighth goes to the boatswain, one Fagg, I believe, another to your sergeant of marines...'

Anson was delighted to hear that his two fellow-escapers from France would benefit, and, he hoped, handsomely too.

'Yes Fagg and Hoover. Both first-rate men.'

'Splendid, splendid. And the remaining quarter — two eighths, that is — will be shared among the rest of the men who took part.'

'That is most gratifying, sir. They're good men and most of them in sore need.'

Adkins nodded. 'Not my place to advise you, Mister Anson, but based here in Portsmouth a mere saunter from the dockyard I have seen many a sailor with back pay or prize money burning a hole in his pocket throwing it away in the pubs, wasting it on the dubious charms of raddled whores — or both. Pub walls, sir. They either piss it or knee-tremble it away against 'em, forgive my French.'

Raucous shouts and singing from a group of passing seamen no doubt celebrating the peace confirmed his point.

'Rest assured, Mister Adkins, I will do my very best to keep them on the straight and narrow.'

'I am sure you will, sir. I've no doubt that in the *Égalité* case the money was hard won and I hate to see it pissed away in the back alleys. What's more, now that peace is upon us there'll be no chance whatsoever of further prize money until the French decide to re-open proceedings against us.'

'I take it you don't think the peace will last, sir?'

'Sadly, I do not. This Napoleon fellow is merely catching his breath and happily taking back most of the overseas possessions we have won with blood and guts. I've no doubt whatsoever that he will return to the fray at a time of his choosing.'

Anson shrugged. 'I share your opinion, but meanwhile I fear that the government will put half the fleet in ordinary, get rid of all the volunteers and so forth.'

Adkins sighed. ''Twas ever thus.' But, brightening, he announced: 'Now to more cheery prospects — the matter of the proceeds of the *Égalité* sale and the amount of the various shares. And we must not forget the head money, of course. There were a tidy few prisoners, I see, and at five pounds a head that too adds up to a goodly sum, to be shared according to the prize money equation.'

Anson had forgotten the head money — and there had been around 40 prisoners.

'I tell you, Lieutenant Anson, you've made a pretty penny by not killing all the Frenchmen. They're worth far more alive than dead!'

'Here are the figures.' He slid a document across the table.

Scanning it, Anson could only again exclaim: 'Good grief!'

*

Back at the George, he confirmed his seat in next day's morning mail coach and rested on his bed until it was time to refresh himself and set off for the Keppel's Head, where he was to be the guest of Messrs Adkins, Woolsack and Adkins for dinner.

At the old inn overlooking the Gun Wharf and much favoured by its mainly navy clientele, he met the three partners for a schooner of sherry in the bar before being ushered to their table.

The pleasantries over, the senior Mister Adkins smilingly confessed: 'Remiss of me, Lieutenant Anson, but it was your mention of HMS *Phryne's* Mediterranean foray that put my son, Rupert here, on to it.'

'To what, sir?'

'Well, I was so busy telling you the good news about the sale of the Normandy privateer that I clean forgot an item of information we received recently from our contact in Gibraltar.'

'Gibraltar?' It had been more than two years since Anson had last been there, during the frigate's highly successful prize-taking cruise.

'You will be aware that *Phryne's* prizes were sold there?'

'Indeed, we were paid out and, sad to say, the money long since spent, as is the way with sailors.'

Adkins senior beamed: 'Allow me to inform you that you are incorrect there, Lieutenant Anson. All except one of the Mediterranean prizes were sold and the money distributed. However, there was some dispute over one of them — a large vessel taken off the North African coast, I understand.'

Anson tried to recall it. 'There was one that we took one off Algiers, loaded with leather and timber I believe. They led us quite a chase.'

'Correct — leather, timber and some kind of ingots secreted under the aforementioned cargo. And there lies the reason for the delay in settling the matter. It apparently took a good while to establish ownership of the cargo which had itself been taken by the Frenchman from various coasters, and to ascertain the value of the metal.'

'So he was a privateer, although he passed himself off as an innocent merchantman carrying a few guns for protection! Come to think of it, I did wonder about the large crew he had on board.'

'At any rate, our Gibraltar partners inform us that the matter has at last been settled.'

Anson shrugged. 'Whatever, litigation doesn't come cheap, so I assume any profit from the sale has long since disappeared into lawyers' pockets. They are not my favourite breed.'

Adkins senior laughed. 'But there you are wrong, sir. The delay was caused not by lawyers racking up their fees, but by the length of time correspondence took to-ing and fro-ing, establishing that she was indeed a privateer, where the cargo had come from and so forth.'

'So there's something to come from it?'

'Indeed. The prize was apparently in good nick and was sold at Gibraltar, as was the entire cargo which proved to be of considerable value — and, again, since she was adjudged to be a privateer there's head money to take into account. Altogether a tidy sum for the flag officer at Gibraltar and the rest going to HMS *Phryne*, according to the usual scale, of course.'

Pleasantly surprised, Anson enquired hesitantly, 'So I will receive...?'

'After our, dare I say, modest, fees, a not inconsiderable sum.' He handed over an envelope but, not wishing to appear too grasping, Anson put in his pocket to savour later.

Already he was reckoning that these prize windfalls would surely cover what he felt he owed his father, freeing himself of obligations to his family.

His morale boosted, he downed his glass and a cruising waiter refilled it. This was indeed a time for celebration.

After a hearty dinner and a good deal of wine followed by several glasses of port, Anson finally took his leave of Adkins, Woolsack and Adkins, and made his way unsteadily back to the George.

Although it was still fairly early, he retired to his room, feeling the effects of the drink and still not having fully recovered from the debilitating wounds he had suffered on the Boulogne raid — and at the hands of that maniac MacIntyre.

But he could not get to sleep for a long time, his mind going over and over the news he had received about the prize money.

It could not have been a better outcome. Now, miraculously, he had the wherewithal not only to pay back his father but enough to tide him over for a while at least. And with the prospect of half pay threatening, that would be much needed.

Drifting off to sleep, he imagined himself to be back at Ludden Hall already and strolling in the gardens with Cassandra. It was a delightful prospect.

18

A Ruthless Bastard

Sent for by the leader, MacIntyre did not know what to expect. Could it just be about another run? Or might another of the smugglers have seen him kill that nosey pack-man beside the lighthouse and shopped him?

But when he reported to the churchyard, he knew all was well. There was no way the head man would have met him alone if he was suspected of anything.

'Ye sent for me, boss?' he asked, deferentially.

'You did well the other night, Billy boy. Showed you were willing to get stuck in — and I've no doubt you'd be handy with the bat if it came to a punch-up with the revenue.'

'Thanks, boss. Told ye I was keen to get into the smuggling game.'

'There's just one thing...'

'Aye?'

'You've heard that one of the pack-men was found dead near the lighthouse?'

'I did hear the whisper that some revenue snitch had got his comeuppance, but I did-na know the bloke.'

'The thing is, Billy boy, that one of the other lads reckons he saw you loitering near the lighthouse where Jim Shallow was found.'

'Me? No, whoever said that's got it wrang. Ye saw me yersel', doon by the watter. Ye telt me off fer helpin' unload when I should've bin guardin'.'

'That's right, I did. Look, if the man was an informer, I don't care who did for him. He would have deserved all he got...'

'Aye.'

'But just in case you didn't already know, I'm the law round here. I'm the one who decides what happens to traitors.'

'Right, boss.'

'Anyway, there's one thing I'm quite sure about. I reckon you're a ruthless bastard, quite capable of giving the chop to anyone who crosses you without a second thought.'

MacIntyre made to protest, but the leader cut him short. 'It was a compliment, you daft bugger. I need ruthless bastards to help me control the whole business. It's not just about arranging the runs and getting the stuff ashore. I have to manage the distribution and payments right down to the end users without giving any cheeky sods the opportunity to rip me off.'

'And, like you said, I'm a ruthless bastard?'

'Look, Billy boy, the fellah who takes charge of the pack train and bat-men once the stuff's ashore has gone sick and I doubt I'll get him back any time soon.'

'So?'

'So I want you to take over from him on the next run. You'll be in charge of those protecting the beach and then look after the pack train and get the stuff safely to the dropping-off points.'

'How would I know where they are?'

'You'll be told — and you'll be well rewarded when the job's done. Are you up for it?'

MacIntyre smiled and nodded. One run and he had already been promoted.

The leader reached out to shake his gnarled paw. 'Oh, just one thing to remember, Billy boy. If the revenue or anyone else tries to interfere don't hesitate to give them the same treatment as Jim Shallow!'

*

As yet, Bosun Fagg had not been given a firm date for disbanding the Seagate Sea Fencible detachment.

He grumbled to the master at arms. 'They ain't told me nuffink, 'cept rest on me arms reversed, Tom.'

Hoover shrugged. 'Well, I guess we're still getting paid — and so are the boys.'

Fagg touched his nose conspiratorially, as was his wont. 'Too blurry right, Tom. Until the hammock-counters catches up wiv me I'm gonna dish aht these 'ere king's shillens like it was Christmas. That'll teach them buggers at the Hadmirality to disband this 'ere unit what we've recruited an' trained like they was our own children, like what we 'aven't got. Leastways, none what the muvvers 'ave told me abaht, so far anyways.'

The American had heard Fagg going on about the children he probably hadn't got many a time and had weightier matters on his mind. 'Binning the men will be hard, Sam. They're a pretty good bunch and we need to see them alright agin the time when we'll want 'em back.'

'Yeah, I've said the same fing to Captain Armstrong and 'e said 'e'll fix some sort of party for 'em.'

'Good, but what'll we do about the gunboats, cannons, muskets and all?'

Fagg touched his nose again. 'I'll tell ye 'ow it 'appens, Tom. The Hadmirality'll leave it to the last minute, tell us to return 'em all to Chatham and just as we get 'em there the effin' Frogs'll kick orf again and we'll 'ave to start from bleedin' scratch wiv no boats, guns or men!'

He grimaced in disgust. 'Bleedin' government! Don't know their arses from their elbows. But what'll we do, Tom? I don't know nuffink 'cept the navy — and you don't know nuffink 'cept the marines. To be 'onest wiv ye, I ain't really known much else 'cept the navy and war. I can't get me 'ead round this peace lark.'

'Nor me,' Hoover admitted. 'As a kid all I knew was the independence war back in the States, with my father going off and getting killed and all. And when my mother brought me and my sisters over here to England, well, apart from a spell when she tried to make me into a tailor, I've known nothing but the marines. It's my life now.'

'And now we're both up the bleedin' creek wivout an effin' paddle!'

The American shrugged. 'Mister Anson's due back any time soon and maybe we'll get some news from him about the prize money we're due. I'm banking on that.'

*

Billy MacIntyre, alias Billy Black, was, he told himself, 'as happy as a pig in shite.'

His new-found comparative wealth from the smuggling game had set him up with a rented cottage half a mile from the Crooked Billet and a floozy he'd met there.

She, too, had been to the school of hard knocks, but was only just past her best bed by year and prepared to keep house for him and put up with his nocturnal fumbling so long as he kept the wolf from the door and the booze flowing. And in any event. many a night he left her drinking steadily in the pub while he was out with the smugglers.

MacIntyre filled his days with boozing, currying favour with his fellow-smugglers and learning all he could about the free trading game.

And they were only too willing to boast of past exploits and reveal all the ramifications of the trade.

They told him that a mysterious person known as an investor would put up the money to buy goods in France. This was given by the gang-master to the skipper of a smuggling vessel who would make the run.

MacIntyre learned about the methods of concealment for contraband when bringing it straight ashore was dicey. At such times the smugglers attached barrels of spirits to sinker stones and retrieved them later using a variation of a grappling hook known as a rock creeper. And he learned about the spout lanterns and flashers — barrel-less pistols — used as direction and warning aids.

Ashore, he was told, a large number of people, from pauper to parson, were only too willing to co-operate with the smugglers for a back-hander, usually in the form of illicit booze or tobacco rather than cash.

Why, pretty well all the churchmen, many of whom doubled up as magistrates, were in receipt of smuggled wine or brandy and turned a blind eye to 'free trading' and there were few officials or inhabitants of the inland villages on the contraband routes who were not susceptible to bribes — or threats.

This extensive network of willing and unwilling collaborators meant that the whereabouts of riding officers ashore — and of the revenue cutters afloat — was almost always known to the smugglers, allowing them to plan accordingly.

At each run Black Mac haunted the shore, ostensibly bossing the bat-men who guarded the beach and escorted the pack train inland. But all the time he was watching, listening and learning, intending one day to take over the whole operation himself.

However, for the time being he needed to ingratiate himself with the hierarchy and win their trust.

19

Homeward Bound

Anson breakfasted early, settled his bill and went outside to join the small crowd of gawpers in front of the George, awaiting the mail coach.

He was hoping that the guard might prove to be that resourceful ex-soldier Nat Bell with whom he had made the same journey three years earlier when carrying vital official papers at the time of the naval mutinies.

But no such luck. The guard today was a humourless bewhiskered fellow full of his own importance and clearly not one to indulge in chit-chat with the passengers.

Questioned by Anson about the whereabouts of the redoubtable Bell he answered, blankly: 'No idea, mate. I ain't privy to the rosters — only get told when I'm on and orf.'

Anson shrugged and determined that he would forego tipping this man. It would have been a fine coincidence if Nat, whose place he had taken when the guard was wounded in an attempted robbery the last time he did the Portsmouth to London run, had chanced to be on duty today.

Not one to be thwarted, he decided to ask after him along the route, and if there was no joy, he would enquire on arrival in London at the General Post Office in Lombard Street. He was in no great hurry this time and it would be good to reminisce about that eventful journey and make sure that Nat was in good fettle.

It soon became clear that he had missed Bell by a day or so. At Liphook the guard coming on duty told him: 'Saw Nat at Kingston last Wednesday, or was it Guildford on Thursday? Anyhow, he said he was taking a day or two orf on account of a terrible cold he's caught. These here coaches are the very devil for catching yer death of cold.'

Anson knew all about that from his one-off experience as a guard. He had ended up with a fever, but the outcome was fortunate in that it led to his convalescence at Ludden Hall with Josiah Parkin — and Cassandra.

At last the mail coach clattered through the London streets and he disembarked, aching and fatigued, at the Angel Inn in Wych Street just off the Strand.

He enquired at the coach office for directions to Lombard Street, left his bag there and made his way to the financial district where he joined the throng outside the General Post Office.

Fruit-sellers were mingling with clerks from the banks, insurance offices and other businesses, together with servants bringing mail from their masters and mistresses for delivery. Not least, Anson noted a good many idlers presumably there merely to gawp at the nightly comings and goings of the mail coaches.

Entering the square four-storey building via the imposing main door flanked by pillars supporting a balcony above, he was taken aback at the sight of an army of uniformed officials standing at desks sorting piles of packets to be put into the appropriate mail bags destined for towns throughout the country.

Joining a queue at one of the counters fronting the sorting desks he waited his turn and then asked if he could be told the whereabouts of the guard Nathanial Bell.

The counter clerk looked him up and down with a supercilious stare and snapped, 'Not policy t'give out information about employees. Next!'

But Anson was not to be browbeaten. 'Look, this is not an idle query. I simply need to know where the guard Nathanial Bell can be found or when he is next on duty.'

The clerk looked down his nose. 'Told you, it's not policy to tell. You might be a debt collector or some legal wallah trying to serve a summons. Next!'

Anson felt his anger rising. 'Do I *look* like a debt collector? I'm wearing the king's uniform, for goodness' sake. I'm a naval officer merely trying to meet up with a man who saved me from being robbed!'

'Can't be helped. It's not policy.'

'Then fetch me your superior,' Anson ordered coldly. 'I'll not leave this spot until you do.'

Those queuing behind him were growing restless and someone called out: 'Get a move on admiral — some of us ain't got all day!'

The clerk said, loudly so that those in line could hear: 'Move along, now. You're holding up the rest.'

Anson folded his arms and stood his ground. He hated making scenes and was beginning to regret that he had made a stand from which it would be difficult to extract himself without losing face. But the clerk's attitude had riled him.

'Very well,' the man snarled. 'You're holding up the mail business and you leave me no choice.' And he flounced off to where a couple of large men in uniforms were lounging beside the sorting desks.

Now acutely conscious of the muttering in the queue behind him and sensing that his stand was not going to end well, Anson decided that discretion was called for, abandoned his quest and abruptly turned and marched off towards the door.

He had only taken a few steps when he felt a hand on his shoulder. Turning, expecting to see the security men about to take him in hand, he was astonished to see a familiar face.

'Nat Bell! Why, you're the very man I came to find, only that damned counter hugger gave me short shrift. The cretin annoyed me and was about to set the beadles on me, so I decided to abort my mission.'

Bell guffawed. 'Good to see you, Mister Anson, ain't it? Take no notice of them desk monkeys, sir. They're just jumped-up pen pushers, too big for their boots, they are.'

He gave the offending clerk a piercing stare. The man shrugged and went back to his counter while the two burly guardians resumed their lounging.

Bell explained: 'I've been orf fer a couple of days wiv this 'ere cold, but I'm just about t'go back on duty. The Portsmouth run again, but I 'ad business 'ere first, rosters and suchlike, so the driver's bringing the coach round from the Angel and I got a bit of time to spare.'

*

In a nearby coffee house, they filled each other in with details of what they had been up to since the dramatic events of the fleet mutinies.

Anson gave a watered-down account of the part he played in helping bring the Nore mutiny to an end, his capture during the cutting out expedition in Normandy, taking command of his Sea Fencible detachment and being wounded on Nelson's Boulogne raid.

Nevertheless, Bell was impressed. 'Gor blimey, you navy men don't 'alf get up to some stunts! Make's a mail guard's life look 'umdrum! I'm gettin' fed up with the life meself, but don't know what I'd do if I gave up guarding.'

'That's two of us,' Anson admitted ruefully. 'Now that peace has broken out it'll be life on the beach on half pay for me, no promotion — nothing.'

'So what will yer do?'

Anson rolled his eyes. 'Your guess is as good as mine. I'm not trained for anything but the sea. I'd be totally useless at anything else.'

'I dunno. You made a pretty good fist of mail guarding!'

'Kind of you to say so, but after being wounded at Boulogne I wouldn't have the stamina to lurch about on top of a coach, even supposing the mail would take me on.'

'You're too good fer it anyway,' Bell assured him. 'There's got t'be other fings someone like you could do.'

'To tell the truth Nat, there's nothing else I want to do right now, except perhaps take a long holiday to recover before war breaks out again, as I feel certain it will.'

'Yeah, why not take a 'oliday?'

'Well, I do have something rather special in mind and it could involve you if you want. That's why I was seeking you out.'

'What might that be?'

'I don't want to say until I've discussed it with friends. If they don't like the idea it's a dead duck before it starts. But if we do go ahead, I'll get in touch and see if you want to be part of it.'

'Wiv you involved, sir, I'd volunteer like a shot, whatever it is.'

Anson was delighted. 'Jot down where I can contact you — ideally not via that damned counter clerk! Then I'll get in touch when the time comes.'

Back outside the General Post Office the crowd of sightseers had thickened.

Bell explained: 'There's more'n 20 mail coaches turn up 'ere every evenin' and these daft buggers come to gawp at 'em comin' and goin', rain or shine. Can't see the attraction meself.'

They parted amiably, with Anson promising to be in touch when the time came, and after collecting his baggage at the Angel he set off to call on the Admiralty before taking the stage coach down to Kent.

20

The Admiralty

Making his way to Whitehall, Anson crossed the cobbled courtyard trodden by so many of his naval heroes past and present, strode purposefully up the steps and entered that holy of naval holies — the Admiralty.

Intercepted by one of the fearsome porters, he stated his business and was directed to the infamous waiting room where generations of sea officers, including him, had been left to stew and fret while awaiting their fate.

There were a few other supplicants nervously awaiting the summons that would almost inevitably confirm that there was no sea-going berth available for them, condemning them to remain on the beach on half pay.

But to his surprise, Anson did not have long to wait for his summons. All the waiting officers looked up expectantly as the porter appeared at the door and announced: 'Lieutenant Anson!'

He rose to his feet and hastened after the messenger, noting the knowing nods exchanged by the other petitioners. His surname could still open doors, even though he was only a very distant kinsman, many times removed, of Admiral Lord Anson.

Captain Arthur Wallis greeted him warmly. The taking of the Normandy privateer and Anson's participation in Nelson's Boulogne raid ensured him of a good reception.

'Ah, Anson! Very good to see you. And you're much recovered from your wounds, I hope? Bad business that, but you will have heard that we've got shot of the man responsible for the debacle? That idiot Hoare is now cooling his heels in the Isles of Scilly and will stay there until we can get rid of him without attracting unwelcome attention from the politicians and the gutter press.'

'I am aware, sir, although I don't know how the Admiralty learned the truth about him. It was certainly not from me. Anyway, may I say how delighted I am that Captain Armstrong has replaced him as divisional captain of the Sea Fencibles? He's a most deserving officer and morale has shot up since he was appointed.'

Wallis nodded enthusiastically. 'Good, good! We Whitehall warriors sometimes get it right, you know. I may as well tell you that you were also in line for promotion — to commander.'

Anson was somewhat taken aback 'Promotion, me? You astonish me, sir. I thought I'd have to wait to fill dead men's shoes.'

'Look Anson, what you did to help bring the Nore mutiny to an end has not been forgotten, nor has the taking of the privateer and your services at Boulogne. Why, if that had been a success you would quite possibly have been made post then and there.'

'Kind of you to say so, sir.'

Wallis massaged his forehead with his fingers and sighed. 'But I fear this peace agreement has thrown a spanner in the works. Our political masters can't wait to run the army and navy down.'

'I feared as much, sir.'

'Yes, and the Sea Fencibles are the first to go, along with the army's volunteer battalions. You're required to

149

disband pretty well forthwith and I am afraid Armstrong will be back on half pay, along with many whose ships will be laid up for the duration. So I fear your promotion will have to be put on hold for the foreseeable future.'

Anson smiled wanly.

'But you're not the only one whose career is affected...'

'Like many other mere lieutenants?'

'Not only lieutenants. Here at the Admiralty with an ear to the ground we tend to know well in advance what our future holds. I was in line for a squadron, but now I'm likely to be put out to grass. The best I can expect is to be yellowed.'

Like all sea officers, Anson was familiar with the promotion ladder. For senior post-captains like Wallis the achievement of flag rank was automatic and in normal times his next step would be promotion to rear-admiral of the blue squadron.

But peace meant fewer sea-going commands, so now he could expect to receive only a nominal promotion to the rank of 'rear-admiral without distinction of squadron'. So in reality, promotion as rear-admiral of the non-existent 'yellow squadron' was thinly-disguised retirement.

Anson was sympathetic. He rated Wallis highly and knew that the kudos of such a meaningless elevation and an end to his career would rankle.

'I am extremely sorry to hear that, sir. So we'll both be without a job?'

'Well, not necessarily in your case, Anson. Despite the unfortunate outcome, you did well in that mission over the other side with what's-his-name — that French royalist...'

'Lieutenant Hurel.'

'Yes, if only the intelligence you gathered had been acted upon, but that was Hoare's fault, not yours. Anyway,

Colonel Redfearn, who as you know looks after intelligence matters on the invasion coasts, appears to think you are God's gift and wants to continue using your services during the peace.'

Anson was pleasantly surprised. 'I had assumed I'd go on half pay like the rest, sir.'

'No, if you agree you will remain on full pay and carry out any tasks he may have for you, but covertly, mind. The Channel ports are full of inquisitive eyes and ears, no doubt many of them only too willing to keep the French well informed, whether for ideological reasons, or simply for money. It would be ill-advised to say the least for you to become labelled...'

'As a spy?'

'Precisely. So chew it over Anson, and go and see him at Dover Castle. He'll tell you what he'd like you to do and you can make up your mind one way of another.'

'I will, sir, and it could be that a venture I have in mind might suit his book.'

21

Happy Reunions

Leaving the coach at the turning off the London to Dover road that led to Ludden, Anson walked slowly down the lane, perspiring from the effort of carrying his dunnage. It was a reminder that he had still not fully recovered from his Boulogne wounds and the knifing he had received at the hand of MacIntyre.

He turned into the Ludden Hall driveway and was thrilled to see a young woman in a bonnet sitting in the arbour beside the small lake.

But as he got closer he was astonished to find that it was not Parkin's niece Cassandra, but his own sister Elizabeth, sketchbook on her knee, evidently drawing the moorhens cruising the lake.

'Good grief! Elizabeth! What on earth are you doing here?'

She smiled and patted the bench beside her.

*

After hearing how Elizabeth had come to be staying with the Parkins, Anson quickly worked out what was behind it and asked: 'I assume our father engineered this as a way of seeking a reconciliation with me?'

She smiled. 'No doubt. He knew we have always got along better together than with Gussie and Anne, so I think he arranged for me to come to Ludden in the hope that I'd entice you back into the bosom of the family.'

'And you're comfortable with that role?'

'Not at all. Well, as father would say, "Blessed are the peacemakers" and I'm quite sure that was why he engineered my visit. But I know about them trying to marry you off to Charlotte Brax and I'm glad you resisted them. She's an extremely scary person and you would have been dreadfully unhappy.'

'Nevertheless, you were willing to intercede?'

'In no way. You are your own man, Oliver, and I know you'll do whatever you decide to do, but, you see, it gave me the opportunity to escape the rectory myself and anyway, I wanted to get to know Cassandra.'

'Escape?'

'Yes, since I met Commander Armstrong...'

'Captain now,' he corrected her.

'Of course. I heard from Cassandra that he had been promoted. Anyway, that visit to Fairlight brought home to me that there was more to life than the rectory and parish affairs. Such an exciting day!'

She smiled at the recollection of Amos Armstrong showing her around his cliff-top signal station and spotting a French privateer with his telescope.

'Anyway, now that Anne's marrying that awful Podmore fellow, you know, the vicar of Nether Siberton, it will only be a matter of time before mother and Gussie try to marry me off to some other clergyman, and for me that would be a fate worse than death.'

Anson nodded sympathetically. Elizabeth, although she had hardly ever been allowed out of the cloistered, claustrophobic atmosphere of the rectory, was more like him than any other member of the family. And neither were what he called 'God-botherers'.

He asked: 'You've taken a shine to Armstrong?'

She blushed and nodded shyly.

'Well, I sense the attraction's mutual. He's forever asking after you and now you're here there's every chance that you'll meet up with him again soon.'

Elizabeth's eyes shone at the thought.

'But now, if you please, let's put family matters aside. It's been a while since I saw Josiah and his niece, and I'd very much like to rectify that.'

*

He found Cassandra in the dining room with cook, planning menus. 'Mister Anson... Oliver, how very good to see you!' Clearly taken by surprise and somewhat flustered, she turned to the cook. 'That will be all for now, Mrs Dodman, but as you can see, there'll be one more at dinner.'

'Then we'll be needing more vegetables. Mister Anson likes his veg, he does.'

Waiting until the cook left, Cassandra smiled at Anson — and he could have sworn he noticed a slight blush on her cheeks.

'Uncle Josiah told me you had returned, but then run away to sea again!'

'But as you may have heard, peace has broken out and here I am, cast up on the shore once again.'

'And a most welcome castaway you are. You know that Elizabeth's here?'

'I was astonished to find her at Ludden Hall. I saw her at the lake, sketching moorhens, and gather that she's another member of the Anson family to be inflicted on you, like me.'

'Pah! She is most welcome. As my uncle's so fond of telling people, we country mice see very few visitors and already she's brightened up our dull existence and become a firm friend. She's far more agreeable than my cousins.'

'And now you have me to put up with too...'

She took his hand. 'Nonsense, I am happier than I can say to have you both here. Please don't rush off again this time.'

'I promise.'

'And by the by, is there any chance now we're at peace that the gallant Mister Armstrong can be prevailed upon to visit us here at Ludden? Elizabeth talks about no-one else and she would be so thrilled if he were to join us. She and I would be able to chaperone one another. What fun we'd have!'

*

Anson sought Parkin and found him in his study, poring over the Reverend Gilbert White's *A Natural History of Selborne.*

'Ah, Oliver, you're back. Welcome. You must tell me all about your voyage in your old ship. But first, tell me, were you aware that the swift is the only bird that can mate on the wing? Extraordinary, isn't it? Even in my younger days I found it tricky enough to attempt procreation on the ground let alone at altitude!'

'Really?'

'Yes, yes, singular birds, swifts — ancient and mysterious creatures. Some call them "the devil's bird" because of their inaccessibility and others believe they hibernate in the mud below ponds. Gilbert White himself paid labourers to dig up likely places to see if he could find any, but he didn't of course. My theory is that they migrate south in winter.'

'I confess that knowledge of avian mating habits has not come to my notice, possibly on account of spending so much of the past decade trying to avoid being killed off by the French. That's tended to get in the way somewhat.'

Parkin, having grown used to Anson's gunroom humour, chuckled and asked: 'But you have come to see me, evidently, and here I am bombarding you with trivia. Is there something you wish to discuss?'

'There is, and it concerns your banking experience.'

'If it's about investing your prize money, I'm very much afraid that I am far from current...'

'Well, I learned at Portsmouth that I am due a substantial sum, but this is not about investing it. No, I want to ask if you will kindly use your banking expertise to arrange for a substantial part of it to be transferred to my father's account.'

'So you are still of a mind to repay the allowance you received from him?

'I am, and what with the sale of the privateer and some unexpected extra money from Gibraltar I have enough to pay back every penny.'

'Knowing him from meetings of the county antiquarian society, I deduce he is by no means grasping when it comes to money — and don't you think it will hurt him to have the allowance thrown back in his face, as it were?'

'I realised only recently that it came from tithe money squeezed out of the farmers and smallholders who can ill afford to give a tenth of what they earn, through the sweat of their brows, to the church.'

Parkin raised his eyebrows quizzically. 'But giving the money back to your father won't help them, will it?'

'I hope it will. You see, I intend to write to my father explaining why I'm returning the money and suggesting that he might consider using it for the good of the poor of his parish.'

Parkin was somewhat taken aback. 'Well, that would be a most honourable, creditable gesture, yet no more than I would have expected of you. But from what you've told me I don't imagine it will find favour with your mother and brother.'

He shook his head. 'Frankly I don't care what they think of it. They are the ones who caused the rift in our family. One day, perhaps, I will become reconciled with my father, but not with my mother and Gussie.'

'But if you repay the allowance will there be anything left of your prize money windfall?'

'Enough to keep the sharks from the raft for the immediate future at least.'

'Sharks?' Parkin smiled at the thought. 'Ah yes, now I come to think of it there are plenty of the human version, attracted by the smell of gold or profit rather than blood. My own cousins who now run the family bank are cases in point. I have to take great care in keeping their hands out of my pockets!'

22

Black Mac's Threat

In the event, Armstrong needed no persuading to visit Ludden Hall. He turned up next day, intent on updating Anson about the fate of the Sea Fencibles and was similarly astonished — and delighted — to find Elizabeth staying there.

When Anson was eventually able to prise his friend away from her, they took a stroll in the garden intent on catching up with service news.

'Well met, mon vieux! I gather you have only just returned yourself after a restorative sea cruise?'

'Correct, via Chatham, my old ship *Phryne* and Portsmouth.'

'So you know all about the peace?'

'I heard it from the French navy themselves.'

'Really? You must fill me in about that. But have you also heard of the fate of the fencibles?'

'I have. On the way back from Portsmouth I called at our old stamping ground — the Admiralty — spent hardly any time at all in the dreaded waiting room only to be informed by Captain Wallace that the Sea Fencibles are to be scrapped forthwith—'

'Along with a general run-down of the navy. Will the politicos never learn?'

'Probably not. Much to everyone's surprise Bonaparte will kick off again as soon as he's ready, and then the navy will have to be resuscitated and we'll be several steps behind the French. I despair.'

'Well, mon vieux, I've come in person because I felt sure you would wish to go and thank your men for what they've done and so forth.'

Anson nodded wryly. He chose not to mention the intelligence role Captain Wallis had discussed with him. 'Thoughtful of you. I gather I've got until the end of the month to wind everything up.'

'Yes, but before that I'm going to visit each of my detachments to collect nominal rolls and whatnot so that we can keep tabs on the men.'

'That makes sense, so when we're required to reform as I'm certain we will be at least we'll be able to contact them quickly.'

'Then there are guns to be laid up and goodness knows what else to sort out.'

'I'll go to the Seagate detachment with you. As you say, I need to thank the men and try to explain to them that they are valued despite the politicians throwing them on the scrapheap.'

'Amen to that.'

*

In the Weald of Kent, the once heavily-forested country between the North and South Downs, the line of pack animals made its way slowly through the village of Woodhurst.

The smugglers had delivered their contraband and were on their way back to the Marsh, but there was a task to perform here.

In most of the villages hereabouts the smugglers could expect whole-hearted cooperation or at least token support. The inhabitants were used to making themselves scarce when a pack train passed through and anyone who happened to be about would avert their eyes. That way, they could truthfully tell inquisitive revenue men that they had seen nothing, knew nothing.

But Woodhurst was different. It was more of a God-fearing community than most and a number of the inhabitants had got together and vowed not to put up with being ordered about by the smugglers and forced to break the law.

The last straw had been when one of the village elders had refused point-blank to allow his barn to be used for storing contraband until it could be moved on.

It was a normal thing to be required to do. All the owner had to do was turn a blind eye, keep his mouth shut and be rewarded for his trouble. Who would refuse that?

But William Philpot had. He was a lay preacher whose religious beliefs forbade him to involve himself in criminal activity of any sort. So he had refused the use of his horse and barn, threatening to report the next run to the revenue. And he had paid for his non-cooperation with a beating that left him with a battered face and a broken arm.

Shocked by such treatment, others had withdrawn their tacit support of the smugglers and Billy MacIntyre, alias Billy Black, had been told to deliver the villagers an ultimatum. Either they agreed to cooperate, or else.

He sent the pack-men on ahead. Now that they had got rid of their loads, they were safe in the unlikely event of being accosted by revenue men, so no longer needed the bat-men's close protection.

Gathering three of his bruisers, he sent for Woodhurst's movers and shakers and when they were gathered in the pub delivered the ultimatum as instructed.

'Look, yous. Yon man who would'na give a lend of his horse or hide the stuff threatened to go tellin' tales to the revenue. Well, he's gone an' got ye'all into a spot of bother. All ye have t'do is look the other way when ye're tellt and ye'll get yer rewards. If ye dinna, then...' And he drew his index finger across his throat.

The village shoe-maker, a Baptist like the man who had been beaten for non-cooperation, looked around his fellow villagers and at their nods spoke for them all.

'But what you're trying to make us do is against the law.'

MacIntyre guffawed and banged his bat down on the table, startling them all. 'The law? *We* are the law frae here to Dungeness and ye'll do what we tell yous!'

The shoe-maker flinched but would not back down. 'We cannot. It's against our religious beliefs.'

'That's twaddle. God does'na gie a damn if ye join in a bit of free tradin'. Like as no he's up there right noo, knockin' back brandy the Archangel fuckin' Gabriel's smuggled fer him!'

Visibly shocked at the smuggler's blasphemy, the villagers muttered among themselves and one or two were clearly ready to make a stand.

MacIntyre would dearly have loved to set about them now. There was little he enjoyed more than what he called 'kicking the shite out o' fuckin' southern worms', but he was short-handed now and had a mission to complete.

So he banged the table once again and warned them: 'I've no got the time to deal with yous now. So I'll be kind an' leave ye to think on it. We'll be back here after the next run. If ye cooperate we'll forget all aboot this fuss you've bin making and ye'll get yer rewards.'

The shoe-maker looked him in the eye. 'And if we don't?'

MacIntyre grinned evilly. 'If ye dinna cooperate, we'll come back an' slaughter the lot of yous and burn every house in the village to the ground!'

There was a shocked silence and the villagers glanced nervously at one another.

One protested: 'But the law will protect us.'

'Oh no it wilna! Like I tellt ye, we are the law round here, and if any one o' yous tries t'call in the revenue men or the military we'll know and we'll put paid to him and every member of his family. Think on it!'

23

A Sporting Challenge

As they made their way to Seagate, Armstrong confided: 'By the by, when I was visiting my Dover detachment, I bumped into Colonel Bumstead of the yeomanry. Silly name, and the man's a trifle stuck-up with it.'

Anson remembered the name from the dinner party his mother threw when he escaped from France after the St Valery raid. He sniffed: 'I could be wrong, but I thought riding the high horse was obligatory in the yeomanry.'

'Anyway, the impudent fellow said he pitied me for losing my job now that the Sea Fencibles are being scrapped. Boasted that the yeomanry will be kept on to deal with the peasants if they get restive!'

Anson registered disgust. It was just the sort of thing his bête noir Chitterling would say, too.

'Came close to calling him out but managed to keep my cool and agreed that before we disband, we'll have some sort of social event, a feast for the men with a sporting theme to mark the peace.'

'Is that strictly necessary?'

'Well, I'm committed to it now. The colonel and I agreed it can't involve horses as that would favour his men and of course most of ours can't ride. Nor can it be anything to do with boats as most of the yeomanry can't row and would be sea-sick on a millpond.'

'So?'

'So it's to be cricket.'

Astonished, Anson could only splutter: 'What!'

Armstrong looked suitably embarrassed. 'You know, the crack of willow on leather and all that, or is it leather on willow?'

'But our boys are not sportsmen and I haven't touched bat or ball since I was at school. With the greatest respect, sir, you're a naval officer, so you should be aware that there's not a lot of cricket played at sea. You'd keep losing balls overboard.'

'When you call me "sir", Anson, and I might remind you that's not often, I am aware that it is a kind of verbal insolence and an implied reprimand for something I've said or done of which you disapprove.'

'I can't argue with that, but cricket, I ask you...?'

'How difficult can it be? You just throw the ball at the enemy batsman and he tries to hit it.'

'Bowl — you're meant to bowl it.' Anson demonstrated with an underarm gesture.

'Yes, I meant bowl. And all the batsman has to do is hit the wretched thing out of sight and run back and forth, scoring runs every time he crosses his oppo. Simple!'

'And you really have committed us to this match?'

'Well, not necessarily your boys. I can get a team up from all my detachments. I've already got two volunteers from Folkestone and three more from Dover.'

'With you as captain?'

'Obviously. Rank has its privileges.'

'So you'll want half a dozen from Seagate?'

'Excellent, Anson! Good of you to offer. Expected nothing less of you.'

*

164

The detachment building was full of expectant fencibles, the old hands eager to learn how much they would get in prize money.

They were all there: Sampson Marsh with his nephew Tom, and other long-serving men including Bishop, Shallow, Oldfield, Hobbs and Boxer, the undertaker and expert number-cruncher, with whom Armstrong was closeted for a while, before the bosun called for order.

Anson told them: 'It's good news and bad, men. Most of you are in for a fair bit of prize money but the downside is that all Sea Fencible units around the coast are being stood down on account of the peace.'

They had already known that was coming, but the prize money sweetened the bitter pill.

Not wanting to witter on, Anson searched for something they would remember. The blood and guts of the Normandy privateer affair and the Boulogne raid came to mind. 'I've been proud to serve with you all. When we started out, we were, well, somewhat—'

Fagg couldn't resist piping up: 'Shambolic!'

Smiling amid the ensuing laughter, Anson added: 'Thank you bosun for your help in finding the right word. Yes, we were shambolic, but with good training and good old British guts you have come through two major scraps with the enemy with flying colours.'

Armstrong, seated beside him, nodded enthusiastically: 'Hear, hear!'

'And we have truly become a band of brothers, like Henry the Fifth's men at Agincourt I told you about on the way to Boulogne. Thank you all and as the agent warned me: don't piss all that prize money away!'

It was Sampson Marsh who stepped forward to speak on behalf of the men. 'We're right proud to have served with you, sir, and the bosun and master at arms, too. And I know the boys would agree, if the trumpet blows again we'll all be back quick as a flash.'

Amid muttered agreement from the fencibles, Armstrong rose and the bosun called for order.

'I'd like to echo everything Mister Anson has said, men, and I have two things to add. My personal thanks to you all and if you'll see Mister Boxer afterwards, he'll give each man jack of you a final payment of a guinea on behalf of a grateful nation!'

The officers left to cheers and, outside, Anson looked his superior in the eye. 'A grateful nation? Since when? That money's coming out of your own purse, isn't it?'

Armstrong shrugged. 'It's no more than the nation should have done. It'll be a while before they get their prize money. Anyway, I can afford it, mon vieux. If nothing else it'll ensure that we won't have any trouble enticing them back when the time comes!'

*

There was much jollification in the Seagate pubs that night as the fencibles celebrated their windfall, and the bosun was somewhat bleary himself when he met the annoyingly bright-eyed and smartly-turned-out master at arms the morning after.

Fagg moaned: 'It's alright for the likes of you, Tom, what don't 'ardly drink. I got slapped on the back and stood tots all bleedin' night and this mornin' I've got a poundin' 'ead and a mouf like a dog what's ate somefink rotten.'

'Yeah, I noticed.' The marine smiled the superior smile of the sober. 'Anyhow, you'd best get what's left of your brain around the problem Captain Armstrong set us.'

Fagg put his head in his hands and groaned. 'Oh Gawd, that cricket lark what 'e was on abaht.' He fumbled for a pencil. 'Well, I can't play on account of not bein' able to run wiv me game leg. But you're a fit bloke, Tom, so I'll put you on the list.'

But the American protested. 'Oh no you won't! I've learned a lot about the English and their strange ways but cricket is something else. Never got my head around it. In the States we played a game a bit like your English rounders.'

'Rounders? That's a game for girls!'

'Well, I guess there's a similarity. You hit the ball and run from base to base. I reckon we should call it baseball. That wouldn't sound girlish. Anyhow, ain't no use explaining the rules of cricket to me. It'd be the same as trying to get me to understand Pythagoras' theorem.'

'Pythagerarse? Never 'eard of him. So 'oo's 'e when 'e's at 'ome then? And what's his theoro-majig?'

'He was a Greek mathematician and I think his theorem was something to do with right-angled triangles, but I never quite got my head around that either.'

'Annuver bleedin' foreigner. Any'ow, triangles is a waste of rations — no use whatso-hevver. I got this far in life wivout ever catchin' sight of one!'

'You were a top-man, weren't you? Ain't some of your sails triangular — the ones with three corners instead of four?'

Fagg pondered for a moment. 'Gor, blimey, 'ooever said you learn somefink every day got it abaht right! Who'd of thought, some Greek bloke called Pythagerarse invented sails!'

Hoover raised his hands in mock surrender. It was way too late to set Sam Fagg off on the path to knowledge, so he changed tack.

'Anyhow, I won't be playing cricket any day soon. The Baptists are agin it.'

'Yeah, I know you was brung up a Baptist but yer 'ain't 'xactly done much time on yer knees since I've known yer. I'm a Christian meself, but I don't lose any sleep over it. Them religions is against all kinds of fun, like drinkin', 'aving it orf wiv tarts an' all that. Nah, I don't s'pose Gawd cares if you play cricket or not. Anyway, like Mister Anson says, the Almighty's got enuff on 'is plate already wivout the likes of us botherin' 'im all the time.'

'Well, Phin's against cricket so I won't play.'

'Yeah, but 'e's a preacher, ain't 'e? And 'e 'as to pretend to be agin anyfink what's fun!' Fagg thought for a moment. 'Ah, 'ang abaht. It's just come to me. If Phin Shrubb 'as to pretend to be agin cricket, then 'is daughter 'as to go along wiv it!'

'That's right. Sarah wouldn't want me to play.'

'So now we knows! I reckon ye're abaht to pop the question an' ye're scared of rockin' the boat in case her father finks you're a sinner what's not fit to marry 'is darlin' daughter.'

Hoover reddened, but held his tongue.

'There y'are! I knew I was right! So when are yer goin' to ask 'er?'

'It ain't as simple as that, Sam. First I have to ask for her father's permission to propose to her.'

'Well, that won't be no problem. Phin finks the sun shines out of your whatnot.'

'Mebbe, but I can't offer her much as a sergeant. And now that it looks as if the fencibles are finished — I can't expect her to follow me here, there and everywhere if I stay in the marines, even supposin' they keep me on. So I'll have to find some other way of making a living. And it'll have to be something her father approves of.'

'Strewth! What'd that be? You ain't goin' to turn devil-dodger or apothy-what's'it? From killin' to curin', eh?'

'Me, preacher or apothecary? I don't think so! No, but I need to find something Phineas and Sarah feel kind of comfortable with...'

''Ow abaht Pope or Harchbishop of Canterbury?'

*

Back at Ludden Hall the dinner conversation centred on the forthcoming match and Armstrong told the company: 'I've made it clear to Colonel Bumstead that I insist we play by agreed rules.'

Anson asked, apparently innocently, 'Rules? Are there any?'

'Of course there are rules. They are essential if chaos is to be avoided.'

'I seem to recall that down at Hardres Minnis they simply play it as they always have.'

'You may have *local* rules, yes, but the next village will have variations. Don't you see that by having agreed overall rules you can avoid confusion and accusations of cheating?'

'So, what are these overall rules?'

'Well, you have two stumps at each end and one bail. The batsman is given out if the bail is knocked off, but not if the ball passes between the stumps.'

Parkin commented: 'That's what happens round here, mostly.'

'Then there's underarm bowling only and four balls to an over. All runs must be run and you can be run out if the

169

fielders place the ball in the block hole on the batting crease.'

Anson looked perplexed. 'You're beginning to lose me.'

But Armstrong ploughed on. 'Batsmen can be changed at any time by the team that's in — and spectators can stand anywhere they like, but only two are allowed beside each umpire.

His friend's quizzical look turned into one of complete bewilderment.

'The correct rig is important. All players must wear white shirts, trousers and boots, and the batsmen wear top hats at the crease — as does the wicket keeper. Oh, and one other thing...'

'What's that?'

'The overall rules clearly state that local rules will also apply...'

*

Anson came across Cassandra and Elizabeth strolling in the gardens and found them animatedly discussing the forthcoming match.

Cassandra was insisting: 'There's no doubt in my mind, as it doesn't involve players grappling with one another, as it were, I firmly believe ladies should be allowed to play.'

Elizabeth grimaced. 'Oh no, that's out of the question. Some of the men are most uncouth. It would not be ladylike to indulge in such a sport.'

'But ladies have played before. Oliver, don't you agree we should be allowed to play against the yeomanry?'

He sensed he was on dangerous ground here and bought time with a diversion. 'Well, at least one man believes you should play. I read that the Duke of Dorset said, "What is human life but a game of cricket? And if so, why should not the ladies play it as well as we?"'

'There you are,' Cassandra announced triumphantly. 'So we should be allowed to play, shouldn't we?'

Anson laughed. 'From what I hear of our grand neighbour over at Knole, the Duke could easily drum up a cricket team from among his mistresses!'

'Really?'

'Yes, really, and I reckon he'd be happy to! Apparently, his twin passions are l'amour and playing cricket.'

Anson had heard of the Duke's prowess both on the cricket field and among the fair sex, and that when he went to Paris as an ambassador-extraordinary to the court of France before The Terror he had promoted cricket among British expatriates and the French with limited success.

The Times had reported in racially prejudicial terms on a match played in the Champs-Elysees: 'His Grace of Dorset was, as usual, the most distinguished for skill and activity. The French, however, cannot imitate us in such vigorous exertions of the body so that we seldom see them enter the lists.'

Cassandra insisted: 'So you agree that we should play?'

'No, I'm afraid I don't. If you were to play in the Sea Fencible team then Charlotte Brax, now Chitterling, and her sisters would no doubt play for the yeomanry. How would you like that?'

24

Travel Plans

Midway through dinner, Josiah Parkin tapped his glass and announced: 'Oliver and I have been closeted in recent weeks discussing the possibility of taking advantage of the peace...'

All eyes were on him as he confirmed the worst-kept secret. '... by going on tour to enjoy the sights and delights of Paris. And you are all cordially invited!'

Cassandra and Elizabeth smiled knowingly. Of course, they had long known all about it. So many little clues had been easy for them to interpret.

Only Armstrong was taken by surprise, but his reaction was one of delight and the secret smile he exchanged with Elizabeth spoke volumes.

Over a decanter of after-dinner port, Parkin, Armstrong and Anson considered their mode of travel.

Anson maintained: 'There is but one way to cross the Channel, so all that needs to be decided is whether we go by packet boat or some other vessel.'

But Armstrong protested playfully: 'No, that's where you are wrong, mon vieux. Now that peace reigns, there's a Frenchman, an engineer by the name of Albert Mathieu who's advocating the digging of a tunnel under the sea.'

'A Channel tunnel? Ridiculous! Which asylum is he in?'

Laughing, Armstrong protested: 'No, no, the man's not mad. He proposes to dig a tunnel that horse-drawn coaches can use to make the crossing by candlelight.'

'What a crazy idea! It would leak! No, it's not going to happen any time soon, if ever. It'll never catch on — and if it did, it wouldn't be ready in time for us.'

'Fair point, but—'

'But nothing. Why, if ever a tunnel was dug the French wouldn't have to outwit our navy to invade. They could march through it and attack us without getting their feet wet! We'd no longer be an island.'

Clearly enjoying the banter, Armstrong countered: 'Britain is already no longer an island. Remember that Blanchard fellow? He's made it across the Channel in a balloon, so how long will it be before our enemies catch on and fly over England dropping bombs?'

Anson was temporarily silenced. He did indeed recall that the French hot air balloon pioneer Jean-Pierre Blanchard and his American backer had made the first successful crossing from Dover back in '85.

He thought for a moment. 'But Blanchard's crossing almost came to grief, did it not?'

That's true. They lost height a few miles short of the French coast and had to jettison everything, clothes and all. But they made it.'

Parkin, who had listened to the repartee with amusement, could contain himself no longer. 'Great heavens! I absolutely refuse to show off my naked nether regions to a parcel of grinning Frenchmen! And I'm sure the ladies in our party would be quite horrified at the mere suggestion of such a thing!'

Armstrong and Anson had a fit of the giggles.

'Good point, well brought out,' the captain admitted. 'So it's back to the drawing board and a sea passage it must be — fully clothed!'

Packet boats were an attraction — fast, well-crewed with experienced captains. Anson had also done some research on Dover-based commercial vessels and mentioned that several schooners had come down from Harwich to take advantage of the increased passenger demand created by the peace.

Parkin warned: 'Sadly we will not be able to take our own conveyance and horses with us, so it will mean hiring when we arrive in Calais. I've corresponded with various former banking contacts there and they assure me it can be done. In fact the French are keen for the business, particularly if we pay in gold. We can either hire a carriage to take us all the way, or do it in stages.'

Nodding in agreement, Anson suggested: 'I propose that we check into a Calais hotel for a few nights on arrival to give the ladies a chance to recover from the passage and use the time to arrange our onward journey.'

And he added: 'Not least it will give Armstrong and I the opportunity to have a surreptitious look around Calais — the fortifications and so on, against the time when war breaks out again.'

*

It having been agreed that Cassandra and Elizabeth should be accompanied by a maid, they discussed the relative merits of Annie and Bessie, the two young girls employed at Ludden Hall, but reached no conclusion.

Neither really fitted the bill and when the Paris trip was mentioned to them both expressed horror at the prospect of visiting an alien country where, thanks to Dodman's oft-declared prejudices, they believed the daily diet consisted snails or frogs' legs and horsemeat, and that foreigners were guillotined in town squares on a weekly basis.

It was Josiah Parkin who came up with the solution. He announced: 'Emily, from the village, would be ideal. A sensible woman with all the necessary skills, and capable of looking after any member of the party who falls ill, why, she'd be perfect!'

Cassandra happily agreed and when the proposal was put to Emily she readily accepted. It would make a change, she said, from administering to the sick and laying out the dead of the parish.

Anson, when he heard, reddened at the memory of being given bed baths by this angel of mercy —— built like a stevedore — when he was racked by fever, but he had to admit that she was an excellent choice. No Frenchman would dare to mess with this formidable woman with her noticeable moustache, work-coarsened hands, and a tongue to match, who had raised five sons and seen off two husbands. Cassandra and his sister would be well shepherded.

*

After some further discussion with Parkin, Anson wrote a brief letter to Nathaniel Bell.

You will recall that when we met in London recently, I spoke about wishing to take a long holiday and that I wanted you to be involved but did not want to say more until I had discussed it with friends. Well, they are equally enthusiastic about the idea and we are planning to be off to France next month.

The peace gives us a wonderful opportunity to visit and sample the delights of Paris. Our intention is to hire a carriage and horses in Calais and make our way to the capital at a leisurely pace (a far cry from your mail coach speed!) stopping at wayside inns overnight.

After many years of war between us and the French we cannot be sure what sort of a reception we will get on the journey and I have convinced my friends that we need a reliable and experienced man, used to handling all aspects of the security of coach, passengers and belongings, to accompany us — in short: you!

I should tell you that the party includes my superior officer in the Sea Fencibles, Captain Armstrong, my particular friend Mister Josiah Parkin, a retired banker and avid antiquarian, his niece Cassandra, my sister Elizabeth and a ladies' maid.

I very much hope this invitation appeals to you and that you will be able to secure, say, two months' leave of absence from the Royal Mail. My friends and I will better than match your current wages and we will foot the bill for all accommodation, messing etc.

Please send word via the mail to me at Ludden Hall, Ludden, near Faversham, to let me know one way or another and if affirmative Mister Parkin will include you in his request for passports for the whole party. I will then notify you when to join us here.

We will travel in civilian clothes and, if you come, you will need to bring the necessary tools of your trade (but not your 'yard of tin'!). Kindly acquire what you think will be needed for the security of the party and I will reimburse you on arrival.

Yours ever
Oliver Anson

25

Visit from a 'Faceless One'

Anson was in the summerhouse with Cassandra when Dodman appeared. 'Gent calling himself Colonel something-or-other is asking for you, sir.'

'Colonel something-or-other?' Anson was puzzled. 'Ah, could it be Colonel Redfearn?'

'That's the one, sir.'

'Kindly bring him here. Cassandra, I suspect the colonel has come on confidential business, so...'

'I'll make myself scarce — and perhaps send some tea?'

'Delightful!'

She disappeared and a tall gentleman with a military bearing but in plain clothes hove to on the verandah.

'Colonel Redfearn! How very good to see you. The last time was at Dover Castle, was it not?'

'Correct, for a briefing before your Boulogne mission.'

Anson well recalled visiting the castle, known as the Key to England, where 'faceless ones' like the colonel who master-minded the gathering of intelligence on the invasion coast were based.

'What brings you here, sir?'

'I gather from Captain Wallis that you have called on him at the Admiralty.'

'Correct, sir, I went, cap in hand as usual to get him to read my fortune. I thought he would tell me I was to go on half pay on account of the Sea Fencibles being disbanded, but he indicated that you might have some employment for me.'

'Yes, he tells me you are planning to go to Paris.'

'That's so, with my particular friend Mister Josiah Parkin, who lives here at Ludden Hall. He's a retired banker and a keen antiquarian whose motivation is most likely to bring back Bonaparte for dissection and stuffing!'

Redfearn laughed. 'It would do the man — and the rest of the world — a lot of good! Look Anson, your mission to Boulogne was most successful—'

'I'd hardly say that, sir, since the information about the French ships being chained together didn't reach Nelson and as a result he failed to cut them out.'

Redfearn snorted: 'True, but that was due entirely to that idiot Hoare who stupidly withheld the information for his own misguided reasons.'

'I wish now that I'd not stuck to the chain of command,' Anson admitted ruefully.

'No blame whatsoever is attached to you. Anyway, Hoare's paying the price now, exiled in the Isles of Scilly with all the time in the world to reflect on his fall from grace.'

'I suppose so, but men died for nothing.'

'Not for the first time, Anson. At any rate, that's all water under the bridge. Whatever the outcome, you and Hurel carried out your mission damned well and if it hadn't been for Hoare, why, Nelson's attack on Boulogne might have been spectacularly successful.'

'It's kind of you to say so, sir.'

'Look, what with your escape from France after the St Valery affair and the Boulogne recce, well, you've won yourself quite a reputation for tip-toeing around northern France.'

'Thank you, sir.'

'When Home Popham and I arranged for you to be posted to the Sea Fencibles, we envisaged you being suitable for the odd clandestine mission over the other side — and you were made aware of that?'

Anson thought for a moment and remembered that the oddly-named commodore had used the self-same expression about being well fitted for tip-toeing around France when he was first appointed to command the Seagate detachment. Home Popham had told him he would be expected to do 'some sniffing around' on the other side of the Channel for intelligence, assisting French royalists and the like — and he had certainly done just that at the time of Nelson's bombardment of Boulogne.

'Fully aware, sir, but—'

'But what?'

'Well, sir, I thought, what with the peace and all—'

The colonel laughed. 'Armed truce, you mean, Anson. The French won't be downing tools just because some politicos have signed a piece of paper. No, although our own government is already rushing to run down the fleet and disband large chunks of the army we must make sure we don't drop our guard — at least as far as intelligence is concerned.'

They were interrupted by the arrival of Bessie the maid carrying a tray with tea and cake. Redfearn helped himself to a slice and chortled. 'You naval fellows certainly know how to live when ashore, Anson. Makes up for all that salt beef and weevil-riddled biscuits, I suppose.'

Laughing, Anson protested. 'That's all landsmen's folklore I'm afraid, colonel. Actually we eat pretty well at sea, except on a long voyage when the only fresh meat is rat or seagull!'

Redfearn raised his eyebrows. 'Disgusting! Anyway, back to business. When the whole thing kicks off again as it surely will, we must ensure that we have a pretty good idea of what the French are up to, particularly in the Channel ports, and that's where you come in.'

'But I have no status now that the Sea Fencibles have been stood down.'

'You're still a sea officer, and if you agree to carry out the task I have in mind you will stay on full pay'

'And after that?'

'You can be certain that the fencibles will be cranked up again the moment the peace breaks down and you will no doubt be required to re-form your detachment.'

Anson's disappointment was self-evident. 'I had hoped that when that happens I will have earned a sea appointment, sir.'

'Sadly, no. You're too damned good at what you do ashore to be wasted at sea. Mark my words, Anson, the French are even now making plans for an invasion via the Kent coast.' He tapped his nose. 'Believe me, I know, I have seen copies of some of their latest planning documents.'

It was Anson's turn to raise an eyebrow.

'Yes, we have our sources. Before I leave, we'll take a look at my map of the Pas de Calais coast and I'll tell you exactly what I need to know.'

He fumbled in the satchel he was carrying and fished out the map which he proceeded to unfold, announcing: 'By the by, there's someone I'd like you to include in your party.'

'Oh?'

'Yes, an imposition I know, but this fellow is known to you.'

Anson was there already. 'Hurel?'

Redfearn beamed. 'Yes, the French royalist who went on that recce of Boulogne with you! Well, he's still alive and well after a long spell of taking the waters at Tunbridge Wells with his émigré friends.'

'I'm glad to hear that, sir. He can be extremely annoying, especially around females, but he's a good man.'

'Well, he's willing, no *eager*, to return to France and has volunteered to gather what you might call political intelligence from his royalist contacts who are in the know. So between you we should get a fair picture of what's going on over there.'

Anson looked doubtful. 'But won't he be a marked man, after Boulogne and all? I know to my cost that he's not very good at keeping a low profile.'

'He managed well enough while serving in the republican navy and as a prisoner in the hulks.'

'But after Boulogne the French intelligence people must have marked his card.'

'Nevertheless, he's happy to go back, ecstatic at the prospect in fact. So will you take him?'

'Well, sir, I must ask my companions.'

'If it's a question of paying his way, that's not a problem. I have access to certain funds and will advance you both a goodly sum to cover all your expenses.'

Anson thought for a moment. This was good news. He had enough left over from his prize money to pay his share of the Paris expedition, but a windfall like this would mean he would not have to concern himself about his bank balance and, more importantly, he would not be a financial burden on Josiah Parkin.

Redfearn leaned forward. 'One thing. Tell your friends that Hurel is merely going to see what's happened to his family home.'

'His chateau?'

'Yes, and he'll be travelling under an assumed name, with a British passport. His English is good enough to convince most Frenchman that he *is* English. But from what you've told me, you'd best try to keep him away from the ladies and make sure he keeps himself under wraps.'

Anson raised his eyebrows once again. He had heard *that* before.

*

They pored over the map and Redfearn indicated where his present knowledge was weak in terms of Channel port defences, dispositions of warships, numbers and types of vessels laid up there that would be suitable for carrying troops and artillery.

He explained: 'We can use the peace to keep up to date not only with what the French are up to in their Channel ports, but politically in Paris too.'

Anson protested: 'I can note what vessels are in Calais and so on well enough, sir, but I'm no politician and won't have a clue what's going on in their corridors of power.'

Redfearn nodded. It'll be a bit more than counting ships. We need to know their state of readiness, morale etcetera, nuances of the political situation and so on.'

'But I'm a simple sailor and know nothing of politics, nor have I any wish to...'

'Come, come, Anson. We both know you are not as naive as you make out. Just do what I know you normally do: ask a lot of questions, note what the senior people are saying, who they are allied with, any personal weaknesses and so on.'

Anson was puzzled. 'Personal weaknesses?'

'Yes, who's living beyond their means, drinking too much, mistresses, sexual peccadillos, that sort of thing.'

'I thought most Frenchmen had mistresses and peccadillos. Look, sir, I don't think I'm cut out for that sort of intelligence-gathering. The military stuff, yes, but sniffing around the upper echelons simply isn't me.'

'Hurel has already been asked to do the same, among other things...'

'But I can't put the rest of the party in any danger. There are ladies involved.'

'You're not the only ones who've been asked to do this, and on your return we will debrief you — and others — put all the jigsaw pieces together and, I hope, build up an overall picture that we can exploit when the peace ends, as it surely will. As long as you are discreet, there's no danger. What could go wrong?'

Redfearn made his farewells and left on horseback for Dover, leaving Anson pondering how he could perform such tasks without endangering the whole party and ending up in a French prison, with the rival intelligence service extracting information from him while pulling out his fingernails.

But he felt he had been unable to refuse to help, and so be it. If he just kept his eyes and ears open, he should be able to observe enough to satisfy Colonel Redfearn without exciting attention from the other side, retain his fingernails — and get the party home safely.

As the colonel had said, what could go wrong?

26

The Match

Heading the little procession into the small village square was Josiah Parkin's coach, driven by Dodman, with the retired banker, his niece Cassandra, Elizabeth Anson and Captain Amos Armstrong on board.

Close behind was Tom Marsh's pony and trap with Anson and Sam Fagg, and bringing up at the rear was a hired wagon drawn by two heavy horses with a dozen Sea Fencibles drawn from various detachments.

Anson looked this way and that, spotted the sails of a mill down a narrow lane leading off from the square and announced: 'Ah, there it is! We'll lead the convoy in.'

Tom Marsh pulled out in front of Parkin's coach and Anson waved to the others to follow them up the lane.

As they neared the post mill Anson could see it was mounted on a huge upright timber that gave it its name. A man he took to be the miller and a lad who could be his son were pushing against a long beam fixed to the mill's wooden steps. This puzzled him, until he deduced that they were swinging the whole building round to keep the sails facing the wind.

He had never thought about it before, but as a sea officer he understood straight away how this ingenious machine — for that was what it was — had been cleverly designed to harness the wind. No doubt when the sails rotated, they turned a shaft from which the power could be taken off to drive millstones and grind grain into flour.

It reminded him very much of a warship, a great creaking, groaning wooden monster driven by sails and totally reliant on the vagaries of the wind unless worked by men who knew their business.

Watching the miller and his young helper straining at the tail-post, his mind turned to ways of doing without the need to turn the mill by muscle power. A cap on top of the mill that could turn independently, powered by a fan-tail, was the obvious answer and although he was yet to see one, he had heard of so-called smock mills that had such a device.

He was jolted back from his musings by a group of cavalrymen, well-mounted and sporting scarlet jackets and high-plumed helmets, overtaking them at the trot. Members of the yeomanry team, no doubt.

The Sea Fencible procession followed the troopers into a large field beside the mill and they were ushered to one side of a small pavilion where wooden benches had been set out.

On the other side of the pavilion, Anson noted, was a long rail beside the hedge where the troopers were tying up their mounts, and more wooden benches.

It being a treat, there were trestle tables of food, covered in cloths to await tea-time, and a barrel of beer guarded by a sergeant he recognised from his clash with the yeomanry troop led by Captain Chitterling on the way to the Mote Park royal review several years earlier.

Armstrong was first out of the coach, to be greeted by Colonel Bumstead of the South Kent Yeomanry, who proceeded to introduce him and his companions to his own officers and their ladies.

Anson noticed to his horror that Chitterling was there with Charlotte, who was followed by a nurse pushing a new-fangled perambulator over the bumpy grass to seats in front of the pavilion. He could not avoid bumping into her at some stage during the proceedings, so when her husband moved away to greet some other new arrivals, he took the bull by the horns and approached her.

'Good day to you, er, Charlotte. I believe I should congratulate you on your marriage?'

'And the birth of our son?'

He flinched. 'Our..?'

She gave him an amused pout, clearly knowing exactly what effect her words had on him. 'Yes, Captain Chitterling and I have a son. Hadn't you heard?'

'No, I'm afraid I've been away a good deal.'

Chitterling appeared, his elaborately-brocaded jacket and scarlet sash now discarded for the match, but still in his overalls with vivid red stripes down the side. 'Why, it's jolly Jack Tar! Still sniffing around me wife, eh? Can't leave her a moment without you randy sailors latching on to her scent.'

Anson tried hard to keep his cool, asking: 'So you play cricket, as well as all your other accomplishments?'

'Normally stick to huntin' and shootin'. Only agreed to play when I heard you'd be in the navy team. Couldn't resist the chance to give you a thrashing, whatever the weapons, eh?

Turning on his heel, Anson muttered grumpily: 'We'll see about that.'

*

Having won the toss, Armstrong elected to bat and to set an example sent himself in first, accompanied by the only other officer in the team: Anson.

All eyes were on the captain as he faced the first ball, delivered by a wiry trooper who had the look of an experienced cricketer, which he was, having turned out for the county on a number of occasions.

His pitched-up delivery was edged by Armstrong into the long grass at the edge of the field and he called to the day-dreaming Anson, 'Run!'

Startled, Anson galloped to the other end and was about to embark on a second run when he spotted his captain's raised hand bidding him to stop. He looked round to see that the ball had been retrieved and was back in the bowler's hand.

Now at the receiving end, he held his curved bat awkwardly in front of the wicket and awaited his first ball.

Released from the bowler at great velocity, it struck the edge of what had until very recently been an active molehill and cut viciously back towards his stumps. Anson attempted to play what he imagined to be a forward defensive stroke but missed completely.

There was a loud groan from the watching fencibles and he turned to see one of his stumps leaning back and the bail on the ground. 'Out!'

Mouthing a curse, and to an ironic cheer from the enemy fielders, he made his way slowly back to the pavilion, passing the triumphantly-sneering Chitterling along the way.

He was still having his bruised ego polished by Parkin and Cassandra when young Tom Marsh hopped over on his crutches.

'What is it, er, Tom?' Now that the Sea Fencibles were disbanding, Anson felt he should dispense with formality.

'Message for you, sir. From Mister Shrubb.'

'What is it?'

'He wants to see you, sir, face-to-face like — and it's urgent, he says.'

'Where is he?'

'Over at the chapel. I'm to take you in me pony and trap.'

Anson shrugged. It was a nuisance. He could happily dispense with the cricket but had looked forward to spending some time with Cassandra and her uncle, talking over their Paris excursion. However, Shrubb was not the kind of man who summoned an officer willy-nilly.

He explained to Parkin: 'Do excuse me. Phineas Shrubb wants to see me and, knowing him, it could be important, some kind of medical emergency perhaps. I'll be back as soon as I can.'

Cassandra smiled. 'Hopefully in time to see your team win?'

'After my pathetic contribution, that would take nothing short of a miracle!'

He walked beside Tom Marsh, hurrying to keep up with the cripple who moved remarkably quickly on his crutches.

As he embarked in the trap at the field gate and they set off down the lane he was just in time to see Armstrong hit the ball over the hedge to the cheers of the Sea Fencibles and their supporters.

27

A Plea for Help

Phineas Shrubb was waiting for them beside the small Baptist chapel with another equally soberly-dressed man at his side.

'Lieutenant Anson, thank you for coming. I could not be seen at a cricket match, you see?'

Anson could not suppress a grin. He knew that the Baptists strongly disapproved of cricket, among a longish list of other pastimes, and wondered to himself what was so sinful about it. Boring, yes, but sinful? And Anson had thought a veteran of the American war like Shrubb would have been more of a man of the world.

He climbed down from the cart and Shrubb shook his hand. 'This is Brother Finch, from the Woodhurst congregation. We know each other through the Baptist Association.'

Anson was aware that Kentish Baptist congregations maintained close links, with representatives meeting together regularly to discuss matters of common interest.

The stranger offered his hand and Anson shook it, asking: 'What can I do for you, Mister Finch?'

But Shrubb put a cautionary finger to his lips. 'May we go into the chapel? Even hedgerows have ears, but we will not be overheard in the house of God.'

Anson was about to say 'except by God, presumably' but checked himself. Although Phineas was a former surgeon's mate used to naval badinage, when it came to his religious beliefs his humour threshold was easily breached.

Inside the chapel they sat on plain wooden benches and Anson took a look around. As the son of an Anglican clergyman he had never set foot in a nonconformist chapel before and was surprised at how simple it was.

It bore no comparison to his father's twelfth-century church, with its colourful stained-glass windows featuring Saints Cosmos and Damian, pioneer makers of prosthetic limbs, and the extravagant memorials — including his own that had been unveiled when it was thought he had been killed in France.

They sat on a bench and Anson asked again: 'So, what can I do for you?'

Finch hesitated, but Shrubb reassured him. 'Lieutenant Anson is totally trustworthy. Tell him what you have told me, brother.'

'Well, sir, the problem is that our village is being terrorised by a ruthless gang of smugglers and we are in dire need of help.'

Anson sighed. He had been on a smuggling run himself, as a way of getting to and from France to gather intelligence just before Nelson's Boulogne raid, and he was aware that some of his own fencibles dabbled in free trading.

'Look, Mister Finch, I am a sea officer, not the law. You should talk to the revenue people...'

Finch shook his head. 'What would they do? Send a few men, or even a troop of dragoons for a few days? Then, as soon as they left the gang would be back to take their revenge.'

190

'That's right,' Shrubb offered. 'A troop of dragoons would have to be stationed in the village on a permanent basis, and that's not going to happen.'

'Can't your people get along with the smugglers like everyone else?' Anson asked. 'What's so bad about that?'

Shrubb answered for the Woodhurst man. 'One of their elders was badly beaten for not cooperating with a gang from Romney Marsh, and when the villagers objected the smugglers threatened to burn their chapel to the ground.'

'That was extreme, I'll grant you.'

'Look, these are simple, God-fearing people. But they've turned the other cheek for too long. The threat to burn their chapel was the last straw and they're now more determined than before to refuse to let the smugglers borrow their horses or use their barns to store contraband.'

'But no doubt you're going to tell me that the gang won't leave it at that?'

Finch nodded. 'They've threatened to come back in a few weeks and if we don't all agree to cooperate by then they've said they'll kill all the elders and burn down not only the chapel but the houses of anyone who resists.'

'Surely they won't do that!'

'They surely will,' Shrubb countered, 'because if they don't make an example of the Woodhurst men, why, others elsewhere will think they can get away with defying them too and they would lose their grip over the whole area. That's how it works.'

'Look, I sympathise, but as I've already said I'm not the law so I don't see how I can help.'

'Knowing you, Mister Anson, I thought now that there's peace and the Sea Fencibles are being disbanded you might go with a few trusted men and advise the villagers on how to defend themselves.'

'To form them into some kind of militia?'

'If that's what it takes. These are God-fearing, peace-loving men. They've no knowledge of weapons or warfare. Perhaps with some basic training, rather like the way you've trained the Sea Fencibles...?'

Anson could now understand why they had approached him. But however sympathetic he felt, the fact was he was now committed to go to France — and not merely as a tourist, but with a mission to fulfil for Colonel Redfearn.

He pondered for a moment before responding. 'Seeing it's you who's asking, Phineas, I would have agreed to do what I could to help. But I'm shortly going over to France, part pleasure it's true, but also on, er, official business.'

Shrubb nodded understandingly. No doubt he could guess what the official business might be. The Woodhurst man did not, and tried further persuasion.

'These men are ruthless, sir, with no religion or scruples, threatening to burn down a house of God and near killing an unarmed man who refused to commit a criminal act.'

'Can you not appeal to whoever leads these men?'

'We've no idea who the overall leader is — someone down on the Marsh, we assume. But the leader of those who threatened to come back and kill us is a Scotsman they call Billy Black, although I doubt that's his real name.'

Anson's interest was pricked. 'Scottish? Can you describe him?'

'He's short, but thick-set with a bull neck, broken nose, and he's completely bald. Looks like he shaves his head.'

'And he's got some wording tattooed on his neck?'

'How did you know? You're right, sir, but I don't know what it says because it's gone sort of dark blue and wrinkled like they do, and he's not the kind of man you want to get too close to.'

Anson smiled grimly. 'I think you'll find it says "Death to Sassenachs!" and if I'm right, this man's real name is MacIntyre and I've met him twice. The first time he punched me without warning and on the second occasion he tried to kill me.'

No-one was more astonished than Shrubb. 'So *he's* the man who knifed you in the Mermaid at Seagate?'

Rolling up his sleeve, Anson revealed the long scar on his forearm that had been tended by Shrubb himself.

'One and the same. Black Mac, as my men know him, must be brought to justice. He's a deserter from the navy, and wanted for attempted murder — of me!'

Shrubb and Finch exchanged a relieved glance. 'Then you'll help?'

'Look, I've explained that much as I'd like to, I cannot get involved personally because I must go to France, but—'

'You'll send some of your men to help these people?' Shrubb asked anxiously.

Nodding, Anson levelled with him: 'Right now I haven't got any men. My detachment's being disbanded, but once the boys know it's to sort out Black Mac there will be no shortage of volunteers! I can think of two in particular.'

*

Anson spent a good deal of time quizzing Finch about Woodhurst and agreeing the outline of a plan to defend the village, a role he would entrust to Tom Hoover and Sam Fagg.

It was therefore much later when Tom Marsh drove him back to the cricket field in the pony and trap that they passed a straggle of riders coming the opposite direction.'

'Must be over?' young Tom suggested.

Anson agreed. 'And the yeomanry off home after their great victory, no doubt.'

But when they entered the ground it was plain to see that it was the Sea Fencibles who were celebrating and tackling the food and ale with great enthusiasm, not their opponents.

Parkin and Cassandra welcomed him back with wide smiles. 'You missed a great victory, my boy,' the old gentlemen told him. 'Your friend Armstrong scored a great many runs and one of your fellows, Bishop by name, bowled the enemy team out almost single-handedly!'

Cassandra enthused: 'Yes, apparently he's played for the county many times and you'll be delighted to hear that he bowled Captain Chitterling first ball. The captain was in such a rage that he threw his bat into the hedge.'

Making a mental note to reward the demon bowler, Anson looked round to congratulate Armstrong and was amused to see his sister Elizabeth gently massaging the batting hero's shoulders as he sat on a bench recovering from his ordeal at the crease and in the field.

'Hmm,' he told himself, 'I had better keep a friendly eye on those two!'

28

'Tools of his Trade'

Nat Bell arrived at Ludden on the mail coach, but seated inside as a paying passenger rather than his usual precarious position on top as guard.

He was not familiar with this route but the coachman knew it well. 'Ludden 'all's just down that lane, mate. You can't miss it.'

Bell climbed down and the guard handed him his luggage, a small trunk and a long heavy canvas bag that clanked faintly as he handled it.

'What you got in there, Nat, the crown bleedin' jewels?'

'That's right, mate, how'd yer guess? I'm goin' to nip over to France and flog 'em to that Bonaparte bloke.'

The guard laughed. 'Good on yer. Anyways, we'd better get on.' He put the post horn — his 'yard of tin' — to his lips, and blew an unnecessary but perfect note in ironic salute. The coachman touched his hat, flicked his whip and they were away.

Bell set off down the lane, turned in at the gates, marched up the long driveway to the iron-studded front door framed by Doric columns and pulled the bell chain.

The door swung open almost immediately and he was greeted by Dodman in his butler role. 'Mister Bell, is it? You're expected. The gents are in the study, so if you'll leave your kit in the hallway...'

He led the way to the study where Anson was with Parkin examining some old coins with the aid of a magnifying glass.

'Ah, Nat Bell, very good to see you. I'm delighted you've agreed to join us. Let me introduce you to the leader of our tour party, the celebrated antiquarian and natural historian Mister Josiah Parkin.'

Flattered at Anson's description of him, Parkin offered his hand. 'Welcome to Ludden Hall, Mister Bell.'

'Nat was formerly a sergeant in the 56th Foot and served at the Great Siege of Gibraltar back in '83.'

Parkin's eyes widened. 'Really? I should dearly love to hear the ins and outs of that — the tunnel digging and all. And you must tell me what you observed of the habits of the famous pouting Barbary macaques.'

Bell grinned. 'Rock apes? They've got 'abits, sure enough, I mind one time—'

'Thank you Nat, but let's keep that for later.' Anson turned to their host. 'Lately Mister Bell has been doing sterling service as a Royal Mail guard seeing off ne'er-do-wells, and now he's to be our guardian angel on the Paris trip.'

'Excellent!'

'He is not merely an experienced guard but will also be of particular use when it comes to arranging onward transport and procuring overnight accommodation for our party. There's no-one who knows the wiles of wayside inn landlords better than Nat, be they English, French or no doubt Hottentots, too!'

Parkin beamed: 'Extremely good of you to join us, Mister Bell. We shall evidently be in very good hands.'

*

Shown to his room in the attic by Dodman, Nat Bell broached what he thought might be a ticklish subject. 'You ain't going on the Paris jaunt then, Mister Dodman?'

'No I ain't, thank Gawd!'

'Oh, only I wouldn't like to fink I was doing you out of what they calls a jolly.'

'A jolly, eh? Ha! That ain't how I see it, Mister Bell. What, risking yer life at sea and then landing among all them Frenchmen what's just waiting their chance to come over here and kill us all? You're welcome to it. It'll be putting yer head in the lion's den, like that there Daniel in the Bible!'

'I don't see it quite like that meself, Mister Dodman. It'll be more of a 'oliday, seeing new places, new people and all that.'

'And eating their disgusting food?'

Bell grinned. It would be a waste of time trying to persuade Dodman against his prejudices, but at least he wouldn't be putting the man's nose out of joint by taking his place on the adventure.

Left to his own devices in his room, he took what Anson had requested him to obtain out of his bag. He had acquired the blunderbuss from a gunsmith he knew who bought ex-service weapons from the Tower of London, no less. It was marked on the stock with two arrows facing each other and 'I CR', indicating that it was a first-class reserve weapon, and it had been refurbished to a good standard.

The pistols were a pair of cannon barrel flintlocks made by Joseph Griffin of New Bond Street and numbered 'one' and 'two' under the barrels, indicating they were a true pair. They had 10-inch barrels and were boxlocks, meaning that the cock was above the barrels, so more compact and less likely to snag on clothing when being drawn, hence being known as 'greatcoat' or 'overcoat' pistols. With them was a powder horn, some cloth wadding, a pouch of pre-cast lead balls, spare flints, a turnscrew and a .38 ball mould for making more ammunition suitable for the blunderbuss as well as the pistols.

Finally, he produced a small double-barrelled tap action boxlock pistol with a sliding trigger guard safety catch — ideal for concealing, loaded, down your boot or at the back of your belt.

Bell handled the weapons lovingly. Mister Anson could hardly fail to be impressed with his choice of 'tools of his trade'.

*

Next to arrive was Hurel, extravagantly attired in a light blue silk cutaway tail coat with black velvet collar and purple neckerchief, tight white pantaloons and short, highly polished hessian boots. He carried a gold-topped ebony stick and a high-crowned round hat.

Armstrong was first to greet him with a hearty 'What-ho, Hurel, still keeping a low profile, I see!'

The sarcasm was lost on the Frenchman. 'Thank you, mon ami. An émigré French lady of my acquaintance in Tunbridge Wells was kind enough to fund my outfit in the 'opes of becoming a baroness, but I am afraid I can oblige 'er in everything but marriage.'

Later he confided in Armstrong and Anson that he had been advised by Colonel Redfearn at Dover Castle to travel under an assumed name lest he be smoked out as a royalist on his return to France and interned — or worse.

His language skills were of course good enough for him to pass as an Englishman in France, and the colonel had been happy enough to provide him with the necessary papers — and give him certain tasks, along with a sizeable cash advance to cover his expenses.

'So I 'ave chosen to travel under the name of Gerald Tunbridge in 'appy remembrance of my place of exile. I would be greatly obliged, gentlemen, if during our visit you no longer address me by my pre-revolution title.'

Tongue in cheek, Armstrong responded: 'Of course, Baron!'

*

At dinner Cassandra announced she had hit upon a way of getting everyone to know each other better before they set off on their tour.

'Thinking about it,' she explained after the soup, 'various of us know at least one other member of the party, but only one person had met all the others before today.'

They were still puzzling it out when Parkin interjected. 'That must be Oliver.'

'Correct, uncle. So why don't we ask him to sing for his supper by telling us how he came to meet the rest of us?'

Anson protested: 'No, no. That would be extremely boring!'

But Cassandra was not to be put off. 'Very well, then, as you are what might be called the common thread that links us all together, let's ask each in turn to recall how they met you!'

Anson was outwitted and amid the laughter Elizabeth volunteered: 'Since I met him first, perhaps I should start?'

Cassandra clapped her hands. 'Excellent, please begin!'

'Well, my earliest memory of Oliver was going ratting with him in the tithe barn near our father's rectory. Our sister Anne was too frightened to join in so my brother and I became, well, quite close. He was a bit of a dare-devil and once lowered himself down from the church tower on a rope, but he wouldn't let me try it—'

'Enough!' Anson exclaimed. 'This is too embarrassing!'

Elizabeth held up her hand. 'I've nearly finished. We didn't hear much of him once he'd joined the navy, you see. But I do remember him putting toads in our beds once. My brother Gussie and sister Anne were terrified! Oh, and before he left, I remember him wearing his pointy navy hat and chasing us around with a dagger when he was supposed to be helping the servants to pack his trunk. Then there was his memorial service after we thought he'd been killed in France—'

Anson pulled a face. 'I protest. That's more than enough!'

Laughing, Cassandra queried: 'So who was the next to meet him, I wonder? Mister Bell, perhaps?'

'I reckon so, miss,' Bell confirmed. 'He travelled to Portsmouth an' back in my mail coach at the time of the naval mutinies. We wus twice attacked, I got wounded and Mister Anson stood in for me on the way back t'London. Wiv a bit o' trainin' he'd make not too bad a mail guard.'

'You've kept that bit of your past under your hat, Anson,' Armstrong commented. 'We must persuade Bell, here, to elaborate about all that during the crossing. So who's next?'

'That would be me, and then Cassandra,' Parkin offered. 'It must have been soon after Mister Bell's encounter. Oliver and I were in a stage coach coming down from Chatham and he collapsed with a fever. I managed to get him to my home here at Ludden to be sorted out by the local doctor and convalesce.'

Cassandra held up her hand. 'And that's when I met him, briefly, before he went back to Chatham where we heard he single-handedly ended the Nore Mutiny.'

'Nonsense! Anson protested. 'I did nothing of the sort. I merely helped one ship to break away from the mutineers. Nothing to write home about.'

Ignoring him, Cassandra went on: 'And then from the Mediterranean he sent Uncle Josiah a box with the remains of stuffed birds that had been eaten by rats and a couple of years later he turned up with Baron Hurel—'

Armstrong interrupted. 'But before that Anson and I met first when we were both fruitlessly pleading at the Admiralty for sea-going appointments, and then at my lonely signal station on the cliffs at Fairlight where we hatched the plan to capture the Normandy privateer. And, of course, he persuaded me to attend a ball at which I met his charming sister.'

He beamed at Elizabeth who looked as if she might swoon with happiness at any moment. Anson noted that his friend had not mentioned that he had met his other sister Anne on the same occasion — and was grateful to him for not mentioning the dreaded Charlotte Brax in front of the Parkins.

'So I am next!' Hurel exclaimed. 'And I 'ad the most unusual first meeting with Lieutenant Anson. In fact, we were introduced just after 'e attended my funeral. It's true!'

Most members of the party knew this story, but were amused at the Frenchman's retelling of it — and how Anson had tried, with only partial success, to keep him 'under wraps' until they were able to slip away to reconnoitre Boulogne.

Cassandra waited patiently for Hurel to finish before announcing: 'So, now we have come full circle. 'It was after the Boulogne raid that Oliver came back into our lives, wasn't it uncle?'

'It was, my dear, down on the beach at Deal where we found him badly wounded and in a sorry state. As soon as we were able we brought him back to Ludden to recover.'

Armstrong quipped: 'So he only stays with you when he's on his last legs or on the run!'

Cassandra smiled ruefully. 'That's true, but for the coming months at least we'll be able to keep a close eye on him and do our best to keep him out of harm's way.'

Touched, Anson caught her eye and they exchanged a meaningful glance. He vowed to himself that as soon as he had the opportunity, he would cut her out from the rest of the company and try to tell her how he felt about her.

29

A Change of Plans

Next morning, Anson was in his room completing an official report he had been required to submit giving details of the disposal of the Seagate detachment's weapons and equipment. It was a task made relatively simple thanks to more or less credible figures supplied by the ever-creative George Boxer. He had been a purser's assistant in the old *Brunswick* but was paid off after being wounded at The Glorious First of June, married into a Folkestone undertaker's business and had been recruited by Anson to become the Sea Fencibles' quartermaster. He was as useful for burying official returns and the like as he was for disposing of bodies.

A tap at his door gave Anson the chance to escape his report-writing and, although he was pleased to see that his visitor was Cassandra, he was concerned that she was clearly not her usual composed self.

'Cassandra, whatever's wrong?'

She raised her hands and shook her head. 'It's Elizabeth. She was walking in the garden with Captain Armstrong. I had been in the arbour, finishing a painting of the lake and heard them. They both sounded happy and were laughing. The mail had arrived and as I walked back to the house, I passed Dodman taking the captain a letter...'

'And?'

'Well, it must have brought ill news. The next thing was that Elizabeth rushed past me in tears, went straight to her room and slammed the door. She's locked it and wouldn't answer when I knocked. I thought I'd best tell you.'

'You were quite right to do so. I've read the signs and believe that Armstrong intends to propose to Elizabeth—'

'And she has told me that if he proposes she will accept, enthusiastically!'

'So whatever has caused her to rush off must be to do with the letter Armstrong received.'

She nodded. 'So will you see the captain and find out what this is all about?'

He took her hand. 'Of course. We don't want anything to put the mockers on our Paris expedition.'

*

Armstrong was in the summer house, looking uncharacteristically gloomy.

'What on earth's happened? Apparently, my sister has locked herself in her room and is wailing like a banshee.'

'I'm so sorry to have upset her, mon vieux. In fact I was on the point of, well, anyway, it was this letter—'

'Bad news?'

'Yes, my dear old father's apparently at death's door and I'll have to go home.'

'To Northumberland?'

'Yes. We must have tempted providence when we spoke of it a while ago and I said I'd much sooner see Paris again and put off managing our estate. But now it looks as if I'll have to take responsibility for it whether I like it or not.'

'So there's no way you can come to Paris with us?'

'Sadly, no, and that's what's upset Elizabeth. But with the old man about to enter the pearly gates it would be wrong for me to go off on a jolly. Not least, I'm the sole heir and there'll be decisions to make about the future. I'm determined to look after the tenants and workers to the best of my ability, just as if they were my ship's company.'

'I understand, of course. But Elizabeth was so looking forward to all of us going to Paris — especially you. Is there no way you can still come?'

'I fear not.'

'What if we were to wait until you return from Northumberland?'

Armstrong shook his head, slowly. I've been away so much in the past ten years that I feel I must spend whatever time the old man's got left with him. Until I get there, I've no idea how long that's likely to be and I couldn't expect the rest of you to wait for me indefinitely. What if the peace ends while I'm away and you're not able to go at all?

Anson put his hand on his friend's shoulder. 'You must do what you must do and we'll all just have to make the best of it.'

'Look, mon vieux, I must be frank with you. The truth is although we've not known one another for very long I was about to propose to Elizabeth when this wretched letter arrived.'

'Now why doesn't that surprise me?'

'You knew?'

'I guessed, not being totally blind and stupid!'

'And you don't object?'

'Of course I don't object! I'm thrilled, delighted. I can't think of anyone I'd prefer to have as a brother-in-law!'

Armstrong grabbed Anson's hand and shook it warmly, but a footstep on the summer house steps made them both turn sharply.

It was Elizabeth, still puffy around the eyes but her tears replaced by a determined look.

Before either of the men could speak, she announced: 'Captain Armstrong, Amos, I have come to apologise.'

Not one for emotional scenes, Anson muttered: 'I'll be off and leave you to it.'

'No, please stay Oliver. I want you to hear what I have to say.'

'Very well, if I must.'

'What I want to say is that it was childish and crass of me to flounce off in tears and I am truly sorry. It was just that I had so been looking forward to us all going to Paris that I, well, now I've had time to think I can see that it was extremely selfish of me to throw a tantrum when I should have been thinking not of myself but of your poor dear father, Amos. Of course you must go to him.'

Armstrong looked mightily relieved. 'Elizabeth, I—'

But she held up her hand to silence him. 'There's something more I want to say, to you both. Look, I know there'll be difficulties but my mind is made up. I am going with you to Northumberland, Amos.'

Both men were completely taken aback and Anson's 'Good grief!' said it all.

*

Within the hour, with Parkin's ready agreement, Anson summoned all to a conference in the drawing room, where Dodman served coffee.

Parkin and his niece sat near the fireplace and Armstrong stood opposite them beside Elizabeth's chair.

Anson waited for silence and looked to their host. Nodding, Parkin told his butler: 'Kindly make yourself scarce and ask Mister Bell and Emily to join us.'

Not knowing what was afoot, Armstrong and the two ladies exchanged puzzled looks.

Nat Bell and Emily entered, looking equally mystified, and Anson got straight to the point. 'Mister Parkin and I have had a brief discussion regarding our expedition to Paris and with his permission I will update you all.'

Parkin nodded. 'Please go ahead.'

'We were, of course, all going to Paris together, but Captain Armstrong has just received news that his father is, er, unwell.'

Armstrong interjected: 'Dying, I fear.'

'So he must go home to Northumberland by the swiftest means.'

'And I mean to go with him,' Elizabeth added, insistently.

Armstrong looked sheepish but happy and Cassandra gave Anson an amused glance.

He shrugged. 'I'm happy to face determined Frenchman on the high seas any day of the week, but we mere sailors are quite lost when ashore and positively crumble before a determined lady — and my sister is a *very* determined lady.'

This produced an amused titter and lightened the mood.

Anson waited for a moment before continuing: 'In the absence of our father I consider myself to be acting in his stead and have given Elizabeth my blessing. I find that, like me, Armstrong here is putty in her hands and is only too keen for her to accompany him.'

Cassandra clapped her hands. 'How romantic!'

Armstrong warned: 'I fear Elizabeth won't find Northumberland quite as romantic as Paris.'

But Cassandra countered: 'Romance, I believe, sir, is far more to do with who you are with, rather than where you are!'

Anson smiled in agreement and paused before continuing: 'But all this does leave us in some disarray vis-a-vis Paris. And of course Elizabeth will require a chaperone. So, having discussed this with Mister Parkin, our solution is this: we would like Emily, here, to accompany Captain Armstrong and Elizabeth to Northumberland both as maid and guardian angel.'

He turned to Emily. 'I fear you will miss out on the fleshpots of Paris.'

Emily snorted: 'Shan't miss them, whatever they are, and at least I'll be fed proper, won't I, Cap'n Armstrong?'

'Certainly! They eat good beef and fresh fish — and the odd haggis, of course, when one escapes across the Scottish border.'

Not being entirely sure what a haggis was, but guessing it must be some kind of sheep, Emily nodded contentedly.

Anson summed up. 'Good, then that's settled. Now the rest of us, Cassandra, Mister Parkin, Hurel — my apologies, *Mister Tunbridge* — Nat Bell and myself will still go to Paris. It will mean persuading one of the Ludden Hall maids, Annie or Bessie, to accompany Cassandra, but that shouldn't be too difficult if we offer her double wages and assure her that she won't be force-fed snails or guillotined the moment she steps ashore!'

*

Amid last-minute preparations, hugs and handshakes, the luggage and a hamper of provisions provided at Parkin's insistence by the cook was loaded on board his coach and Armstrong and a tearful but excited Elizabeth, fussed over by the bossy Emily, departed for London.

Armstrong had confided that his intention was to stay in the capital overnight and seek passage north the following day, quipping: 'At the very least there'll be colliers returning to Newcastle!'

As soon as the coach turned out of the gates heading for the London road, Anson retreated to his room to compose the letter he knew he must write.

Dear Father

I write to inform you that Elizabeth is well, is much enjoying her stay here at Ludden Hall, and has become firm friends with Mister Josiah Parkin's niece, Cassandra.

It was intended that we would all take advantage of this temporary peace to visit Paris along with my friend Amos Armstrong, who you will remember meeting when he stayed at the rectory at the time of the Brax Hall ball. I am happy to say that since then he has been promoted to captain, although the coming of peace means that we are both currently — in sea officers' parlance — 'on the beach'.

However, our Paris plans were thrown awry when Captain Armstrong received news that his father is gravely ill, requiring him to return to the family estate in Northumberland with the utmost despatch.

I must tell you that, although they have known one another for a relatively short time, an understanding has developed between Armstrong and my sister, and that with my approval, acting as it were 'in loco parentis', she has insisted on accompanying him, chaperoned by an extremely fierce maid from Ludden, a formidable woman of middle years. Normally you would have of course been consulted, but there was no time.

Please accept my assurance that Armstrong is an honourable man and, should the relationship develop, there is no-one I would choose above him as a brother-in-law. I hope therefore that you will feel able to write to Elizabeth care of the Armstrong estate address, below, giving your blessing to what has occurred and your consent to her marriage to Captain Armstrong, should that happy circumstance arise while they are in Northumberland. Such a letter from you would delight them both, and me.

I am leaving shortly for Paris with Mister Parkin and his niece, but before we go, I also wanted to assure you that the rift which has occurred in our family was not of my choosing and that I have no quarrel with you in particular. Although I cannot envisage ever being able to forget the position taken by my mother and brother over the Brax affair, it is my dearest wish to be reconciled with you personally. Perhaps the two of us could meet on 'neutral ground' at Ludden Hall following my return from France.

Meanwhile I trust you have received the allowance money I have returned and very much hope that you will use at least some of it for the good of the poor of your parish.

Yours most sincerely
Oliver

30

The Deserted Village

With Tom Hoover riding Anson's horse Ebony and Sam Fagg lording it in Tom Marsh's pony and trap, they made their way into the Wealden village of Woodhurst.

They passed what they correctly assumed was the Baptist chapel that the smugglers had threatened to burn down, and halted in front of an inn with a creaking sign announcing it as the Rose and Crown. A young potboy emerged from the pub and asked: 'What can I do for you, gents?'

Hoover dismounted, massaged his backside and asked the boy: 'D'you know Mister Finch, son?'

'Depends who wants him. Are you blokes smugglers?'

'No, tell him two friends of Phineas Shrubb are here and would like a word.'

The boy touched his forehead and disappeared down a nearby alley.

Sam Fagg got down awkwardly from the cart. His ankle, broken during the Normandy raid, was still troubling him. He observed: 'Ain't much of a welcome, is it? Place is deserted, like what you might call a ghost village. No-one abaht.'

Hoover shrugged. 'I guess after what's happened here, they must be pretty wary of strangers.'

After a while the potboy returned with a perspiring soberly-dressed man who introduced himself as John Finch. 'And you must be Lieutenant Anson's men?'

'That's right, Tom Hoover and Sam Fagg at your service. Now, we'll need somewhere to stay. The pub here will do — and we'll need to talk to the rest of your men.'

'The elders?'

'That's right, and as soon as you like.'

Finch pondered. 'Normally we'd meet in the chapel, but we'd best not attract too much attention. So it'll have to be my barn. Young Ned here will fetch you once you've settled in. Shall we say in about an hour? And, by the way, the landlord's expecting you and your rooms and everything else will be paid for by our congregation.'

Hoover shook his head. 'Kind of you, but no, we'll pay our own way, won't we Sam? And, by the by, tell the men to bring any firearms and other weapons they have.'

Finch gave them what Fagg called a sideways look, but nodded at the inevitability of it, warning: 'I will, but if I were you I wouldn't expect too much.'

*

Sam Fagg glanced uneasily at Hoover, and although the American clearly shared his misgivings, he remained deadpan. They were sitting on boxes and other makeshift seats in a circle of soberly-dressed men in Finch's barn. True, the Woodhurst men did not look remotely soldierly. But then the Seagate Sea Fencibles had not impressed on first meeting yet had gone on to take the Normandy privateer and showed great courage during Nelson's attack on Boulogne.

'I'm Sergeant Hoover of the Marines, and this here's Bosun Sam Fagg. Perhaps you'd introduce yourselves?'

Finch answered for them. 'This is Brother Stephen Clark. He's the village grocer. Brother John Cooper here is the apothecary. It's through him, and the Baptist connection of course, that we know Phineas Shrubb.'

'A good man, Phin, and a right 'andsome daughter, too,' Fagg interjected, only to provoke a disapproving look from Hoover.

'Brother James Morris, here, is the baker.'

Fagg could not help himself muttering: 'We'll not be short o' vittles, then.'

But again Hoover browbeat him to silence and the last two men were introduced as Brothers Moses Lade, the village blacksmith, and George Attwood, a farmer.

Finch explained: 'We're all members of the Baptist congregation. There may be a couple of others who're willing to join us but they couldn't make it tonight.'

'Prayin', I 'spect,' Fagg offered, but yet again Hoover spoke over him.

'Any of you got any military experience?'

There was a general shaking of heads.

'Weapons? You were asked to bring weapons.'

The farmer produced a flintlock shotgun and handed it to Hoover.

The marine checked it over. 'Hmm, not bad. William Parker of Rochester's a good maker. It'll do fine. What else?'

The farmer pointed to a pitchfork leaning against an upright. 'I can bring several more.'

Fagg snorted dismissively, but Hoover stayed him. 'These'll be fine, too. I'm a military man but I'll tell you, I wouldn't want to rush a bunch of determined men armed with pitchforks.'

But, he wondered, did these men have the guts to stand against a ruthless gang of smugglers led by a maniac like Black Mac?

Almost shyly, as if expecting to be ridiculed, the baker handed over a rusty sword that looked to be of English Civil War vintage. Hoover ran his thumb along the blade and pronounced it serviceable but blunt.

'I can sort that easily,' the blacksmith offered. 'And I'll put an edge on anything else as needs it.'

'Good. So let our friend Moses here have any axes, slashers and billhooks you have so that he can sharpen them up. Anything like that's a formidable weapon in the right hands and even if you don't get to use them at least they'll make you look the part. Sam and I will do our best to train you, but there ain't much time and it's vital that you look as if you mean business.'

The only other firearm produced was an old flintlock pistol missing its trigger. Hoover handed it to the blacksmith. 'Can you fix that, too?'

Lade shook his head, but, eager to please, offered to take it to a Maidstone gunsmith to be repaired.

'Do that, and as soon as possible. So, we've got a couple of firearms, a sword and a bunch of tools that can serve as weapons.'

'Ploughshares into swords,' Cooper pronounced. 'Isaiah chapter two, verse four: "They shall beat their swords into ploughshares and their spears into pruning hooks." But, sadly, we'll be doing it the other way around.'

Hoover searched his memory and his Baptist upbringing gave him the answer. 'That's right, but doesn't it say in the psalms: "Blessed be the Lord my strength, which teacheth my hands to war, my fingers to fight"?'

Finch nodded approvingly. 'Well said, Brother Hoover. We don't want to fight, but we must defend our church and our flock against evil. So let's not shilly-shally. If we do, evil will triumph.'

'Right men, let's get to it. I'd prefer to be called Sergeant Hoover, by the by. From this moment on this here's the Woodhurst Militia and I'll expect you all to act in a soldierly fashion. So are you all with us?'

The elders looked from one to another and answered with conviction: 'We are!'

*

Over the following days Hoover did a careful reconnaissance of the village noting all approaches and possible strong points, such as they were.

The chapel was constructed mainly of wood and would be useless for defensive purposes. Use of any of the more substantial village houses would similarly be a bad idea. It was important to keep even those against standing up to the smugglers on side and any private dwelling they selected would surely become a magnet for the enemy.

It quickly became clear to the American that, as Lieutenant Anson had suggested, the church, with its stone-built tower within the walled graveyard was the obvious place to use as a stronghold when attack threatened. It offered an all-round view and was crenelated like a castle keep — ideal for marksmen to use for protection while reloading. But he wondered how good or otherwise the Baptists' relationship was with the established church hereabouts. It would not do to risk sparking a religious hoo-ha by using the churchyard or the building itself without full cooperation from the local vicar.

Over at the blacksmith's forge, Fagg spent time with Moses Lade examining the weapons that had been handed in. They were laid out on a workbench, the axes, handbills, bill hooks and the ancient sword now with razor sharp edges. Even the pitchforks had freshly-sharpened prongs.

The bosun picked one up and tested its points, announcing: 'Good job, blacksmith. I wouldn't want one o' them stuck up me...' He stopped himself saying 'arse' just in time, telling himself that these here devil-dodging country bumpkins wouldn't appreciate sailor-like forthrightness.

Tom Hoover hove to, and together they walked back to the pub. Over a mug of ale he filled Fagg in on his thoughts about defending the village. 'We need to get the nod to be able to use the church tower, even if it's only for stationing a look-out there.'

'They couldn't say no t'that, could they?'

'It's a bit tricky. The people who've asked for our help are Baptists — non-conformists — and the church is Anglican.'

'Strewth, there's only one Gawd, ain't there?'

Not wishing to get into a lower deck philosophical discussion, Hoover ignored him. 'Anyways, that'll need sorting out. I'd dearly love to use the tower for placing marksmen, too. If we can get permission for that we'll be fine and dandy.'

'Marksmen? You got to be joking. I don't fink these blokes'll be able to 'it a bleedin' barn door right in front of 'em, let alone a bunch of cutthroats what's runnin' abaht firin' back at 'em!'

'They'll learn and meanwhile I'll train the youngest and fittest men as a kind of mobile force to attack the smugglers whichever way they approach.'

'So, like Mister Anson said, nuffink could possibly go wrong?'

Hoover grinned. 'That's right!'

31

Dover

On arrival in Dover, Parkin's party checked into the Ship Inn and before dinner he, Hurel, Cassandra and Anson took a stroll along the front and on one of the piers from which they had an excellent view of the castle — and out to sea.

Cassandra had taken Parkin's arm and before Anson could make a move, the Frenchman had latched on to her left. Miffed, he fell in with Nat Bell who was sheep-dogging behind, his eyes ever alert for signs of ne'er-do-wells. Bessie, the maid who had been persuaded to join the party, had chosen to remain at the inn.

Halfway along the pier Parkin, that mine of miscellaneous information, broke ranks to sit on a bollard and take a breather, remarking: 'This pier reminds me of a sad tale, you know.'

'Of a lover's farewell, uncle?'

'No, well, not exactly. Many years ago the harbour commissioners were quite taken aback when a fellow called Henry Matson died, leaving all his estates to Dover Harbour.'

'What's sad about that?' Anson asked.

'There was a condition, you see, that once a year the wooden decking was to be inspected for holes which were to be plugged immediately to prevent gentlemen's walking sticks falling through—'

'An odd bequest,' Cassandra observed. 'What was behind it?'

'Ah, well, he was a substantial local landowner and wanted to marry a young lady called Elizabeth Stokes. She was the daughter of a master mariner who was six times mayor of Dover—'

'But do we take it that Henry and Elizabeth didn't marry?'

'You're there before me! William was taking his customary walk on the pier one day when his gold-topped cane slipped through a hole in the decking and vanished into the sea. And although he was a churchwarden, he was so cross he swore loudly and was overheard by Elizabeth and her mother—'

'Oh dear, so that put her off him?'

'Apparently. At any rate she married someone else and poor Henry remained a bachelor. After he died and left his estate to the commissioners, they carried out the inspections he had stipulated for a good few years and the annual feast held afterwards went on even longer.'

Cassandra pouted. 'What a sad tale, but I have to say that if the minx was put off by a few swearwords she didn't deserve him, poor man. Fancy condemning a man to a lifetime of unrequited love over such a trivial thing!'

Anson observed playfully: 'I'm told that ladies who marry sea officers are advised to close their ears on occasion. What do you say to that?'

'That's sound advice. Elizabeth told me that she developed selective hearing as soon as you became a midshipman. She said your mother was quite shocked when you first came on leave full of lower deck expressions.'

Anson protested: 'What can you expect when we have to live hugger-mugger with rough sailors?'

*

The breeze was freshening, and as they walked back down the pier Anson eyed the choppy sea a trifle anxiously.

It would be no problem for the likes of him and Hurel, but he was not so sure about the others. Parkin was not exactly robust, Cassandra had never been afloat, and a bad crossing would set the Paris trip off on entirely the wrong foot.

They retired early and next morning, on the advice of the hotel proprietor, Anson accompanied Parkin to seek out the captain of a two-masted vessel — the reassuringly-named *Dover Goodwife* — and found him on the pier supervising the loading of stores.

Anson cast a professional eye over the *Goodwife*. Her fore and aft rigged masts were raked very much like a schooner, and her long bowsprit was near horizontal. The courses were gaffsails that could be extended by booms as in cutters. Square topsails could be carried on both masts — and a square course when running before the wind. Clearly, she was built for speed. He reckoned she was of around fifty tons with a crew of under a dozen.

The captain, a genial middle-aged man with well-weathered face, removed his clay pipe to ask: 'Can I help you, gentlemen? Cap'n Thomas Sutton, at your service.'

Parkin looked to Anson, who asked: 'You're on the Calais run?'

'I am, sir. Brought the *Goodwife* down from Harwich recently to run passengers across now that peace has broken out.'

Anson nodded. There would have been precious little passenger traffic out of Dover during hostilities and he knew some skippers had migrated temporarily to East Anglia, where there had been richer pickings. Sutton was clearly one of those who had thought it worthwhile to return.

'We're seeking a passage and we've been recommended to you.'

'That's on account of the old *Goodwife* being the best, sir. Just the two of you for Calais, is it?'

'We have a party of six, all told, staying at the Ship Inn and keen to sail as soon as possible.'

'Very well, sir. I can do you a very good price for five. Let's say two guineas a head.'

As a banker, albeit retired, Parkin had done his homework and would not be dunned although he could well afford to be. 'We'd rather pay a guinea a head, that being more like the going rate.'

'Ha, you should have said you were local! There's a price for locals and another for strangers, especially Londoners. So, when is it you're wanting to sail?'

'Tomorrow, if wind and tide are right.'

'Tide's constant, give or take, but wind's variable. This north-westerly is a trifle strong but should suit us, so unless it changes, I'll plan to sail tomorrow morning on the ebb, around eight o'clock. You'll all need to be on board, bags and baggage by seven, no later.'

Parkin asked: 'And when can we expect to arrive in Calais?'

The captain chuckled indulgently. 'Bless you, sir, 'tis plain you're no sailor! We'll get there when the wind lets us and not before.'

He looked out to sea at the white-topped waves and warned: 'Looks to me as if it'll be a rough passage, but a quick one.'

'Will you be taking any other passengers?'

'I will, sir, but only five others, so you won't be crowded out.'

Before securing the deal, Anson enquired who the other passengers were. With his clandestine role in mind it paid to be careful.

Sutton took off his battered tricorn hat and scratched his balding pate. 'The others? Let me see. There's a military-looking gent with his sister and fiancée. Says they're getting married in Paris, romantic, see?'

'And the others?'

'There's a man of business with a fellow he calls his valet but who looks more like a bruiser.'

'A bodyguard?'

'I reckon so. The business gent's short and chubby and carries a big leather bag around with him that he never lets out of his sight. The other cove keeps watch on him, always looking round, furtive like, as if he's expecting someone to try and rob them at any minute.'

There was something familiar about the packet captain's description of the businessman, but no doubt all would be revealed when they embarked next day.

'Now, gents, if you'll kindly leave a deposit to secure your berths, I'll crack on with loading stores. Oh, by the by, I'd be obliged if you don't mention to the other passengers how much you're paying. They're Londoners, y'see, so qualify for the full rate, same as foreigners.'

Amused at the captain's audacity, Parkin and Anson made their way back to the Ship Inn to announce what was planned, and recommend that after a sight-seeing visit to the famous castle the party should eat and retire early so as to be in good form for the crossing.

32

The Woodhurst Militia

As it grew dark Hoover accompanied Brother Finch to the vicarage, announcing to the servant who answered their knock that they had a matter of the greatest importance to discuss with the incumbent.

After a lengthy wait in the hallway they were ushered into the study, where they found the Reverend Tobias Root smoking a pipe and enjoying a glass of postprandial brandy.

Hoover raised an eyebrow. This didn't augur well. They were about to ask the vicar to cut off his brandy supply, which would surely happen if he co-operated to thwart the smugglers.

But the interview went better than expected.

Seated and offered a glass, which both politely declined, they quickly outlined the situation — the beating of William Philpot and the smugglers' threat to burn the chapel and the houses of anyone who refused to cooperate with them.

The vicar listened without reaction, but when Hoover explained that he was a sergeant of marines and had been sent by Lieutenant Anson of the Seagate Sea Fencibles to protect the village, he beamed.

'Anson? Kin of the Reverend Thomas Anson, rector of Hardres-with-Farthingham?'

'His son, sir.'

'His second son, I think you'll find. The eldest, Augustine, is a canon at Canterbury Cathedral. So this must be...?'

'Oliver Anson, sir.'

'Yes, yes, the young man who escaped from France and captured a French man-of-war!'

'It was a privateer, sir.'

'An enemy ship nevertheless, however you'd care to describe it. I know the young man's father well. So, how can I help?'

An hour later Hoover and Finch left the vicarage with permission to station a lookout in the church tower and to take refuge there should it prove necessary. What's more, the Reverend Root had offered to find a few volunteers 'sound of wind and limb' to join the Woodhurst Militia, explaining with a broad smile: 'If the smugglers do attack the village, I can't have it said afterwards that they were beaten off by half a parcel of non-conformists! No, this must be a joint effort!'

Back at the pub, Hoover updated the bosun. 'The vicar ain't fussed if we post look-outs in his tower and use the church for shelter if we're hard-pressed. I didn't tell him that's where I reckon the action will be, but we won't worry ourselves about that 'til it happens.'

'While you was hobnobbin' wiv the vicar, young Tom Marsh 'as come back wiv you-know-what.'

'The muskets? Has Boxer squared it?'

'Yeah. Young Tom says when 'e took 'im your note George told 'im 'e's already written some orf, wiv bayonets, powder, balls — the lot. Mister Anson's orders.'

All it had needed to win the quartermaster's cooperation was the mention that the smuggling gang threatening Woodhurst was led by one Billy MacIntyre.

Boxer and Black Mac had history, the former bosun of the Seagate detachment having blackmailed him by threatening to shop him to the impress, wounded veteran or not, unless he paid up.

Hoover frowned. 'How come he's managed to write off the muskets? I bet it ain't strictly legal, is it?'

''Course it ain't! They all got lost overboard from the boats when we attacked Boulogne, didn't they? Leastways, that's what the paperwork says. Quartermasters love a bit of henemy action, so's they can write orf all sorts of stuff.'

'But losing half a dozen muskets overboard sounds a mite suspicious.'

'Nah, nah! Ain't yer learned nuffink all the time yer bin in the marines? No, silly, 'e's sent us seven. See, when y'want to put one over on the 'ammock-counters what ye do is give 'em an odd number...'

Hoover looked doubtful.

'Look, it's like if yer was claimin' some money back what ye'd paid aht on be'alf of the navy. Well, never say it was a pound, even if it was. What y'do is claim one pound one shillen and thrupence farthin'. Common sense ain't it? If you claim a round pound they gets all suspicious. Mind you, always claim 'igh rather than low, but never a round figure, see?'

Hoover reacted with a quizzical look at this piece of lower deck economic wisdom but let it go.

'Where are these lost muskets right now?'

'In yer room, mate, under yer bed. Weapons is marines' kit, ain't they? Anyway, if I 'appen to get lucky in the bar tonight I don't want the floozy to trip over a pile of muskets, do I? Might put 'er orf 'er stroke.'

But in the event Sam Fagg did not 'get lucky' in the bar and they both wisely decided on an early night. They had a militia to train.

33

Fellow Passengers

Breakfasting early with the Ludden Hall party, Anson noted a ruddy-faced military-looking type accompanied by a hard-faced woman and a much younger, shy-looking lady at a nearby table. No doubt some of the fellow-passengers Captain Sutton had mentioned.

His exchange of small talk with the Parkins and Hurel about the upcoming crossing was interrupted by the arrival of a short, well-upholstered, purple-nosed man sporting extravagant side-whiskers known in the service as 'bugger's grips' and clutching a large leather bag as if it were a precious child.

Anson near choked on a forkful of scrambled egg and rose to his feet. 'Good grief, Obadiah Pettiworth!'

The man and his companion, a tough-looking fellow with the appearance of a bodyguard, stared at Anson, who immediately realised that he must look different in plain clothes and with considerably more scars than he had when they last met.

'You clearly don't recognise me, Mister Pettiworth. Perhaps if I were in naval uniform?'

The penny dropped and Pettiworth beamed. 'Why it's Lieutenant Anson, my saviour when robbers attacked me at the mail coach stop on the way back to London!'

It had been back at the time of the naval mutinies in '97 and Anson and Nat Bell had seen the villains off, although the guard had taken a pistol ball for his trouble.

'I am still in your debt, lieutenant. Had you not come to my aid those miscreants would have made off with my bag.' He patted it lovingly. 'And, well, I would have lost a small fortune and my counting house might well have gone under.'

'But I see you have your own security now, Mister Pettiworth.'

'Obadiah, please. Yes, this is Crocker. He's an old soldier and there's no-one better at covering my back, barring your good self of course.'

'May I ask what brings you to Dover, er, Obadiah? Might I guess that you are taking advantage of the temporary peace and crossing the Channel to take the benefits of your financial acumen to the French?'

'You've got it in one!' Pettiworth laughed. 'Yes, after years of enmity there will be opportunities galore, so I'm taking passage in Captain Sutton's vessel this very morning.'

'Then once again we'll be fellow passengers. Mister Parkin and his niece, Cassandra here, are off to Paris with me, and this is our friend Hur—, er, Mister Tunbridge. And would you believe it? Nat Bell, the guard who was wounded when you were attacked, is here with us.'

Pettiworth chuckled happily. 'Then from personal experience I can assure Mister Parkin and his niece that we could not be in better hands!'

*

Anson and Bell busied themselves collecting the party's luggage and arranging for it to be taken down to the *Dover Goodwife's* berth. But Bell insisted on carrying what

Anson had called his 'bag of tools' himself. 'I ain't being parted from this,' he announced. 'It's well known that these 'ere Channel ports is swarmin' wiv ne'r-do-wells and it'd be more'n me life's worth to 'ave this lot nicked!'

Parkin paid the bill, ignoring protests from Anson by saying, patently untruthfully, that they could 'settle up later', and Hurel seized the opportunity to continue his campaign to charm Cassandra, who avoided him taking her arm by linking hers with young Bessie.

It being only a musket shot from the pier, they walked together, talking excitedly of the adventure to come.

But Anson's attention was focused on the weather. He did not like the keen nor-westerly that seemed to have increased overnight.

As they approached the *Goodwife* he could see that she was swinging at her moorings and he exchanged a quiet word with Hurel. 'This doesn't augur well for the non-sailors. Do you think we should delay our departure until it quietens down?'

But Hurel shook his head. 'Worry not, mon ami. It's but twenty or so of your English miles and we'll be there before you can flutter an eyelid.'

Anson shrugged. 'I think you mean *bat* an eyelid. A man fluttering his eyelids indicates something quite different in the British navy, but no matter. I was merely thinking of Parkin, Cassandra and her maid who are unused to the sea.'

Captain Sutton was at the gangway to greet them. 'Good morning gentlemen, ladies. With this heavy swell I fear conditions are not as good as I'd hoped, but as I said, we should be in for a quick passage.'

Pettiworth and his man, the ruddy-faced military type, his hard-faced sister and shy — and, Anson noted, now greatly agitated — young fiancée were already on board, and the businessman could be heard lecturing them: 'Yes, the peace brings opportunities for those bold enough to grab them! The blockades have starved the French of the benefits of trade and commerce, but I intend to put that right in short order!'

Anson led his party over the gangway, touched his hat by way of salute and joined the other passengers amidships, where Pettiworth announced him. 'Ah, here's my very old friend Lieutenant Anson, of the Royal Navy.'

The army man looked him up and down and announced himself: '*Major* Trumper, on my way to Paris on a diplomatic mission of the greatest importance.' The emphasis on his rank and the pomposity with which he had described his reason for crossing made Anson take an instant dislike to the man. 'And these people?'

'Lieutenant Hur—'

'No, no, my friend! Remember I am a civilian now. Gerald Tunbridge, at your service, major.'

Trumper sniffed. 'Another jolly Jack Tar, eh? So we'll be well served at sea when we get to all the yo-heave-oh-ing, what?'

'As you might deduce from our plain clothes, major, I am off duty for the duration of the peace and Hur—, er Tunbridge, here is no longer serving, so any yo-heave-oh-ing will be left to the ship's crew, all of whom I am sure are fully up to the task of getting us to France.'

The army man sniffed disdainfully and directed his attention to Parkin, who was watching a cloud of seagulls following a fishing boat into the harbour. 'And you, sir?'

'Me, sir? Parkin's the name, a particular friend of Lieutenant Anson.'

'Really? And why, may I ask, are you going to France?'

Parkin, too, appeared a little put out by the major's directness, but answered civilly enough: 'We see this peace as an opportunity to undertake what you might call a grand tour in miniature.'

'Huh, I'd call that a holiday.' He turned away and Anson shrugged, thinking 'there's always one.' No doubt the pompous major was one of those who had bought his commission, as was possible — indeed normal — in an army that had not shed much blood in the recent war.

Captain Sutton left the gangway and joined Anson's party. 'We're all ready for the off, gentlemen, ladies, but I fear the heavy swell will make for an uncomfortable crossing.'

Parkin looked to Anson, eyebrows raised. Anson glanced seawards. 'Well, there's no rush as far as we're concerned, so if you feel it's best to wait until it abates, so be it.'

But the major had overheard. 'Wait! Why in the devil's name should we wait?'

Anson sighed. 'The captain knows the Channel better than most and reckons conditions will make it an uncomfortable run. With the ladies and civilians in mind, perhaps we should delay sailing until the weather improves.'

'Delay? I have already told you I am on important diplomatic business. There must be no delay! If you and your party are too lily-livered to make the crossing because of a bit of weather I suggest you take yourselves ashore and wait it out.'

Bridling at the slight, Anson was ready to teach the man some manners, but Parkin restrained him with a hand on his arm and muttered softly: 'The ladies.'

Anson paused for a moment and nodded. It would not do to become involved in an undignified squabble with this cretin before they had even set sail. Instead, he gave the major a withering stare and said quietly: 'Very well, let's get under way and hope your stomach is as strong as your tongue.'

'Pah!' The major spun on his heel and went to join his sister and fiancée.

34

'A Bit of Weather'

The increasing swell caused by the 'bit of weather' dismissed so contemptuously by the military man became obvious as the *Goodwife* left the pier behind and headed into the open sea.

Soon the vessel was rising, dipping and rolling from side to side in a corkscrew motion, and Parkin, Bell and the ladies were quick to join the rest of the passengers below deck.

Anson and Hurel joined the captain beside the helmsman, who was struggling at the wheel.

Sutton explained: 'With this nor'-westerly, gentlemen, I'm forced to head for a point to the east of Calais.'

'Anything less would take us too far down-Channel?' Anson observed.

'That's right. Once we're beyond Calais we'll wear round on a port tack and let the tide run us in.'

Hurel asked: 'I take it these fore-and-afters 'andle well in coastal winds and shallow waters, captain?'

'That's right. Makes 'em ideal for going into ports like Calais.'

He broke off to order the helmsman to steer further to larboard and turned to resume his conversation with Anson and Hurel.

'Not the weather I had hoped for, gentlemen, but then this narrow stretch of water can be calm as a millpond and a raging tempest in the space of an hour. It's on account of being at the corner of the North Sea and the Channel, you see.'

Anson offered: 'Can we be of any help?'

'Bless you, no, sir. We've been back and forth pretty well every other day since the peace and a bit of weather's no problem. I just hope that the other members of your party manage to keep their breakfasts down!'

No sooner had he said it than the major, who had gone below with the ladies, reappeared on deck with the suddenness of a jack-in-the-box, bolted to the side and threw up.

Anson had to laugh. 'Poetic justice! I fear that the passenger keenest to make the crossing and never mind the weather has fallen at the first fence, or whatever the sea-going equivalent is!'

Sutton grinned. 'Never suffered with it myself, but I believe sea-sickness is worse than almost any other malady known to mankind other than giving birth, and I'm not planning to try that!'

Tapping the vomiting army man on the shoulder, Anson commiserated: 'Feeling a bit liverish, major? Perhaps it was something you ate?'

The army man heaved again, turned weakly and mouthed what Anson took to be Anglo-Saxon for 'go away'.

*

The *Goodwife* ploughed on through heavy seas, rising then lurching and rolling with waves breaking over the bow and soaking those still on deck.

The major and had disappeared below again and only Anson and Hurel remained with the captain and duty watch.

Clinging to the foremast, Anson found it exhilarating — a reminder if needed of how much he loved being at sea, whatever face it showed. His thoughts turned to what he would do when the peace ended and he determined to find a way to win a sea-going appointment whatever the cost.

He was still musing when, within sight of Calais, the *Goodwife* hit an exceptional wave. The schooner lurched violently, caught Captain Sutton off balance and sent him sprawling. As he went down he hit his head on the corner edge of a grating, knocking himself senseless.

Anson and Hurel looked on in horror as he rolled onto his back, apparently lifeless, blood pouring from an ugly head wound.

'Good grief!' Anson sprang to his aid, and could see immediately that Sutton was badly hurt. Kneeling beside him, he felt the injured man's neck and found a weak pulse.

The mate came hurrying up, blanched and exclaimed: 'Oh my Gawd, is he dead?'

'No, but he's in a pretty bad way. Has he got a cot in his cabin?'

'He has, sir. Shall we carry him down?'

'Yes, and can you find some bandages?'

Still a trifle weak from his recent wounds, Anson stood back as Sutton was carried below, limp and heavy as a sack of potatoes, leaving a trail of bloody drops.

Following them down, Anson just avoided colliding with Cassandra, who had emerged from the main cabin to see what was going on. He answered her unasked question. 'He's alive, but we must stop the bleeding.'

The captain was now on his back on the cot in his tiny cabin and the mate had found a piece of more or less clean towelling.

Anson took it and bandaged the injured man's head as best he could with it, wishing Phineas Shrubb or his daughter Sarah had been there. From personal experience he knew of no-one better at patching damaged bodies than the pair of them.

Leaving Cassandra to keep an eye on the captain, Anson went back on deck with the mate and Hurel.

'Look, Mister...?'

'Abbott, sir.'

'You must take over, Mister Abbott. Are you up to it?'

Abbott's look of alarm said it all — he wasn't. He stammered: 'I'm, well, new to all this, sir. Only joined the *Goodwife* a couple of weeks ago. I'm a fisherman, y'see. When his proper mate went sick, Captain Sutton gave me the job on account of me being his nephew.'

Anson's eyebrows shot skywards. So much for a leisurely crossing. He and Hurel would have to take over in all but name.

'Nevertheless, Mister Abbott, you must take command, but Hur—, er, Mister Tunbridge and I are both navy men and will help as best we can.'

The man was pathetically grateful. 'You're sea officers, sir? So we'll be alright, thank the Lord!'

Anson did not share the man's confidence. Hurel had probably spent more time in a prison hulk than he had at sea, and what was more neither of them had ever taken a vessel of any kind into Calais before, even supposing they could find the entrance.

Nevertheless, he knew instinctively that he must appear confident and make sure Abbott and the rest of the crew were kept occupied.

*

If anything, the weather had worsened in the hour since the captain was injured and those still on deck had to move carefully from handhold to handhold to stay upright.

Shouting to make himself heard, Anson told the mate: 'We'll have a devil of a job getting into Calais in this weather. How familiar are you with the port?'

'Not familiar at all, sir, on account of only having been there twice since I joined the *Goodwife*. And those times the Channel's been like a millpond, so we had it easy. It was what you might call plain sailing. But I do know there's an old watch-tower and there are two spires or belfries, one either side of it. We went ashore and saw them close up. The one to the left is a church.'

Anson took a quick look at his pocket journal. 'L'Église Notre-Dame?'

'Dunno about that, sir, but it's a church sure enough. I remember last time we were here the bells were ringing and all the old biddies were scurrying in there like a lot of black beetles. But how'd you know about the church, if you haven't been here before?'

'A sailing master I know let me study notes he's been keeping for years of his own observations and information he's gleaned from others.' He consulted his journal again. 'There's a fort over to the right of the harbour and a long curving wooden jetty to larboard with a line of stakes to starboard marking the navigable way in. But there are hazards.'

Abbott was looking more anxious by the minute, but Anson ploughed on: 'Yes, apparently the tide sets across the harbour entrance and can be as strong as three knots so it'll be easy to drift off course into danger as we enter. There are shallows offshore to the west and a sandbank one mile north of the harbour entrance with hardly any depth in places.'

The mate pulled a face and exhaled. 'Phew! So it's not going to be easy?'

'No, and the notes warn that in strong northerly winds the sea breaks on the sandbank and it's best not to enter Calais in such conditions!'

Anson turned to Hurel. 'To sum up, we have a strong north-westerly, a vessel neither of us is familiar with, going into a strange port with an inexperienced and depleted crew, and a group of passengers precious to us and expecting that as experienced sea officers we will get them ashore safely. That's about the size of it. We could of course beat up and down outside Calais until the wind drops and take her in then, but...'

Hurel exercised one of his Gallic shrugs and announced: 'Non! Let me go and check on the captain and passengers.'

Anson, left hanging on grimly as the *Goodwife* bucked and rolled in the heavy swell, was beginning to feel a little queasy himself.

The Frenchman returned looking concerned. 'The passengers are in distress, mon ami. Mister Parkin has turned positively green and tells me 'e feels so dreadfully ill that 'e will never, ever again set foot on board a vessel of any kind that floats. I asked him how 'e proposed to get back to England but 'is reply was most out of character!'

'How about the ladies?'

Hurel shook his head. 'Not good.'

Anson considered for a moment. His mind made up, he announced: 'We could pussyfoot around outside Calais all night hoping the weather calms down, so we'll take her in, come what may!'

35

Weapons and Tactics

It was an enlarged band that met in Finch's barn. The Baptist elders had been joined by half a dozen members of the Anglican congregation who brought with them two fireable shotguns and a few edged tools that would do as weapons.

Although they obviously all knew one another, they were divided by their religious persuasions and the newcomers eyed the Baptists warily — and vice versa.

Well used to lower deck cliques, Fagg addressed them as if they were a bunch of street-scrapings newly arrived from a receiving ship.

'Let's get this straight right orf. I'm a proper petty officer in the navy and I ain't bovvered about all this religious stuff, what foot yer kicks wiv and so-forth.'

There was some muttering but they held their peace. The bosun might be a trifle short and scrawny, but he had natural authority and didn't look like someone you'd mess with.

He eyeballed the two groups and announced: 'Don't matter wevver ye're Anglicans, Americans, Baptists or bigamists, ye're all the same t'me and Tom, 'ere. Right? This 'ere militia ye've joined is what matters nah and ye've got to learn to take orders from us, and I'll tell yer fer nothin', the only fing what will bovver us is if you lot don't jump to it when ye're told to jump.'

There was muttered assent, but Fagg glared fiercely at them. 'Look a bit more lively for Gawd's sake. I want all them as is gettin' on a bit or 'as wooden legs or whatnot move to starboard and all them what's sound o' wind and limb to larboard.'

There was some confusion as the villagers first decided which was left and right and then which category each of them fell into.

One elderly specimen who ended up on the left with the fitter men had to be shunted off to the right.

'Nah then, the old and bold lot are mine and the rest of yer now belong to Sergeant 'oover. Tom?'

Hoover looked both groups over and explained: 'We have the vicar's permission to use the church tower as a look-out position, so Bosun Fagg will be in charge of the church group, on account of the game leg he acquired killing Frenchmen.'

'That's right,' Fagg offered. 'We'll keep a watch from the tower.'

'What all of us?'

'No. One maybe two at a time. It'll be easy enough by day and when there's moonlight, but not a lot o' good on dark nights.'

'So what do we do then?'

'That's where Sergeant 'oover's boys come in.'

'Right! On dark nights some of my group will be stationed at the village approaches. Day or night, whoever spots the enemy will fire this flasher...'

He produced a barrel-less pistol that could be used to emit a blue flash as a warning signal. Ironically he had borrowed it from Seagate fencibles who used it on smuggling runs to let an incoming vessel know if the landing was compromised.

'What if no-one sees it?'

'He'll fire a musket, too.'

'Then what?'

'The rest of Bosun Fagg's men must make their way to the churchyard. There're plenty of places you can take cover and fire from if attacked.'

'What, hide behind the gravestones?'

'You got it. Then, if 'ard pressed we go in, barricade the church doors and fire down on 'em from the tower.

'And the rest?' Brother Finch asked.

Hoover explained, with more confidence than he felt. 'The rest will be under me operating as a mobile force deploying to tackle the enemy wherever they appear.'

'But we've got our businesses to run, our work to do,' Morris, the baker, protested.

Fagg glared at him. 'Look mate, we ain't doing this fer fun. If y'want to let the smugglers walk all over yer that's fine with Tom and me. We'll be 'appy to leave you lot to it.'

Hoover was more diplomatic. 'You've got a point about having to do your normal work. I understand that. We'll need a duty roster and with careful planning we can minimise the effect of all this, so you men can cover for one another. Now let's sort out training.'

The baker scoffed: 'Training? What with, three old shotguns and a handful of tools? The smugglers'll laugh at us.'

Fagg grinned smugly. 'Ah, I wondered who'd be fust to bring that up. Well, as it 'appens, Tom and me 'as brung a present fer yer.'

He limped across to a pile of hay, fished in it and held up a musket. 'We got seven o' these, as used in action orf Boulogne, so we know they works.'

242

There were mutters of surprise. He had their attention.

'Tom 'ere, Sergeant 'oover, is goin' to show ye 'ow to fire these 'ere muskets. We'll do what they calls dry trainin' 'ere on account of not wanting to scare the shite outta the village wiv lots o' loud bangs and set the effing barn on fire.'

Hoover took over. 'Excuse the bosun's salty language folks. Comes from mixing with a lot of rough sailors. Anyhow, I'll teach you the basics here — how to handle the weapon, clean and load it, but we'll do the proper firing well out of the way in the woods.'

36

Green Around the Gills

Seizing a speaking trumpet, Anson struggled for'ard and stationed himself behind the foremast, contending with the high wind and drenching spray with the utmost difficulty.

On reaching it he immediately took the precaution of lashing himself to it — otherwise, he reasoned, in these heavy seas a sudden lurch could easily throw him over the side.

Several of the *Goodwife's* hands were reducing canvas. One of them, he noticed was Abbott, the mate. He prayed that they had taken similar care and roped themselves on. The vessel was now level with the harbour mouth, pitching and rolling alarmingly in the cross current and flowing tide, and began her perilous run.

Even with some of the way taken off the vessel, the forward momentum was still alarming and Anson was relieved to see that Hurel had again joined the helmsman wrestling with the wheel.

Shielding his eyes, he could see the triangular outline of a church tower to larboard. That must be l'Église Notre-Dame. A good distance away to its right were two more tall buildings, closer together — the observation tower and the belfry.

Glancing towards the long curving jetty, he could see that the *Goodwife* was well off line and in imminent danger of running into the stakes marking the starboard edge of the channel, or, worse, grounding beyond them on the sandbanks in front of the fort.

He put the speaking trumpet to his lips and made to shout, but only a strangled cry came out so he coughed to clear the frog in his throat, thinking to himself what an absurd expression that was, although strangely apt on this occasion. His mind flashed back, too, to his pathetic attempts to blow a post horn while standing in as a mail coach guard.

'Helmsman there!' This time his voice was strong and clear. Their attention caught, Hurel and the helmsman, clinging to the wheel together, looked up.

'Bear hard to larboard and steer for the left-hand tower!'

The pair fought with the wheel and the vessel swung round almost immediately, but too far, her bow heading for the jetty where a number of locals were lounging, watching proceedings with interest although apparently blissfully unaware that they were in some danger.

Anson yelled again: 'Starboard!' and the helmsmen reacted just in time to avoid colliding with the jetty.

They over-corrected again and the vessel veered dangerously near the line of stakes, but they quickly noticed and made the necessary adjustment.

With the tail wind shooting them down the curving Channel towards the harbour, Anson saw to his horror that in their path was a small rowing boat, with a single oarsman apparently oblivious to the fast-approaching danger.

Anson put the speaking trumpet to his lips again and yelled: 'Attention, attention! Prenez garde, idiot!'

Miraculously the startled boatman managed to row to one side as the *Goodwife* swept past, rocking his dinghy so violently that he had to let go of his oars and hang on to the thwarts for dear life.

The following waves were milder now and, without needing to be ordered, Abbott and his crewmen were feverishly reefing and dropping the remaining sails, taking off much of the way that had brought them so speedily into the channel.

Anson shouted: 'There's a spare berth behind that merchantman. Head for the spot in line with the two right-hand towers.'

Hurel waved his acknowledgement and, in the nick of time, heavy woven-rope fenders were flung over the side to protect the hull. Seconds later the *Dover Goodwife* thumped and slid alongside the jetty in the heart of the harbour sending several crewmen sprawling as they flung mooring ropes ashore.

To the alarm of gesticulating Frenchmen, the schooner's bowsprit ended up inches from the stern of the merchantman in the next berth. It had been a close-run thing.

Allowing himself to relax for the first time in many hours, Anson mouthed: 'Phew!' Whether by luck, judgment, or a bit of both, they had arrived more or less safely, if a little green around the gills, in France.

*

Anson and the mate busied themselves ensuring that the *Dover Goodwife* was properly secured to the bollards and he then ushered Parkin and Cassandra ashore.

A crowd of sightseers had gathered by the time all members of the English party had disembarked and among the gawpers were touts for various hotels. 'This way, milord,' one insisted. 'Follow me to the best hotel in

Calais! Comfortable beds, sheets changed monthly whether soiled or not, no fleas, exquisite cuisine...'

'And a French widow in every bedroom, I hope?' quipped Nat Bell, who was standing guard over the growing pile of luggage being landed by the crew.

'Of course, monsieur!'

But Parkin, already recovering from his bout of sea-sickness and gradually turning from green to ashen pink, appealed to Anson. 'Let's not be diverted by these barkers. We should make our way to the Hôtel d'Angleterre. That, my banking contacts tell me, was the best before the war. Let's hope it hasn't gone downhill.'

Anson turned to Abbott, who was waiting by the gangway. 'Mister Abbott, be good enough to fetch me the speaking trumpet.'

Once again he put it to his lips and shouted: 'Attention, s'il vous plaît! Nous allons a L'Hôtel d'Angleterre de M. Dessein.'

'Monsieur, je suis de cet hôtel. C'est le meilleur!'

Anson lowered the trumpet. 'Bon. Parlez vous anglais?'

'Oui. *Yes*, monsieur.'

'You say it's the best? Then be good enough to engage some trustworthy porters and lead us to the hotel.'

'Of course, monsieur, immédiatement!'

There was a good deal of muttering among the other touts. Although the war was over, at least temporarily, English visitors with gold in their pockets were still as rare as rocking horse droppings in Calais. Anson ignored the grumblers and instructed the guide. 'Before we leave for the hotel, kindly send someone for a doctor to come on board the vessel. The captain has been injured and requires treatment.'

'Certainly, monsieur.'

'Mon ami.'

Anson turned to find Hurel at his elbow, whispering: 'I could 'ave 'elped with these arrangements, my friend, but there will be spies 'ere in Calais and I am trying to keep myself under wraps.'

Anson smiled, remembering when he had urged the Frenchman to do just that before their reconnaissance of Boulogne — with precious little effect. Hurel had blown his cover completely by flirting with every female he encountered and getting involved in a foolish duel with that ass Chitterling. But maybe he had learned the lesson — hence the low profile he was now adopting.

Looking round, Anson noted that Pettiworth and his man had already left the quayside, as had Major Trumper and his female companions.

After a good deal of confusion, shouting and gesturing, his own little procession at last got under way with Nat Bell bringing up at the rear with his pistols in his belt keeping a careful eye on the porters carrying the luggage. No-one was going to make off with any of their dunnage on his watch.

37

Calais

Major Trumper, still green about the gills, was already at the hotel and he and his two female companions disappeared to their rooms as soon as they were allocated.

Dessein's establishment lived up to its official name, the Hôtel d'Angleterre. Its original proprietor had become famous after featuring in a book by the novelist Laurence Sterne, and it specialised in catering for English travellers.

English was spoken by many of the staff, so Parkin was able to negotiate good rooms, with Hurel at his elbow listening for stage whispers in French that might indicate that they were being dunned in any way.

The old gentleman had worked out what he considered to be a suitable exchange rate and the management was more than happy to accept and exchange English gold. It mattered not to them whose head adorned the coins. They were only interested in the weight and would extract a suitable commission for their trouble.

Bell stood guard over the large pile of luggage, so, free from responsibility for a while, Anson was at last able to seek out Cassandra, who was sitting with her maid on a chaise lounge in the foyer.

Both insisted they were fully recovered from the ordeal of the crossing.

'No wonder you sea officers manage to keep such trim figures, Oliver. Bessie lost her breakfast the moment we left Dover, and couldn't possibly have faced lunch. At this rate she'll be positively sylphlike by the time we get home.'

Anson cast an eye over the dumpy maid and thought to himself that she could do with a few more voyages. But he answered sympathetically: 'I promise the sea is not always so inhospitable. If it were, Bessie, none of us would venture out of harbour. And you, Miss, er, Cassandra?'

She smiled at his awkwardness and replied, pointedly, 'I'm quite well, thank you, Oliver. I can't say I enjoyed being tossed about but I managed to retain my breakfast and found the whole crossing quite exhilarating, particularly coming into the port with you clinging to the mast and waving your arms like some great bird.'

He grinned. 'Yes, I admit to flapping somewhat. In the service we don't normally enter port in quite such a rush and I was trying to shoo that small boat out of our way. No, there's a good deal more caution exercised in the navy on account of captains being wary of being court-martialled if they get it wrong. But then, this was a merchant vessel with the captain incapacitated so it was a case of different ships, different long-splices.'

'Different ways of doing the same thing?'

'You've caught my drift.'

'Well, I, in fact both of us, thought you and Lieutenant Hurel were both heroic to take over and bring us in safely, didn't we Bessie? If I'd felt well enough I would have sketched le Baron wrestling with the wheel.'

Anson was less than impressed, but confined himself to warning: 'While we're here we must forget his silly title and string of names. Please remember, he's Gerald Tunbridge now.'

*

250

The hotel buildings formed two squares, with attractive gardens and vines lining the walls. Parkin's party was shown to handsome apartments in the inner square at one side of which there was a theatre and other places of entertainment including coffee, reading and billiard rooms.

Once they were all settled in and been reunited with their luggage, Anson, freed from responsibility, persuaded Cassandra to accompany him on a walk around the harbour area with her sketchbook. It would give her a chance to record the busy quayside scene and him the opportunity to take a closer look at the fort that lay to the west of the entrance — and to memorise the layout of the port, so that he could commit it to his journal back in his room.

The most striking features were the long curving wooden pier or jetty that swept out from the shore fronting the old watch tower and the matching arc of wooden piles marking the extent of the navigable channel they had entered so rapidly just a few hours earlier.

The sea was calmer now and the channel was empty except for the boat they had almost run down, now tied up against the pier.

A few pedestrians were strolling about, one with a dog, and others including a woman in what appeared to be traditional local costume with white bonnet and colourful shawl. She and her man, in broad-brimmed hat and wearing a kilt-like creation over loose trousers, were leaning over the jetty's protective wooden wall, where there was an excellent view of the port.

That gave Anson an idea. He shepherded Cassandra and her maid beyond these idlers and they took up a similar stance further along.

Looking round to make sure no-one was paying them particular attention, he borrowed Cassandra's sketchbook and drew the outline of the port's main features — the curving pier and piles, the position of the three towers and old wall to his left and the fort to his right. He had been taught drawing as a midshipman for just such eventualities and reckoned he made a pretty fair fist of it.

Before handing the book back he noted down approximate distances, the width of the channel and so on. If nothing more, the information would be a useful addition to Josiah Tutt's notes.

They strolled back down the broad jetty, nodding to the idlers as they passed, and when they reached the berths he was not surprised to see the *Dover Goodwife* was still tied up there.

But he was disconcerted to see Hurel approaching from the direction of the hotel.

'Ah, Cassandra, I believe you mentioned that my struggle with the wheel during the crossing would make an excellent sketch and I will be delighted to pose!'

'Of course you will!' Anson muttered, but if he heard the remark the Frenchman ignored the sarcasm.

Anson spotted the mate, Abbott, who was at the gangway seeing off a Frenchman who had the look of a medical man, and went on board.

'Ah, Lieutenant Anson. Settled into your hotel, I hope?'

'We are, thank you. But more importantly, how is your captain?'

'Not too bad, sir. The Froggie doctor seemed to know his business. He's sending men with a stretcher to take him ashore on account of how the motion of the ship, even alongside, isn't doing him any good.'

'Is he conscious?'

'Drifting in and out, you might say. But the doc seemed to think his skull isn't broken and he'll recover with complete bed rest for a couple of days at least. I've given the doc some money from the ship's imprest to tide him over.'

'Well, that's good to hear. So what will you do?'

'I'll sail tomorrow on the ebb, sir. Now that the weather's calmed down I reckon I can get her out without hitting anything. The Dover end will be a pushover. The crew are used to slapping her alongside there, no problem. I'll report what's happened and likely as not the next packet to call here will be told to check up on the skipper.'

'Good man.'

'By the by, sir, I'd like to thank you and Baron Hurel for helping to bring her in. I don't think I'd have made it without your help.'

Anson winced. So much for Hurel's low profile. He had clearly revealed his true name and title to the *Goodwife's* mate — and who else?

The Frenchman had ushered Cassandra on board and took up an exaggerated heroic pose at the wheel. Catching on, Abbott produced a crate — and to Anson's annoyance she sat and started busily sketching the scene.

He could not resist asking: 'Shall we ask Mister Abbott to fetch the proper helmsman for authenticity?'

Again, he was ignored and Cassandra continued for a while before announcing: 'I've more or less sketched the outline of you at the wheel and perhaps you could pose for me again in the hotel so that I can capture your features, Gerald?'

Tunbridge, alias Hurel, said he would be only too delighted to accommodate her, a remark that made Anson seethe. Why, she was actively encouraging the man and if this was an attempt to make him jealous, it had succeeded.

A small crowd had gathered to see what these 'Rosbifs' were up to and, wary of attracting unwanted attention and anxious to bring the sketching session to an end, Anson thought it wise for them to return to the hotel.

There they learned that Parkin and Bell had successfully hired a suitable carriage and four that would be available in a week's time. That gave them plenty of time to recuperate from their exhausting crossing, enjoy the delights of the hotel, and obtain anything they might need for the onward journey.

'My dears!' Parkin exclaimed on hearing of their sketching foray. Have you not heard of William Hogarth's misadventures here for the self-same activity?'

'No,' Cassandra admitted hesitatingly. Nor was she quite sure of who Hogarth was.

Anson had heard of the artist and cartoonist famous for his moral representations of *A Harlot's Progress* and *A Rake's Progress*, and asked: 'Why, did he visit Calais?'

'He did. It was during a previous peace some fifty years ago, and he got into a great deal of difficulty through sketching the ancient gate. The French arrested him as a spy, thinking he intended to draw a plan of the fortifications.'

'Good grief!'

'He was marched in front of the governor and his sketchbook was scrutinized page by page.'

'And did they find anything incriminating?'

'Not at all, in fact they made him prove himself to be a genuine artist by getting him to draw some of them, and of course his talent was obvious! Nevertheless they told him he was lucky they didn't hang him from the ramparts!'

Cassandra put her hand to her mouth. 'So we were lucky to escape the same treatment?'

'You were! But he got his own back by painting a scene at the Calais gate showing the French as emaciated, cringing creatures watching an enormous side of beef arriving, symbolising British prosperity and superiority. He called the painting *O the Roast Beef of old England: The Gate of Calais*.'

Thinking back over their own sketching trip, Anson reddened, embarrassed that he had put Cassandra into a compromising position. If they had been challenged by the authorities and her sketchbook subjected to the Hogarth treatment, his drawing of the port and fort would certainly have been discovered and there could have been hell to pay.

'Hmm,' he ventured, considerably chastened: 'I think we'd best keep sketchbooks in our baggage while we're in Calais and commit scenes to memory.'

But all that — and the ordeal of the crossing — was forgotten over dinner that evening which was a happy occasion of good food, wine and excited conversation, auguring well for the adventure that lay ahead of them.

38

Pinning Tails on Donkeys

On the other side of the Channel the volunteer militiamen of Woodhurst were gradually growing familiar with the workings of the sea service musket, shorter than the infantry's Brown Bess to make it easier to handle in the confines of a warship.

They practised over and over again with its flintlock firing mechanism and the loading drill via the muzzle using a ramrod. Once Fagg was satisfied they had mastered it sufficiently, they were sent one by one to rendezvous with Hoover in the woods, where at last they were able to forget the dumb show and fire for real. Anyone hearing occasional shots would no doubt think someone was out hunting.

Hoover had rigged up a kind of scarecrow, dressed in a ragged jacket and with a turnip for a head, as a target, figuring that men who spent a good deal of their time praying needed to be faced with the reality that sooner rather than later they would be required to fire at their fellow men, albeit ruthless ruffians.

Although the musket was effective for about 100 yards against a close-packed enemy, he stationed them a mere 20 yards from his target. He wanted to make them feel confident that they could hit it — and in any event when it came to action it was likely they would fight at close quarters.

To that end, he showed them how to fit the bayonet, charge and thrust it into the dummy. But although they were doing it before his eyes only, the men went about it as if they were playing a pin-the-tail-on-the-donkey game at a children's party.

They exhibited about as much menace as mice trying to frighten off cats.

He despaired but hoped when the time came they would find some grit from somewhere.

From among the old and bold of his churchyard section, Fagg appointed one of the Anglicans, Jacob Fairbrother, a middle-aged farmer, as his corporal, and for the mobile squad Hoover chose Moses Lade, the tall, well-built man who doubled as village blacksmith and unpaid constable.

The man's policing role had so far merely involved impounding straying livestock and sending the occasional drunk home with a flea in his ear, but he gave every indication of being up to this stiffer test — and, importantly, he was well respected by his fellow villagers whatever their religious persuasion.

Fagg's men took turns as church tower look-outs during the day, and at night the whole group met for an hour or so in the churchyard. With the rest of the village in virtual lock-down, Hoover and Fagg were able to rehearse the men in what they were to do when the smugglers attacked.

For ease of recognition after dark they wore white cross-belts and white bands round their hats. Hoover explained: 'This is how we do it at sea. We marines wear uniforms but the seamen are dressed every which way, so we lend 'em white belts so's we'll know who's who.'

Brother Finch bearded Hoover and Fagg after the latest training session. He warned: 'We've sworn everyone in the village to secrecy about what's going on, but I fear that word will get back to the smugglers.'

Hoover shrugged. 'Sure, we have to expect that they'll find out about it but if they hear you've formed an armed militia prepared to defend the village maybe they'll stay away. So it'll be mission accomplished.'

'But surely they'll just wait until you've gone and then attack us anyway?'

'Not if they know you're organised, well-armed and determined to see them off. The man who leads them is a bully and won't attack if he's convinced you'll stand up to him no matter what.'

But behind his back, the marine was crossing his fingers.

39

A Maiden in Distress

Anson was surprised by a knock on his door. He put down his razor, patted his chin with a towel and on opening the door was astonished to see Cassandra, clearly somewhat agitated.

He asked: 'Is something wrong?'

'Oliver, may I come in? There is something I feel I should tell you.'

'Of course.' He ushered her in and closed the door.

'What's afoot? You have decided you no longer wish to mix with rough sailors like me?'

She blushed. 'Far from it, and kindly stop fishing for compliments. No, this is serious — and excruciatingly embarrassing.'

'You know you may tell me anything. Is it, er, personal?'

'No, no. It concerns Major Trumper.'

'The surly conceited soldier?' His face darkened. 'He hasn't insulted you?'

'No, it's something his fiancée, Miss Ward, has confided in me — and I'm not sure I'm at liberty to tell you, but I feel I must.'

'You know it will go no further.'

She nodded. 'Well, it was when I left you after dinner last night. She was clearly upset about something and asked if she could come to my room.'

'Where was he? I assumed he was still suffering the after-effects of the crossing and couldn't face dinner.'

'So did I, but when we were alone she burst into tears and told me that when she went to his sister's room she found them in bed.'

'The major and his sister? But surely they were just lying on the bed, conversing perhaps?'

Cassandra reddened. She had enjoyed an enlightened upbringing, thanks to Josiah Parkin teaching her biology and the mysteries of animal reproduction with his dissections of toads, rats and other creatures. But she was not quite so well versed in the couplings of the human species and there were some things she found difficult to put into words.

'She tells me they were *in* the bed rather than on it, and they certainly were conversing, but they were both stark naked, enjoying what I believe is politely known as criminal conversation...'

'Good grief! I took an instant dislike to the man but I can hardly believe that he would do such a dastardly thing! Even army officers usually behave with decency and decorum! And with his own sister, for pity's sake!'

'But Miss Ward tells me that the so-called sister is his real wife.'

'What?'

'Poor Helen confronted them, but they were both drunk and laughed in her face. He even invited her to join them in bed and when she refused, furiously, he told her the awful woman posing as his sister was really his wife.'

'I can hardly believe it.'

'Nor I, but I'm sure it's true. He told Miss Ward that he had only offered to marry her for her money and he would be calling at the bank this morning to withdraw the funds he had persuaded her to transfer there before they left England. He told her she could go hang herself for all he cared.'

Anson was horrified. 'Good grief! I thought I'd heard everything, but this takes the biscuit.'

'It appears that she's an heiress. They met less than a month ago at some ball in London. She had a sheltered upbringing and he appeared so dashing, and paid her such attention, that she was swept off her feet.'

'Didn't her parents warn her about such men?'

'They did, and cautioned her not to rush things, but he persuaded her to elope with him on the understanding that they'd be married in Paris. He told her his so-called sister would chaperone them. Apparently he had acted the perfect gentleman until they stayed overnight in Dover where he went to her room and attempted, well...'

'Attempted?'

'Yes, but she resisted him, telling him he must wait until their marriage and he stormed off.'

'To his wife's bed, no doubt!'

'Helen was not to know that at the time and blamed herself for unintentionally leading him on. She thought all would be well once they were married. But then she found them...'

'Poor girl!'

'I insisted she stayed in my room overnight. She was most grateful and this morning she pleaded with me to protect her from him.'

'Well, we most certainly can't abandon her to that swine.'

'She is too terrified to leave my room and fears nothing can be done to prevent him stealing her money.'

Anson thought for a moment. 'Bring her to my room and when I leave make sure she stays here with you and with the door locked. I'll send for Bell to stand guard. Meanwhile the shark nearest the raft is this swindler's plan to get his hands on her money. How much is involved?'

'Five hundred pounds, I believe.'

'Good grief — a fortune!'

'And this is just her own money. She will inherit much more eventually and I suppose that's the real prize this dreadful man was after.'

'Then we must move fast. I know just the men who can help sort out things at the bank and Nat Bell will make sure that the cad and his woman don't bother Miss Ward again.'

*

Anson's plans were in place by the time Hurel sought him out to say farewell.

Shaking his hand, Anson wished him 'Au revoir et bon chance! I hope you find your chateau in good nick. Now perhaps I will be able to spend some time alone with Cassandra.'

The Frenchman smirked. 'She is very beautiful and like most of the ladies she 'as a great affection for me, but you 'ave my blessing to try your 'and with 'er.'

With heavy sarcasm, Anson responded: 'Good of you. I know I'm forever in your shadow.'

'Thank you, my friend. I know that you would 'ave been 'appy to accompany me but it is better that I go alone. I can easily talk myself out of trouble, but if you were to come with me and we were challenged...'

'They would smoke out that I am an English sea officer.'

'Exactly, and an escapee. We would both end up in prison for espionage — or meet a worse fate...'

He drew his finger across his throat. 'As it is, I will arouse no suspicion. I am just another Frenchman headed for Le 'avre.'

They shook hands. 'Take care Hurel.'

'And you, mon ami, and we'll rendezvous in Paris in maybe two or three weeks.'

*

Armed with a signed instruction from Miss Ward, Parkin and Pettiworth were ushered into the manager's office, where they were treated as honoured guests.

The manager, whose English was impeccable having represented his bank in the City of London before The Terror, sent for wine and quizzed them eagerly about wartime life in England. 'We are told you were starving and this peace is more like your surrender, but I have long doubted that is true.'

Pettiworth patted his ample belly. He was what the navy called 'provisioned for a long voyage' and assured the Frenchman: 'Don't look as if I'm exactly starving does it, monsieur?'

The manager smiled. 'No doubt both sides are subjected to false information by their leaders. But I like to think that we in the banking profession are above mere politics and sabre-rattling squabbles.'

His British guests quaffed the excellent vintage and agreed wholeheartedly. Pettiworth chuckled. 'Quite right, monsieur. Money knows no borders, it merely changes its name as it travels hither and thither!'

It transpired that Parkin's family bank was known to the Frenchman and he announced himself happy to accommodate any financial transactions they cared to put his way.

Within the hour they left, to mutual assurances of undying friendship and the certainty that Miss Ward's money was safe from anyone, with promissory notes drawing on it only to be accepted with her personal authority coupled with that of her temporary self-appointed, guardians — Messieurs Parkin and Pettiworth.

*

While this was occurring Major Trumper, having worked out where his victim must have spent the night, presented himself at the door of Miss Parkin's room.

'Helen, dear. Please open the door and we'll sort out last night's little misunderstanding and take ourselves down to the bank.'

He was about to knock again when the door opened suddenly almost hitting his nose and he found himself staring into the steely eyes of Nat Bell, former sergeant of the 56th Foot, and down the barrel of one of Griffin of New Bond Street's overcoat pistols.

'What d'you want?'

The bluster had temporarily deserted the major and he stammered: 'I'm, er, looking for my fiancée.'

Bell stared him down and said quietly and coldly: 'Ain't one wife enough for you? I'm to tell you that you ain't got a fiancée no more and a stop 'as bin put on her money. So push orf and don't bovver 'er agin unless you want me to teach you some manners.'

The major hesitated, tempted to persist, but discretion won over valour and he turn away and beat as dignified a retreat as was possible in the circumstances.

Within the hour, he and his real wife had left for Paris, telling the hotel management that Miss Ward would settle their bill.

40

Return to Old Haunts

Flushed with their success at the bank, Parkin and Pettiworth returned to see what could be done to assist the damsel in distress.

They met with her, Cassandra and Anson in a secluded part of the foyer, with Bell lurking in the background just in case Trumper had the audacity to return. Offered the opportunity to join the Paris party, Miss Ward shuddered at the thought. 'Oh no, gentlemen. It's most kind of you, but what if I bumped into that dreadful pair there?'

'Good point, well brought out,' Anson agreed. 'So it's to be a passage home?'

She nodded sadly. 'My dear parents will be dreadfully worried and I have treated them abominably in running off without their approval, but the major was *so* persuasive.'

'Then we must return you to them forthwith,' Parkin insisted.

'But I fear travelling alone, sir.'

Pettiworth held up his hand. 'I think I have the answer. With Nat Bell here looking after us all, my man Crocker has little to do. He is not enamoured of France and would seize the chance to accompany Miss Ward back to England. I propose he returns with her and once at Dover she can send word asking for her father to collect her.'

Parkin asked: 'Is Crocker reliable?'

'Of course! He wouldn't be in my employ if he wasn't. He looks — and is — a hard nut, but he's also a respectable family man, devoted to his wife and nine children.'

Anson stood. 'Then the way is clear. I'll go straight to the harbour and seek out the mate of the *Dover Goodwife*. He's planning to sail for Dover on the ebb and will be glad to take on two extra passengers.'

Cassandra smiled. 'While you're at it, could you kindly ask him if he can find a less choppy way across?'

*

Parkin was happy that the rest of the party, now to include Pettiworth, should remain in Calais until their onward journey to Paris while Anson went off to revisit some contacts he had made during his escape from France three years earlier, explaining: 'I'm sure you'll understand I cannot be more specific.'

The old gentleman was clearly under the impression that this mysterious mission must be connected in some way to intelligence-gathering and readily agreed.

He pointed out: 'There's plenty to divert us here: theatrical performances, fine dining and so on. It will give us the opportunity to regain our land legs — and stomachs — and quiz returning English visitors for their tips on making the most of our stay in Paris.'

Cassandra was more reluctant to see Anson go, gripping his hand for far longer than was necessary and urging him: 'Please take care and come back to us soon — and all in one piece this time.'

*

Settling Miss Ward's account before escorting her to the *Dover Goodwife* for passage home, Parkin and Pettiworth were horrified to be told that she was expected to pay the Trumpers' unpaid bill.

'There is no way that any member of our party can be held responsible for that fraudster's debt!' Pettiworth shouted at the unfortunate hotel clerk. 'May I suggest, monsieur that you set the law on him, have him imprisoned in your darkest dungeon and throw away the key!'

The Frenchman bowed politely. 'Of course, monsieur, leave it with me.'

*

Anson left for St Omer by coach and on arrival there he hired a horse for the onward journey. He spent the night in a remote auberge and was up early, keen to push on yet apprehensive as to what might transpire.

As he rode on, the countryside became more recognisable. He had travelled this way before, only then as a wounded prisoner after the abortive boat attack at St Valery-en-Caux.

Although he had been semi-conscious much of the time he remembered the undulating fields and woods, reddish soil, occasional wayside inns and timber-framed farmhouses and barns with their high-pitched roofs.

No natural horseman, he dismounted and led the horse up the occasional slopes, more to ease his aching backside than to rest the animal.

Nevertheless, he made good progress and as the miles fell away his mind strayed back to the aftermath of the St Valery raid when he, Hoover and Fagg had been captured and bided their time until they were fit enough to make their escape.

A lot of water had passed under the bridge since then, but the further inland he got the more vividly he recalled that exhilarating time. It had been hard but against all the odds they had managed to make their way to Dunkirk and coerce a Kentish smuggler into giving them passage home in his lugger.

Anson knew he could not have had two better companions for the escape and wondered how the marine and the cheeky foretop-man turned bosun of the Sea Fencibles were getting on swatting smugglers away from a Kentish village. He wished he could be with them, but had already committed himself to the Paris visit when the call for help had come. So be it, he told himself. The Woodhurst mission could not be in better hands.

At last the long straight road led him to a village he remembered well and he turned into the tree-lined central square dominated by a twin-spired church.

And there to his right, dominating one side of the square, was a familiar sprawling ramshackle building with a weather-worn sign bearing a naive painting of a seaman and a name: Auberge du Marin.

*

It was as Gerald Tunbridge, rather than under his true name and pre-revolution title: Gérard, Baron Hurel de Pisseleu-aux-Bois, that Anson's occasionally annoying friend hired a horse in Calais and made his way homewards.

Riding the familiar roads alone, his mind naturally turned to the loss of his family, estate and title during The Terror.

The republicans had murdered his father, mother and elder brother — all guillotined during the revolution. He himself had served in the navy of the ancien régime, escaped when his family were taken, and when he learned of their fate changed his appearance and re-joined under an assumed — or at least abridged — name, reasoning it would be best to hide in plain sight.

The republicans had been glad enough to recruit any experienced sea officer not to bother with making too many enquiries. As far as they were concerned, he was willing to serve the new régime under the tricolour and that was sufficient.

Captured by the Royal Navy and a prisoner in the Medway hulks, he had volunteered to help the British, been spirited away, given a fake funeral that Anson had attended, and went with him to reconnoitre Boulogne just before Nelson's bombardment and subsequent raid on the port.

His motivation for what some would consider turning his coat had been revenge for the assassination of his immediate family — and doing whatever he could to hasten the restoration of his ancestral home. To him, it was the republicans who were the traitors to king and country, not him. The memory of his happy childhood at the family chateau and the prospect of winning it back had kept him going these past years.

But now, he was so close to it he was full of trepidation. Would the chateau have been burned or razed to the ground, as he knew some aristocrats' homes had been, or commandeered and occupied by some republican upstart?

At last he reached the side road leading to his former home and kicked his horse into a trot.

The entrance gates were still there and beyond, down the long carriageway, stood the chateau, surrounded by its moat and dominated by twin towers either side of the main entrance.

He rode on, noting with disgust the overgrown park, now full of thorn bushes, bracken and gorse, with no sign of the deer that had grazed there before the revolution. No doubt they had been poached close to extinction. From a distance the chateau itself appeared intact, but as he drew closer he could see that it was in a pitiful state of repair. Tiles were missing from the roof, the great oak doors were hanging off their hinges, almost every shutter and window appeared to be broken and the moat was full of rubbish.

Dismounting, he tied the horse to an iron ring beside the mounting block he had used from boyhood and pushed his way through the broken doors into the once immaculate entrance hall.

He was deeply shocked at what he saw. His cherished home had clearly been used as a temporary barracks, with revolutionary slogans painted in red on the walls and broken furniture and other detritus littering the floor.

Hurrying through to the library, he was horrified to see that many of the precious leather-bound albums had been pulled from the shelves, ripped up and scattered around, some burnt remnants showing that the violators had used the pages to light fires in the great fireplace.

But there was worse. His ancestors' portraits, his murdered father, mother and brother, his grandparents, great grandparents, even his great-great aunt, the mistress of a king and of whom he had been so proud, had clearly been used for target practice and were riddled with holes.

Fearing to look further in case he discovered even worse vandalism, the inheritor of the Chateau de Pisseleu-aux-Bois sank to his knees, put his hands to his head and wept.

After a while he roused himself and went outside, remounted his horse and rode off towards the Seine. There was work to be done and intelligence to be gathered to use against the republican cochons who had murdered his family and desecrated his ancestral home.

Anson well remembered the first time he had seen the auberge. As the wagon bringing him, Hoover and Fagg as wounded prisoners of war had come upon it the landlord had been observed urinating against the front wall. But today it appeared deserted.

He tied his horse to the rail beside the door, tried the handle and entered to find there was some life there after all.

It was gloomy inside, just as he remembered it, with little outside light showing through the small grimy windows and smoke from several pipes creating a thick fug. The pipe-smokers ignored him and carried on drinking, as did the landlord, now even chubbier and shabbier than Anson remembered him.

'Bonjour, monsieur, souviens-toi de moi?'

The innkeeper screwed up his eyes and studied the newcomer. 'Mon dieu! Lieutenant Anson, n'est ce pas?'

'Oui, c'est moi.'

'Un verre?'

'Oui, vin rouge.'

There was no sign of Thérèse, nor her son from her marriage to a soldier who had been killed in action before Anson first met her.

'Où est Thérèse?'

'Marié, à un fermier près de Rouen.'

Anson sipped the familiar rough red wine. 'Est elle heureuse?

'Bien sûr. Elle espérait que tu revientrais, mais la guerre...'

So she had hoped he would return. Anson nodded and shrugged. 'Oui, la guerre.'

The inn-keeper rattled off something Anson understood to mean that after his departure she had met a widower, a farmer, they had been happily married for a year and now had a baby daughter, a sister for Thierry.

The arrival of a group of farm-workers eager for a thirst-quencher after their days' work interrupted them, and once they had been served, the landlord, being a man who clearly remembered prompt payers, was only too happy to agree to put Anson up for the night, stable his horse and provide a meal.

The so-called beefsteak offered was of the same suspiciously blueish tinge as that which he, Fagg and Hoover had been served when they were first washed up at the auberge three years before. But Anson was so hungry he did not care if it was horse-meat or not. When he retired for the night it was to the room he had occupied before, only this time there would be no amorous visitation from Thérèse.

As he drifted off to sleep he went over what he had learned and consoled himself that at least by her father's account she was happy and secure — and that her new child could not possibly be his. He had been very fond of her, and their intimacy had filled a need that both had at the time. But it had not been love.

41

A Final Warning

Down on the Marsh, Billy MacIntyre had already heard about the formation of the Woodhurst Militia and who was leading it.

He cursed, remembering with anger that the cretin who'd replaced him as bosun of the Seagate Sea Fencibles and his marine mate were the ones who had foiled his attempt to kill Lieutenant Anson in the Mermaid pub.

And now they were standing in his way again.

He had been given carte blanche by the gang leader to sort out the uppity villagers of Woodhurst who had refused cooperation and if they weren't punished and made to toe the line others elsewhere might well follow suit.

So they needed to be taught a lesson they would never forget, and a sure-fire way was to carry out his threat to burn down their meeting house and make examples of a few of them.

But first, the American and his sidekick would find out what a mistake it was to cross Billy Black.

*

A musket shot scared pigeons away from the church roof and sent the few villagers who were out and about scuttling indoors. Hoover and Fagg, who were demolishing a lamb pie in the Rose and Crown, dropped their eating irons and grabbed their muskets.

'This could be it.'

'Yeah, unless some idiot's 'ad a haccidental discharge.'

'Well, like they say, there's only one way to find out!'

Outside, the village appeared to be deserted except for a lone figure waving at them from the church tower.

'Looks like Attwood.'

They hurried into the churchyard. As a former man-of-war foretop-man, Fagg had a voice that could be just as easily heard from ground level to church tower as from mast-head to deck. Cupping his hands to his mouth he yelled, 'What's up, George? Was that what they calls haccidental?'

Attwood peered down. 'No, there are strangers approaching!'

'How many?'

'I've seen about half a dozen but there could be more.'

'Where are they now?'

'That's the funny thing. When I fired they disappeared behind the chapel, but two of 'em's just come out in the open the other side of the churchyard wall carrying something. Looks like a makeshift white flag!'

Hoover exchanged a puzzled glance with Fagg and called up to the lookout: 'Could be some kind of trick. Reload, with ball this time, and keep them covered.'

'Right, sergeant, and there's some of our lot heading for the church.'

'Sam, when our boys get here send some up the tower and get the rest to take cover behind gravestones. I'm gonna find out what's occurring.'

Happy to defer to the marine in a scrap, Fagg raised his thumb and took shelter behind a tombstone.

'And make sure they've loaded their muskets!'

Crouching low, Hoover threaded his way through the graves towards the white cloth that was being waved back and forth the other side of the five-foot rag-stone wall. Peering over it, he was taken aback to see the battered features of a face he had last seen in the Mermaid on the night Lieutenant Anson was attacked.

'MacIntyre!'

The Scotsman, accompanied by an evil-looking wall-eyed, lank-haired companion carrying a forked pole with a sheet hanging from it, responded with a surly grin. 'It's Billy Black now. And you's that clown Anson's minder! Ye're a lang way frae the sea, laddie.'

Hoover guessed, correctly, that they had raided someone's washing line for their flag of truce. 'What d'you want?'

'We just want these worms to cooperate with the free tradin' like everyone else does.'

Hoover glanced up and could see that several more men had joined the lookout in the tower. MacIntyre had clearly spotted them, too.

'And what if we don't agree to cooperate?'

'Then we'll be back in force. Whatever they're paying yous is no enough. If ye've got any sense you and your hop-along friend will be long gone afore we come back and this stupid militia will 'ave packed it in and agreed to toe the line.'

'We ain't being paid. Not a penny. We're doing this on account of how much we enjoy seeing off scum like you.'

'Then ye're even dafter than ye look. Anyways, we'll be back wi' a lot mair men to sort yous lot out.'

And if we're still here?'

'Then we'll kill ye both, burn down yon chapel and the houses of anyone stupid enough not to have got out o' this pathetic militia.'

And without waiting for a reaction MacIntyre signed to his side-kick to throw aside the white flag, and they turned and stalked away.

Warily, in case of tricks, Hoover backed away to the cluster of gravestones where Fagg was sheltering.

'You heard?'

'I 'eard. So if we don't piss orf they're comin' back to top us?'

'In a nutshell, yes. I reckon it's time to send for a few reinforcements and prepare some surprises for Black Mac and his men.' He thought for a moment. 'Oh, by the by, we'll need a drum.'

Fagg frowned. 'A drum?'

'Yeah, can you put your feelers out? Someone around here must have a drum and know how to bang it.'

Nodding, the bosun knew he wouldn't get anything more out of Hoover when he was in his enigmatic mode. But if there was a drum to be had within a ten-mile radius, Sam Fagg, ace procurer, would surely find it.

42

Paris

In Paris, as arranged, Anson found Parkin and Cassandra at the fashionable Richelieu Hotel, to which they had been recommended by the old gentlemen's banking contacts.

It was a happy reunion. The Parkins were abuzz about their week in Calais enjoying the theatrical productions and excellent dinners at Dessein's and meeting other English travellers both coming and going.

'Cassandra met a quite a number of fellow art enthusiasts, you know,' the old gentleman recalled. 'One was a rather odd man, a Mister Turner, risking arrest by sketching a packet boat entering the harbour in stormy weather. Don't know if the picture he paints will amount to much, but you never know.'

They were full, too, of tales about the trials and tribulations of their journey to Paris. At one village they had been held up by a bunch of hostile locals. 'But Mister Bell saw them off with his blunderbuss. One shot over their heads and they scattered!' Cassandra recalled.

It had taken four days including overnight stops en route, but the excitement of arriving in the capital outweighed all that.

Pettiworth, they told Anson, was spending his days 'passing on the benefits of his business acumen' to the French, so was not a burden on his fellow-tourists' time.

Parkin had already taken his niece to see some of the sights, shadowed at all times by Nat Bell to ensure that they were not dunned or insulted. The blackthorn walking stick that he carried around the capital was a fearsome weapon, and clearly not there simply for decoration.

The old gentleman, Cassandra and Anson found comfortable wicker chairs in the hotel foyer and took tea.

Anson was anxious to talk to Cassandra, but in company conversation was stilted, so he confined himself to enquiring what she had seen of Paris so far.

'Uncle took me to the site of the storming of the Bastille, but of course since it was demolished there is little to see—'

Parkin interrupted. 'However, I was able to purchase — at some expense I might add — one of the original bricks carved into a replica of the fortress. It is secreted in my room and I will show it to you later.'

Deadpan, Anson assured the old gentleman: 'I will be on tenterhooks until I see it.' But privately he wondered just how many such bricks had survived from the once massive fortress and were being similarly chiselled out by the locals for sale to gullible foreigners.

'We've also been to look at the old Marie in the second arrondissement where Napoleon and Josephine married. They say he was very late for the ceremony and eventually rushed in ordering "Marry us quickly!" So romantic!'

'Do I detect you have become an admirer of the First Consul?' Anson asked.

'In some ways, yes. When they married he gave her a pendant, you know, inscribed "To Destiny".'

'Yet by all accounts she cheated on him almost immediately.'

'Oh, Oliver, at times you are so cold-hearted!'

He frowned. Was that how she saw him? He made a mental note to come up with some sort of romantic gesture, but for the life of him he couldn't think of one at the moment.

Oblivious to such nuances, Parkin spoke again. 'Cassandra also insisted I took her to see the house in Rue de la Victoire where Napoleon and Josephine lived. But of course after his coup d'état he moved to the Luxembourg, which they've now renamed the Palais du Consulate.'

Cassandra added excitedly: 'We've yet to go there, or to the Notre-Dame — or the Tuileries and the Louvre, let alone Versailles and Fontainebleau, so there's still much to be see now we're all together.'

'All of us except Hurel, or perhaps I should say Gerald Tunbridge. I take it there's been no sign of him as yet?'

Cassandra shook her head. 'No, I hope he arrives soon because he's promised to help me with my French conversation.'

'Hmm. I hope he will not get in the way of our sight-seeing.'

She sighed. 'I must confess that since we've been here it seems we've spent more time being stared at than we did sightsceing. Frenchmen are very...' she groped for the word, 'forward, I find.'

Anson smiled ruefully. He could sympathise with the Frenchmen and would prefer looking at her to peering at monuments any day. There was no doubt she was an extremely attractive woman, with a handsome figure, raven hair and fine complexion, and he thanked his lucky stars that after his visit to the Auberge du Marin he was no longer carrying any emotional baggage.

And now he was determined not to be passed over in Cassandra's favour by 'le Baron'.

Changing the subject, he asked the old gentleman. 'And you, sir? Is Paris living up to your expectations?'

Parkin took a sip of his tea. 'Do please call me Josiah. We are surely old shipmates by now, are we not?'

'Very well, er, Josiah. Have you managed to make contact with fellow antiquarians and natural historians?'

'I have indeed been welcomed by a distinguished body of Parisian luminaries.'

Anson raised an eyebrow.

'Yes, luminaries, persons who have obtained eminence in their fields of endeavour and become an inspiration to others. Why, some of the world's leading bird and bat stuffers base themselves here in Paris.'

'You amaze me.'

'Then there are a good many botanists, antiquarians — and more eminent etymologists than you can shake a stick insect at!'

'Awesome. If you'd care to spend more time with them I can always take over your role of escorting Cassandra.'

'Would you, my dear fellow? How kind. There's a lecture tomorrow about the microscopic examination of rat droppings to identify their eating habits. Quite fascinating and not something I would wish to miss. So you'll kindly take my niece off my hands?'

'With the greatest pleasure!'

*

Parkin excused himself to update his journal, leaving Cassandra and Anson together.

She asked, a little shyly, 'How was your journey? I shall quite understand if you feel you are not able to discuss it.'

'There was someone I needed to see, something I had to check.'

'From the time of your escape after the St Valery raid?'

280

Yes, a ghost to lay to rest.'

'Was it something to do with where you recuperated while waiting to escape?'

'It was — and someone I knew while I was there.'

'I think I understand. And have you laid the ghost?'

He nodded. 'I have.'

*

On board the river craft, Hurel was bored. He was fulfilling a particular mission seeking information about a new terror weapon but, truth be told, he did not believe there was such a thing — and if there was he doubted very much that he would come across any trace of it.

He had kept his eyes open and his ears flapping throughout the slow passage down the Seine, but he had not seen or heard anything of interest.

But as the vessel neared Le Havre and stopped to pick up some passengers, he struck gold.

He fell into conversation with a farmer bound for the port and enquired as casually as he was able about strange goings on in the estuary that he claimed to have heard about — as indeed he had from Colonel Redfearn before leaving Dover.

The man guffawed. 'Oui, monsieur, ils ont capturé un monstre — un monstre marin!'

43

The Gold Anchor

At breakfast, Parkin asked: 'Cassandra, my dear, will you kindly remind us what is on our list of essential places to visit?'

'In Paris?'

'Yes, we'll visit Versailles and Fontainebleau later.'

'Well then, I've always longed to stroll along the banks of the Seine to the Notre-Dame. So romantic!'

'Then so you shall, this very day.'

He thought for a moment, put his hand to his forehead and exclaimed: 'Ah, no, I almost forgot the lecture about the microscopic examination of rat droppings. But you indicated that you are free to escort Cassandra, my boy?'

'Of course!' Anson smiled. He would be alone with her at last and was determined to reveal that, despite her accusation of cold-heartedness, he also had a romantic side.

While she went back to her room with her maid to prepare for the outing, Anson made enquiries at the reception desk and slipped out of the hotel, headed for the piazza of the old Palais Royal.

There among the coffee houses, milliners and booksellers he found a jeweller's shop that had exactly what he was seeking and was happy to pay the asking price without a murmur.

Later, as they crossed the bridge to the Île de la Cité with Bessie the maid trailing behind, they were taken aback by the grandeur of the Gothic cathedral of Notre-Dame.

It was as imposing, Anson thought, as Canterbury Cathedral where his brother Gussie was a minor canon — if not more so, with its two massive towers, three great rose windows, daring flying buttresses and numerous stone carvings.

They entered, leaving Bessie to stand alone outside, since she preferred to risk being kidnapped and sold into white slavery rather than set foot in a Roman Catholic building. Anson supposed, correctly, that she was blissfully ignorant of the fact that her own local church in Ludden, where she worshipped every Sunday, was originally of the same persuasion.

In the dimly-lit nave Anson took Cassandra's hand protectively and they wandered around the great building together, not really taking much in but content to be in one another's company.

They did register the damage and neglect the cathedral had suffered as a result of the revolution and she insisted fervently: 'It was Napoleon who rescued it from destruction, you know!'

Anson smiled secretly. Clearly, had the First Consul not been otherwise occupied with his wife and mistresses he could well have been a serious rival for Cassandra's affections.

Outside they blinked in the sunlight, took the greatly relieved Bessie back in tow, and made their way to a wooden bench overlooking the Seine.

The package Anson had obtained earlier at the jeweller's was burning a hole in his pocket, but with Bessie hovering nearby he was hampered. He whispered to Cassandra:

283

'There's something I wish to tell you, but...' and he nodded towards Bessie.

Cassandra caught on immediately and told her maid: 'Bessie, I think I may have dropped my lace handkerchief near the cathedral doors. Please see if you can find it.'

Bessie walked reluctantly away, glancing warily to left and right, and Cassandra turned to Anson. 'So, Oliver, we are alone. What is this confidential matter you wish to mention?'

He stuttered: 'You said I was cold-hearted.'

'It was in jest.'

'Yes, but I wished to make a romantic gesture, so I bought you this.' He fumbled in his pocket and produced the package tied with a tiny red ribbon.'

She took it, asking: 'May I open it now?'

'Of course.'

Untying the ribbon she smoothed out the paper to reveal a small red leather box and opened it expectantly.

'Oh, Oliver — a golden anchor!'

'Yes, it can be worn as a brooch or a pendant. There's a delicate gold chain with it, you see?'

'How lovely! May I wear it straight away?'

He nodded happily. It seemed his romantic gesture had paid off, but his hopes to capitalise on it were dashed with Bessie's return.

'Ah, Bessie, I fear I sent you on a wild handkerchief chase. It was here up my sleeve all the time. But perhaps you'd help me put on this lovely pendant that Lieutenant Anson has kindly given to me.'

Frustrated, Anson couldn't help pulling a face. His plan of campaign had been to kiss Cassandra's neck as he draped the necklace around it...

*

Next day, the old gentleman had no luminaries' meetings or lectures about rat droppings to attend so opted to join them on a visit to the Louvre.

As they approached it on the right bank of the Seine, he explained: 'It was originally a fortress and then Francis I occupied it as a royal palace. But Louis XIV chose Versailles instead so it's become one of the civilised world's greatest museums and galleries.'

Anson wondered, facetiously, if there were any museums and galleries in the *un*civilised world, but held his tongue. Parkin burbled on. 'Napoleon has appointed its first director, you know, his art advisor, Dominique Vivant, Baron Denon. He's something of a polymath: archaeologist, artist, author, diplomat, you know. He accompanied Bonaparte's expedition to Egypt and inspired the discovery of the Valley of the Kings.'

Cassandra, wearing her gold anchor as a brooch today, commented: 'Fascinating, but it's my greatest wish to see Leonardo da Vinci's *Mona Lisa*.'

'And so you shall, my dear. We are extremely lucky to see anything at all because the Louvre has only recently reopened after structural problems.'

They wandered the galleries, with Parkin exclaiming in admiration at many of the masterpieces. Louis XVI's collection formed the core of it, along with great works seized during Bonaparte's campaigns. Strangely, Anson thought, Parkin appeared to admire the First Consul for that, although many might consider it looting.

There were not enough scenes of sea battles for Anson's taste and he was staring, by now rather bored, at yet another classical depiction when he felt a tug at his elbow.

It was Cassandra. 'Oliver, don't make it obvious, but look at that woman at the other end of the gallery.'

He followed her glance. 'Good grief! It's that ghastly Trumper's wife! So they *are* in Paris.'

'Should we do anything?'

He thought for a moment, then shook his head. 'I could follow her discretely to find out where they're staying, but to what purpose? Miss Ward is free of him and I very much doubt that the French, of all people, have a law against attempted seduction while already married!'

44

Time Runs Out

The deadline Black Mac had given the Woodhurst Militia by which to disband and for Hoover and Fagg to make themselves scarce was fast approaching.

The mood, when the men gathered in the barn, was sombre.

'Well, men, this is it. They've threatened to attack any time from tomorrow and I reckon they will,' Hoover confided. 'If they don't, they'll lose face and their grip everywhere else will be weakened.'

Fagg, his pipe in the corner of his mouth, but unlit on account of his not wishing to burn the barn down, nodded his head vigorously. 'Tom and me was told to eff orf and you lot to disband an' crawl back 'ome. But we 'ain't and you lot ain't. We're still 'ere and ready to stand up to 'em, right?'

The militiamen did not appear to be entirely convinced, but Lade the blacksmith offered: 'There's only one of us that isn't here.'

'Clark, the grocer? Why not?'

'His mother's been took bad and won't let him leave her side.'

One of the Anglicans put up his hand, 'My wife's been on at me. Keeps moaning about what's going to happen to her and the little ones if I get killed.'

Several others began muttering, clearly sharing his misgivings, and Morris, the baker, said darkly: 'Those that live by the sword, die by the sword. Maybe we should give up all this militia foolishness and turn the other cheek.'

Fagg began spluttering, as if prior to explosion, but Hoover held up his hand to quieten the waverers. His Baptist upbringing in America came in useful now and then. 'Remember Samuel 2, verse 22?'

Finch got there first. 'You mean, "I call upon the Lord, who is worthy to be praised, and I am saved from my enemies"?'

'That's it. We are in the right and the Lord is on our side. If you melt away your enemies will triumph and you'll never be able to lift your heads up again. But if you stand up to them they will learn a lesson they will never forget and leave this village in peace.'

He picked up his musket. 'Right now it might seem like you're facing Goliath and the Philistines, but remember what David did, and this here sea service musket is a whole lot more powerful than his slingshot. It's your choice, brothers.'

Fagg watched, first mystified and then astonished at the effect of the marine's words. The reluctant militiamen were galvanised and when dismissed to get a good night's rest before the coming battle, went off with a spring in their step.

When they were alone, Fagg shook his head in disbelief. 'I got to 'and it to yer, Tom. I ain't never seen a bunch o' ditherers like that lot stirred up wiv a sayin' out o' the Bible afore. Dunno 'ow you can remember all that stuff. Sounded like you meant it, too.'

The American grinned. 'Sure, I meant it, but I had to spend an hour in the church this afternoon looking up a suitable verse, in case they started to wobble!'

*

The deadline arrived but there was no sign of the threatened attack. The Woodhurst militiamen took time off from their work to patrol the approaches and man the church tower, but as evening wore on the smugglers had still failed to put in an appearance.

Eventually, Hoover felt he had no choice but to stand most of the men down so that they could eat and rest. They could be in for a long night.

Trying to put himself in the smugglers' shoes, he pondered what he would do and decided he would wait until it was dark — or attack next day at first light. Either way they would need to harbour up not too far from the village, wait until all was quiet and then attack. Leaving Fagg in charge of the duty men, he tacked up Ebony and rather than keep to the main road, set off down a side lane.

A mile from the village his attention was drawn to a plume of smoke rising almost vertically on the near-still evening air. It came from the far edge of the wood he was skirting, so he dismounted, tied the horse to a tree, took his musket from its makeshift holster and set off into the wood.

As he neared the spot where the smoke was rising he could see the outline of a small barn and hear raucous voices. Creeping closer, he found a large recently-fallen branch and hid among its foliage, thankful that he was not wearing his scarlet uniform jacket and that his brown civilian coat camouflaged him well.

There appeared to be up to a dozen men beside the barn, and he gathered that they were eating and drinking. Two broke away from the rest and stood relieving themselves not more than twenty paces from him. He could see that both were armed with muskets, pistols and swords. They were clearly not military or revenue men, but smugglers: Black Mac's gang.

One of the men made a crude remark about 'sticking this in one of them militiamen's wives come nightfall', and his companion cackled in reply. When they had finished relieving themselves they turned and walked back to the others.

Having seen and heard enough, Hoover set off at a crouching run back to where he had left Ebony, but just before he reached the edge of the wood he had an idea, turned and fired his musket in the direction of the barn.

That would set the cat among the pigeons and get the gang running around in confusion, fearful that they were being attacked. At the very least it would jolt their confidence and make some of the nervy ones begin to wonder if they were about to bite off more than they could chew.

*

Back in the village, Hoover called a council of war with Fagg, the militia corporals, and Sampson Marsh, George Boxer, Joe Bishop and Jacob Shallow, who had answered the call for reinforcements from their lately-disbanded Sea Fencible detachment.

Shallow had more reason than most to hate MacIntyre, having been blackmailed by him and pressed into the navy when he couldn't pay up. The Seagate greengrocer had been rescued from naval servitude by Lieutenant Anson and knew better than anyone which side his bread was buttered.

Hoover briefed them on what he had seen. 'There's a dozen of them holed up at a barn the other side of the woods to the west and they're planning to attack tonight. I stirred them up with a musket shot, so they'll be a bit edgy.'

Moses Lade asked: 'So which way will they come?'

'Your guess is as good as mine. Depends on how well they know the area. Myself, I'd come through the woods, but—'

He was interrupted by the arrival of Tom Marsh, who had been sent out to reconnoitre the main road in his pony and trap.

'What's afoot, young Tom?'

'There's men approachin' up the main road a couple of miles from the village, sergeant. Soon as I saw 'em I turned and headed back.'

'How many?'

'Dunno, p'haps twenty, maybe a few more or less.'

'Armed?'

Young Tom nodded.

Hoover thought for a moment. 'This lot young Tom's seen ain't the same as the ones I saw the other side of the woods. They couldn't have gotten a couple of miles south in that time.'

'So there's two groups?'

'Yeah, about thirty or more all told.'

Fagg raised his eyebrows. 'Strewth! And there's only about fifteen of us, some as can barely fire a musket, even if we 'ad that many, which we ain't.'

The American smiled. 'But the militia's on its own ground. We know they're coming tonight, we've sorted out our defensive positions, and above all we've got our own fortress — the church tower. Now let's get to it.

Corporals, turn out your men and deploy 'em like we've practised!'

*

At the crossroads a mile from Woodhurst, Billy MacIntyre waited until the inland group that had been harboured up by the barn joined up with the larger contingent he had led up from the Marsh.

It was dark now, but there was sufficient moonlight for him to be able to see what was what and for the men to avoid stumbling into one another. He barked out his orders and, noisily with much excited joshing, his little army headed off down the road.

A few mounted men were left to secure the road behind them just in case the defenders had tried to summon up reinforcements, but the rest moved on to the outskirts of the village.

Some now carried flaming torches — MacIntyre's idea to put the fear of God into the pathetic militia and remind them that if they didn't give in straight away, their chapel and their homes would be set on fire.

His confidence was high. There was no way a handful of Bible bashers, even if led by that marine and his mate from Seagate, were going to stand against a gang of hard-nut smugglers in full cry. It would be a walk-over and he savoured the prospect of punishing those who had dared to defy the free traders. Not least, he had heard some of his men discussing in lurid detail what they would do to the defenders' wives — and he was not averse to participating in that bit of sport himself.

All told, it would be a lesson the village — and the rest of the county — would never, ever forget.

They pushed on noisily, but then over the chattering and laughter he heard a noise familiar to old sea dogs like him: the rat-a-tat-tat of a drum beating to quarters.

45

The Sea Monster

After further sightseeing over several days, sadly all with either Parkin or the maid Bessie tagging along unknowingly playing gooseberry, Anson was puzzled to hear that there was a fellow English gentleman awaiting him in the hotel vestibule.

Among the potted ferns in a quiet corner he found Hurel, ostensibly reading a tattered copy of the London *Times*, but actually using it to hide behind.

'Ah, Hurel! How very good to see you! Back from revisiting your vast estate?'

Hurel's face was a picture of horror. 'Shush, my friend! I am keeping myself in the low profile, under what you call wraps! I would be much relieved if you addressed me as Gerald Tunbridge, my nom de guerre.'

Anson grinned. 'Of course, mon ami, I mean… Gerald. But never fear, there's no-one near and you are very well concealed behind *The Times* in this forest of aspidistras!'

'This is not a joke, Anson. P'haps you do not realise there are spies everywhere in Paris and some are paid just to observe the comings and goings of we English?'

'You, English?'

'Well, temporary English.'

'Anyway, no-one can overhear us here.'

'You are wrong, Anson. Here in Fouché's Paris, even the aspidistras 'ave ears. Please, let us take a stroll where we cannot he 'eard.'

Anson had become well aware of the iron grip the Minister of Police had on the capital and was happy to oblige. They left the hotel and walked towards the Jardin des Tuileries. When no-one was near, Anson asked: 'Well, er, Gerald, I am itching to know how you got on. So, did you find your family home in good order?'

Hurel shook his head sadly. 'No, I did not. The republicans had used it as a barracks and left it in a disgusting state. Although as you know I am not an emotional man...'

'Perish the thought.'

'Yes, even I was reduced to tears. They 'ad strewn rubbish everywhere, broken some of our finest furniture and burned many of the precious books in our library. Mon Dieu! They had even used my family portraits for target practice!'

'What, even your great-great aunt, the mistress of a king?' But even as he said it, Anson regretted being facetious.

Hurel, downcast at what his own countrymen had done to his cherished family home, had not registered the sarcasm and answered sadly. 'Yes, mon ami, even her.'

'Look Hurel, I mean Tunbridge, you must not let this get you down. If and when the war is truly over, you will be able to return and restore your chateau to its former grandeur.'

'Do you really think so?'

'Of course, but for now you must put it out of your mind and concentrate on two things, enjoying the delights of

Paris while we may and gathering whatever information we can that could help overthrow our enemies.'

'In that connection I believe I 'ave outdone myself.' Hurel looked around to make sure no-one was on their heels and tapped his nose. 'I 'ave met with many fellow royalist contacts in Normandy and they will 'elp us if we need to leave in a 'urry, but more importantly I 'ave seen incredible things, mon ami, incredible things!'

Anson was intrigued. 'Really?'

'Indeed. Before we left England, Colonel Redfearn mentioned to me that a man called Fulton 'ad approached the French government some time ago offering to build a mechanical engine that could attack British ships from under water.'

'How did he learn that?'

'From spies, of course, especially a man called Johnstone who informed him that this engine was to be trialled in the Seine and then at Le 'avre.'

'So that's why you went south?'

'Yes, the colonel wanted me to check on this story and it proved easy enough to learn the truth. Le 'avre is awash with tales about it. In the mouth of the Seine there has been much talk of a sea monster. One farmer I met on the way told me that one had been captured!'

'Good grief! You didn't believe that?'

'Of course not.'

'But you believe they have built such a craft?'

'I know they have, mon ami. I have seen it for myself!'

'Good grief! Does it work?'

'Please do not keep saying "good grief" with your mouth 'anging open, Anson. It is not what you English call officer-like.'

'But I truly am astonished!'

'I can assure you it does work. It is shaped like a fish and maybe as long as a jollyboat, twenty foot or thereabouts. It 'as a copper 'ull with a diameter of perhaps seven feet.'

'Not big enough to carry many men, then?'

'No, I saw only three men go on board 'er, but I 'eard she can take more and remain submerged for eight hours.'

'But how do they propel the beast?'

'On the surface they rig a sail and when they wish to dive below the surface they use a 'and-cranked propeller.'

'Did you see her dive?'

'I did, and she remained under water for more than half an hour.'

'But how can this machine attack surface vessels?'

'This I did not see for myself, but I was told that when underwater the submarine boat can attach explosive devices to the hull of a surface ship to be detonated by a timing device, or they can moor the mine to the seabed beneath it to explode on contact.'

'So it represents a real threat to our ships if war breaks out again?'

'Yes, of course, but the strange thing is that Bonaparte is apparently sceptical about it and will not continue to fund this man Fulton's efforts. So it might be possible to persuade 'im to work for the British instead.'

'Well done, Hurel, sorry, Tunbridge! This information will be of the utmost value to the Admiralty.'

'And there is something else, mon ami, I am told that the man Johnstone who is involved in all of this is also 'ere in Paris.'

'Really? Then we must find him!'

As they made their way back to the hotel Anson asked: 'By the by, does this strange vessel have a name?'

'It does. They call it the *Nautilus*.'

46

The Battle of Woodhurst

At the sound of the drum, MacIntyre stopped in his tracks and the rest of the men followed suit, all quiet now and waiting for his orders.

He had expected nothing short of capitulation — but the drum told him otherwise.

Could the villagers have sent for the military? Unlikely. No, this was a naval alert calling men to their action stations, so it must be Anson's pet marine and the hop-along bosun from Seagate.

But, he reckoned, the drum was not only being used to call out the defenders. This was some kind of attempt to put the attackers off, or at least buy time.

He called out: 'Tak nae notice o' the drummer boy, men. He'll be wearing it round his fuckin' neck soon enough!'

The men nearest him laughed and his pock-faced henchman asked: 'What's the plan then, Billy Boy?'

'The drum's coming frae the church tower and that's where their look-outs are. We'll tak cover behind the churchyard wall and gie 'em a taste of musket balls. That'll shut the buggers up!'

The order was relayed and the smugglers advanced towards the flint wall that surrounded the church. But to MacIntyre's astonishment an explosion nearby sent several of his men reeling and one shouted: 'They've got a cannon!'

He yelled: 'Have they bollocks! Get to the wall and open fire at the church tower!'

But as some of the men rushed to obey another explosion scattered them and they fell back.

'What now, Billy Boy?' his henchman asked, with more than a touch of sarcasm.

'That's nae but a few fuckin' fireworks. They've set charges wi' long fuses. Get to the wall men and open fire on the bastards!'

Nervously now, half a dozen of the men ran forward, but most still hung back, fearful of more explosions. Those who made it to the wall took aim at the crenelated top of the church tower and began firing one by one.

But to their horror, shapes rose up from behind headstones in the churchyard like ghostly creatures rising from the grave and a calm, firm voice ordered: 'Present, aim, fire!'

A ragged volley sent musket balls screaming over the attackers' heads and shotgun pellets hit the flint wall sending splinters and sparks flying. The men at the wall crouched low behind it, pinned down, and there was no need to call on the rest to fall back. Some of them were already running to shelter behind any cover they could find.

From the churchyard the same voice could be heard calling on the defenders to reload, watch for a target to present itself and fire at will.

MacIntyre's sidekick, now crouching low like his leader, enquired drolly: 'As I was saying, what now, Billy Boy?'

'There's nae but a handful of 'em, so we'll spread oursel's out and attack from several places at once. Get some o' the boys to rip up yon garden fences to use as ladders to get o'er the wall!'

'Wouldn't it be a good idea to send some men through the village? If these blokes in the churchyard think their families are in danger they'll panic.'

'Aye, do that. Tell the boys to break into some o' the houses and drag some womenfolk back here. No auld crones, mind!'

*

Leaving five of Fagg's men crouching behind tombstones with instructions to fire at anyone poking his nose over the churchyard wall and retreat into the church itself if hard pressed, Tom Hoover joined his mobile team waiting on the far side of the churchyard.

Joined by the drummer boy who had come down from the tower as planned, they went out through the lych-gate into the village.

Apart from some shouts from the smugglers on the far side of the church there was no other sign of life. Using hand signals to avoid giving their positions away, the marine fanned his men out and they made their way slowly down both sides of the main street, moving silently from doorway to doorway. He intended to make sure the village was all quiet, circle round and take up position on the flank of the main body of MacIntyre's men.

But when they reached the crossroads in the village centre they were rooted to the spot by screams coming from somewhere over near the chapel — women's screams.

*

Three women were pushed forward and flung at MacIntyre's feet. The smugglers who had broken down their doors and dragged them out had gone for the younger ones and by the looks of their torn dresses, the girls had already been groped.

301

Black Mac looked them over. 'Ye've chosen well, lads. Nae auld crones here, eh? Now, you men get into three groups, use these fences as ladders and get o'er the wall in three different places. The rest of us'll keep the bastards' heads doon while you go o'er the top'

'What then, boss?'

'The bastards'll run, for sure. Top any as don't, and the first three of you back here when they've surrendered can have some fun wi' these tarts.'

*

Atop the church tower, feeling like he was back aloft in his foretop days, Sam Fagg watched the smugglers' flaming torches concentrating at three different points around the churchyard wall.

It was what he and Hoover had anticipated. They were going to make a three-pronged assault and there was no way the five defenders left crouching behind gravestones could stand against that. He leaned over and yelled down: 'They're gonna come over the wall at three different places, boys. Fall back on the church like what we told yer!'

A few musket and pistol balls whizzed overhead as the five left their protective gravestones and hurried into the church, locking the great iron-studded oak door behind them.

As planned, two took cover behind pews that gave them a clear line of fire at anyone who managed to break down the door and the others, breathing heavily, climbed one by one up the ladder steps to join Fagg and his lookouts at the top of the tower.

The dozen or so of MacIntyre's men who had made it over the churchyard wall moved cautiously forward,

302

expecting defenders to rise up from behind tombstones. But none did.

'The beggars have run away!'

Up in the tower Fagg yelled: 'No they ain't. They're up 'ere ready to fire dahn on yer!'

The attackers looked up in confusion and as they did so musket balls screamed down, some striking chips off the tombstones. Fagg pushed three more of his men forward while the others reloaded. 'Take aim, boys, and fire when ye're ready!'

Pinned down, the attackers dared not press on or retreat. The churchyard wall had become their temporary prison.

Frustrated at not knowing how the attack was going, MacIntyre sent his henchman forward. 'Find out what the fuck's going on, will ye?'

But before his order could be obeyed the beating of a drum to his right made his blood run cold.

Someone yelled: 'The bastards have flanked us! They're in the houses!'

Sure enough, he could see several men looking down on him from upstairs windows and almost immediately they fired a volley that sent one of the smugglers reeling with a ball in the head.

It was time to get the hell out of there, and Black Mac saw a way. He reached down, grabbed one of the girls and pulled her to her feet, calling to the men nearest him to do the same.

Three figures emerged from one of the defenders' houses and approached, muskets at the ready.

In the lead was Tom Hoover. 'It's time to surrender, MacIntyre. Half your men are trapped in the churchyard and the rest of you are covered by the boys in the houses.

If you want to get out alive throw down your weapons — now!'

MacIntyre pulled the crying girl in front of him and ripped the top of her dress exposing her breasts. The men who had grabbed the other two girls did the same. 'Ye dinna wanna harm these wee lassies d'ye?'

'Let them go. If you don't you'll swing for it.'

MacIntyre sneered. 'I fuckin' thought so! Ye're that bastard marine. I thought ye'd have had the sense to fuck off hame to America. Well, we'll leave right enough, but these wee girls'll come wie us. If ye fire at us ye'll kill them, so...'

Hoover stepped forward but with his free right hand MacIntyre took a pistol from his belt and aimed it at the marine. 'One mair step and ye're a dead man!'

As Hoover was about to take another step a shot rang out and he froze, thinking MacIntyre had fired. But it was the smuggler who fell, a neat bloody hole in his forehead.

The hysterical girl pulled herself free and fell at the feet of her saviours.

Hoover looked round. 'Who fired?'

Jacob Shallow held up his hand. 'Guilty, sarge. I thought the bugger was goin' to shoot you and anyway, I owed him.'

'Thanks.' He turned to the smugglers holding the other two girls. 'Come on lads, you don't want to follow Black Mac to hell, do you?'

The lank-haired, wall-eyed smuggler raised his pistol but was shot down by Bishop.

The rest looked uneasily at one another and released the girls.

'Now, all of you, you're covered by my boys. If you throw down your weapons we'll let you leave unharmed.

If you don't...' He pointed his musket at MacIntyre's crumpled body.

They dropped their weapons.

'Good, now make yourselves scarce. We'll give you an hour to get clear of the village. After that, any of you we find will be strung up.'

Leaving Shallow and Joe Bishop to collect the smugglers' discarded weapons, Hoover returned to the churchyard where a similar scene was enacted.

Under the cover of Fagg's musketeers up in the church tower, the marine called on the attackers to throw down their arms and walk out via the church gate. They did, leaving one of their number sprawled across a grave, stone dead.

To speed up the smugglers' withdrawal, Sam Fagg aimed his musket just behind the rear-most and fired, yelling: 'Jump to it, ye bastards!'

*

Job done, the Seagate men left next morning.

The dead smugglers had been buried hastily in what was intended as an unmarked grave in a neglected corner of the churchyard. But already someone had stuck a wooden board in place of a gravestone with 'All they that take the sword shall perish with the sword' painted crudely on it.

Most of the villagers turned out to see their saviours off amid much hand-shaking and back-slapping from the men of the Woodhurst Militia, Anglicans and Baptists alike. Brother Finch, who had enlisted their aid through Phineas Shrubb, expressed their heartfelt thanks and asked Hoover and Fagg to name their reward.

But Hoover shook his head. 'We didn't come here for any reward, friend. There was a score or two to settle with Black Mac and I doubt that gang will bother you again.'

'We'll keep the militia going and if the smugglers give us any trouble we'll send them packing again, brother. Anyway, we've got all their weapons now so we don't need the muskets you brought us.'

Boxer overheard that with relief. 'That's good news. I didn't really believe the hammock-counters would swallow that tale about them being lost off Boulogne!'

47

Versailles

The hired carriage sashayed up the long broad drive that led to the Palace of Versailles, sometime home of kings.

Parkin and his niece had chattered happily throughout the ten-mile journey but fell silent as they approached. One look at the unkempt park, weed-filled formal gardens and waterless fountains told a sad story of neglect since The Terror.

'What would the Sun King make of it now?' Parkin pondered aloud.

It had been not only Louis XIV's palace but the seat of his government, too.

Entering the palace itself they found much of it almost empty except for a few old pots and items of furniture that had somehow escaped the organisers of post-revolution sales. To their astonishment, they found that one of the great buildings where once officers of the court were accommodated had now been converted to an arms factory.

But the Hall of Mirrors still impressed, and the visitors were somewhat mollified to hear from a friendly Frenchman that Bonaparte was believed to be ordering a complete renovation of the entire complex.

Back outside, Anson took an interest in the mile-long canal that had in earlier years, he was told, been used for naval demonstrations held to entertain royals who enjoyed being rowed along it in gondolas.

Cassandra begged him to join her and her uncle on a visit to the Grand Trianon, which the Sun King had used as a private refuge to escape the constraints of court life. She was even keener to see the nearby Petit Trianon which had later been used for similar purposes by Louis XVI's queen, the ill-fated Marie-Antoinette.

'And there's the Temple of Love she had built for her. So romantic!'

Anson would have agreed with her wholeheartedly and would have suggested they sit in it for a while together to see if its aura still worked, but with her uncle in tow romance would have to wait for another day.

*

On their way back to Paris, Parkin spoke of his ambition to see Bonaparte himself in the flesh.

Cassandra exchanged an amused smile with Anson and asked facetiously: 'What, pinned to a dissection board, uncle?'

The old gentleman protested. 'Not everyone thinks ill of him, my dear. One of my correspondents sent me a cutting from an English newspaper. Here.' He fumbled in his pocket and handed it to her.

There was a likeness of Bonaparte with a poem beneath. She read it aloud so that Anson could hear:

It was a maxim in ancient Greece,
To learn the art of war in time of peace;
But he found out a better maxim far.
By conquest to make peace in time of war;
And through all Europe, bidding discord cease,
Gave to France; liberty; to the World, peace.

Anson shrugged. Whichever way you looked at it, Bonaparte had come a long way from his Corsican birthplace and service as a lowly artillery officer to the upper political and military echelons of Republican France. And now he was swanning around as First Consul being fawned upon right, left and centre by all and sundry — apparently even the otherwise enlightened Josiah Parkin.

Why, Bonaparte was already well on the way to becoming as much a dictator as a Roman Caesar. It might be impolitic to proclaim himself a king now, for sure. But how long would it be, Anson wondered, before the Corsican assumed the full powers and trappings of an emperor?

*

Hurel had stayed behind in Paris and was beside himself with excitement when the Versailles party returned.

He grabbed Anson's arm and almost dragged him to a secluded corner of the vestibule among the aspidistras. Anson protested: 'What on earth's got into you? Has war broken out again?'

'Not just yet, mon ami, but I 'ave seen 'im!'

'Who's 'im, I mean him?'

'You know, the smuggler, Johnstone!'

'The fellow involved in the *Nautilus* business?'

'Precisely — 'e is 'ere, in Paris, and contacts of mine are keeping their eyes on 'im.'

'Good grief! Have you met him?'

'No, mon ami. That is a role better suited to you, is it not?'

*

Within the hour, one of Hurel's contacts had shown them to a drinking establishment on the left bank.

The Frenchman remained outside wishing Anson 'bon chance' as he entered with some trepidation, although he had the pocket pistol with him in case of trouble.

At the bar he ordered a glass of red wine and looked around as nonchalantly as he was able, but none of the clientele looked English. He decided to wait for a while and as he sipped his wine a man entered from a rear door, evidently having been to relieve himself in the urinoir. Anson noted that the man had the curious rolling gait peculiar to those who had spent a good many of their years keeping their balance on heaving decks. His face was well-weathered but not unhandsome, with bright blue eyes, jet black hair and luxuriant side whiskers, and he was as tall as Anson — a little over six feet.

The man took a seat at the bar near Anson who said: 'Your face is familiar. English?'

'Depends who's asking.'

'It's a treat to be able to speak to a fellow-countryman amongst all these Frogs. Can I get you a drink?'

The man smiled, glanced at his near-empty glass and nodded. 'It's brandy, and yes, I'm fed up with trying to make myself understood.'

His manner of speech was featureless — certainly not refined and clearly Kentish, but not that of sailors like Fagg, whose conversations were littered with dropped aitches. This man could fit into pretty well any company without standing out one way or another.

He asked: 'What're you doing here, taking a holiday?'

'You could call it that. After so many years of hostilities it's good to be able to come here openly. My name's Anson, by the by.'

'Navy?'

'Yes.'

'Any kin of *the* Anson?'

'Only very distantly, I'm afraid.'

'So where do you think you've seen me?'

'In Deal perhaps, after the Boulogne raids, or maybe in Seagate. Before the peace I commanded the Sea Fencibles there. Now? Well, like many another I'm washed up on the beach and over here with friends to see the sights.'

'Ah, Seagate! That's where it could have been. You may not know it but a number of your men were believers in free trade, much like myself.'

Anson smiled at the euphemism smugglers used to describe themselves. He had himself benefited from their efforts to import wine, brandy and other luxury goods without handing over large sums to the revenue.

'I didn't catch your name.'

'I didn't throw it, but I've no reason not to tell you. It's Tom Johnstone, known as Captain Johnstone to most.'

'Then I most certainly do know who you are. You've earned quite a reputation, being imprisoned by both the French and back home for smuggling, escaped from a press-gang and been posted as "run".'

Johnstone's eyes twinkled. 'But since then I've become almost respectable.'

Anson laughed. 'Respectable? Well, yes, but if the rumours are true while you were in the Netherlands you seduced your host's wife.'

'Doesn't everyone?' He ordered another round and soon Johnstone was reminiscing about piloting the Duke of York's expeditionary force off Den Helder.

'But it didn't go well?'

'Not my fault that most of 'em fell sick ashore and the whole thing turned into a jar of worms. Anyway, since then I've led a perfectly respectable life and helped the

Admiralty with scraps of information I've picked up here and there.'

'Such as your friend Robert Fulton's plunging boat, and the fact that Bonaparte won't fund it anymore?'

Johnstone laughed. '*Nautilus*? How the hell did you know about that?'

'I try to keep up to date. Look, I know people back home who would give a lot to know chapter and verse about it — and maybe make an approach to Fulton through you.'

Shaking his head, Johnstone countered: 'I can't see him cooperating with the Brits. He's a republican.'

More wine and brandy flowed and by the time they parted Anson had extracted a promise that Johnstone would contact him once they were back in England, which the fragility of the current peace indicated could well be sooner than later.

48

A Pencil Shortage

Anson and Cassandra were happy to accompany the old gentleman to places of interest, galleries and so forth, but drew the line at attending meetings of the learned societies.

Instead they were content to stroll together beside the Seine or in the public gardens followed at a discreet distance by Bessie the maid, who, rather than keeping an eye on them, was forever glancing behind, fearful that some randy Frenchman was creeping up intending to ravish her.

They marvelled at the view from the top of the Panthéon and, over a number of days, took in the Invalides, Place de la Concorde, Champs-Elysées and the Jardin des Plantes, in addition to paying several more visits to the Louvre.

Just back from one such trip, they were taking tea in the vestibule when the old gentleman returned, attended by Nat Bell.

Parkin had been at a session of natural historians and was positively glowing. 'They were so welcoming,' he announced. 'It was as if we had never been at war. A love of the natural sciences transcends all human pettiness!'

Anson was sceptical. 'I'd hardly call the past decade of conquest and blood-letting mere pettiness.'

Parkin chuckled. 'Touché, as the French say. But you know what I mean. We put aside politics and national animosity and spent a delightful afternoon looking at specimens and discussing truly important matters.'

Bell couldn't contain himself, muttering: 'What 'e means is, they spent bleedin' hours passing round dead hanimals and great big hinsects pinned to boards.'

'Thank you, Nathaniel, for your frank summing-up of the proceedings. No doubt you'd like to run along and get your supper.'

Alone with Anson, Parkin confided: 'There is something I should tell you — quite remarkable. When I took my pocket book out to make some notes about a particularly large dung beetle, the entire room fell silent.'

'Really?'

'Yes, to a man they were staring lustfully at my pencil!'

'Good grief, what narrow lives they must lead!'

'No, don't you see, owing to the war they have not had access to English graphite and therefore over the years their supply of pencils has dwindled to nothing.'

Anson pretended astonishment. 'Frenchmen with no lead in their pencils! Couldn't they obtain graphite elsewhere?'

'There is none in France, and although there are some deposits elsewhere on the Continent the supply has been severely disrupted by war. No, England is their main hope. Of course I donated my pencil to the president who was pathetically grateful and flaunted it to the envy of his peers.'

'Naturally.'

'Afterwards one of the members approached me and asked if I could obtain a supply of graphite and send it to him, so that he could arrange the manufacture of pencils for the society's use. I readily acquiesced of course. It's the least I could do to repay their hospitality.'

Anson was puzzled, wondering why they hadn't simply asked for a supply of pencils. But he did not want to prick his friend's balloon so held his peace and confined himself to suggesting that the French might name some insect after him out of gratitude.

Again, Parkin did not detect his young friend's playful sarcasm but instead glowed at the thought. 'What an honour it would be to have some newly-discovered beetle or fly called after me! Why, that would be the next best thing to immortality!'

49

An Encounter with Bonaparte

Excitement mounted in the cobblestoned courtyard fronting the Tuileries palace as a haughty Imperial Guard drum major, hand on hip, swanked past brandishing his baton followed by two lines of drummers beating out a slow roll that quickened the blood.

Behind them marched a band, playing an unfamiliar but unmistakeably military air, and then came rank upon rank of guardsmen, stepping smartly through the Arc de Triomphe du Carrousel, their bearskins giving them the appearance of near giants.

A formidable foe to face in battle, Anson acknowledged as he stood with Parkin, Cassandra and Pettiworth among the crowd of spectators. Dogs, excited by the drums and bustle, ran about yapping and he smiled at the sight of small boys with toy drums and penny whistles aping the bandsmen.

A guards' officer shouted an order and to cheers the First Consul, Bonaparte himself, appeared on horseback and trotted through the ranks.

The review over, Pettiworth led the way to the gardens behind the palace where a reception was getting under way.

He showed an official-looking paper to a sentry and they were waved through.

'Contacts, you see?' he announced to his fellow tourists. 'English gold can still open any door, anywhere.'

'Or any garden in Paris that's already open to the public?' Anson countered, tongue in cheek.

But Pettiworth was not one to allow himself to be put down. 'Ah, that's where you're wrong my friend. It may be open to the hoi-polloi on ordinary days, but today's reception is exclusive.'

Exclusive or not, the gardens were already rapidly filling with fabulously coifed and dressed — some might say half-dressed — ladies on the arms of extravagantly uniformed military officers. They were overwhelmingly army men and Anson was able to spot only a few naval types — and those evidently admirals.

The cavalrymen included cuirassiers with shining breast-plates and elaborately-plumed helmets, hussars in tight sky-blue overalls with pelisses slung apparently nonchalantly over their left shoulders, dragoons in green coats with scarlet facings and leopard-skin fronted brass helmets, and lancers and chasseurs in equally extravagant uniforms. The infantry, and particularly members of the Imperial Guard, were almost as colourful, and Anson pointed out to Cassandra a marshal of France, his green jacket festooned with crimson and gold, and his decorations flashing in the sunlight. But, predictably, Cassandra was more interested in the ladies' fashions, and Anson himself was not averse to having some of them pointed out to him — especially those with deeply-plunging necklines.

Anson had been happy to wear his civilian mid-blue coat when they set out that morning but the sight of all this brass made him feel a trifle inadequate and he rather wished it had been appropriate to wear his naval uniform, which of course it was not. Cassandra, too, was clearly feeling overwhelmed by all the high fashion and her mauve dress that her uncle and Anson had said suited her so, now made her feel drab.

At least their subdued outfits meant that no attention was drawn to them — a relief to Anson, who was afraid he would have struggled to conduct a conversation with any French officer in such a twittering throng.

He noticed a good many others in civilian dress, no doubt ambassadors, functionaries and tourists like themselves.

Pettiworth excused himself to mingle with his 'contacts' and Parkin wandered off in the hope of finding some of the fellow antiquarians and naturalists he had become acquainted with at meetings of the learned societies.

Anson was relieved and delighted to be left alone with Cassandra, the more so when she slipped her arm through his. He smiled at her protectively and they walked slowly through the throng, content to be alone together even in such a crowd.

After a while their people-watching was interrupted by the return of Pettiworth and the old gentleman, who was smiling broadly.

'Did you find any luminaries, uncle?'

'No, I imagine that there are precious few among all these preening militarists, but I did have the pleasure of conversing with General Bonaparte!'

'Good grief!' Anson was truly amazed and would have given his eye teeth to have bumped into the man many Britons rated a monster. 'You actually met him?'

'I did, and we conversed. In fact I instigated the flow of conversation.'

This could be important. What valuable gem had Parkin heard from the Corsican's lips that could be passed on to the faceless ones back in Kent?

'What did you say?'

Parkin beamed. 'I saw him approaching and said "Bonjour General"!'

'And he replied?'

'Yes, he nodded to me and said "Bonjour!"'

'And?'

'Well, I had intended to ask him if he thought the peace would last, but unfortunately some extremely tall guardsmen with huge moustaches moved him on to a group of ambassadors from vassal states who were clearly desperate to curry favour with him.'

Anson could not disguise the ghost of a smile. So, no pearl of wisdom or hint of useful intelligence from the lips of France's First Consul, then?

*

Back in Seagate, Sam Fagg was contemplating his future with some misgivings.

'Why the long face, Sam? I thought you'd have bought the Mermaid and be looking for a couple of plump barmaids by now.'

'Never 'appen, mate. I changed me mind. After what we just done up at Woodhurst I got the taste fer a bit of action, like, and can't bear the thought of settlin' dahn. Not yet, anyways. I'm gonna take a few weeks orf, boozing, wenchin' an' that, and then I might see if the revenue'll take me on.'

'You, on the side of the law? Like they say, set a thief to catch a thief!'

Fagg ignored the sarcasm. 'What abaht you, Tom?'

'Dunno. I'm going to report back to Phineas about the Woodhurst business...'

'And his daughter?' Fagg asked archly.

'Yeah, and his daughter.'

'So can we expect a weddin'?'

Hoover smiled. 'Mebbe. But like you I ain't ready to settle down. What would I do? I don't fancy sitting around out in the sticks twiddling my fingers. She'd soon get fed up with me.'

'So what will you do?'

'Officially I'm still in the marines, so I might take myself up to Chatham and see if they've got a berth for me. But with the peace and all, well, there's not much chance of any action.'

Fagg sucked on his pipe and blew a plume of smoke skywards. 'It's a funny fing. When you're in the navy — or marines, I s'ppose — all you want is to get aht. But once ye're aht you wish you was back in.'

'Yeah. It's a pity Mister Anson ain't here. I reckon he'd feel the same and come up with something we could all do.'

50

Ghosts from the Past

Temporarily separated from the Parkins, who had wandered over to the Tuileries palace to join others apparently trying to peer through the windows of what they had been told was Josephine's suite, Anson spun at a tap on his shoulder.

He was confronted by a small, balding, cadaverous man wearing civilian clothes.

The man took off his thick spectacles and blinked as he polished them with a handkerchief, asking in excellent if heavily accented English: 'Lieutenant Anson? Your name is very familiar to me.'

'How did you know——?'

'Your name was on the list of foreigners granted access today and Englishmen of military age are easy enough to identify.'

'If my name is familiar you may be thinking, perhaps, of my illustrious namesake Admiral Lord Anson, the great circumnavigator and reformer of our navy? I'm afraid I'm only a very distant kinsman.'

Replacing his spectacles, the Frenchman shook his head. 'No. I recall your name because we came close to meeting in Boulogne when your Admiral Nelson saw fit to bombard the port and later to mount a...'

He paused, searching for the right word, and Anson offered: 'Disastrous?'

The Frenchman smirked. 'Thank you, yes, a disastrous boat attack. At the time of the bombardment you were there in the company of a renegade, were you not, Hurel by name?'

Anson was now convinced that this was the sinister colonel of intelligence who had questioned Hurel during their reconnaissance mission in Boulogne. He thought for a moment. There was little point in denial. 'Hurel? Oh yes, a royalist rather than a renegade, I believe.'

'And where is this Hurel now?'

Praying that Hurel would not suddenly appear, he answered as nonchalantly as he was able. 'He went off to take the waters at Tunbridge Wells, I understand. The spa is popular with French émigrés, especially the ladies, hence Hurel's keenness to take the cure there.'

'The cure? He should 'ave come to Paris with you, monsieur. I know ways of curing such men without the need of spas.' He stared at Anson, his thick lenses making his eyes appear to bulge. 'And what I have in mind is a permanent cure.'

Anson imagined the intelligence man's remedy would involve torture and a date with a firing squad — or guillotine.

'Fortunately Hurel will not be needing your cure, colonel.'

The Frenchman started at the use of his rank. It confirmed beyond doubt that Anson clearly knew exactly who and what he was — briefed no doubt by Hurel — and it killed the politesse of the conversation stone dead.

'So you know who I am, monsieur, and you are aware that Hurel was unmasked when genuine escapers from your filthy prison hulks reported your spying mission to me?'

Anson chose not to respond.

'On my orders they pursued you and you escaped from Boulogne only by what you English call the skin of your teeth. But I warn you that the men who pursued you are now on my staff. They know who you are and while you are in France they will be keeping their eyes on you. Take one step out of line and poof, you will be taken, peace or no peace.'

'I am obliged to you for that advice, colonel. My companions and I are here merely as tourists, sampling the delights of Paris that have been denied to us by years of war.'

'If that is so, you have nothing to fear, monsieur. Enjoy your stay, although you would be well advised to depart immediately should war suddenly break out again. If it does it will be what 'unters call open season — on Englishmen.'

A moustachioed officer in a gaudy hussar uniform approached, with fur-edged jacket — the pelisse — hanging from his left shoulder like a dead animal and a lady on his right arm dripping jewels and displaying a large expanse of chest.

Anson used the opportunity to back away and disappear into the melee in search of the rest of his party.

He spotted Parkin and Cassandra near the refreshment tables, availing themselves of un-smuggled French wine for a change. But as he made his way towards them he started at seeing another familiar face: Citoyen Bardet — the French officer who had escaped from a Medway hulk and pursued him in Boulogne.

The intelligence colonel had mentioned that this man and his fellow escapers were now on his staff but spotting him here, so close, was a shock.

He slipped behind a statue so he could observe Bardet without being spotted.

Yes, it was definitely him — a coarse-featured individual with thick curly hair, looking about him as if seeking someone: him!

When Anson had first met the 'Citizen', as the hulk guards called him, he'd had a straggly, unkempt beard and was wearing tattered sulphur-yellow prisoner-of-war garb. But now he was in a smart blue naval officer's uniform and sporting a neatly-trimmed beard. In view of what the intelligence colonel had told him there was little doubt in Anson's mind that Bardet had already been set to keep an eye on him and his party.

The last thing he wanted was to endanger his friends. What's more, Bell was an old soldier in possession of a stash of firearms. The French could easily make something out of that if they so chose. And what if they were to discover that Hurel was with them?

As he watched, two men in plain clothes joined Bardet — no doubt 'Citizen's' bodyguards on the hulk who had escaped with him. From the information he had been given at the time by Captain Wills, Anson knew that one of them was a Parisian called Girault, a butcher in civilian life, and the other a Corsican known as Cornacchia, the crow, who looked as if he would cut your throat as soon as look at you — and probably would.

Bardet appeared to be briefing the other two and while their attention was engaged, Anson slipped away, joined Parkin and Cassandra and hurried them away.

'Ah, my dear boy! I was about to send out a search party.' Then, noting Anson's anxious look, he asked: 'Are you alright? You look as if you've seen a ghost!'

'I'm very much afraid I just have come across one from my past. I've been sought out and chatted up by a sinister intelligence colonel, the man who questioned Hurel during our recce of Boulogne.'

'Really? What on earth did he want?'

'Truth be told I think he wanted to chain me up in a dungeon and remove my body parts bit by bit. But fortunately, as we are at peace, he restricted himself to barely-veiled threats.'

'Surely it was merely a chance encounter?'

'No, he's not the sort of man who has chance encounters. I believe he knew exactly where I'd be.'

'Good heavens! Do you really think you're being followed?'

'Yes. Remember having to provide details when checking into the hotel and when Pettiworth acquired tickets for this reception?'

'But that's normal over here, surely.'

'Maybe, but I've no doubt such details are immediately reported to the intelligence people. I believe this colonel, the one I know as 'Pebble-eyes', intends to keep me, us, under observation and when, not if, the peace ends I fear we will be detained. And then—'

'Pebble-eyes?'

'That's what Hurel called him, on account of his thick spectacles. I've no idea what his real name is and he didn't offer it when we met a few minutes ago.'

'But there are thousands of English visitors in France just now, and there's no way Bonaparte can detain us all.'

'Nevertheless, Hurel has his ear close to the ground and he believes the minute the peace breaks down, all Englishmen between 18 and 60 will be rounded up. And that means me, Hurel, Bell and Pettiworth.'

'So Cassandra, Bessie and I would be left to get home by ourselves?'

Anson thought of Parkin's ignorance of all matters practical other than finance, the collection of antiquarian objects and the dissection and stuffing of specimens, and shared his friend's concern.

But Parkin was clearly still in denial about the threat of detention. 'I simply cannot believe the French would scoop you up, my boy. Not least that would be against all accepted rules of international behaviour. And they must surely realise that if they detain us our government will retaliate by rounding up all their nationals.'

Anson shook his head. 'I reckon almost all French nationals in England right now are royalists, or spies posing as royalists. What's to attract Frenchmen to what they call "perfidious Albion" anyway? May I remind you of Shakespeare's Henry V?' Anson had studied it at school and it was his favourite play.

'Please do.'

'Well, when the French heard Henry's weakened army had crossed the Somme and was offering battle, the bard has the Duke of Bretagne calling Britain "that nook-shotten isle of Albion" and the Constable of France crying out "where have they this mettle?" because he can't understand how we could breed such fighting men in our miserable "foggy, raw and dull climate".'

Parkin was taken aback. 'Extraordinary, Anson! How can one small head carry all you know? But what, as your bosun would say, is "nook-shotten" when it's at home, or should I say 'ome?'

'I think it means full of nooks and corners — a tin-pot little island. Anyway, Shakespeare was trying to show that the French despised our homeland but marvelled at our mettle.'

'But no longer, eh, if the news-sheets are to be believed, with Napoleon himself calling us "a nation of shopkeepers"? Whatever, with all this literary stuff I've rather lost the thread.'

'The thread, my dear sir, is that although we Brits may have flocked to Paris in large numbers, your revolutionary Frenchman has no desire whatsoever to visit London or anywhere else in "nook-ridden Albion", so detaining foreign nationals the minute peace breaks down will be a one-sided affair. And what's more, I strongly suspect that as an enemy sea officer already known to "Pebble-eyes" I will be among the first to be taken.'

Parkin was suitably chastened. 'So you could well end up—?'

'Most likely in a Paris prison having my fingernails extracted by that intelligence colonel...'

Cassandra had overheard and exclaimed anxiously: 'We can't let that happen. So do you propose we get out while the going's good?'

'I do. The peace is fragile and I believe we should make urgent preparations to leave France right away, before it's too late, so after dinner let's meet with the others and come up with a plan.'

Anson looked round to see if they were being followed and spotted Pettiworth hurrying to catch them up, beaming happily.

Parkin asked: 'May we take it from your smile that you have secured some lucrative business deal, Obadiah?'

'Better than that, my dear fellow. I spotted that dreadful rogue and his woman who made the crossing to Calais with us and attempted to dun that poor sweet Miss Ward.'

Startled, Anson spluttered: 'Did you speak to them?'

'No, they didn't notice me and Trumper was in earnest conversation with a strange-looking French cove wearing thick glasses.'

'Pebble-eyes!'

'That's a good description of him. Anyway, Trumper appeared to be handing the French chap some sort of document surreptitiously.'

'So he could be a traitor as well as a cad?' Cassandra asked.

'Could well be. Anyway, I think I've dropped him in it. I let slip to one of my Paris contacts who's well in with the police that the major is one of England's most successful intelligence agents.'

'Good grief!'

'I mentioned it to my contact in the strictest confidence of course, so by tomorrow the whole of Paris will know!'

51

Fontainebleau

Floorboards squeaked as Pettiworth, Anson, Hurel and Bell made their way one by one to Parkin's room.

As he crept there, hoping not to bump into hotel staff or fellow guests, Anson could not help thinking this was all very like a French farce in which lovers attempt to avoid marital partners or chaperones to canoodle illicitly.

But this was no romantic rendezvous. By flickering candlelight in Parkin's room, the five met, talking in whispers in case someone was listening at the door.

Anson described meeting the intelligence colonel, an occurrence he was now convinced was not accidental, and repeated the thinly-veiled threat that all Britons of military age visiting France would be detained the moment the peace broke, as it was showing every indication of doing.

'Once that happens it would be risky trying to obtain a passage home when the military authorities will no doubt be shutting down cross-Channel travel.'

Parkin was clearly rattled. 'Dear me, dear me! Let me tell you, gentlemen, that without you I would never have made it to Paris and as to running the gauntlet back to Calais alone with Cassandra and Bessie, well...'

'Hur—, er, Tunbridge, do you have any ideas?' Anson asked.

'I do, mon ami. There are still many royalists, Jacobins, discontented bourgeois and others in my country who despise the republicans for what they did and the present government for what they are doing.'

'And you are in touch with these people, I'm sure?'

'With some I am, and knowing that the peace is coming to an end I 'ave made enquiries for just this eventuality.'

Pettiworth asked anxiously: 'So do you have a plan for our escape, monsieur?'

Hurel held up his hand in protest. 'Please, Mister Littleworth—'

'Pettiworth. It's Pettiworth.'

'No matter. Please do not "monsieur" me. Please remember that while we are 'ere in France my name is *Mister* Gerald Tunbridge! My papers show me to be an Englishman.'

Anson intervened. 'Gentlemen, please keep your voices down and let's all take care to remember to use our friend's alias at all times. His life is at stake.'

'Thank you, mon ami. Yes, I 'ave a plan. It involves us disappearing from 'ere and 'iding up until my friends can organise a passage back to England.'

'Disappear, but how? I may already be under surveillance here and wherever we go in Paris. So the authorities can pick us up whenever they choose.'

'Exactly, so we must act as if we are totally unaware that you are being watched and go about our visits to places of interest as if we 'ave no intention of making a run for it.'

'That's easily said, but if the peace really is about to be broken we can't be wandering around taking in the sights of Paris for much longer. We need to go into hiding now. In any case we've already been just about everywhere of interest there is to see.'

'Indeed, but you 'aven't yet been to Fontainebleau, so that's where you must go next. Or at least, that's where you must say you're going.'

'So where will we go?'

'Fontainebleau is en route to my family home, the Chateau de Pisseleu-aux-Bois, but we must make sure we are not followed.'

*

Next morning Anson slipped out of the hotel and headed nonchalantly towards the Seine, as if taking an early constitutional, followed by a dark curly-haired man with cauliflower ears and a rolling gait, who had been lurking outside.

Nat Bell, waiting among the aspidistras in the foyer, left it for a few minutes and set off behind them.

Before reaching the river Anson paused, as if uncertain of the way, and turned down a side lane. His pursuer followed suit. Ensuring no-one else was around, Anson stopped as if he were about to urinate against the wall.

Unaware that he was himself being followed, his pursuer slid into a doorway to wait, but a footstep sounded behind him and a blow behind the ear laid him out cold.

*

Back at the hotel, Parkin and Pettiworth informed the management that they had arranged to visit Fontainebleau, burbling on about longing to see the famous chateau that had been a royal residence since the time of Louis VI, known as 'Louis the Fat'. Settling the substantial account, they let it be known that they would be returning to Paris in a few days when they would again require rooms.

To make the story more convincing, they left a few items of luggage for safekeeping. The truth was that these contained non-essential clothing. But if the authorities searched them there was nothing to suggest that they would not be returning.

The party's main baggage was brought down and they embarked in a four-horse carriage that had appeared without being booked through the hotel, as was normal.

In his usual loud stage whisper, Hurel informed them: 'This is the carriage of, shall we say, friends.'

They set off slowly out of Paris, to all appearances just another party of tourists off sightseeing. When they reached the outskirts the carriage pulled up briefly for Anson and Bell to clamber on board.

It was early evening before they reached an auberge near the Forest of Fontainebleau, and harboured up for the night.

*

As at Versailles, the extensive formal gardens and ornamental lakes surrounding the Palace of Fontainebleau had clearly suffered from neglect since the revolution.

Nevertheless, the party could not fail to be impressed by such a magnificent showcase of French architecture evolving from the twelfth century onwards. As usual, Parkin was full of information, recalling that the palace could be said to have been the cradle of the Age of Enlightenment and that among famous events here was the signing by Louis XVI of a trade agreement with the British at the end of the American Revolutionary War.

But in Anson's case all this went in one ear and out the other. His mind was on the onward journey to Hurel's estate and what they would do if challenged en route.

With a Frenchman driving the coach they could hardly claim to have taken a wrong turning, and they were in no position to make a fight of it.

After what seemed an age, Hurel gathered the party together and called the coach forward.

He put his hand to his mouth and told Anson conspiratorially: 'We 'ad to rest the 'orses, mon ami. It is a long way to my chateau.'

They re-embarked and the carriage crunched off down the long driveway.

But when it reached the main road instead of turning north towards Paris it turned left and headed towards the Channel coast.

*

As yet unknown to Anson and his companions, the Peace of Amiens had come to an acrimonious end that very day and Bonaparte had already ordered General Junot, Governor of Paris:

All Englishmen from the age of 18 to 60, or holding any commission from His Britannic Majesty, who are at present in France shall immediately be constituted prisoners of war. I am resolved that tonight not an Englishman shall be visible in the most obscure theatre or restaurant in Paris.

52

Le Chateau de Pisseleu-aux-Bois

It took two days to reach Hurel's former home. Their first overnight stop was at a large farmhouse belonging to a royalist sympathiser, and it was there that they learned of Bonaparte's edict.

Undaunted, as they were about to set off next day, Hurel and the driver appeared in military uniform.

Hurel smiled at Anson's reaction. 'Attention to detail, mon ami. If we are stopped our story will be that we are escorting some English tourists to prison. We 'ave the necessary papers.'

Anson laughed. 'I'm sure you have!'

With two uniformed military men in plain view, no-one gave the coach a second glance and they completed the day's journey unmolested.

That night's stop was in another sympathiser's home, well off the main road, and the following day was also without incident.

It was early evening when at long last the coach turned into the side road leading to Hurel's ancestral home.

The coach negotiated the entrance gates and set off down the long carriageway towards the chateau. But relief at their safe arrival turned to alarm when Nat Bell, now riding as guard beside the coachman with his blunderbuss in his lap, turned to warn the passengers that he could see armed men gathered at the bridge over the moat that led to the twin towers either side of the main entrance.

Hurel's head appeared out of the carriage window and, shielding his eyes with his hand, he stared ahead.

Satisfied, he flopped back into his seat and informed his worried fellow passengers: 'Fear not, they are my friends!'

Pettiworth spoke for them all. 'Phew! Are you sure?'

'I am perfectly sure, monsieur. They are royalists, summoned from Normandy to guard my chateau while we are 'ere and to aid our escape.'

The coach rumbled over the wooden bridge and they disembarked, watched by half a dozen alert-looking armed men.

Anson knew the importance of establishing a rapport with such allies and went over to introduce himself: 'Anson, Lieutenant, Royal Navy' — and shook hands with each one.

Hurel was pointing out the sad state of repair of his ancestral home, but was cheered somewhat to see that the great oak doors were no longer hanging off their hinges and the broken shutters had been repaired.

Inside, the revolutionary slogans painted in red on the walls when it had been used by republicans as a temporary barracks had been over-painted in whitewash and some attempt had been made to clear the main rooms of broken furniture and other detritus.

He led his visitors into the library, close to tears to see that it was still in a mess with books that had been thrown from the shelves scattered everywhere. Parkin noted his anguish and offered: 'Most distressing, Baron, but while we are here Cassandra and I will do what we can to put things to rights.'

Pettiworth agreed. 'Count me in, monsieur.'

Unashamedly tearful now, Hurel showed them the family portraits, ruined by musket and pistol balls. 'Even my great-great aunt, the mistress of a king of France, no less, was not spared.'

'Damned shame,' Pettiworth sympathised. 'Must be hard to tell who's who with all the damage.'

'I would be able to tell, monsieur. I 'ave gazed at these pictures since I was a tiny child. They are precious to me and I am devastated at their loss. With my family murdered by the filthy republicans these portraits were all I 'ad left — and now they too are gone.'

Pettiworth was deeply affected and when the rest moved on he hung back and beckoned to Josiah Parkin.

'Dear me, Josiah, what a tragedy! We two are in this gentleman's debt for arranging our escape, so I believe we must see what can be done to bring these portraits back to life.'

'How so?'

'Maybe we could get some clever artist-wallah to patch 'em and touch 'em up so you wouldn't be able to tell they'd been damaged.'

Parkin was ahead of him. 'We could not encumber ourselves with the frames, of course, but with the Baron's permission we could remove what remains of the canvasses and roll them up. They would then be easily portable.'

'So we can take them home to England?'

'Indeed, and find some clever restorer able to repair them.'

'At our joint expense?'

'I believe that would go some way towards repaying him for the trouble he is going to in order to get us out of France.'

For a man obsessed with money, Pettiworth was exhibiting a generosity of spirit that he had kept well-hidden up until now, and Parkin shook his hand warmly. This was one useful thing that the pair of them could do.

*

The visitors were allocated beds in cleaned-up rooms and gathered for dinner — venison stew — and some fine wine that had evidently been brought with them by their guardians, Hurel's cellar having been stripped by the republicans.

At dinner the English party had been introduced to a silver-haired, aristocratic-looking Frenchman, who appeared to be the leader of their guardians, but when Anson asked his name he smiled: 'It is better that you do not know, monsieur. Suffice it to say I am a friend.'

When Cassandra and her maid retired, Hurel tapped a glass and announced: 'We must address ourselves to our escape, gentlemen.'

The silver-haired man nodded: 'The ports nearest the Kent coast will be under close surveillance. They are of course the most likely escape routes for the English fleeing France.'

Hurel agreed. 'That is the obvious way out, but from 'ere in Pisseleu-aux-Bois it will be better for us to 'ead for Étaples where our friend 'ere 'as contacts. We 'ave been in touch with them and they are agreeable to borrowing a boat in which we can escape.'

Anson was doubtful. 'You mean steal. But surely, being a port, Étaples will be watched, too?'

Hurel raised both hands. 'Of course, but it is less obvious than Calais, Boulogne etcetera. And we will not enter the port boldly demanding instant passage as if we were Englishmen abroad.'

'But we are Englishmen abroad! At least you may not be but the rest of us are.'

'I, too, am a paper Englishman, remember? You still 'ave not mastered my Gallic sense of 'umour, Anson. You will be escorted to the port, where you will join our friends, all Frenchmen with apparently the correct papers, take one of the invasion craft moored there and sail pretending to be 'eading further down the coast to Dieppe or Le 'avre.'

'What of us?' Pettiworth asked.

'The rest of us will make for a place to the south of Étaples. My party will be rowed out by boat and rendezvous with Anson at sea.'

'And then?'

'We will 'ead for England, praying for a wind that will take us to the Kent coast.'

'But if caught, your friends' lives will be forfeit. Are they really prepared to undertake such a plan to help a handful of English tourists get home?'

It was the silver-haired man who replied: 'I think you underestimate the 'atred some of us royalists 'ave for the republicans, monsieur. Those of us who lost relatives during The Terror would 'appily give our own lives to avenge them.'

*

As it would take a good while for their guardians to put the necessary plans in place, the English party got to work on the chateau.

Parkin set about the library, doing what he could to repair damaged books and returning them in some sort of order to the shelves. What he considered to be the most precious volumes he put in a trunk to be taken back to England for safekeeping.

With Hurel's approval, Pettiworth removed the damaged family portraits from their frames and rolled them up carefully, tied them with ribbons and placed them in a large canvas hold-all.

Meanwhile Cassandra, sleeves rolled up and looking like a maid herself, spent the days with Bessie washing clothes, cleaning and tidying as best they could.

When she was not fully occupied, Hurel insisted on continuing his French lessons, and Anson couldn't help hearing their laughter with irritation.

Communal meals were cooked by a couple of the Normandy men, who clearly knew what they were about, and Anson took a share of guard duty.

Bell did the same and passed the rest of his time helping the coachman look after the horses. The carriage would be key to their escape.

*

After a week without any interference or contact from the outside world, a messenger arrived on horseback from the coast and went into a huddle with the leader, Hurel and Anson.

The man was clearly of good breeding and spoke excellent English, but like his comrades remained anonymous, other than suggesting that the English party call him Pierre, which Anson guessed was almost certainly not his real name.

He reported that there were many invasion craft gathered in the harbours bordering La Manche.

'So their intent is to invade Britain, possibly in the near future?'

'Of course,' the Normandy men's leader spread his hands dismissively. 'The peace was a mere interlude. Bonaparte knows 'e must overcome the power of your navy to secure Europe and 'is overseas territories. Your strangle'old by blockade frustrates that. If 'e cannot destroy you at sea he must defeat you in your islands.'

Anson asked the messenger: 'How many of these invasion craft are there at Étaples?'

'Maybe already 20 or more.'

'And the other ports: Dunkirk, Gravelines, Calais, Boulogne?'

Pierre shrugged. 'I do not know. But I believe there are as many already in each place and very many more building. It is rumoured that Bonaparte will 'ave as many as 2,000 for 'is invasion.'

'What types are they?'

'The biggest are prames, three-masted vessels of the premier class carrying 12 guns. Then there are chaloupes cannonière with two masts, péniches that carry 'owitzers, and many gunboats.'

'How many men can they carry?

'They say the chaloupes and péniches can embark maybe 100 men and their weapons.'

Hurel exercised his Gallic shrug: 'I tell you my friend, the Bonapartists 'ave been very busy during this sham peace.'

'When we get to Étaples I must sketch these craft. Such intelligence could be of the utmost value to the Admiralty.'

'You need not sketch the chaloupes, my friend. We are going to steal one, sail it to England and when we are safely in the dockyard there your shipwrights can crawl all over it to their 'earts' content.

'Good grief!'

*

As the time drew near for Anson to leave, he sought out Cassandra, who was taking a brief respite from her self-inflicted chores and French lessons.

A trifle awkwardly, he told her: 'I must leave for the coast with Pierre. We have to acquire a boat. Tomorrow the coach will take you and the others to another safe place Hurel knows and later we will rendezvous off the coast.'

She asked anxiously: 'Oliver, do you trust these men?'

'I do. They are risking their lives for us.'

He saw that she was wearing the anchor brooch he had given her in Paris.

Her eyes followed his and she asked: 'Tell me before you go, why an anchor? I understand the connection with the navy, but...'

Colouring slightly, he took her hand and confessed, almost shyly: 'It's close to your heart, where I long to anchor myself forever.'

It was her turn to blush, but their tête-à-tête was rudely interrupted by Hurel, announcing: 'It's time to be gone, Anson, tide and time don't wait for any man, as we English say!'

'It's "time and tide wait for no man", but no matter.'

Parkin and the other members of the party came to make their farewells and before he could speak to Cassandra again he had been hustled outside where Pierre was waiting with his horse and another that had been conjured up for Anson.

Grimacing at the thought of having to spend many hours undertaking his least favourite mode of travel — horseback — he mounted the beast awkwardly.

Hurel reached up to shake his hand and Anson seized the opportunity to ask him quietly: 'About your intentions towards Cassandra, you know I have strong feelings for her?'

'Intentions?' The Frenchman laughed. 'Don't worry, mon ami. I 'ave merely been flirting with 'er to pull your legs! Can't you see she is in love with you?'

Anson was about to tell his friend that you pulled someone's leg, not legs, but realised the import of what he had just heard and instead told him: 'Thank you, Hurel. I should have remembered our vow to one another: honour and trust.'

It was a commitment they had exchanged on the Boulogne mission and Hurel repeated it now: 'D'accord, mon ami. Honour and trust!'

*

It was beginning to grow dark when Pierre and Anson reached the outskirts of Étaples after three days of dogged travel, mostly by night, spending a few hours resting in safe houses and isolated barns during the day.

They dismounted and Anson massaged his aching thighs and rubbed his sore behind, vowing to himself that he would never ever climb on board a horse again.

Pierre told him: 'I am taking you first to a place close by the harbour. If all has gone well we will meet some men who like me detest the regime. They are experienced sailors and will have procured some suitable clothing. It is easy enough to buy what you need from the French navy. Like you British they are not well paid.'

'So we'll dress like French sailors?'

'Certainly. It is our best chance of moving around the area unnoticed. We will blend into the background.'

'And we steal one of the invasion craft?'

'Precisely. My friends will have already selected which one and forged orders that say we are to take her out on

342

trial. It is a believable story because the one we will take will have recently been fitting out. It will be like taking milk from a baby.'

'Or, as my bosun would say, it could all go tits up!'

Puzzled, the Frenchman shrugged. His English might be good but it did not extend to lower deck sayings of the Rosbifs' navy.

They left the horses at an inn's stables — Pierre telling the ostler he would be back for them in a day or two — and approached a shabby-looking detached house in a side street.

The Frenchman rapped softly on the door and it opened slightly, as far as the chain fitted on the inside would allow it, letting out a wedge of pale light. There was some low muttering in rapid French that Anson could not follow, the chain was unfastened and the door swung open. Pierre beckoned him and they entered, blinking at the light from an oil lamp.

The door was immediately shut behind them and the chain replaced.

As Anson's eyes adjusted to the light he found himself being stared at by three Frenchmen, one with a loaded pistol in his hand. For a split second, he wondered if he had been betrayed, but the man who had opened the door stuck his pistol in his belt and smiled reassuringly.

The guide announced: 'Mes amis, allow me to present Lieutenant Oliver Anson, of the Royal Navy. His French is, shall we say, of the schoolboy variety, so while we are here it is better that we speak in English. Anson, these gentlemen are friends, royalists like me.'

'I am happy to make your acquaintance, gentlemen.'

He shook hands with each in turn.

The oldest and evidently their leader, a tough-looking man with greying hair and what appeared to be a duelling scar on his cheek, told him smilingly: 'My men call me "le Compte", but we do not introduce ourselves to you by name, m'sieur. It is not out of impolitesse, you understand. If we are captured by the republicans it is better that you do not know who we are, n'est pas?'

Anson nodded. 'Nevertheless I am deeply grateful to you, gentlemen.'

'Ça ne fait rien. Now, m'sieur, you must put on the clothes of a French sailor and we will get to work.'

53

Rendezvous at Sea

Pierre slipped outside to satisfy himself that the coast was clear and they left the house one by one to form up in the road outside, kitbags over their shoulders.

The leader, now in the uniform of a French naval petty officer, gave a quiet word of command and they marched off confidently towards the harbour. To call this marching was somewhat over-egging it, Anson thought, but then he doubted that French or any other sailors would ever come close to matching guardsmen.

He disliked wearing headgear at the best of times and had pulled on the blue stocking hat and threadbare jacket and striped trousers with reluctance, thinking that with his scarred face in this outfit all he lacked was an eye-patch to make him look the quintessential pirate.

On entering the port area they were challenged by a sentry, but waved through with a smile when the leader replied with some apparently amusing remark that Anson didn't quite catch. He thanked his lucky stars that being among these Frenchmen he would not have to do the talking as he had during his escape after the St Valery raid.

As they approached the waterfront, Anson could see what he took to be a chaloupe — a two-masted vessel at any rate — drawn up on a slipway apparently awaiting repairs. Another, which appeared to be fully operational, was moored nearby.

He cast a professional eye over the one on the slipway and at a glance could tell it had been designed to be a troop carrier that could easily negotiate mud and sandbanks and be run up a beach, no problem. However, his seaman's instinct told him that her shallow draught, small keel and low sides would make her the very devil to handle in heavy weather. Loaded with troops and with artillery embarked she would be vulnerable anywhere other than on a millpond.

But for now, whatever the weather, the moored chaloupe, new and clearly still being fitted out, would have to do. He noted with some misgivings that it rejoiced in the name of *Tortue* — Turtle or Tortoise, he supposed — and he hoped it handled better than its name suggested. Anyway, getting one to England intact for the experts to crawl over would be a wonderful coup.

While he was cogitating, the 'petty officer' grunted an order and the group came to an untidy halt. The leader muttered to the rest to stand easy and walked confidently to the gangway.

It was then that Anson spotted a marine armed with a musket sitting on a crate beside the main-mast observing them with vague interest. A sentry? This was unexpected but not surprising in view of Bonaparte's edict ordering the rounding up of all British men of military age.

Vessels of every kind would no doubt by now be under guard all along the Channel coast.

The leader strolled nonchalantly over the gangway and raised a hand to his stocking hat as he went on board.

Shown some paperwork which he did not — or could not — read, the sentry indulged in a few Gallic shrugs, tilted back his shako and fished a clay pipe from his jacket pocket.

Le Compte turned to call the rest of the party on board, and without further ado they set about preparing to sail.

Anson busied himself as best he could, keeping a careful eye on the sentry who began to gather his kit as if about to go ashore.

Sidling up to the leader, Anson indicated the sentry and whispered. 'What are we going to do with him?'

'We must take 'im with us. If we leave 'im 'ere 'e might raise the alarm. I 'ave told 'im we are just moving to a different anchorage, but 'e is just a little suspicious. A drink would keep 'im occupied.'

Fishing in his kit bag, Anson produced a flask of brandy he'd brought along for just such emergencies. He approached the sentry, pretended to take a swig, wiped his mouth with the back of his hand and handed the flask to the Frenchmen.

The man grinned, took a swig himself and handed it back. But Anson shook his head, muttered gruffly 'Pour vous' and went to help cast off, leaving the sentry happily downing another shot.

It was early evening and no-one on the waterfront took the slightest interest in the *Tortue* as she slowly left the mooring. After all, the vessel was crewed by French sailors and the sentry was still on board, so they could well have merely been changing berths.

*

Once out of the harbour they tacked slowly down towards Berck.

With no duties to perform, Anson fell to wondering how Cassandra and the others were faring ashore. He consoled himself that at least they had Nat Bell to look after them but otherwise were totally reliant on Hurel and the royalists he had enlisted to escort them to the rendezvous.

A cackle of laughter startled him. It was the sentry, now three sheets in the wind, and apparently finding everything hysterically funny. The brandy flask had done its work.

'What'll we do with him?'

Le Compte spread his hands and shrugged. 'I 'ave taken 'is musket and bayonet. Soon 'e will be asleep and when 'e wakes up and finds 'imself in England I expect he will decide to become a royalist.'

Anson smiled. 'Very wise.'

He tried to catch some sleep with his head resting on his kitbag, but his mind was still churning over and over all the things that could go wrong for the shore party. They could so easily have been betrayed or fail to make the rendezvous for a dozen different reasons. And it would be his fault for agreeing to such a hare-brained scheme.

Exhausted from his travels, he did doze off eventually and woke much later to find the chaloupe hove to and the Frenchmen scanning the moonlit coast and the lights of Berck to the south, anxiously.

He joined them and suddenly there it was: the outline of what appeared to be a rowing boat.

Le Compte had seen it too and within minutes a lantern showing a green light was swinging from the chaloupe's mainmast.

*

Boarding *Tortue* was a trial for Parkin and Pettiworth who made heavy weather of scrambling over the side. But, shoved by Bell from below and eagerly pulled on board by Anson, Cassandra and her maid coped without mishap.

On deck Cassandra appeared to stumble and fell into his arms — or was it intentional? Whatever, he held her tightly for a few moments and she whispered to him: 'You see, I am wearing my anchor and we are moored alongside one another once again.'

He smiled happily at the thought but broke away reluctantly to help hoist their luggage on board. Bell came next, clutching his blunderbuss, and finally Hurel clambered on board.

At the last minute le Compte decided to send the drunken sentry ashore with the returning boat rather than taking him to England and he was lowered unceremoniously over the side.

With cries of 'au revoir' and 'à bientôt', the royalist oarsmen pushed off, gathered themselves and struck out for the shore — rowing more easily with their lighter load.

54

Who Winks First

With everyone on board at last, *Tortue* headed out to sea to take advantage of the south-westerly that they hoped would drive them down Channel to the Kent coast.

Happy to be reunited with Cassandra and the others, Anson set about trying to make them as comfortable as possible.

She told him: 'We've had such adventures since we left the chateau, Oliver, but they are for the telling later when we're safely home.'

Parkin was positively effervescent, announcing: 'Now I've got over the Calais crossing, I'm quite taken with this maritime life. It's so much more exciting than dissecting toads!'

But the sudden crack of a cannon back towards Étaples turned his smile to a look of alarm.

Anson exclaimed: 'If I'm not mistaken that's a Frog trying to bisect us! What's afoot, Hurel?'

The Frenchman was already peering through a glass. 'A sail, 'eading this way.'

'Can you make out what it is?'

'Not enough light to be certain, but it looks like a frigate.'

'Ours or theirs?'

Le Compte answered for him: 'French for sure, maybe the *Rapide* out of Boulogne. She patrols this coast.' He ordered a crewman to hoist the tricolour, telling Anson: 'It may fool them into thinking we are trialling the chaloupe.'

Anson doubted that would work and stated the obvious: 'Unless they turn away we must run.'

'Certainly. If we are taken by the republicans we can expect no mercy. We will be executed as traitors and you English will become guests of Bonaparte for the duration of the war.'

The cannon sounded again, closer now, and the ball could be heard splashing nearby.

Still studying the frigate through the glass, Hurel called out: 'They 'ave run up a flag signal, but without their code book there is no way we can know what it says.'

Anson offered: 'I think I can tell you. What I would be hoisting if I were the French captain is "Heave to and prepare to be boarded" or something very like it.'

'Then let's 'eave to and see what 'appens.'

Hove to, *Tortue* wallowed in the swell. Anson borrowed the glass and peered at the French frigate. 'They're lowering two boats and it looks like they have marines in them!'

Le Compte warned: 'Then they 'ave made up our minds for us. If we were just Frenchmen we might be able to bluff it out, pretending that we are on some official mission. But with you English on board we cannot risk a search.'

'Very well, let's wait until they are almost alongside then make a dash for it. We will have a few minutes' grace. The frigate won't risk firing at us for fear of sinking her own boats.'

Hurel looked doubtful. 'I 'ope you are right, mon ami. Our lives depend on it!'

The two French boats were now in hailing distance and Le Compte shouted to them in rapid French. Anson caught only the gist of it — words to the effect that they were shipyard men trialling the chaloupe following repairs. But whether he was believed or not, the boats kept coming and the marines crouching in the thwarts could be seen readying their weapons.

'There is nothing more we can do. They intend to board us and if they do...' Hurel drew his index finger across his throat.

Anson looked this way and that, noting that the chaloupe's crew were arming themselves and Nat Bell was checking his blunderbuss and the two pistols.

Looking to Cassandra and Bessie, Parkin and Pettiworth huddled together aft, he wondered for a moment if for their safety the best thing would be to surrender without further ado.

But he understood that the royalists were in graver peril so they would have to attempt a last-minute dash and if that failed at least make a fight of it, reasoning that the enemy would not harm the civilians intentionally.

Hurel, musket in hand, shouted to Anson: 'If it comes to it we will show them we are armed and we will see which side winks first, mon ami!'

Amused despite the imminent danger, Anson corrected him: 'It's blinks, not winks!' But a sudden hail from *Tortue's* helmsman drew his attention to another sail coming up fast from the west.

He trained the telescope on the newcomer. Another frigate — and there was something most familiar about her rakish lines. As he watched, colours were hoisted and he saw to his delight not the tricolour but the Union flag.

'She's British!' Anson was about to add: 'Looks like my old ship *Phryne*!' But he hesitated, unsure.

'The Lord be praised!' Pettiworth exclaimed.

Parkin gave him a questioning look. 'I didn't realise you were a believer, Obadiah.'

'Only at moments of great extremity!'

But Anson warned: 'We're not out of trouble yet. Hurel, strike the tricolour. We don't want these Brits to get the wrong idea!'

'Immediately, mon ami! And shall we run up the royalist flag? Le Compte 'as one with 'im.'

'If you please. That will at least get them thinking and hunting through their signal book.'

The British frigate had also been spotted from the pursuing boats which, from being hunters, had suddenly become the prey.

55

'Beat to Quarters!'

On board HMS *Phryne,* Captain John Howard rubbed his hands in expectation.

Newly promoted, now that George Phillips had been posted to a shore job, he was relishing the command that he had craved for so long. With the resumption of hostilities he had been despatched from Portsmouth to take a look at the Normandy coast from Dieppe northwards to the Straits of Dover to monitor any enemy activity. And now, with the peace only ended for a matter of days, here was a chance to distinguish himself in action against a French frigate.

What's more, running before the prevailing south westerly, he had the weather gauge.

'Mister Allfree!'

'Sir?'

'Beat to quarters!'

Allfree beamed. 'Bosun, beat to quarters!'

As the continuous roll was thundered out by the marine drummer there was a thumping and clattering of feet throughout the ship, suddenly seething like a disturbed anthill, as men rushed to their action stations.

The few old lags and landsmen who were a little tardy were hurried on their way by the bosun's mates. But for most, no goading was necessary. The drumming excited the blood and stirred men to action — a summons to glory, or death.

Howard planted his legs apart to steady himself and peered through his glass to study the scene ahead. It was puzzling. There was enough moonlight to see a French frigate hove to right enough, but two of its boats appeared to be closing on a two-masted vessel that was wallowing in the swell apparently about to be boarded.

And as he watched, the smaller vessel suddenly lowered the tricolour and hoisted a white flag.

'Well I'll be damned!' His mind jumped back to the time when a French warship had appeared out of the fog flying a white flag. But that had been a flag of truce and they had first learned that peace had been signed.

If this two-master was French there would be no way the crew would be surrendering to the first British sail that appeared — not when backed by a French frigate.

No, it appeared that the vessel was about to be boarded by the Frenchman's boats, so there had to be another explanation.

'Mister Allfree, I do believe the crew of the smaller vessel might be royalists, trying to escape. See if the gunner can frighten off those two boats with a bow-chaser, but mind, he is not to endanger the vessel flying the white flag.'

'But why a white flag, sir?'

'Because that's what French royalists use — and they are on our side. So let's get to it!'

Allfree touched his hat and hurried for'ard, calling for the gunner.

*

The sighting shot from *Phryne's* bow-chaser skimmed the water and caused consternation among the marines in the two boats.

Amid much shouting, order and counter-order, the crews brought them round and headed back towards the French frigate.

The Frenchman could not risk firing at the chaloupe while his own boats were in the way, and the unexpected arrival of the Royal Navy was giving the captain something more important to concern himself with than boarding a suspect vessel. Oarsmen rowing furiously, the two French boat crews parted, clearly intending to go one to starboard and the other to larboard to shelter behind their mother ship.

As *Phryne* came up to the chaloupe, Howard leaned over the side and shouted into his speaking trumpet: 'Attendez, messieurs. Nous...' But his French was not up to it. He was about to say 'retourner', but something told him that meant overturn, and they would not appreciate that, so he fell back on English, shouting: 'We'll come back for you!'

There was a cluster of civilians and crewmen on deck and something very familiar about one of them, a tall slim man with dark hair and a scarred face. 'Good Lord, it's Anson!'

But before he could do a double-take, the chaloupe was already behind him and he focused instead on the French frigate looming up. Behind him, the chaloupe's crew seized the opportunity to escape and bore away nor'west.

Ahead of *Phryne*, the boats had disappeared behind the Frenchman, and Howard imagined the marines were by now scrambling back on board on the lee side. He called for the master. 'Mister Tutt. She's caught bow on to seaward. I intend to run past raking her as our guns bear, is that clear?'

Tutt touched his hat, shouted his orders to the helmsman and warned the captain: 'We have the weather gauge, sir, but we must be mindful of the shore batteries behind Berck and the fort south of the Baie de l'Authie.'

Howard recognised that this was Tutt's polite way of telling him to stay the hell out of range, but he accepted it readily. The French were known to have 24-pounders or even 32-pound monsters commanding entry to their harbours and capable of blasting anything that could float out of the water.

They were well protected behind embrasures five-foot-thick and eight-foot-high, and had furnaces for heating shot — a frightening prospect for men in a wooden warship unable to elevate their own guns enough to counter them.

The gunner was hovering at Howard's elbow.

'Mister Rogers!'

'Sir?'

'Load alternate guns with bar. As we pass the Frenchman's bow I want the starboard guns to fire one by one as they bear: pop, pop, pop, pop! This is not about killing Frenchmen. I intend to disable her, so we'll go for the top hamper: masts, sails and rigging.'

'Aye, aye, sir.'

'We only have one chance before the shore batteries come into action. So each shot must count. Pass the word.'

He turned to the first lieutenant. 'Mister Allfree!'

'Sir?'

'Our sharpshooters are to target anyone anywhere near the Frenchman's bow chasers. I don't want to see any return fire.'

As the gap between the opposing frigates closed, *Phryne's* alternate gun crews were scrabbling in the shot lockers for the double headed bar shot designed to shred canvas and rigging and damage an enemy's superstructure.

Boys had already scampered back from the magazine with charges that were quickly rammed down, followed by the ball or bar. Wads were inserted and rammed home and guns were manoeuvred into position with handspikes and elevated.

Finally, gun captains pricked the cartridges through the vents and stood by, slow-match in hand ready to fire.

*

On board the *Rapide* the captain had been taken by surprise by the fast approach of the British frigate.

One minute he had been carrying out a routine stop and search operation of a suspect chaloupe reported missing from Étaples, and now, hove to and with two of his boats on his lee side with marines scrambling back on board, he found himself at the mercy of an enemy frigate that had the weather gauge on him and was coming up fast on a run.

Seeing what was coming, he gave orders to bear away — boats or no boats — so that his own larboard guns could be brought into action, but it was already too late. *Phryne* was almost on her and as she drew level the British frigate's starboard 18-pounders began to thunder out, one by one, the detonations almost simultaneous.

With her guns elevated, *Phryne's* ball and bar shot screamed across the Frenchman's deck from end to end tearing gaping holes in the frigate's canvas, bringing rigging tumbling down, smashing anything within its path and sending deadly splinters flying. From such close range, no more than 100 yards, *Phryne's* gunners could not miss and Howard punched the air in triumph.

The detonations continued, with the unoccupied larboard crews helping to drag the aftermost guns to an angle enabling them to get their shots in as they swept past.

There was a brief deafened silence after the last gun had fired and the Frenchman was left rocking with tattered canvas and rigging raining down on deck. And then a loud creaking was accompanied by cheers from the *Phryne*, as the crippled enemy frigate's foremast toppled and came crashing down.

It had been struck at least twice at head height and its fall covered the *Rapide's* bow completely with canvas and detritus.

Delighted, Howard quickly calculated the possibility of turning to windward to gain sea-room, then bearing away and heading up to pass the stricken Frenchman again to have another go, this time with his larboard guns. Boarding and taking an enemy frigate was an enormously tempting proposition and would mean glory and prize money. But, if only slightly misjudged, such a manoeuvre could expose *Phryne* to a battering from the enemy's starboard guns — and there were the shore batteries to consider.

He had only a few moments to make the decision and in the event it was made for him. Puffs of smoke appeared as one of the shore batteries opened up. The French gunners had clearly worked on the ranges and the first shot splashed in *Phryne's* wake.

Given time, they would no doubt do even better. So Howard resigned himself to the reality that there was no chance of a second run even supposing he could claw his way back.

A cheeky skirmisher called down from the rigging: 'Can't we have another go, sir?'

Howard forgave forwardness from keen hands. 'I fear not, Adams. Much as I'd love to, we can't risk the shore batteries. One heated shot from them in the wrong place and we'd all be shaking hands with the devil!'

Obvious disappointment showed on every face, but no-one from the first lieutenant to the newest landsman questioned his decision. All knew that he would win no laurels for hazarding his ship. On the contrary, he risked a court martial. The French frigate was clearly out of action, but with it under the protection of the shore batteries it would be madness to continue the engagement.

Not least, there was the mysterious chaloupe to investigate — and he was anxious to find out what Anson was up to.

Well past the stricken Frenchman, *Phryne* rounded to larboard and once far enough out to sea and well beyond the reach of the batteries tacked back to intercept the chaloupe.

56

A Surprise for the Colonel

The chaloupe bumped alongside *Phryne*, a rope ladder was thrown down and an officer climbed down.

'Allfree!'

Phryne's new first lieutenant grinned broadly. 'One and the same, and very good to see you, Anson! Been pestering the Frogs again?'

'We were merely taking a peaceful holiday in France when all of a sudden Englishmen were in season again and we had to hide up for a while and then make a run for it.'

'And you've brought some Frenchmen with you, I see.'

'Yes, royalists. We owe them — and *Phryne* — our freedom, if not our lives.'

'Good, good. Well, we'll get your party on board and send an officer and some hands to help your tame Frenchmen bring her over to England. I take it that's where they want to go?'

'It's their dearest wish.'

'Excellent! Now, I'll need to have some kind of bosun's chair rigged to haul up the ladies.' He gave the elderly Parkin and the chubby Pettiworth the once-over. 'Hmm, and we'll need it for these two gentlemen, too.'

*

There was a joyful reunion in the great cabin of HMS *Phryne*.

Anson introduced the party to his old shipmate Captain Howard and one by one they thanked their saviour effusively. Pettiworth, still clutching his leather satchel, assured him: 'Their lordships will hear of this, captain. I quite thought we were done for and then suddenly you appeared and went straight at 'em — just like Nelson himself!'

Later, alone with Howard on the quarter deck, Anson enquired how his friend had come to command *Phryne*. 'The last I heard was that she was one of many ships going into ordinary.'

'You're right. She was earmarked for mothballing and a few weeks after you left us at Portsmouth we paid off.'

'What happened to Captain Phillips?'

'Much to his surprise, he was offered a shore job down in Plymouth. He was delighted because he'd expected to be on the beach like so many others. As it is he was able to send for his wife from Pembrokeshire and they've set up home near the dockyard. He's happy as a sand-boy.'

'And you?'

'Like you, I was sent packing on half pay and crawled back to my family home, wondering what the hell to do with the rest of my life. But then their lordships had a change of heart — that is, if they have a heart between 'em.'

Anson smiled knowingly. Their masters at the Admiralty were not known for kind-hearted gestures and the right man did not always get the right job, but more often than not they did get it right by inserting a round peg in a round hole.

'It appears that when the dockyard people were preparing to mothball *Phryne* they noticed she was in far better nick than most. Someone dug out the paperwork about what amounted to a recent refit at Chatham and their lordships decided to keep her after all.'

'But you'd gone home?'

'Yes, but to my astonishment they recalled me from darkest Yorkshire, promoted me and offered me command. Naturally I hesitated for a few seconds and then accepted graciously!'

'Anson laughed. Well, it was no more than you deserved and I wish you joy of it.'

'I'm sure George Phillips had a hand in it.'

'It wouldn't be surprising. He was a good captain. You say the old ship's company was paid off, but I notice some familiar faces: Mister Tutt, Allfree — now your first lieutenant, I note — and a few others.'

'Yes, I managed to track quite a few down and they were only too pleased to come back. There are a lot of new men, too, but with so many on the beach because of the peace I was pretty much able to pick and choose.'

'So they're a good lot?'

'They are, and now that we've seen some action they'll be cock-a-hoop, especially if prize money is forthcoming for this vessel of yours.'

'Well, she's technically an enemy vessel and I doubt the crew will be concerned about what happens to her. As royalists all they want to do is undermine Bonaparte in any way they can.'

'This chaloupe you've commandeered, d'you reckon it was part of an invasion flotilla?'

'No doubt. I saw for myself three-masted prames and chaloupes like this. Then there are gunboats, barges and caiques. The bigger vessels are designed to carry artillery, cavalry horses and a great many men — and this is merely what they have at Étaples. I'm led to believe they're gathering similar flotillas in ports from Dunkirk in the north right down to Le Havre.'

'So the French haven't been idle during the peace.'

'No, as many of us feared, the peace was just an excuse for them to take a breather, build up their strength and begin preparations to invade England.'

'And you have details of what they're up to?'

'I have been keeping my eyes open and my ears flapping all the time we have been in France, just as the faceless ones in Dover Castle had requested. Add what I know to what Hurel and his royalist friends have picked up, and between us we have a good deal of intelligence.'

'So you'll both need to debrief back at Dover Castle.'

'We will.'

'Very well, I was planning to tow your chaloupe into Portsmouth, but in view of the intelligence you've gathered and with this strong south westerly behind us it would make better sense to head for Dover and put you ashore there.'

*

Landing at Dover next day, Parkin and Pettiworth hired porters to carry the luggage and the whole party — including the Frenchmen — made their way somewhat wearily to the Ship Inn.

There Pettiworth bagged a seat on the next London mail coach and made his farewells, telling his fellow travellers: 'Must get back to my counting house forthwith — there's urgent business for me to transact on behalf of my new French contacts before the world and his wife wake up to the fact that we're at war again!'

After making sure the rest were settled, Anson reported first to the port captain and then he and Hurel made their way up the hill to Dover Castle.

Colonel Redfearn was delighted to see them. 'I feared you'd both be trapped in France, but I should have known that resourceful fellows like you would find a way out.'

'When you have an hour or two to spare we could tell you the tale, sir. Our return was not without incident. The good news is that we bring much information about French preparedness, news of Robert Fulton's terror weapon, and of a suspected British traitor we've scuppered.'

'Splendid, splendid! Where did you sail from?'

'Étaples.'

'And were you able to see what types of invasion craft they're gathering?'

Hurel smirked. 'Better still, colonel, we 'ave brought one back for you, a chaloupe. It's anchored 'ere in the 'arbour!'

Redfearn registered astonishment. 'Great heavens!'

*

They disembarked from the Dover to London stage at the turning to Ludden and, leaving Parkins, Cassandra and the pile of baggage in the charge of Nat Bell, Anson set off on foot for the hall.

As he neared the house, the butler-coachman Dodman appeared, smiling broadly.

'Welcome back, Mister Anson. I trust you haven't left the master and Miss Cassandra in France!'

'It was a close-run thing, I have to say, but no, we managed to make it back across the Channel, caught the London stage from Dover and they're waiting at the crossroads.'

'Then I'd best get the horses tacked up and go down there and fetch 'em.'

'Yes, quick as you can, Dodman. They're bone weary after the journey which hasn't exactly been without incident. Is all well here?'

'It is, sir, but you've got visitors, over in the summerhouse.'

An educated guess proved right. It was Armstrong and Elizabeth, holding hands and sitting together far more closely than necessary, with no sign of his sister's chaperone, the redoubtable Emily.

'Ah, Anson, mon vieux — returned safely from your holiday in France!'

Elizabeth rose and pecked his cheek and Armstrong shook his hand vigorously.

'Yes, Bonaparte wanted to clap us in irons and throw us into a dungeon, but we managed to evade his clutches. We've just arrived on the Dover stage and I've sent Dodman down to the crossroads with the coach to pick up the others.'

'Splendid! When I heard that the peace had come to an end I feared that the Frogs would slam the door with all the English tourists on the wrong side of it.'

'They tried, believe me, they tried. And you pair of...' He was about to say 'lovebirds' but checked himself. 'You managed to escape from the barbarous north? How is your father?'

'Dead, but he lived long enough to meet Elizabeth and give us his blessing—'

Elizabeth interrupted. 'He was such a kindly man, so brave and considerate of others right to the end. I'm so glad to have known him, albeit very briefly.'

'I'm extremely sorry to hear of your loss, Armstrong.'

'Thank you, but as you know yourself we sailors leave home so young to join the service that we're already well used to being sea orphans, as it were, are we not?'

Anson nodded understandingly. 'That's very true. It's hard to feel too deeply about families we haven't seen for years on end.'

Elizabeth protested: 'I do hope you didn't mean to include me in that remark, Oliver. Oh, I must tell you: Northumberland is so beautiful, not an ugly place full of shipyards and mines like mother described it!'

Anson smiled faintly. 'She'd never been there, of course. It was just the usual southern bias against anything north of London.'

His sister burbled on: 'And Captain Armstrong is the heir to the estate, which is, well, huge!'

Clearly a trifle embarrassed, Armstrong attempted to rein her in. 'Much of it unproductive moors, of course.'

But she cantered on. 'Oh, and I learned that a haggis is not some creature, as Captain Armstrong led Emily and I to believe, but a kind of savoury pudding they eat over the border in Scotland. In fact, I've eaten one!'

'Really? You never cease to astonish me, Elizabeth.'

'And here's the strangest thing. While we were at Captain, er, Amos's home a letter arrived for me from our father, giving us his blessing. He could only have learned from you or Mister Parkin that we had gone to Northumberland.'

Anson could but confess. 'Yes Elizabeth, I admit to having sent word to him that you'd gone north and what the circumstances were. I thought it best that he be told rather than getting the impression that you had eloped. So can I take it that you two have spliced the knot?'

Elizabeth blushed. 'Oh no, Captain Armstrong was insistent that we should wait until we got back to Kent, so that we can be married in father's church.'

Anson thought to himself that they might well have waited to tie the knot officially, but all the billing and cooing told him they were already lovers in every sense of the word.

'I am delighted to hear your news and wish you both joy of it.'

He was genuinely delighted, of course, that his favourite sister was to be married to a brother officer he admired and was proud to call his friend. But a wedding at Hardres Minnis would mean he would have to bury the hatchet, at least temporarily, with his mother and brother Gussie, when, ideally, he would prefer to bury it in his priggish brother's back.

What's more, he knew his mother would insist that the awful Sir Oswald Brax, who had the advowson — the right to select the incumbent of the parish — must be invited. And that meant Charlotte and her oafish husband, Dickie Chitterling would be there.

He would sooner face the French in battle. But although the prospect of mingling with the Brax-Chitterlings and his own estranged family appalled him, he tried not to show it.

Smiling radiantly, Elizabeth announced: 'Captain Armstrong has something more to tell you, haven't you, Amos?'

'I have. I'd very much like you to be my best man,' Armstrong beamed.

'Kind of you, and of course I'm flattered, but a family wedding in father's church could prove a trifle awkward...'

The return of Parkin's coach interrupted them and Elizabeth skittered off to welcome Cassandra back and no doubt enthuse all over her about her Northumbrian adventures and forthcoming marriage.

Armstrong hung back. 'I didn't want to say anything in front of Elizabeth, but Sergeant Hoover was here a few days since, looking for you.'

'Back from Woodhurst?'

'Yes and unscathed. There's been something of a battle and Hoover, Fagg and their makeshift militia have apparently seen off the smuggling gang that was threatening the village.'

'Excellent news! Any casualties?'

'Three or four of the smugglers dead, and one of 'em's your former bosun and would-be assassin.'

'MacIntyre?'

'Yes, Black Mac himself.'

Anson nodded. 'And very good riddance to him! I'll go and see the boys and get the full story. But, changing the subject, there's something that bothers me about your wedding.'

'What is it, mon vieux? Are you unhappy about being my best man?'

'No, of course not. I'd have been deeply offended if you'd asked someone else. As I was about to say before, it's just that the rift with my family will make things a touch awkward, but for me, not the happy couple.'

'We can steer through those troubled waters, mon vieux, and once I'm a member of the family perhaps we can pour some oil on them.'

Anson was unconvinced. 'Perhaps, perhaps not, but there's something else I wanted to ask. Now that you've inherited will you remain in the navy or go back to manage the family estate?'

'Now that war's broken out again? Of course I'll stay in the service. In fact... well, first things first. There's a most competent steward who's been looking after the estate during my father's illness. I've upped his salary and asked him to stay on indefinitely, so that's not a problem.'

'You were about to say something else?'

'Yes, the fact is, when we returned via London I took the opportunity to call on the Admiralty...'

'And you were not kept waiting too long, I trust?' They both remembered only too well being left for what had seemed like infinity in the infamous waiting room where unemployed half pay officers were washed up from time to time.

'Imagine — I was ushered straight in to see my appointer!'

'And?'

'To my astonishment, they've offered me command of a frigate! She's laid up in some creek in mothballs at present, and I'll have to see her through some refitting at Chatham, but that will mean Elizabeth and I can be together for a while after the wedding.'

Anson exclaimed: 'Oh, very well done! A frigate, eh? And if the war carries on it'll then be a ship of the line and in no time you'll get your flag!'

But as he congratulated his friend, he did a quick calculation. This meant that there would be a vacancy for a new divisional captain for the Sea Fencibles. And he had been told that had it not been for the peace he would have been promoted anyway, so that must surely now be on the cards again.

However, Armstrong was clearly not thinking along the same lines.

'Yes, it's early days to be talking about ships of the line and flag rank, but I'll be back afloat at last, mon vieux. And there's something else I should tell you. I've asked the appointers if I can have you as my first lieutenant!'

Historical Note

In Lieutenant Oliver Anson's day, naval officers drank toasts to 'A bloody war or a sickly season', as dead men's shoes were the best chance they had of advancement.

Following his exploits during the 1797 naval mutinies, his escape from France after the St Valery-en-Caux cutting out expedition, the taking of the Normandy privateer and the part he played in Nelson's Boulogne raids, Anson could now surely expect promotion.

But his career, like so many others, was interrupted by the cessation of hostilities known as the Peace of Amiens. It resulted in a great number of ships being placed in ordinary — mothballed — and many sea officers finding themselves beached on half pay.

Anson's dreams of a sea-going appointment were put on hold yet again — and the disbandment of the Sea Fencibles meant that even the shore-based command of his oddball 'Dad's Navy' detachment was binned.

However, all was not lost. The 'faceless ones' who oversaw intelligence-gathering from Dover and Walmer Castles on Kent's invasion coast, still had tasks for him.

The peace — concertinaed somewhat in this story — was a mere interlude in the middle of the Revolutionary and Napoleonic Wars, enabling the warring nations to gather their strength for the next round. But it also gave the British, starved like Josiah Parkin and his party of continental travel, the opportunity to enjoy the delights of Paris. And it gave some, like Anson and his sometimes-annoying French royalist friend Hurel, the chance to engage in espionage.

As they discovered, the French used the peace to prepare for an invasion of England and were gathering a flotilla of troop-carrying vessels in ports from Dunkirk in the north to Le Havre in the south.

Extraordinarily, the story of Robert Fulton's submarine, *Nautilus*, and the enigmatic smuggler-spy Captain Tom Johnstone is true and the intelligence Anson and Hurel gained could prove of enormous value to the Royal Navy, as will no doubt be revealed in the story of their next adventures.

Paris during the peace was a city full of intrigue. But it was also undergoing tremendous change as the First Consul, Napoleon Bonaparte, exerted his now immense power to embark on massive slum clearance and rebuilding schemes, creating a new street plan, dramatically improving public services — and even remodelling the Louvre, stocking it with looted masterpieces from his campaigns.

When the peace ended the door was slammed shut and Bonaparte moved swiftly to detain all British male tourists between the ages of 18 and 60. Parkin's party was fortunate to evade the authorities and escape. Many of those who did not spent many years as unwilling guests of the French.

Back in Kent, most of the smugglers Anson's men came across — including some of his own Sea Fencibles — were merely trying to make a dishonest living out of what was euphemistically known as 'free trading'. The majority sought no trouble, but others like Billy MacIntyre and his cronies were undoubtedly ruthless and violent criminals.

One such group was the Hawkhurst Gang that terrorised the uncooperative Kent village of Goudhurst in 1747. But a former army corporal, William Sturt, formed the villagers into a militia and when the smugglers attacked they were beaten off — much as the men trained and led by Tom Hoover and Sam Fagg saw off Black Mac's ruffians half a century on.

That narrow gap between England and France can indeed be a cruel sea, as the author's own maternal grandfather, Thomas Poile, well knew during his 30 years of cross-Channel ferry service in the old paddle steamer days. And it was something the author learned from personal experience many years later, enduring a storm-lashed Channel passage in a minesweeper and afterwards suffering the ignominy of handing his naval uniform jacket to the cleaners with the request 'Please remove vomit stains'.

Thanks are due to Jeremy Speakman and Neil McDine for sharing their experience afloat in these waters. Like them, Oliver Anson, as distant kinsman many times removed of the great circumnavigator and reformer of the navy Admiral Lord Anson, is of course made of sterner stuff and will no doubt be itching to obtain a sea-going commission in his next adventure.

Ominously, shortly after the renewal of war, Bonaparte was writing:

We have the insults of six centuries to avenge... From the cliff at Ambleteuse I had a sight of the English coast. I could make out houses and movement. The thing is a ditch, and with a pinch of courage it can be jumped... At the end of February I shall be at Boulogne with 130,000 men. With a good wind we need the fleet for only 12 hours.

About the Author

David McDine, OBE, is a Deputy Lieutenant of Kent and a former Royal Navy Reserve officer and Admiralty information officer. He is the author of *Unconquered: The Story of Kent and its Lieutenancy*. His fiction output includes his humorous novels *The Five Horseshoes* and *The Animal Man*, and more recently his popular historic naval fiction series featuring Lieutenant Oliver Anson. The series prequel, *Strike the Red Flag*, and the follow-up adventures, *The Normandy Privateer* and *Dead Man's Island* are all published by Endeavour Media and are also available as the *Blood in the Water Trilogy*.

Made in the USA
Coppell, TX
13 January 2020

14281835R00217